THE GARRITY TEST

Books authored or coauthored by Brenton G. Yorgason

The Garrity Test
The Power of Intimacy in Business and Personal Relationships
Six Secrets of Self-Renewal and Relationship Enhancement (private printing)
The First *Christmas Gift*
Georganna Bushman Spurlock: My Story (private printing)
Obtaining the Blessings of Heaven
To Mothers and Fathers from the Book of Mormon
Receiving Answers to Prayer
Prayers on the Wind
Spiritual Survival in the Last Days
Here Stands a Man
Roger and Sybil Ferguson Biography (private printing)
Sacred Intimacy
Little-Known Evidences of the Book of Mormon
Pardners: Three Stories on Friendship
In Search of Steenie Bergman (Soderberg Series #5)
KING—The Life of Jerome Palmer King (private printing)
The Greatest Quest
Seven Days for Ruby (Soderberg Series #4)
Dirty Socks and Shining Armour—A Tale from Camelot
Tarred and Feathered
The Eleven-Dollar Surgery
Becoming
Tales from the Book of Mormon
Brother Brigham's Gold (Soderberg Series #3)
Ride the Laughing Wind
The Miracle
The Thanksgiving Promise
Chester, I Love You (Soderberg Series #2)
Double Exposure
Seeker of the Gentle Heart
The Krystal Promise
A Town Called Charity, and Other Stories about Decisions
The Bishop's Horse Race (Soderberg Series #1)
Windwalker (movie version)
Others
From First Date to Chosen Mate
From Two to One
From This Day Forth
Creating a Celestial Marriage (textbook—out of print)
Marriage and Family Stewardships (textbook—out of print)

BRENTON YORGASON
and RICHARD MYERS

THE GARRITY TEST

A NOVEL

BOOKCRAFT
Salt Lake City, Utah

All characters in this book are fictitious,
and any resemblance to actual persons,
living or dead, is purely coincidental.

Library of Congress Catalog Card Number: 92-72666
ISBN 0-88494-840-4

First Printing, 1992

Printed in the United States of America

We tenderly dedicate this story to our children: to Rick's daughters,
Melinda and Megan, and to Richie, his "Little Jack"; and to
Brent's daughters, Jennifer and Angela, as well as to his seven sons—
Jason, Aaron, Jeremy, Josh, Don, David, and Jordan.
After all, these children *are* our reasons for living.

Author's Note

My coauthor, Richard (Rick) Myers, and I met a full quarter of a century ago. At that time I sensed an unusual sparkle of creativity in his nature—a very fertile mind. Our friendship grew, and over the years we have enjoyed sharing countless magical moments of creativity with each other.

Then several months ago, during one of these remarkably energized sharing sessions, Rick mentioned a story line idea that had been roaming around in his mind. I challenged him to put his thoughts to pen and we would see where the journey led. Rick accepted my challenge, and the next time we met, it was a two-hour session of my enjoying Rick's passion for a plot that was beginning to take hold.

Rick then spent several days in seclusion penning his thoughts, which seemed to explode into his mind faster than he was able to write them down. When Rick invited me to write this story with him, it just seemed natural that I do just that. I became consumed with the concept, the plot, and the charisma of the relationships coming to life in the story.

And now our journey into the life of Little Jack is at an end—or is it? We're not sure, but we are hopeful that you, the reader, will enjoy what for us has become a most powerfully exhilarating story.

Brenton G. Yorgason

Acknowledgments

We wish to extend our special thanks to those who assisted us in making this story come to life. First, we thank our dear friend, Kevin Lund, who assisted in the ongoing creation of some of the scenes of the story, as well as for his efforts in editing the various drafts of the manuscript.

We thank Staff Sergeant Jack W. Goode of the 2852nd Security Police Group at Hill Air Force Base, Utah, who provided countless insights into the intriguing world of the United States armed forces. This information, together with Brent's experience in the Army in Vietnam, provided a necessary foundation for the military setting of the story to unfold.

We also thank Velta Sawyer, Lew Day, David and Sheila Zolman, Tom Myers, Jr., Art and Dallas Berg, Roger Berg, and Margaret Yorgason, who gave us encouragement to pursue this story, and who read through various drafts and assisted with story line consistency and continuity.

And finally, though most important, we wish to thank Thomas G. Myers, Rick's father and a true friend to both of us, who read and re-read various drafts of the story, and who provided continual encouragement and assistance.

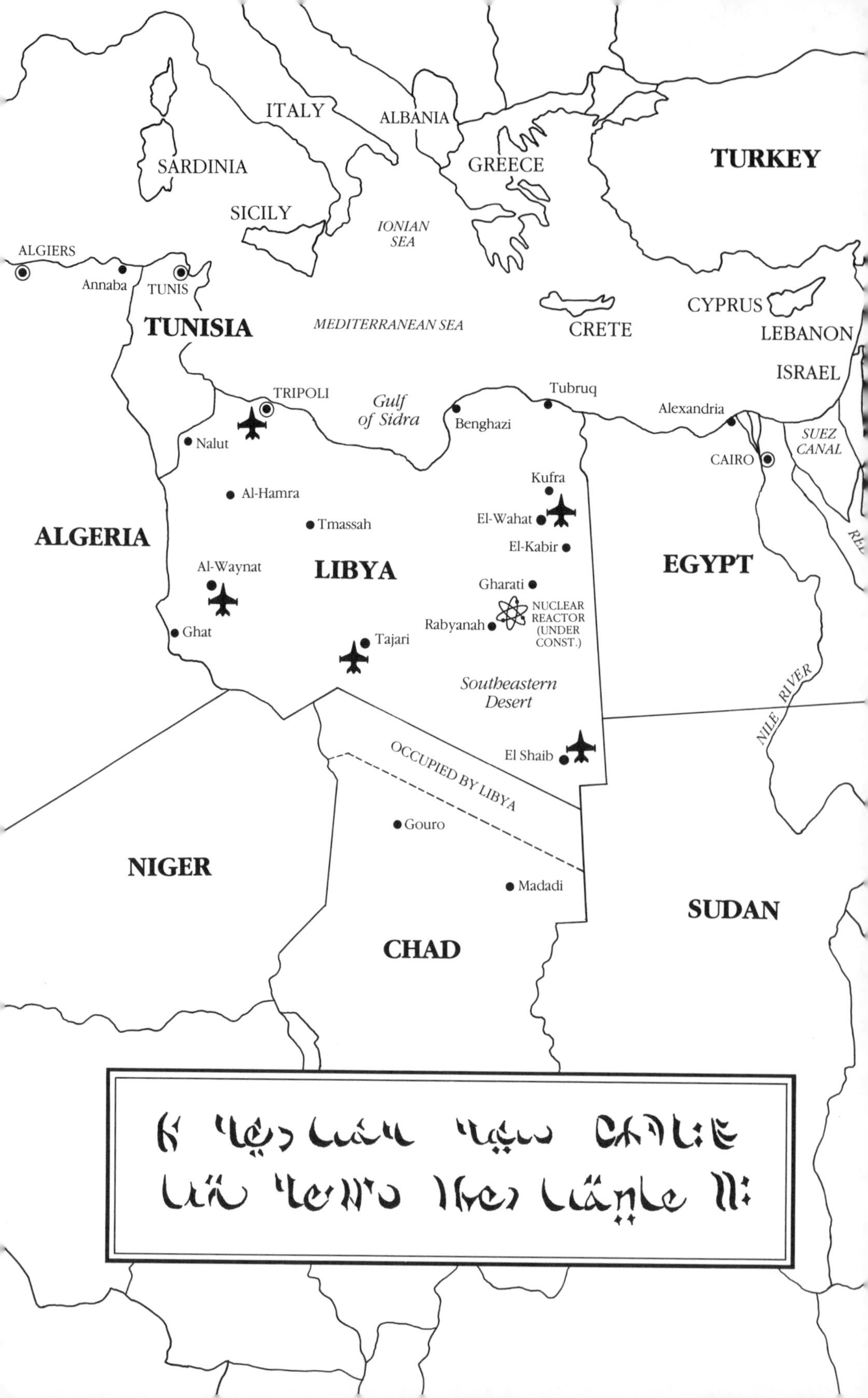
ITALY
ALBANIA
SARDINIA
GREECE
TURKEY
SICILY
IONIAN SEA
ALGIERS
Annaba
TUNIS
TUNISIA
MEDITERRANEAN SEA
CRETE
CYPRUS
LEBANON
ISRAEL
TRIPOLI
Gulf of Sidra
Tubruq
Alexandria
Benghazi
Nalut
SUEZ CANAL
CAIRO
Kufra
Al-Hamra
El-Wahat
Tmassah
ALGERIA
El-Kabir
EGYPT
Al-Waynat
LIBYA
Gharati
NUCLEAR REACTOR (UNDER CONST.)
Rabyanah
Ghat
Tajari
NILE RIVER
Southeastern Desert
OCCUPIED BY LIBYA
El Shaib
Gouro
NIGER
Madadi
SUDAN
CHAD

Prologue

Christmas Eve, 1991
Outside the Village of Rabyanah
Southeastern Desert of Libya

With a slight wind blowing steadily in from the east, stirring the loose sands and dust in its path, Haman Al-Rashid—military mastermind and supreme commander of the prestigious Libyan Elite—was forced to squint his eyes cautiously. It was too dark for his protective sunglasses, so he squinted as he surveyed the area around him.

The small, carefully disguised concrete bunker just to his left was perfect. It could not be seen from the air, or from anywhere else nearby, and so its invisible position gave the pensive commander a sense of triumphant satisfaction.

"Perfect," he whispered into the night. "Perfect, indeed!" Haman Al-Rashid's thoughts centered momentarily on the truly historic role this particular place and its people would play in the glorious rebirth of the North African Phoenix—in the rise of the next world power—Libya.

"Behold, Tajim," Haman whispered excitedly to his young helicopter pilot, pointing off into the distant horizon. "The beginning of a new world order! *Our* world order! Just as the great prophet has foretold!"

Commander Haman Al-Rashid and the young pilot, Tajim, boarded the sleek military gunship, then waited patiently, almost reverently, for Executive Officer Lucca Rovigo to complete his task. At that moment the Greek-born Libyan military officer was lifting the latch on the small concrete bunker. He then flipped on his flashlight and went inside.

Inwardly, the Grecian Lucca was nearly overwhelmed with excitement. This was the moment he had waited for. His moment! What power! What awesome, magnificent power lay before him! Supreme power—at *his* fingertips!

Slowly and cautiously Lucca Rovigo lifted a small panel in the spherical device in front of him, automatically activating the three tiny switches.

With each audible click of a switch, a small, bright red light illuminated.

"Good!" he whispered, breathing more intently now. "And now to ready the timer."

He pressed a button on the extreme right side of the panel.

Immediately a reddish-orange digital display lit up, reading 00:00 (zero minutes, zero seconds).

Then, licking his lips as if savoring a delicious taste in his mouth, Lucca Rovigo reached for and extracted the strange-looking key attached to a gold chain hanging around his neck.

Lucca Rovigo inserted the key into the slot just under the electronic display and turned it one quarter turn to the right.

Click.

It was set; all was now ready for the numbered-sequence commands that could be given by phone.

He withdrew the key and replaced it, with the chain, over his head.

With perspiration beading on his forehead, he breathed deeply, for he knew that *finally* it was done!

He knelt there for a moment, feeling mysteriously hypnotized as he looked admiringly at the soccer-ball-size metal globe.

"Fascinating!" he whispered, turning toward the small door that led into the bunker.

Quickly, Lucca Rovigo squeezed out through the small opening, turned around to shut the door from without, then decided to have one last look.

He flipped the flashlight back on and poked his head inside.

The massive cone-shaped device, to which the small metal globe was attached, gleamed in the light, and some letters on it now caught Lucca's attention. They were English words, not the usual Arabic figures he was accustomed to seeing. They read simply: *Pluton Nuclear Warhead.*

Lucca smiled eerily. He understood the monumental significance of this moment and thought about the great, rapidly unfolding project in which he would play a major role.

For indeed, now that the crumbling infidels inside what was the Soviet Union no longer posed any serious threat, the void that had been left by them needed to be filled.

Soon the entire world would unite under one powerful banner, and Libya would claim its predestined seat of global rule!

Operation Holy Power had begun—Lucca had been the one to "flip the switch!"

He turned once again and left the small bunker for the last time. Moments later the only sound left in the night was the whirling rotors of the distancing chopper as it made its way back toward Benghazi, in the Gulf of Sidra.

Unbeknownst to the sleeping citizens of the remote desert community called Rabyanah, instantaneous death lay close at hand in the form of an explosive device fifty times more powerful than the atomic bomb that had been dropped on Hiroshima. . . .

PART ONE

Prelude to Crises

If ever there's a time of need,
With back against the wall . . .
Just lift your eyes and ask for help
From Him who gives to all.

1

Christmas Eve, 1991
Edwards Air Force Base, California

Major Jack Garrity sat alone at his desk with endless thoughts racing through his mind. Each thought contained a scenario of events that, for the moment, he could only imagine were to come. He blinked his eyes once, then twice, before looking again at the unfolded piece of paper in his hands. He had never seen an actual signature from the president of the United States. He held the letter close to his eyes, trying to imagine the president's own pen actually stroking the signature at the bottom, his hand smudging the paper with fresh ink. But the paper was clean with no visible mark other than that of the evenly scribbled signature.

The phone rang, jarring Jack Garrity back to reality.

"Hello!" he shouted, feeling at once apologetic for his tone of voice.

"Jack?"

It was his wife, Linda. He recognized her voice, all right, but she seemed to be a trillion miles away. He pictured her calling him from the supersonic F-14 fighter he had flown that very afternoon.

"Jack? Jack, are you there?"

"Hi, honey," he answered, snapping out of his unintentional daydream.

"What are you doing, sweetheart? You sound like you're a trillion miles away!"

Funny she should say a trillion, he thought, trying to gather enough composure to tell her they would have to postpone their skiing vacation.

"A trillion miles away?" he questioned. "And just how far is a trillion miles, anyway, Linda?"

"Oh . . . ah . . . I see," she countered. "We're trying to play the who's-smarter-than-who game tonight, are we? Well, Major Garrity, if you must know, a trillion miles is exactly one billion billion! But it's also going to be equivalent to the number of apologies you're going to give to Little Jack and Trish if you don't hurry and get your handsome body home for dinner! Did you forget what night this is, honey?"

Jack glanced at the clock on the wall—1835! It was almost a full hour past dinner time, and Jack knew he had blown it. As he considered how he had inconvenienced his lovely wife, he absently gazed at the wall calendar she had recently hung in his office. She had picked it up at the novelty shop in Palmdale, and the picture before him depicted three T-38 chase planes flying in perfect formation. They flew to the front and on both sides of the space shuttle *Atlantis* while on its final approach toward Edwards's dry lake bed just south of the base. It wasn't just the photo of the space shuttle that Linda had liked. It was a picture of her "handsome, dark-haired husband" flying the T-38 on the right flank. It was a picture that made Jack proud.

"Hello! Calling Major Jack Garrity! Are you there, Major?"

"Oh, pardon me, sir!" he snapped back laughingly. "Is this Brigadier General Linda A. Garrity?"

"You're absolutely right, Major! And I'm giving you a direct order to come home this instant, or—"

"Christmas Eve!" he shouted, interrupting his wife's feeble attempt at impersonating General Walker, his commanding officer and closest friend. "Isn't that what you asked me, smarty pants? You thought I forgot, didn't you! It's 1830 hours on Christmas Eve, nineteen hundred and ninety-one, and I haven't forgotten the date at all! Instead, my beautiful, enticing brigadier general, I shall be leaving my post momentarily, and will navigate home and into your open arms before the palace meal is spread upon the table."

"I love you, Jack, all thirty-eight years and six-foot-two inches of you," she said, smiling on the other end of the line.

"I love you too, dear."

"Jack!"

Jack caught her voice just a split second before hanging up.

"What?" he answered, swinging the receiver back to his ear.

"It's 1838, Jack!" she said. "It's 1838, not 1830 . . . and . . . uh . . . Santa Claus . . . you do remember Santa Claus, don't you? Well, Santa is reported to have been sighted flying along the Northern Hemisphere, and is forecasted to arrive at the Garrity Palace at approximately zero one hundred hours. Merry Christmas, Jack!"

Without waiting for a reply, the phone clicked, and Jack knew his wife had made her point. He looked back at the clock on the wall, and sure enough, it read 1838, just as Linda had said. What a funny gal she was, always making a fuss about his custom of military time-telling. She would break him of the habit yet.

6:38 P.M., he thought. That's what time it was to everyone else in the civilized world around the air base. Six thirty-eight P.M.! He'd try and remember that when addressing the civilians.

Civilians! It suddenly occurred to Jack that he was not a civilian. He was an Air Force major with a job to do—a job he'd not been able to tell even his wife about. The sealed orders made it perfectly clear that he wasn't to tell anyone, not even his beloved Linda—and that hurt.

Signed in person by the president of the United States! Did that mean that the president knew him personally? Well, maybe not personally, but no doubt the president was well aware of his file records. In a way, Jack felt honored, but at the same time a terrible sense of foreboding was in his heart, and a feeling of impending doom. That was the hard part—wondering now if he'd make it through alive. But this letter was what it was all about! This was the primary reason he'd joined the Air Force in the first place, although it had never occurred to him that he would actually become one of the nation's best Air Force pilots. Nor had he considered that he'd be hand-picked to carry out such an extraordinarily high-security, highly classified combat mission.

The meeting with General Walker had seemed like a dream. Jack had been thinking about his family, the traditional holiday festivities, and the tentative "R & R" he'd been promised. In fact, the whole idea of a skiing trip up at Snow Valley with his wife and kids, and of getting away from the pressures of the base, had made this Christmas a special one indeed. Snow Valley's famous Big Bear was his favorite resort, and how his spirit soared when he went there! Oh well, so much for R & R. So much for special holidays.

Jack picked up the classified papers and looked at them again. The three eight-by-tens were spread out on top of his desk. As he looked down at the images in the glossy photos, he envisioned two things—the clairvoyant instructions from the general about the target sites, and the unbelievable technology that had enabled the United States to acquire the photographs in the first place: high-powered lenses positioned in satellites orbiting the earth.

The first two photos presented detailed images of two specific targets in Libya, a uranium mine just south of the capital city, Tripoli, and an almost-completed nuclear reactor plant on the outskirts of Gharati. But it was the third photograph that was most astounding—a colored eight-by-ten glossy of a highly secret aircraft known to exist only to a handful of top brass officials at the Pentagon and the White House.

General Walker's description of the futuristic-looking flying machine had left Jack's mouth hanging wide open.

"Major," the general had said just hours ago, "you're looking at the most sophisticated airplane ever devised by man. We're talking Star Wars technology, son, right out of a sci-fi novel! The F-31 Banshee supersonic fighter plane is, as its name suggests, a highly sophisticated stealth tactical fighter—totally invisible to radar, and faster and more maneuverable than anything else in the world! And I mean a whole lot faster!"

"A whole lot faster!" The words echoed over and over in Jack's mind. He was going to fly the fastest fighter jet ever developed, and take it on a top-secret mission to the Middle East!

"Now," the general had directed, "read these operation plans carefully, Major, and study those photographs until you're absolutely certain of your target sites, even with your eyes closed! You're scheduled for your first test flight of this baby just three days from tomorrow, so you'll need to have your gear packed and ready to go no later than 0400 hours on the twenty-eighth. Got that?"

"Yes, sir. I understand, General. Uh . . . this may sound odd, General, but just what do I tell Linda?"

"As per the directive, Major. No more."

"I understand, sir. Do I report to you directly, sir?"

"No, Jack, you don't."

The general had been quietly studying Jack, and felt a sense of pride for his closest friend—a man who was actually more like a son to him than was his own son. Jack was the best! He knew it, the president knew it, and if there was anyone who could pull this mission off, it was Major Jack Garrity. But suddenly a feeling of loneliness seemed to sweep over the general's heart. If something went wrong, and it easily could, Jack would be lost—and for the first time since he and the president had made the decision to proceed, the general shuddered in fear.

"Report to Major Barry, Jack. You know him, don't you?"

"We've met, sir," Jack answered, still standing at attention in front of the general's glistening walnut desk. He was proud that he and the general were all business.

"Barry is the only other officer on base who has any knowledge of Operation Screaming Ghost."

"Screaming Ghost, sir?" Jack queried.

"That's the code name, Jack. A banshee, as defined in the dictionary, is a flying, screaming spirit that warns of certain doom. A ghost of doom, Jack. You and Major Barry are considered two of the most qualified pilots in the Air Force, and you both will be trained to fly our baby. Barry will learn of his assignment in two days upon his return from Maui, so don't make contact with him. He's been assigned to fly the Banshee to Italy, and then he'll be backup for you during the mission."

"Thank you, sir. Uh . . . have we built more than one Banshee, sir?"

"No, Major, we haven't. But funding for the second prototype was just approved, so a second and a third will be assembled shortly. Unfortunately, we need the technology of the F-31 right now, as well as the support and confidence of you and Barry. Are you with me on this, Jack?"

"One hundred percent, sir."

"Good! Now, go on home, spend a good Christmas with Linda and the kids, and take the opportunity to review your directives. When you're certain you have a clear understanding of your mission, destroy the documents. I don't think I have to say it, but *no one* can know anything whatsoever about Screaming Ghost! Am I clear on that, Major?"

"You are indeed, sir."

The general closed his eyes, sat back in his chair, brushed his fingers back through his wavy white hair as he took a deep breath, and then folded his hands across his chest. When he opened his eyes and looked up at Major Jack Garrity, he saw the man's eyes fixed on the wall behind him. Jack was solemn and completely still. Goodness, was he standing tall! He had, the general thought, the confidence of a king.

As he looked up at Jack, it again occurred to the general that he may never see his friend again, and the general found himself struggling with a lump in his throat, fighting back a tear.

"Any questions, Major?" the general asked at last.

"Only one, sir. Is the F-31 Banshee hangared here at Edwards?"

"No, Jack, it's not. You'll learn of its whereabouts in three and a half days. So don't worry about it, okay? That's Major Barry's stewardship. Just get on home to your family and enjoy the holiday. Merry Christmas, Jack."

"Thank you, sir. Same to you, sir, and to Betty. We're lucky men to have our wives . . . uh, aren't we, sir?"

"That we are, Jack. That we are."

The general stood then, and the two men who were friends and yet professional soldiers clasped hands firmly, and gazed anxiously into each other's eyes.

It had begun.

2

Jack spent the entire fifteen-minute drive home doing all within his power to force the word *Banshee* from his mind. His car, an early and long-planned-for Christmas present from Linda, was a Porsche 911, and seemed to have a mind of its own as he absently pulled into his garage.

For a moment Jack sat in silence, wondering how he was going to give a normal Christmas Eve to his family. Traditionally, this was the most favorite night of the year for him and Linda as they shared stories with the kids, opened a selected gift together, and then joined in a special prayer kneeling next to the Christmas tree. Their goal was to instill the virtues of proper gratitude into the hearts of their children, Little Jack and Trish. They taught them the true meaning of Christmas, the celebration of the birth of the Christ child in Bethlehem, and the spirit of giving. They focused their attention on the teachings of the Bible, and tenderly reminded their children that although Santa Claus and presents were part of the overall celebration, the true happiness that came from the Christmas tradition was in remembering the great blessings that came from the Lord.

At last, realizing that he was giving the evening a review in advance while his family eagerly waited for dinner, Jack cleared his mind, pulled himself up out of the car, and powered the door down behind him as he entered the house.

The next three hours for the Garrity family were memorable. Little Jack, who was almost fourteen, was very much aware of *who* Santa was, and had, in recent years, developed a healthy and reverent love for the stories he had heard in Sunday School about the life of Jesus

Christ. He loved the story of baby Jesus, born in a manger, and the shepherds who had seen an angel of the Lord.

But most of all, Little Jack loved the traditional tale of the young shepherd boy who, having no other gift for the Christ child, gave up his sturdy shepherd's staff. This act, Little Jack had learned, was a real sacrifice because the shepherd boy had injured his leg and had relied on the staff for support.

It was the miracle in this story that had touched Little Jack's heart. He believed in miracles. He knew that Jesus loved him, and would answer his prayers just as he had answered the prayers of the shepherd boy—for upon delivering his staff to the baby Jesus, the shepherd boy immediately discovered that his injury was healed. Somehow Little Jack knew that if he ever really needed a similar miracle, the Lord would hear his prayers and provide him with one.

Trish, on the other hand, had turned seven the previous June. She still firmly believed in Santa Claus and waited eagerly for Christmas to come—knowing full well that Santa would come sliding down their chimney, deliver all kinds of wonderful toys, and hungrily eat up the plate full of cookies she and her mother would leave on the kitchen counter.

In Sunday School, Trish had been taught to recite verses 11 and 12 of Luke, chapter 2:

"For unto you is born this day in the city of David a Saviour, which is Christ the Lord. And this shall be a sign unto you; Ye shall find the babe wrapped in swaddling clothes, lying in a manger."

The last verse was Trish's favorite part of the story, for in her young mind she could clearly see baby Jesus all wrapped up in a blanket, sleeping peacefully in a manger of hay. She often wished she could hold baby Jesus in her own arms—she was going to be a terrific mommy; she was sure of it.

As it came time to put the kids to bed, Jack asked Linda to allow him a few moments alone with them. Something seemed to be tugging at his heart—he needed his kids so desperately.

Looking a little surprised with her husband's request—but definitely agreeable, given all of the tasks before her—Linda said, "They're all yours, Major!" And with that, she resumed her work in the kitchen while Jack shuffled Little Jack and Trish off to their room for the night.

"All right, kids," Jack said, tucking Trish in as he spoke. "Santa comes early in this part of the country, so you'd best get those eyes closed."

"Aw, come on, Dad," Little Jack moaned. "You promised me a back rub, which I think is a bribe for me to sleep in Trish's room tonight."

"You used to *always* sleep with me," Trish countered. "And you said that you liked keeping the boogeyman away, too."

"I've told you a thousand times, Trish, there's no such thing as a boogeyman. It's just your little-girl imagination."

"I don't care. I'm still scared."

"All right, you guys, let's think of Santa and reindeer and tomorrow morning. Why, when I was Trish's age, I heard bells and reindeer on our roof, and it was about this time of night, too."

"Aw, you're just kiddin' us, Dad," Little Jack answered, his eyes closed and a smile on his face as he began to enjoy one of his father's famous back rubs.

"You've got to rub my back, too, Daddy," Trish said, doing her best to keep her eyes closed.

Without answering, Jack patted his son's back, and then shifted over to Trish's bed and repeated the ritual for her. And as he did, he found his eyes welling up with tears—tears of gratitude, and of impending loneliness for his two beautiful children. They were life for him and Linda, and already he was missing them terribly.

"I sure love you two," he whispered, at last breaking the silence.

"Love you, too," Little Jack sighed matter-of-factly.

"How much do you love *me*?" Trish asked.

"Oh, I'd say about seven zillion," Jack answered, anticipating the predictable response that would now come from the pillow below him.

"Love you more," Trish said, smiling in the darkness.

"How much more, darling?"

"Oh, googalong and infinity."

"Yeah, I guess you do," Jack replied. Then, kissing his two children goodnight, and turning on the night-light, Jack quietly stepped to the door.

"Dad?"

"Yeah, son, what is it?"

"Why do you keep calling me Little Jack?"

"That's easy, son. You wouldn't call a four-foot dwarf Big Jack, now would you?"

"Dad!"

"Okay, four-foot-one-inch dwarf."

"I'm serious, Dad. You and Mom have called me Little Jack ever since I can remember . . . and when we're at Grandpa's house, he calls *you* Little Jack. How can I be Little Jack if you're Little Jack?"

The major stood silent. It became suddenly clear that it was time to spend some quality time with this growing young man—there was a tale to be told. He remembered telling it several years earlier, but evidently Little Jack had not remembered it.

Jack could see a longing in his son's dimly lit eyes. It was almost as though Little Jack knew that his father was going away and wanted to spend these last precious moments with him.

There had been a reason why his own father, Jack Garrity, had named *him* Little Jack.

Jack quietly moved to where his son lay and silently positioned himself on the edge of the bed.

"Grandpa named me Little Jack a long time ago. Do you remember when we were driving to Los Angeles to pick up that roll-top desk we gave your mother for her birthday last fall?"

"Yeah."

"Do you remember what happened when we were driving along the Coast Highway, out by Malibu Pier?"

"You mean when we got that flat tire and you nearly ran us off the road?"

"Well, yeah . . . but I don't know that *I* nearly ran us off the road. The flat tire definitely made it difficult to steer the Blazer. But we got out of it all right, if you remember. Anyway, do you recall what we had to do to change the tire?"

"What d'you mean?" the boy asked seriously.

"Well, think for a moment. There was a tool in the trunk, a special jack that we used to lift the car so we could change the tire."

"Oh, yeah, I sure do. You let me push the handle up and down, and you called me the elevator man. I lifted the Blazer up all by myself!"

"You sure did that. But do you think you could have lifted the car by yourself without that special jack?"

"Maybe, if I ate a whole can of spinach!"

The major reached over and tickled his son until he curled up into a ball. "Spinach, huh? Now, are you gonna be silly all night, or do you want me to tell you this story?"

"Tell me the story," his son answered, sitting back up in his bed while trying to become serious.

"Okay, then listen up." Jack swung his feet up onto the bed, and sat next to his son. As he did so, he glanced over and saw that Trish was fast asleep, dreaming of Santa and toy dolls.

"When I was about ten years old, Grandpa and I were driving through Utah and Nevada along the old Highway 91. Suddenly, just like the time you and I got our flat tire in Malibu, we had a blowout and were forced to pull over to the side of the road. It was a bad one, too. Well, anyway, after we stopped the car, my father showed me where to fetch the special jack that would lift the car while he loosened the lug bolts. And, just like you, I got my first assignment as the elevator man.

"I remember how amazed I was that a little jack with a small lever could lift such a heavy car all by itself. So I asked your grandpa what made it work like it did. He told me that the little jack was built so that it could lift a heavy car one step at a time. Each time the lever was lifted, then pressed downward, a small but strong steel finger would swing in and out of a series of notches—kind of like climbing a set of stairs. And as it did, it would lift the big, heavy automobile one step at a time.

"Dad then told me that it didn't matter what I wanted to be in this life—I could be anything I desired if I just took my time and did things one step at a time. The idea was that each time I learned another lesson, it would be like stepping up onto another stair. Eventually, if I worked hard, he said that I would climb all of the stairs and become a concert pianist, if that was what I desired. And there you have it. That's when he named me Little Jack.

"The problem is that too many people try and skip a stair or two along the way, and that's how they slip up. You see, that little car jack *never* skips a step. It can't! It has to lock onto each notch on its upward climb, grab a new hold, and then lift again, one step at a time. If it skipped even one notch, without grabbing a proper hold, the weight of the car would send that little elevator crashing back to the bottom. And, of course, that's when someone trying to change a tire could get seriously injured."

As he finished speaking, Jack looked intensely into his son's eyes, trying to determine whether the boy was getting the message.

"Both of us are Little Jacks, son. I was one to my father because he expected me to climb as high as I could in life, and you're one for the same reason. Whatever you decide you're going to do, I suspect you'll get there 'cuz you know the secret—the one-step-at-a-time secret."

"Is that how you learned to fly those jets, Dad?"

"Yes, it was."

"Was it hard?"

"No, not really. I mean, flying is something that seems to come natural for me, kiddo; but all the years I spent learning about airplanes, weather, and so on—that's what took the most time. I had to spend many hours in what they call a ground school, where I had to read books and take tests just like you and Trish have to do at your schools. But gradually, one step at a time, I learned, until I took my first flight, putting into practice what I had taken so long to learn."

"Trish doesn't take tests, Dad."

"Sure she does. She just doesn't have to write them down at this point. But you can bet that she's learning something new every time she goes to her first-grade class, just like you and I did."

"The hardest test I had was in fifth grade. We had to memorize all of the states and capitals. Boy, was that hard!"

"How'd you do?"

"I only missed two," the boy mentioned with pride. "Delaware and Rhode Island."

"Sounds like you remember them now, though."

"Yeah, I do. I learned 'em for good!"

"That's my Little Jack," the major said, throwing an arm around his son's shoulders and pulling him close.

For several moments the two lay in each other's arms. Then, without speaking, and realizing by his heavy breathing that his son was asleep, Jack quietly arose and left the room—feeling, as he did, that he was the luckiest father in the entire world.

"What was that hour all about, Jack?" Linda asked as her husband walked quietly into their bedroom.

"What . . . I—"

"Hey! You know what I was thinking, honey?" she interrupted.

"Thinking?"

"Yeah. About our trip to Big Bear," she said, not really paying attention to anything except the corners of the gift she was wrapping. "I saw this ad on TV last night that said for just forty dollars or so down, we could get one of those nice camcorders. It'd be cheap, really, just a few extra dollars each month on a rent-to-own basis. And, if we decide we wanna keep it, well, each one of those rent payments we make will be applied to the purchase cost. Oh honey, do you think—?" And at that moment Linda looked up and saw the pained expression on her husband's face.

"What's wrong, Jack? What did I say?"

"Nothing, hon." It was a lie.

"Nothing, huh?" she questioned searchingly, and then her eyes widened. "Is it Trish, or is it Little Jack?"

"No, no . . . nothing's wrong. They're fine. I tucked 'em in bed, and they're both sleeping like a couple of logs."

But Jack could tell by his wife's expression that he had not convinced her with his words. "Relax, Linda . . . they're okay, really. I'm just a bit tired is all."

Another lie. He hated lies! He then looked at his wife and forced one of those famous Jack Garrity smiles. He finished pulling on his powder blue silk pajamas, wondering how long he could keep faking it before Linda saw through his words and demanded an explanation.

Was this a good time to tell her about the cancellations? He knew she had her heart set on the Big Bear trip as much as any vacation he could remember. How was he going to explain what he *couldn't* explain. He had always told her that the moment might arrive when she couldn't know about his mission. But that had never been a reality—not, that is, until this very moment.

Eventually she would understand, he thought, and would quit probing for even a hint. She knew that the military was cloaked with secrets that for "national security reasons" (and he knew how she hated that particular phrase) could *never* be discussed. She'd get over it. And besides, if all went well, the whole mission would be completed almost as quickly as it had begun.

In the end, Jack reasoned that for now—well, it just wasn't fair to lay the Banshee thing on Linda on Christmas Eve. He could distract her sensitive inquisitiveness by discussing the camcorder thing.

An hour later, after all was made ready for a beautiful and extravagant Christmas, Jack held his Linda in his arms, not being able to get close enough to her.

It was amazing, he thought, as the two lay close together, the tremendous support and strength such an embrace could provide. How thankful he was that their marriage had been one of relative ease, with each passing year more joyful and fulfilling than the one previous.

"Merry Christmas, Major," Linda whispered.

"And you, too, lovely lady," he said softly into her ear, noticing as he spoke that she had already passed the threshold of consciousness and was clearly floating off into the world of dreams.

It was going to be a great Christmas, he thought, and he was determined *not* to ruin it with the announcement that they would have to postpone Big Bear.

The curtains were pulled back to allow the cool breeze to flow into the bedroom, and as Jack looked up, he noticed that he could actually make out a couple of constellations in the heavens above. The Big Dipper's handle was always the first thing that caught his eye whenever he gazed at the stars.

The digital clock on the nightstand read 0038 hours, and across the Atlantic Ocean things had already been set in motion.

3

3:00 A.M.—
Trieste, Italy

Beep! Beep! Beep! Beep!

Armando Palumbo opened his eyes with a start. The little beeper on the clock radio was annoyingly loud. He reached over and flipped the switch on the side to turn it off. Meanwhile, he cleared the sleep from his eyes and sat up in his bed. The bright red glow from the digital display read 3:01 A.M. He'd have about thirty minutes or so before the phone would ring, and he wanted to be dressed and wide awake to receive the message.

Armando shivered as he climbed grudgingly out from under the warmth of the bed covers, then reached over and picked up the matches he'd left on the nightstand. The small satellite heater with its attached propane-filled *bombola*, or fuel tank, was more than efficient for heating the one-room apartment he had rented only hours before. He quickly lit the heating coils to soothe his hands and feet in the immediate warmth it provided.

The man sat there a moment, never quite able to capture enough heat in his limbs. It'd be a few minutes before the frigid chill in the room abated and he could move about with a degree of comfort.

It was cold outside, really cold! Winters in Trieste were sometimes unbearable, especially when those formidable winds blew in off the Adriatic. "The *Bora!*" he muttered out loud. That's what the Triestini called it. And sometimes the wind was so strong that people had to hang on, literally, to one of the hundreds of handrails bolted onto the sides of the buildings that lined the steep streets of the ancient city.

Tonight, however, there was no *Bora*. But it was still cold, and this annoyed Armando. Quickly he pulled on a pair of American-made jeans, an extra T-shirt, and a dark grey sweatshirt with a hood. Of course, before he left the apartment he'd have to put on a wool-lined army jacket and gloves. No sense in freezing to death, he reasoned, his head at last beginning to clear.

It was 3:19 A.M. Just a few more minutes. He walked over to the phone to make sure there was a dial tone. He certainly didn't want any mess-ups—not now, anyway. They were much too close to allow simple problems to botch things up.

"*Molto bene!*" he said softly, setting the phone back onto its cradle.

Armando then walked to the window and drew back the green shutters. There was a thin icy frost on the two panes of glass, but outside it appeared crystal clear. His apartment commanded a scenic view of the bay, and he stared down at the shipyard below. There were several large tankers in port, each one brightly lit with an array of lights fore and aft, outlining the familiar contours of each great vessel. He wondered, arbitrarily, how many gallons of oil those tankers carried on their journeys back and forth across the oceans, then moved slowly over to his small kitchenette. He flipped the switch on the little hot plate and began heating a small pot of water for a desperately needed cup of *Espresso* coffee.

Rrrrinnngg! The telephone!

He had the receiver in his hand before the second ring.

"*Pronto*," he said quietly.

The voice on the other end of the line asked Armando if he knew what time it was.

"*Si*," he responded impatiently, "*Sono le tre è mezzo*."

"How many days until Christmas?" the voice asked in broken English.

"Not many," Armando responded.

"Good!" There was a short pause, then the voice continued, "*Piazza del duomo* . . . in Udine . . . okay?"

"*Si*," Armando replied, "what time?"

"Five o'clock." And then the line went dead.

Five o'clock, Armando repeated in his mind. That would be more than enough time. And at this time of the night, nearly all of the streets and short stretches of *autostrada* would be virtually empty. Armando replaced the telephone quietly back onto its resting place next to the clock radio. The red electronic digits read 3:34 A.M., and the water on the hot plate started to boil.

Armando Palumbo drove his grey Fiat van at a reasonable speed along the *Coastal Autostrada* to avoid attracting any unnecessary attention from one of the occasional *carbinieri* that patrolled at night. He knew, of course, that there was little likelihood of his actually seeing one, because the *carbinieri* were not nearly so motivated as to stay awake and alert all night long. Still, he wasn't taking any chances.

Ten minutes later, Armando saw the sign that signaled the approaching turnoff for Gorizia and Udine. Twenty more minutes, he thought, and then he wondered if he would have any trouble meeting with his man at the *piazza del duomo*. He knew the place well. Every Italian city had a *piazza del duomo*. These public squares were the so-called centers of each city, and marked the city's central Catholic activity from the great cathedrals the Italians called *duomos*—easy to find.

The *piazza* was dark, except for the dim glow of several street lamps positioned at the four corners of the square. Four different cobblestone roads fed into the circular thoroughfare surrounding the cathedral and the *piazza*. Armando did not know from which of these the American would emerge, but since there was no visible traffic and only a few parked Fiats and motor scooters, it was likely that the first or second mobilized vehicle would be the one he was to meet.

He would wait. It was 4:46 A.M. according to his Timex. He was fifteen minutes early. Better than being late. He prided himself on punctuality and was very meticulous about his contracts. His reputation depended on that.

Suddenly he saw lights coming from the opposite end of the *piazza*. He could see the dancing shadows on the walls that lined the streets. Someone would merge into the square in just seconds.

Armando waited, slumped down in the driver's seat of the van. If it was a passerby, he didn't want the driver to see his silhouette at this time of the night in a parked vehicle.

The automobile approached the square slowly. It entered the circular thoroughfare and drove straight toward Armando's van, pulled up alongside without slowing down further, and then drove quietly past. Armando remained crouched in the front seat, his heart beating rapidly, his eyes barely level with the bottom of his side window.

He watched cautiously as the tail lights of the passing automobile slowly, but surely, dimmed from his view out of the side mirror of the van.

Keeping his head down, Armando pressed the little side button on his Timex and read the illuminated digital display again. It was nearly ten minutes to five.

He wondered again what kind of vehicle the man would be driving. An American car? He was sure that the American was a military man. More than likely, he was in the Air Force, stationed at Aviano Air Force Base just a few miles north of Udine.

"The *Americanos*," he whispered to himself, "they have military bases all over the world! And so many in our country." To Armando, it just didn't seem right. He was not necessarily anti-American, or anything like that. But he did feel that the Italian people, *his* people, should defend themselves. His own people should be in control of all those military install—

Tap! Tap!

"What was that?" he whispered audibly, his heart in his throat.

A quick, but light tapping noise sounded again on the window at the passenger's side of the van. He jumped, his heart racing, and turned his head to the right. There was a man standing at the door.

For just a second Armando froze. The man at the window did not move. He simply stood there, staring at Armando's barely perceptible figure crouched in the front seat.

Finally, after what seemed an eternity to Armando, the man tapped on the window again, seemingly unconcerned with fear or any other emotion.

Armando sat upright, leaned over instinctively, and rolled down the window a full inch.

"*Si*," was all he could say, his heart beating so loudly he could actually hear it in the silence.

"*Ma, scusi signore*," the man said in Italian, and then switched over to English. "You know what time it is?"

"*Si*," Armando said, realizing the coded question. "*Sono le tre è mezzo*."

"How many days until Christmas?" the man asked.

"Not many," Armando said shakily.

"Good." There was a moment's pause again, and finally the American said, "May I get in?"

"*Si, certo!* Get in . . . get in!" And with that he leaned over one more time, unlocked the latch, and lifted the lever on the door.

4

0600 Hours, Christmas Morning—
Palmdale, California

"Mom! Dad! Get up! Santa came last night! Come and see!"

By now Trish had the covers halfway pulled down, and Linda and Jack were struggling to shake themselves free from their sleep-induced confusion.

"Come on, Mommy! Come on, Daddy! Little Jack is by the tree, and he wants you to see what Santa left us!"

"Okay," they answered in unison, finally getting a grip on the reality of this magical moment.

"Santa Claus was *here?* He really made it?" Major Garrity asked with a startled expression, while at the same time taking hold of his daughter's hand.

"Well, my goodness, Trish," Linda exclaimed, equally spirited by her daughter's infectious enthusiasm. "When did he come? I never heard him!"

"I don't know, Mommy!" Trish shouted, obviously beside herself with joy. "He just did!"

When they arrived in the family room, Little Jack was already studying a set of fairly sophisticated instructions that had come attached to an expensive radio-controlled airplane kit. It was what he had asked for again and again, and despite the stack of unopened presents still tagged with his name, the radio-control unit had the boy mesmerized.

Seeing his parents enter the room, Little Jack jumped up, ran over to them while still clutching the instruction booklet, and threw his arms around both of them at the same time.

"Thanks, Dad," he said, triumphantly jubilant. "Come on, Dad. Let's go fly it!"

"Whoa . . . hold on there, big guy. Aren't you even going to peek at your other gifts?"

"Oh, yeah," the boy remembered. And with that, he made a beeline to the tree, and to the greatest Christmas ever.

After Little Jack and Trish had carefully identified each new treasure, they categorized their gifts according to that special value so common to children on Christmas day. For Trish, the prized Baby Suzi doll that would actually cry, wet, and even crawl like a real baby, was the priceless "special gift." And for Little Jack, there was no dispute. The P-51 Mustang World War II fighter plane, with its miniature gas engine and true-to-life features, was the bonanza of gifts. But what really made it special was the custom-made decals on the tail section. In bright red, with yellowish-orange blocking, the words *Little Jack* clearly identified this particular remote-control aircraft as the finest there ever was.

By mid-afternoon, Little Jack's P-51 was airborne. It had taken the collective intellects of father and son to piece together the carefully crafted parts, but eventually their efforts paid off.

"Remember what I told you about proper wind conditions, son?" the major questioned just after the first successful taxiing maneuvers.

"Yeah," the boy answered.

"All right, then." Jack hesitated, holding the remote control unit firmly in hand.

"All right, *what*, Dad?"

"Well, look around you and tell me what you see." He hesitated again, waiting for some type of assurance that his son was beginning to understand the basics of assessing wind conditions. Then he continued.

"How can we expect to take off without clearance from the tower?"

"You gonna fly it, Dad?" Little Jack asked excitedly.

"*Me?* No, not me. *You* are!"

The major held the remote unit toward his son, signaling the boy to come over and join him. Little Jack stepped up and carefully retrieved the controls, and he could sense that his father was clearly proud of his gentle handling of the expensive hobby equipment. He then reached into his back pocket for the small card his father had printed out at the office—a special checklist, for takeoff.

"Remember what I told you last night, Little Jack," the major said, pointing to the shining laminated index card in his son's hand. "Just take things one step at a time."

The major and his son read through the checklist, discussing when necessary the meaning of each step. They concluded, unanimously, that conditions for flying were excellent. The major was pleased with the obvious patience exhibited by his son, because he knew that lack of such would likely result in a crash. But Little Jack was clearly in command of his emotions, and understood that by not following instructions, he could and *would* likely destroy a several-hundred-dollar investment.

"Remember, son, the P-51 is not a toy. It requires thorough maintenance and a skilled pilot at the controls."

And so, after two tankfuls of expended fuel from taxiing around the parking lot, and learning confidently the sensitive nature of the battery-powered remote, Little Jack said, "I'm ready, Major! Let's refuel and turn her into the wind!

"This," the boy continued, "is the Little Jack Mustang P-51 two-niner-two-tango ready for takeoff. Over."

"Two-niner-two," Jack responded, cupping both hands over his mouth to sound like a radio communication from the control tower. "You are cleared for takeoff. Proceed to runway three-one, over."

"Runway three-one, roger. Two-niner-two clear!"

"Now, remember what I said, son," the major coached. "Watch your airspeed, keep your nose into the wind, and watch your tail section. It's gonna lift off slightly ahead of the rest of the plane."

"Okay, Dad," the boy said, still very much in control. Jack wondered, for a moment, if he was perhaps more nervous than his son. A warm, affectionate smile drew across his face, and sure enough, as the little plane raced off across the parking lot and leaped, finally, into the gentle breeze, the major noticed an obvious increase in his heart rate.

"Yea!" Jack shouted, throwing his hands up into the air. "That's it, Little Jack. Keep her steady now!"

The excitement of the day' activities had had a numbing effect on the major. There had been the luncheon with Linda's mother, who lived in nearby Lancaster, the ever-enthusiastic energy of Trish and Little Jack, the late-afternoon flights at the school parking lot, and finally the winding-down efforts, thank yous, and good-byes. It had indeed been a memorable Christmas.

Now, however, stretched out in his easy chair in front of the TV set, Jack's thoughts floated hauntingly close to that painful decision he knew he needed to make. Tonight, after careful study of his upcoming military objectives and commitment to memory of all of the data concealed in the government pouch, he would tell Linda what, unbeknownst to him at the time, would unalterably change the course of their lives.

The clock on the mantel struck 1900 hours, and far away in Udine, Italy, events continued to uncontrollably unfold.

5

0521 Hours—
Udine, Italy

Armando Palumbo turned the small brown envelope over once, then twice in his left hand. He hadn't opened it yet, but he could clearly feel the outline of the key inside. It was still dark out, and he was glad to be free of the American. There had been something profoundly unsettling about the man. He had kept his face forward, and not once during their five-to-ten-minute conversation did the American make eye contact. If anything, Armando had noticed an occasional side glance, but nothing more. Rigid!

That was another thing—the man had sat perfectly still, like a stone statue. In fact, thinking back, Armando remembered very little about what human features were noticeable. The man had been dressed like a thief. A deep black sweater with a black or dark grey turtleneck underneath, and a pair of Mario Andretti leather driving gloves covering his hands. Armando knew the gloves' logo, as they could be purchased there in Italy.

The man's dark cap had made it impossible for Armando to determine what color of hair he had, but there was a moustache—and although it had been ghostly dark inside the van, Armando was certain it was either dark brown, or perhaps even black. None of that mattered, anyway. Yet still, the entire event had seemed eerily frightening.

"You will follow the instructions carefully," the American had whispered. "You do understand English, yes?"

"*Si*," Armando replied. He was whispering, too.

"There is a map inside of this envelope with a set of instructions and a key. The instructions are in English. Read them, follow them precisely, and then see that they are disposed of." He handed the envelope to Armando. "Questions?"

"No . . . no questions," Armando stammered. He then took the envelope and set it between his legs on the seat. Then, for a moment, there was silence between the two men. Both stared out into the darkness and the dimly lit *piazza* beyond. Finally, as if prompted by some unseen cue, the American said, "You know Al-Rashid?"

"I . . . I know of him . . . that is all."

"You have never seen him, then?" the man quizzed, still focusing on the shadows outside the van.

"I only know his voice. We have never met."

"He is Haman Al-Rashid. You must ask his name to be repeated before you deliver the package. He has a chipped tooth that was crowned with a gold cap, and when he pronounces his name *RA-Sheed*, he lifts his upper lip so that if you are looking, you can see the shine from the gold. If you do not see the shine, do not deliver the merchandise! *Capisce?*"

"*Si . . . Capisco!* Do not deliver package unless I see shine!"

The American's eyes shifted slightly to the left, then quickly back forward once more.

"When you are sure that you have seen the gold tooth, ask the man where he studied English." The eyes shifted again, and Armando noticed a slight tilt of the man's head as it also turned to the left and back again. "You understand?"

"*Si, certo*," Armando responded. "Ask him where he studied English."

"If it is truly Al-Rashid," the American continued, "he will raise his left hand and point somewhere off in the horizon—somewhere in the western sky—and will answer, 'Boston University.'"

"*Va bene*," Armando whispered urgently, "Boston University."

"When you have established absolute contact with Haman Al-Rashid—when you are certain it *is* Al-Rashid—deliver the package to him, at which time you will be paid, as promised."

"But . . . how will *he* know who I—"

"Read the instructions," the man interrupted, "and follow them precisely!"

Armando Palumbo knew not to ask further questions. He simply sat still and watched the man in the dark clothing exit the van and slip inconspicuously out into the night. The two would never see each other again. Armando knew he wouldn't recognize him even if they did.

Armando waited for a full five minutes, still sitting in the crouched position in the front seat of his van. He wondered where the American had vanished to, because despite the passing time, he neither saw nor heard another automobile engine turn over. He rose slowly and turned his head in an effort to peer out the rear windows of the van.

Nothing!

He strained his eyes, attempting to adjust them to the darkness of the cobblestone street behind him. No movement at all. The man had simply vanished!

An uneasy feeling suddenly overwhelmed him. He remembered that he had forgotten to relock the passenger door, and so he reached over to press down on the latch. In that split second, a strange fear flooded into his already overactive imagination, and he shivered.

Armando determined to leave his present location before examining the contents of the envelope, which still rested on the seat between his legs. He turned the key in the ignition, the engine responded immediately, and he sped away. His plan was to drive beyond the *piazza del duomo*, find a side street, and pull over and park again, where he was sure to be alone.

Like most Italian cities, Udine was a virtual spiderweb of crisscrossing roads and alleyways, and it wasn't long before Armando found what he was looking for. Making a right turn off the *Strada Maggiore*, he turned his van onto the circular thoroughfare that surrounded the *duomo*, and continued on *Via Del Aprosio* until he was able to turn left onto a small street called *Viale Del Mare*. From there it was less than half a city block before he found an even smaller dead-end alleyway with an appropriately named sign attached to an adjacent building. It read simply *Fine*—the end.

Turning off the motor for the second time that night, Armando peered once again out into the darkness. He was completely surrounded by tall buildings, and with the single lamppost at the alley's end allowing a minimal amount of light to filter in through the tinted windshield, he decided that he was, at last, alone, and could now safely study the material.

As described by the American, three individual items were inside the envelope—a copper-colored key wrapped neatly in a sheet of clear cellophane, a handwritten set of instructions, and a well-drawn, detailed map of Udine's city center and surrounding area.

He looked at the map first. This American had gone to an awful lot of trouble, Armando thought, as he quickly pinpointed his immediate location at the dead-end alley called *Fine*. He worked his way along the map back to where he had parked near the *piazza del duomo*, and realized in a sudden rush of needless panic that he'd stationed himself slightly less than a block away from the local police station, the *carbinieri*, which was undoubtedly the courthouse as well. Interestingly, however, he had not seen a single squad car the whole time. Yet, so what if he had? He wouldn't have been noticed anyway.

As Armando's eyes continued scanning the map in search of where the American might have disappeared to after leaving the van, he suddenly noticed a boldly drawn arrow at the top center. It pointed to a small building at a junction of two side streets perhaps a half mile or so from the *piazza del duomo*.

"*Via Breno* . . . and *Via Vicenza*," he whispered to himself. "I wonder what that place is . . . an apartment, maybe? More important," he continued, as though verbally reasoning with someone else in the van, "what's *in* there?"

He stared stupidly at the arrow and the slightly darker-colored apparent destination point, allowing his imagination to again run wild. He did not have the slightest clue as to what he was to transport, and he thought of himself suddenly as an international spy! He knew, however, that his agreements with the "money people" in the past strictly prohibited him from viewing any of the objects he transported. Most of the items were packaged tightly, and although the curiosity was at times overwhelming, he'd never tampered with any of the goods. It was his personal code of ethics. Still, he continued staring at the location, holding the map close to try and second guess the kind of building that was detailed at the corner junction.

Suddenly Armando remembered the instructions. Setting the map over to the side on the passenger seat, he focused his attention on the handwritten list of things to do.

"Must be some sort of garage," he whispered to himself again as he read the three lines of instruction.

"*The wooden crate is fairly heavy*," the handwriting said. "*You must be extremely careful not to damage it in any way*."

Suddenly Armando's eyes caught sight of something unbelievably sweet written at the very bottom of the sheet of paper. It read simply:

Deliver the crate in due time and without damage, and there will be an extra $10,000 on top of your normal fee waiting for you at the rendezvous point.

"Ten thousand dollars!" he blurted out in sudden uncontrolled excitement, "*Santo Cielo!* What could possibly be inside that crate that is worth—?"

Whump!

Armando's head bolted upright! His heart suddenly energized with adrenalin, jolting into high gear! Something had just slammed into his van!

He froze solid, unable to flex even a single muscle in his body. Slowly, he moved his eyes first to the left and then to the right. He couldn't see a thing. So *what* was it? Was there something, or someone, behind him? He was too frightened to turn around for a glance out the rear windows. Something was out there! Wait a minute. Right overhead. On the roof . . . yes, something was moving slowly on top of the roof of the van!

Closer now. Yes . . . moving slowly toward the front . . . only inches away from the windshield . . .

What!

There, peering down into his eyes, was nothing more than a large cat.

6

It took a moment for Armando to get ahold of himself. He struggled in the aftermath of the adrenalin rush to oxygenate his blood to a level of calm that would allow him to think clearly again. Strange, he thought, how intense fear has such a paralyzing effect on the body.

Armando then watched as the dark grey tomcat leaped effortlessly from the roof of the van to the top of a trash can a few feet away. It halted there for a moment, and turned its head toward Armando. Then, in what appeared to be a look of catlike indifference or unconcern for the emotional fear it had caused the human, the sleek night prowler simply licked its lips, meowed once, and vanished behind a stack of discarded boxes piled alongside the wall at the far end of the alley.

There had been a moment, just prior to the cat's exit from sight, when Armando nursed an attitude of vengeance against the animal. He thought that if he'd had a gun, or some other weapon, he would not have hesitated to use it. He disliked cats, anyway. But, such thinking was irrational, at best. After all, the darn thing was only a cat—probably hungry and undoubtedly on a nightly prowl for something to eat.

Armando turned his attention back to the task at hand. It was time to get moving again. It was getting light, and he was feeling a sense of urgency that was almost impossible to bear.

The corner of *Via Breno* and *Via Vicenza*, like so many small cobblestone streets of Europe, was a narrow junction, poorly lit, and essentially better adapted for the pedestrian than for even the small cars so typical of the country. But with a little effort, Armando found a place to park the van, and made his way on foot to the building designated in the upper area of the map.

There he found a row of five single-car garages in the lower quarter of an old building. To one side, there was also a single green door. This, he surmised, was undoubtedly the entrance he sought. But when he tried to fit the key into the locking device, he discovered that it would not go in. Puzzled, he scoped the garage door to his left and immediately noticed that it, too, had a small keyhole just under the handle. Seconds later he found to his relief that the key slid effortlessly into place.

The garage was empty except for the wooden crate. Hanging from a nail on the left wall were a pair of blue pants, a light blue T-shirt, a matching windbreaker, and a name tag that read *Rovenji Shipping Lanes*, with an official-looking typed alias, *Paulo Terracini*.

All of this, of course, made perfect sense to Armando, who had carefully read and already disposed of the instructions from the envelope. He tried the windbreaker on for size. It fit. Then, peeking cautiously outside for signs of early-morning activity, and relieved at the sight of a still-quiet street, he carried the clothing, then the heavy crate, to the van.

As Armando made his way back through the city center and on toward his destination in Trieste, the increasing light of day signaled the advent of Christmas morning. Everywhere around the modern world, he thought, sleepy-eyed children would be feverishly tearing into gifts of all kinds and shapes, anxiously hoping to discover treasures left by the white-bearded man in the bright-red costume.

It had not been easy for him to leave his wife and children the day before, but Armando knew that Flavio and Michalina were going to have a wonderful Christmas this year, even in his absence. Besides, he would be able to spend the rest of the week with them, and he planned to do just that after delivering the crate to his contact at the shipping yard. From there, he figured, if he drove all day he could reach Taranto, his home in southern Italy, by late evening. He would be back in his wife's arms and surprise her with his ten-thousand-dollar bonus for a job well done. Of course, she'd never know *what* job he'd done.

Entering once again the *autostrada* freeway headed south toward Trieste, Armando allowed a smile of satisfaction to draw itself across his face. He thought about the wooden crate in the back of the van, and of the bonus money that was to be *his* Christmas gift. He was still quite curious about the crate's contents and would have liked to peek inside, but he thought again that it didn't really matter. Whatever the cargo, it had been purchased apparently by Mr. Al-Rashid, whoever *he* was—and was *his* gift this Christmas Day.

Curious, Armando turned around one last time to check for markings that he might have missed in the dark. The crate was plain enough; nothing seemed to be written on the outside. Yet, wait a minute. Maybe there *was* something. In the corner farthest away from his line of vision, there was a small but identifiable inscription. He couldn't possibly read it from his position at the wheel, and so once again he tried to dismiss this unexpected information from his mind.

Armando's foremost defect of character was his insatiable curiosity.

Without thinking further, Armando pulled over to the side of the *autostrada*, put the manual gearshift lever in neutral with the engine still running, and climbed into the back for a closer look.

The marking on the corner of the crate, he observed, was strangely simple. He learned nothing from it that would help to explain what might be inside and supposed it was probably just a trademark. After all, it was simply a miniature drawing of a rattlesnake baring two poisonous fangs—one of which had just released a drop of venom. To the right of the coiled and ready-to-strike serpent was a single word, a secondary name by which the rattlesnake was known in its native habitat of America. It read simply, *Sidewinder*.

7

Late Christmas Night— Palmdale, California

"You can't be serious!" Linda challenged. "You're telling me that after more than a year of planning, you're cancelling the most important vacation our family has ever decided upon?"

"Hold on a minute, Linda, I—"

"No, *you* hold on a minute, Jack! What I don't understand is why you led me to believe that all was fine . . . all was well. . . . 'No problems, Linda!' 'I'm just tired, Linda!' 'Don't worry about a thing, Linda!' How could you do that to me . . . to *us*, Jack? You knew how much this getaway meant."

"Will you hang on for a cotton-picking second, Linda?" Jack shouted back defiantly. "This wasn't *my* decision! You know that!"

"Then tell me, *Major*—just whose decision was it?" She was beginning to be irrational. She knew, despite what she *didn't* know, that in the event of some national emergency (what national emergency was there now? she thought furiously) he'd be called away from her and the kids—and there wasn't a thing either of them could do about it.

"You didn't *have* to volunteer!" she added, knowing full well how ridiculous her words sounded. But she was angry.

"I *didn't* volunteer," he snapped back.

"Then why can't you at least tell me where you're going, or how long you're going to be gone?" she countered, at the same time knowing quite well that such information was classified.

"Linda, I—"

"Oh, never mind!" she interrupted. "Look," she continued, snatching her purse from a nearby table, "I'm going for a little drive."

"Wait, Linda!" he called to her. "Where're you going? It's already after 2200 hours."

"Just keep an eye on the kids, Jack," she said, her voice more controlled than it had been in the entire outburst. "I'm all right. I just want to drive around for a while, okay? Just give me some room, will you? I'll be back in a little while."

With that Linda walked through the kitchen doorway leading to the garage, punched the garage door button, climbed into her Blazer, and drove away.

Jack felt defeated, but he knew things would turn out all right. Linda would let off some steam, think about the situation for a while, and then come home. He really didn't blame her for her outburst, but felt badly that his military work at times painfully interfered with his domestic life. He wished he could telephone General Walker and tell him that the answer was a resounding "No!" He wasn't going to fly some stupid political mission into some strange country, either for him, for the president of the United States, or for anyone else!

Emotionally spent, the major collapsed onto the couch in the living room. He then put a hand up to his head and rubbed his eyebrows, a habit he fell to in times of extreme stress and fatigue. His mind was flaming with the days ahead, about Linda's justified anger of perceived betrayal, and the seemingly unfair reasoning of his having been selected for this mission. "There's a million fly-boys who could do equally as well as I can," he mumbled to himself," and some of those guys aren't even married!"

"Dad?" the quiet voice said, interrupting Jack's thoughts.

"Little Jack?" the major answered, pulling himself up from the couch. The boy walked cautiously into the living room. "What's up, big guy?" he asked.

"Oh, I don't know," his son replied, walking over to his father. "I heard you and Mom fighting."

"We weren't fighting, son."

"Sure sounded like a fight to me," Little Jack countered.

"Sorry about that, little buddy," Jack sighed, sliding over to the left so that his son could join him on the couch. "Your mother's a bit upset, that's all." He didn't want to tell Little Jack about the mission, but after a moment of awkward silence, he determined that he might as well get it over with.

"How come she's upset, Dad?" the boy inquired.

"Well, you know that vacation we've been planning up at Big Bear? The ski trip?"

"Yeah, sure."

"Well, I'm not going to be able to go with you guys."

"How come, Dad?"

"Well, I got a job that I gotta do for Uncle Sam."

"Uncle Sam?"

"Yeah. You know Uncle Sam, don't you?" Jack laughed, trying to take the edge off the conversation.

"I . . . I don't think I do," Little Jack said, somewhat puzzled.

"Uncle Sam is my boss," the major said. "His other name is Mr. United States of America."

"Oh, yeah! I know who *he* is. I seen his picture. But he's not real, Dad. He's just a poster of a bearded man pointing his finger."

"You're absolutely right, son. He is a pretend person, but he really does represent the U.S. of A. You know that, don't you?"

"Yeah, I guess I do."

"Well, there's something I've been asked to do for our country's security, and I'm afraid that the timing of my mission interferes with our plans to go skiing at Big Bear. But you guys are still going to get to go, and if all goes well with me, I might be back in time to join you. We still might do some skiing together!"

"Is that why Mom's mad?" Little Jack questioned again.

"I'm afraid it is. She's justifiably upset 'cause I didn't tell her about the assignment until just tonight. I didn't learn of it, myself, until yesterday, and I suppose I should have told her then, but . . . well, you know . . . I just didn't want to spoil her Christmas, that's all."

Jack hung his head, and his son could clearly see the strain in his father's face. At last, breaking the silence, he said, "It's okay, Dad. We can go skiing some other time. Mom'll understand. She knows it's not your fault that you gotta do a mission."

The major hugged his son close, and felt more grateful than ever for a son who was truly becoming a reasoning young man.

"Where're ya going on your mission, Dad?" Little Jack said with youthful interest.

"I can't really say, son," Jack replied. "They don't let us talk about it, as you know."

"Is it *classified?*" the boy inquired eagerly.

"Yeah, it's classified. It's top secret stuff. Me and James Bond are gonna go and get some bad guy."

"Dad, can we be serious for a minute?" There was a look of concern in the boy's face.

"I'm sorry, son," Jack said, sensing the boy's need. "I was just trying—"

"I had a dream a couple of nights ago, Dad, that really scared me." Little Jack had twisted in his position so that he could look directly into the eyes of his now fully attentive father.

"A dream?" the major questioned.

"It was real horrible!"

"Well, we all have nightmares. You know that. Remember when—"

"It wasn't like a nightmare, Dad," Little Jack insisted. "It was real life. There weren't any monsters, or silly stuff like that; but it was . . . it was different."

"How do you mean?"

"Well . . . it was about you, Dad."

Little Jack suddenly lost his ability to continue the narrative, and so he put his hands in front of his face in an attempt to conceal the embarrassment of tears that had welled up in his eyes.

"Hey, big guy," his father said, reaching out to pull his son close to him. "What's this? Tears? What's wrong, son? It was just a dream—don't dwell on it. Don't let—"

"I don't want you to go, Dad!" Little Jack managed to say, "cuz you won't come back!"

"Hey now, you just hold on there, buster. What do you mean I won't come back?" The major paused for a moment, contemplating the sudden chill that had swept over him upon hearing his son's prophetic-sounding announcement. "Nothing in all the world could stop me from returning to you, Trish, and your mother! Nothing!"

The two sat there on the couch and held onto each other, drawing strength from one another as they each tried to control their emotions. Each was lost in thought. Jack would never know the depth of his son's subconscious dream state, or the graphic and lingering images that had haunted him for days thereafter. And although Little Jack was aware of something—*what* he did not know or understand—he could not be told of the mission. But for the moment they had each other, and that was all that seemed to matter.

"Where's Mommy?" came the little voice from the hallway. Jack and his son released themselves from the embrace and turned simultaneously toward the direction of the adjoining hallway where, standing in the light that filtered in from the kitchen, little Trish was cradling her Baby Suzi doll.

"Hi, Trish, honey. What're you doin' outta bed, doll?"

"Is Mommy gone?" Trish asked, rubbing her eyes and walking over to her father's lap.

"Just for a while, pumpkin," Jack assured her. "She'll be back anytime now."

"Well, we didn't have our prayers, Daddy, and I'm scared."

"I'll tell you guys what. . . . Let's all kneel down now, and Little Jack will do the honors. Make sure that you tell Heavenly Father how grateful we are for a wonderful Christmas, and for being such a close family."

"Yeah," Trish interjected, "and thank him for Baby Suzi, too."

"We don't pray for pretend dolls," Little Jack corrected.

"It's okay, son," Jack interjected, "we pray for whatever's in our hearts."

And so, each with a different agenda running through their minds, Little Jack prayed. He even thanked God for Trish's doll, knowing it would make her happy, though he almost started to laugh when he heard her say "Yeah." He finally closed, insisting that God watch over his dad, who was going on a secret mission. Just then the telephone rang.

"Hurry . . . climb into your beds, guys," Jack insisted, rapidly rising to his feet to grab the phone in the kitchen.

"Good night, Daddy," Trish called, scurrying down the hall ahead of her brother. "No wetting the bed tonight, Suzi," she said into the doll's ear.

"Oh brother!" Little Jack said in a grown-up way, while shaking his head. Then he called back to the kitchen, "Good night, Dad. Thanks for the great Christmas!"

"Yeah, Merry Christmas, Daddy!" Trish echoed.

"You, too! Both of you!" and Jack rushed out the door and into the kitchen.

"Major Garrity?" the voice on the other end of the line inquired.

"Yes."

"General Walker has a message for you, sir." There was a slight pause. "Will you hold the line, sir?"

"Yeah, sure, I'll hold."

Jack thought about the voice at the other end. Must be a young fellow from the sound of his voice—didn't recognize it, though. Had to be some new aide the general was using for temporary assistance over the holidays.

"Jack?" It was the general's voice.

"Yessir . . . Hello, sir," Jack responded.

"Jack, I need you down here right away! The operation's been moved ahead of schedule. There's a crisis."

"A *crisis*, sir?"

"Can't discuss it over the phone, Major!"

"Yessir . . . I understand fully, sir. You need me *tonight?*"

"Don't bother packin' a thing. Just get here as quickly as possible. I'll see you when you arrive."

The phone went dead.

Suddenly the reality of the call slammed into the major's mind like a thunderbolt. "Right *now?*" he questioned in a whisper. "But . . . what about Linda? I can't leave without saying good-bye to Linda!"

Slowly the words came back to him. "A crisis!" He was perfectly aware of what that meant. For one thing, it meant that he didn't question his commanding officer, who in this case was General Walker. It also meant that there was no time for delay. An alert had been sounded, and Major Jack Garrity was a commissioned Air Force officer with a specific task to perform. He had to go that very moment!

But where was Linda?

Frantically, Jack ran to the front door, opened it, and went outside. It was definitely dark outside, but at least there was a full moon. His watch told him that it was 2300 hours. The general would have hung up the phone at approximately 2255 hours. He could kill a minute—maybe two—waiting, hoping for Linda to return. But what if she didn't?

"Come on, Linda!" he whispered urgently, looking up and down the road in front of his drive. It was now 2304 hours! No sign whatsoever of his wife's Blazer. She'd been gone about an hour. She'd surely be on her way back by now, surely. No time to wait, though. He had to get someone to keep an eye on the kids. He couldn't just leave them alone. But then, Little Jack was responsible, he knew that. He could watch out for Trish, couldn't he?

The neighbors—Alex and Mariam! Their bedroom light was still on.

Jack ran instinctively across the street, glancing again at his watch—2314 hours. It couldn't be! Time had actually speeded up. Only seconds ago the darn thing had read 2312—or had it been thirteen?

He knocked on the door. He tried not to bang on it, but he was sure that he had. He hadn't wanted to startle them or to awaken their kids. But where were they? He raised his hand again, formed a solid fist, and was just about to pound on it when it swung open.

"Jack?" It was Alex. "You look white as a—"

"Listen, Alex, I need your help," Jack began, breathing hard, as though he'd just run a mile and not fifty feet. "There's been an alert, a crisis of some sort, and I've been called to the base. Linda's not here right now, and the kids—"

"Sure! Sure, Jack! No problem! Me and Mariam, we'll go over there right now! A crisis?"

"I'm sure it's nothing big, Alex, so don't panic on me. But I've been called to the base, and so I've gotta leave the kids. Just check on them, will you, till you see Linda pull in with her Blazer."

At that moment Mariam walked up behind her husband, tying a knot in her bathrobe.

"What's—?"

"Tell ya later, honey," Alex said, cutting her off. "Jack's gotta go. Come on, Major. I'll walk you to your car." Turning back to his wife, he said, "I'll be in their living room, Mariam. You go back to bed, and I'll see you when Linda gets back."

"Are you sure?" she questioned. "Something wrong, Jack?"

They didn't answer her.

Jack went back into his house with Alex on his heels. "Hit the garage door opener, will you, Alex? Linda closed it when she left."

"Okay, buddy," Alex said, turning toward the kitchen.

Jack went quickly into his and Linda's bedroom. He took a pen from the little desk in the corner, sat down, and quickly scribbled a note:

My Beloved Linda,

How dreadfully sorry I am that I didn't
have time to say good-bye! Alex and Mariam
will explain everything. But I wanted to
tell you how dear and beloved you are to
me. You are my life, Linda, as you know!
I'm so sorry about tonight and the ski trip.
There's a serious situation developing in
the Middle East—and that's probably
telling you too much already! General
Walker just called and summoned me. But
I promise you this—I'll be back! Because,
well . . . I love you, and I won't ever leave

> you! Be careful at Big Bear—I might even meet you there! Stay well, and take care of the greatest kids in the world, 'kay?
>
> Forever yours,
> Jack
>
> P.S. I've got the medallion. I'll wear it next to my heart. Promise!

Folding the note, Jack quickly placed it on top of Linda's pillow, and then glanced around the room.

His flight jacket—he needed that! He grabbed it out of the closet, and took one last look at their bed. He was going to miss that woman—he already did.

The kids were asleep—good. He poked his head into their room, went to their beds, and gave them each a kiss on the cheek. "Good-bye," he whispered. "You guys are the greatest!"

He never saw the tear trickle down his son's cheek as he closed the door and then proceeded down the hallway.

"Thanks, Alex," Jack said as he backed out of the garage. He'd told Alex briefly about the call from General Walker, given his friend a few last-minute instructions, and pleaded with him to relay a message of love to Linda when she returned—and to assure her that everything would be okay.

"I mean it, man . . . thank you!" Jack said, extending his hand out the car window.

"Hey, don't think any more about it. We'll take care of Linda and the kids. Not to worry, buddy."

For a moment longer Jack hesitated, desperately hoping to see Linda before he had to leave. But when her Blazer didn't appear, he threw his Porsche into gear, and headed up the street toward Edwards Air Force Base.

Jack's watch now read 2320 hours, and although he didn't know it, his life was about to change forever.

8

Aviano Air Force Base,
Northeastern Italy

Lieutenant David Guant drove past the checkpoint just at the break of day. There should have been two guards posted at the main gate, but there was only a single tired-looking sentry who, upon recognizing the lieutenant's car, snapped quickly to attention, offered a salute, and allowed the officer to pass through. He'd failed as a sentry, Guant thought. He never even asked me for my ID.

As a commissioned officer, Guant enjoyed the complete privacy of his officer's quarters. He drove the Alfa Romeo—his personal plaything—around the back of the PX and parked. It was a short walk from there to his quarters, and as tired as he was, even that seemed too far. Once inside, however, he scanned the room for normality, then walked over to the closet.

Secured to the back wall, near the floor in the east corner, was a small wooden box barely visible to anyone but himself. Inside was an electronic sensory device he had built some time ago, to detect—by way of microchip-size sensors placed at strategic locations throughout his living quarters—if anyone had been snooping around in his absence. Two small lights, one red and the other green, just inside the box, would tell the story. If there was an intruder, sensors would pick up the movement, and the red light would remain lit if the reset button wasn't pressed within thirty seconds after entry. With no disturbances, the green light would simply remind the lieutenant that his system was still operational.

There had been only two times when anyone had come into Guant's quarters in his absence. The first occurred after he absentmindedly left a folder stuffed with electronics data in the lounge at the officers' club. The base commander, Colonel Mavers, had hand-delivered it to Guant's quarters, apparently hoping to find the lieutenant home for some reason or another. Finding the place empty, the colonel had walked into the kitchen area, placed the folder on Guant's table, and then had "nosed" around.

Guant later discovered the intrusion, and had actually watched the colonel's probing activities on his hidden TV monitor. A video camera mounted within the closet's interior recorded—through a wide-angle lens—the curious colonel as he poked through this and that, obviously just looking around. Nothing to worry about, Guant had reassured himself. And more important, Guant had seen how cleverly reliable his electronics equipment had been. A good test. The camera, which recorded its scenes through a small decorative two-way mirror hanging on the wall, was activated immediately when the red light on the sensory device lit up; and except for a small area in the kitchen that remained out of view, the camera saw everything. The whole thing was simple, really, though Lieutenant Guant was quietly proud of his accomplishment.

The second intrusion, also captured on video, was a test he had arranged with an unsuspecting friend who'd gone into Guant's quarters in search of a wallet. Guant had stashed the wallet in his briefcase—ready to "discover it" later on that night in his friend's presence. The friend had searched everywhere, including a brief scan of the inside of the closet, never suspecting for a moment that his every move was being filmed.

Later that night, while watching as his friend looked under the bed, in drawers, in cupboards, and so on, Guant was amused when, to his great surprise, his buddy had walked over to the lieutenant's refrigerator, pulled the top off a bottle of milk, and taken several gulps right from the bottle. Afterward, he wiped the milk jug clean with his shirt, replaced the cap, and stuck the bottle back into the fridge.

Guant later retrieved the defiled jug and poured its remaining contents down the kitchen sink. Some things he could tolerate, but that was not one.

Tonight, however, there had been no intruders. The green light inside the sensory device was glowing just as it should. He closed the lid on the wooden box, got down on his hands and knees, and reached—as far as he could—to the opposite end of the closet. There he found and retrieved another box and pulled it slowly toward him. He then lugged it out of the closet and lifted it onto the kitchen table. The box was filled with a vast assortment of tools, mostly for finite work on miniature electronic components. He was also equipped with base plates and servicing slides that housed micro computer chips that he could work on and refine under his microscope.

Dave Guant was an electronics genius. He was a commissioned officer, having earned a master's degree in computer electronics, and was well on his way to a doctorate when he decided to use the military to accomplish his "plan." He had received his commission through the ROTC, and with his obvious knack for electronics engineering, he'd pretty much been able to pick and choose his way to his present assignment in Italy.

Interestingly, though, no one had the slightest clue as to just how truly brilliant in electronics Guant was. If they did, he undoubtedly would have been commissioned to work under some military science team instead. No, he played it just right. He had showed them just enough. No more.

"Christmas morning," he breathed to himself. "Should be fairly quiet all day long."

The high-tech homing transmitter that Guant had been working on was nearly complete. He knew that time was of the essence and had worked nonstop to get the device functional before the final testing phase of the F-31, which was at that moment hangared out by the flight line. That might be anytime now, according to what he'd been able to monitor from his buddy in intelligence. In any case, he had to complete the project as quickly as possible, for he knew full well that even *his* access to the Banshee would be strictly monitored.

Guant then removed his Andretti gloves, the stocking ski cap, and other garb, and stuffed them into his *borsa*. Then he made one final precautionary scan of the base from his kitchen window and went to work.

His plan was entering its final phase, and nothing—*nothing*—could go wrong from this point on. There was no margin of error!

9

9:00 A.M.— *A Few Miles Away*

Armando Palumbo pulled his van over to the left-hand side of the dock. A mammoth sign across the back of the tall building just beyond the gate read *Rovenji Shipping Lanes*. He was sure that this was the place the American had instructed him to meet the man.

There were, as far as Armando could see, just a handful of workers on the docks. Like himself, each was dressed in a uniform similar to what he had found back at the garage in Udine—blue pants, the T-shirt, and the windbreaker. A couple of them wore an extra turtleneck sweater. All of them, however, had the bright orange name tag clipped to their clothing—somewhere clearly visible to anyone who might want to check. Armando looked down at the one clipped to his own collar and purposely read the alias out loud. "Paulo Terracini," he said with a smile. "I like that."

Armando wondered how many full-time workers the shipping company employed. Surely the few he could see scurrying about the dock this morning—Christmas morning—were nothing more than a holiday skeleton crew. Would they recognize him as being a stranger if he had to walk among them? Or would they simply ignore him?

Just then someone exited a side door of the building before him. It was a man dressed in the company's blues. He stood there for a moment, casually looking Armando's way. Armando thought he caught the man's eye for a brief second, but then, maybe not—because at that instant he simply turned and walked back inside the building.

Two minutes passed.

Then, appearing once again at the same door, the man exited and walked toward the gate that separated Armando from the main docks.

Never looking directly at the van or its occupant, the man

inserted a key into a padlock, lifted it, and slowly pulled back on the gate. There was plenty of room now for Armando to pass through.

Leaving the gate hung wide, the man walked over to Armando's van and up to the driver's window. He held a clipboard with a pen attached in his hand.

"What a pity one must work on Christmas Day . . . yes?" the man said in English, handing the clipboard to Armando.

"A pity, indeed!" Armando responded with equal fervor.

"You have delivery, yes?"

Armando said nothing.

"You are Signore Terracini, no?" the man said, extending a courteous hand. "I am Al-Rashid—Haman Al-Rashid."

Armando saw the gold tooth and extended his own hand in response.

"Where did you study English, Mr. Al-Rashid?" Armando inquired passively.

"I was a student years ago in America," Haman said. "I studied at the prestigious Boston University." He waved his left hand outward as if pointing toward the western horizon. "And you, Signore Terracini? Where did *you* study English?"

"I learned it from the Americans at a U.S. Naval base near my home in the south, when I was a lad."

"Then," Al-Rashid said, "you have a package for me?"

"*Si*," Armando nodded.

"This is good! Take this dispatch form to docking bay number 7. Ask for Lucca Rovigo. He will sign the order and secure the merchandise on board. Once you have done this, bring the order back to me in the shipping office. Then I will pay you, Signore Terracini, okay?"

"You do not want to inspect the cargo now?" Armando asked, thinking about the ten-thousand-dollar bonus he would receive.

"Lucca will inspect it," Al-Rashid said. He then turned and reentered the door whence he had appeared.

Armando drove his van down onto the main dock. A young fellow driving a slow-moving forklift passed him on the left and waved a friendly hello. Armando returned the gesture, thinking that he had apparently fit well into the overall picture. He was simply another worker.

Docking bay number 7 was a good drive south of his meeting place with Al-Rashid, yet each of the giant portholes were numbered clearly. A few of them even had sub-docking. There was, for instance, a main dock with a number 1 designating a voluminous waterway that housed a magnificent ship called *Constantine*. Alongside it were three smaller bays, marked 1-A, 1-B, and 1-C. A and B were both empty, but in 1-C, dwarfed by the great tanker in docking bay 1, but immense and awe-inspiring nonetheless, a truly beautiful ivory-colored yacht announced someone's personal wealth.

"How would it be?" Armando whispered, unable to peel his eyes away from the stately cruiser. Whoever owned such a vessel would no doubt be worth millions! There was a name on the hull, *Amalias*.

The *Argos*, another magnificent oil tanker, much newer than any of the others he had seen, was poised and obviously ready to set sail. He noticed right away that docking bay number 7 was the largest in the chain of portholes accessing the shipping company. It also lay farthest south in the Triestine bay.

Lucca Rovigo identified himself immediately. He was not a pleasant man, and used few words other than a very informal greeting.

The man waited with obvious impatience for Armando to walk around to the back of the van and open the rear doors. The crate was secured tightly to one side of the van's interior with a set of nylon ropes fastened to two hooks on the paneling. Armando quickly untied them and slid the case outward where, after a quick confirming glance toward Lucca, the two of them hoisted it carefully onto a flat pushcart.

"You have the dispatch form with you?" Lucca said, wheeling the pushcart to the long ramp that ascended upwards and eventually disappeared. Before waiting for a reply, he disappeared into a darkened portal about midway up the hull of the ship's bow.

"*Si*," Armando replied, "up in the front seat. *Momento prego*, and I will retrieve them."

Lucca reappeared, then lifted each end of the wooden crate, peering over and under it and then on both sides of the box, apparently looking for something. Armando suspected the little rattlesnake logo, and was about to point it out when he thought it might be suspicious, if indeed they had not wanted him to examine the merchandise in any way. Besides, he thought, the little marking was small but clearly visible to anyone inspecting as thoroughly as this man was. Certainly this fellow Lucca Rovigo had already seen it.

He was looking for something else.

Armando stood silently curious.

Lucca was inspecting a corner of the crate now and running a finger slowly back and forth over something that was obscured from

Armando's view. At length, the man set the tilted side of the case back down onto the pushcart and squatted in front of it—all the while keeping a finger firmly pressed against whatever he had found.

Then, with his free hand, he reached into his shirt pocket and withdrew what appeared to be a small metal rod about the size of a sixteen-penny nail, though not nearly as thick in diameter. Armando watched closely as Lucca carefully inserted one end of the small device into a hole that was, obviously now, what had been the focus of his search. When a small red light at the end of the device suddenly blinked, and then remained fully illuminated, Armando found himself blinking his own eyes in astonishment.

Lucca bobbed his head slightly up and down once, slowly withdrew the metal rod, instantly extinguishing the miniature red light, and stood on his feet.

"Okay," he said, turning to Armando and reaching for the clipboard that Armando had nearly forgotten was now hanging at his side.

"Oh, *si*," Armando said, handing the clipboard to the man. He wanted desperately to ask questions about the little metal thing with the light at the end and satisfy his curiosity about the contents of the wooden crate. But he didn't. He simply remained quiet and waited for the man named Lucca to sign the document—whatever *it* was.

Lucca scribbled an illegible signature at the bottom of the form, handed it with the clipboard and pen back to Armando, and without a word, started up the boat ramp, pushing the cart with the wooden crate out in front of him. They eventually disappeared into the darkness of the portal beyond. Armando would never know what had been inside the box, and he hated that.

"*Grazie, Signore Al-Rashid*," Armando had said upon receiving the envelope filled with U.S. dollars. There was, by the feel and his brief inspection of the contents, a great deal more than the sum they had originally agreed upon. Once again, he thought, the American had been true to his word. There was easily an additional ten thousand U.S. dollars.

"It is our pleasure, Mr. Terracini," Haman had said. "We will do business again, yes?"

"Anytime!" Armando said delightedly. "You have the number to find me. You call anytime, as I am always at your disposal. It has been my pleasure to meet you at last."

Armando left Trieste at a little past ten in the morning. From there he took the *autostrada* toward Venice, where he would veer south and begin the long drive down the coastal route of the beautiful Adriatic toward his eventual destination—his wife and family in Taranto.

It had been the most wonderful Christmas ever!

10

0350 Hours,
26 December 1991—At an Altitude of 25,000 Feet
Somewhere Over the Atlantic Ocean

Like most of those rare individuals who have flown inside the spacious hulks of massive military transport planes, Major Jack Garrity was awestruck by the 141's incredible size. He had flown several times in the equally impressive C-5s, but this was his first time aboard an airborne command center. The large interior of the ship had been converted into a virtual Crystal Palace with its seemingly endless equipment of computers, radar, intelligence operations, and linkage with the office of the president. From here, he thought, an entire war could be fought, while its commander viewed the battle from forty or fifty thousand feet in the air.

"We'll be refueling in the air over the Atlantic, Major, so I would suggest, after the briefing, that you get yourself some sleep."

General Walker had spoken, and with just the sound of his voice Jack experienced a calming sense of security. "We've got a lot to go over," the general continued, "with an even busier schedule in the morning, so I guarantee you'll need the rest."

"What's the nature of the crisis, General . . . sir?" Jack asked, simultaneously viewing images on a nearby computer screen.

"The crisis?" the general answered, pausing for a moment as if to thumb through several pages of previously recorded thoughts. "Oh, nothing too serious," he sighed, his voice raising uncontrollably as he spoke. "Just a simple aboveground detonation of a nuclear device in a southern desert inside Libya. It wouldn't bother us so much if we'd even known a little about it beforehand; but someone messed up! I can't imagine our not having been on top of it!

"For years we've been duped into thinking that Qaddafi was the power player in Libya. But that's not so. He merely has been the spokesman, the figurehead. The real darkness in that country has the name of Al-Rashid. Haman Al-Rashid. We don't know when the power shifted, but we are confident in our intelligence gathering."

Seeing that Jack was not wanting to respond but was simply absorbing the data he was providing, the general continued. "How Al-Rashid was able to get his hands on nuclear weapons, I'll never know. But one thing is certain. We cannot and *will not* allow him to keep them, or to keep the technology to manufacture them!"

"But, how—"

"I'm sure we'll learn soon enough, Jack. What matters at the moment is the strategy of shutting that man down. From what we *do* know, he doesn't have any missiles yet. But that possibility could come about in a matter of days. And, if intelligence reports are even remotely accurate, the crazy idiot has at least two or three fully armed warheads set and ready for detonation in neighboring oil fields inside Algeria. This could be bigger than Hussein's debacle in Kuwait! Al-Rashid threatened the war office at the Pentagon late yesterday afternoon just after our satellites detected and recorded the blast—and I'm asking you, Jack, what kind of psychopath explodes nuclear bombs on Christmas Day? He threatened that if we attempted in any way to interfere or neutralize his country's 'nuclear defensive capabilities'—what horse rubbish!—he'd not hesitate to burst one or both of the devices, killing who knows how many innocent civilians!"

The general paused for a moment, shaking his head in disgust. Then, in an after-thought, he said to Jack and to the crew chief seated close by, "And you know something? I honestly think this terrorist jerk would really do it! You know what I mean?"

Neither of the two men said anything. They simply glanced at each other with obvious disbelief, then turned their silent attention back to the brigadier. There was real concern in the general's face, as though even he was not quite sure how or if their impending mission could succeed.

Jack found the concern contagious, and wrestled with the slight discomfort of sudden excess stomach acid. He turned to the general and broke the eery silence that had closed in around them. "Let me get this straight, if I may, sir." He then reached down and cracked a knuckle, pausing for just a second. "You're telling us that the Libyans exploded a nuclear device just today? Er . . . well . . . yesterday, I guess it would be?" He quickly glanced at his watch, interrupting briefly his train of thought, while becoming aware that it was now

0400 hours—the day after Christmas. Continuing, he said, "And you're saying that we didn't even know they had such a weapon, let alone were in the process of developing them? How could that be, sir? I mean, I'm aware that intelligence is sometimes . . . well . . . you know what I mean. But completely *oblivious*, sir?"

"Not quite oblivious, Jack," the general answered. "But sadly miscalculated, I'm afraid. We knew, as the outset of this operation clearly detailed, that they had nuclear potential and were even close to completing certain objectives. But I'm afraid we had no idea just how close they really were!

"Most of our efforts lately," the general continued, "have centered on the recent war in Iraq, and what few reports we had coming out of intelligence about Libyan nuclear weaponry were discounted as being overstated. We know now that our lack of concern was a grave mistake, but we also have reason to believe that there has been somewhat of a cover-up! More important, it would seem—at least in my opinion—is that the Libyans had some *inside* help. That someone, somewhere, has sold Al-Rashid parts, as well as technology. All of this hardly matters right now, though. We'll look to the OSI or the CIA to unravel the espionage, if there is, in fact, an inside cancer somewhere. Meanwhile, gentlemen, we're going in there!"

"The Banshee, sir?" Jack asked timidly.

"It's the only way, Major. I'm convinced, as is the president, that we can pull this off if we play our cards right."

Major Jack Garrity shifted uneasily in his seat. He tried to comprehend what some of the specifics of the upcoming events would reveal. He knew he had to put fear out of his mind completely. Whatever happened, he'd deal with it. It was, however, a bit sobering to think that his eventual targets would be intensely defended. His primary concern was whether or not the F-31 was really cloaked with the stealth technology its designers and engineers claimed made it purportedly invisible. If that were so, he just *might* successfully neutralize the enemy's chances of success, as the general and the president believed.

Jack turned to the general and asked, "No doubt War Plans has a specific strategy in mind?"

"We think we do, Jack. Let's move into the war room. I'll lay it out for you."

In a small room near the midsection of the 141, various maps and satellite photos were neatly arranged on two tables. A young second lieutenant named Rickie Lee Weiss was sitting at a command station of computers, radar equipment, and other electronic devices that reminded Jack of the Houston-based NASA Flight Control Center.

Neither the general nor the crew chief, a quiet fellow named De Bourge, introduced Jack to the young lieutenant, and Jack noted that the guy didn't seem to flex a muscle or blink an eye when the three of them entered the room. He just went about his business as though he were completely alone.

Meanwhile, the three men moved in around the two tables.

"The F-31," the general said, using a pointer stick he'd retrieved from the wall beside him, "is hangared here at Aviano Air Force Base in northeastern Italy."

"It's already in Europe?" Jack questioned with a puzzled look on his face." I thought you said that Major Barry and I would be the first to fly the jet."

"That's correct, Jack. Major Barry took off from Nellis three hours before our departure and flew nonstop directly over the North Atlantic to Iceland, where he was refueled in the air by a KC-135. He will have landed the Banshee by now at Aviano. There've been no reports from anywhere or from anyone in the world having screened him on radar. We couldn't track him ourselves. The stealth characteristics worked marvelously well, wouldn't you say?"

"Why Aviano?"

"Part of the strategy, we hope. Obviously, most of the civilized world, especially the superpowers, have voiced real concerns about a nuclear device being tested aboveground in defiance and blatant disregard of the World Test-Ban Treaty. Of course, we're not dealing with a sane or reasonable government here, and the governments of the world believe that Libya's detonation of this weapon is sort of a challenge, if you will."

"A *challenge?*" the major asked.

"Yes, Jack, a challenge to see just how far the Libyans can push us with their newfound power. Al-Rashid is like a spoiled kid. He's got a new toy, though I assure you he has no idea what he's toying with. He wants the entire civilized world to know that he's got the bomb. I honestly believe that if any country attempts an invasion or any other hostile act aimed at disarming the madman, he'll not hesitate to detonate every nuclear device in his possession. And we think that he has at least three of them ready and armed.

"Al-Rashid won't concern himself with the annihilation ideology that has kept the superpowers in check for so many years. Heavens, he'll simply blow up as many people as he can if we launch a nuclear attack against him! Complete obliteration of his *own* people would not bother him in the least if he thought he was going to be destroyed anyway. Can you understand our dilemma, Major?"

"Certainly, General. But that still leaves me in the dark about why we would have the F-31 hangared at Aviano, so far from the target. Why not on a carrier out in the Mediterranean?"

"That's what I'm getting to, Jack. You see, Al-Rashid has scrambled *his* air force to patrol all borders. You can be sure that he'll be keeping a fairly close watch of all major activities offshore, as well as inland. We think he's actually *hoping* for a confrontation, the suicidal maniac! And if F-14s or F-16s, or anything else, come anywhere near . . . Well, you know!

"The Banshee will fly out tonight. It will maintain an altitude of eight hundred to one thousand feet. And, while we and our allies fly normal precautionary maneuvers in the Mediterranean with conventional warplanes, the F-31 will sneak speedily along the coast of Yugoslavia, across the Adriatic from Italy, and then cross unseen over Albania, then Greece, and finally over the Ionian Sea. Here," the general pointed with the stick, "and across the Mediterranean to Libya . . . right over here.

"Its first mission will be a high-speed photographic run of the region surrounding the facility for nuclear development. As Al-Rashid keeps his attention focused on the allied warships in the Mediterranean performing normal maneuvers, but always keeping our distance, he'll begin to believe that we are taking his threat seriously, and that we don't want a confrontation.

"Now," the general continued, clearing his throat, "the satellite maps and photos we have are good, to be sure. But we need some clear close-ups that will hopefully help us pinpoint the targets we seek. Of course, our main objective will be to find Al-Rashid, himself, and his top aides, who will undoubtedly be convened in their own war room, where detonation of the nuclear devices will be at their fingertips.

"If we can locate *that* target, then the second and final mission of the Banshee will be, of course, to eliminate Mr. Al-Rashid and his men, and thereby terminate the threat of a nuclear war."

The general paused briefly, holding the pointer stick against his chin. He continued staring at the map in front of him, as did the other two men, each apparently lost in thought.

Over at the electronics console, Lieutenant Rickie Lee Weiss held a hand over the headset pad pressing against his left ear, then turned to the general and said, "It's Colonel Monson, sir. We're hooking up with a KC-135 out of Tinker. He says we should get ready . . ."

"I'll need to get up to the front," De Bourge said. "If you'll excuse me, sir?"

"Fine, Jerry, go ahead. Jack and I will see if we can't get ourselves a little shut-eye. We can get into the specifics when we touch down at Aviano. Okay with you, Jack?"

"Suits me fine, sir," Jack said to the brigadier. "I need some time alone, anyway, to sort things out . . . if you know what I mean."

"I do, indeed, Jack," the general responded reassuringly.

The KC-135 made its rendezvous with the 141 just off the coast of Iceland, about ten degrees longitude and sixty-five degrees latitude, over the Norwegian Sea. Major Garrity watched with mild curiosity what he could from a window by his cot. Refueling in the air was a tricky maneuver, but with the skilled hands of Colonel Monson, the senior officer at the controls in the cockpit, and Captain De Bourge in operations, the event passed uneventfully.

Jack had been watching the quick rise of the sun as it rounded the Eastern Hemisphere. He was tired, and though he knew sleep was vital, he couldn't put himself to it. His thoughts were thousands of miles away in the Southwest, where Linda and his two beautiful children were undoubtedly still sleeping in their beds through the early hours of dawn.

He craned his neck a bit so as to get a better glimpse of the stark blue ocean thousands of feet below. He shuddered to think about being suddenly stranded in that vast desert of water, should for some reason the 141 suddenly lose power and drop out of the sky. Ridiculous, he thought. With her four powerful engines, losing one—or perhaps even two—would be of little or no consequence. Modern aviation was truly the safest form of travel.

"Better get some sleep," he told himself, readjusting the two pillows that were stuffed behind his head. He hoped Linda was okay when she got home the previous night. If he just could have spent a little time with her before he had to leave. He felt suddenly more lonely than he could remember being in his entire life. Some unseen, all-consuming power seemed to take hold of his body and paralyze his every muscle. Concentrating with all of the energy he could muster, Major Jack Garrity began to pray silently. But before he could finish, his mind was again thousands of miles away, only this time in the land of dreams, flying model airplanes with his son, Little Jack.

11

Little Jack Garrity had felt very alone after the urgent call from General Walker at Edwards had forced his dad to leave him and Trish alone. Sure, their neighbors Alex and Mariam Salinger were there to make sure all would be okay. But still Little Jack was terribly lonely.

He wished his dad would have understood a little better the dreams he had been having. They had all seemed so real. What was worse, they had something to do with the Air Force. Little Jack wanted so badly to convince his dad to retire from active duty and get a civilian job somewhere. But he knew that was not going to happen. His dad had always been in the Air Force, and always would be.

It had been pretty much impossible for Little Jack to drift off into that sometimes frightening world of sleep. Instead, sensing the near-panic element in his father's rushing about before reporting at the base, Little Jack had tiptoed to the bedroom door to keep a vigilant watch.

He had managed to climb back into his bed only seconds before his dad had come into Trish's bedroom where the two were sleeping. He saw him go over and kiss Trish good-bye—and he had almost jumped up right then and there to plead with his dad not to go. But he knew better. He was beginning to—how did the adults say it? Oh yeah, beginning to *mature*. That was a grown-up word that had to do with something about accepting responsibility and being brave. So when his dad had come over to his bedside and had quietly bid him farewell, Little Jack had only pretended to be asleep. In his mind, he had said good-bye to his dad and had tried to remain brave. But what he had really wanted to do was suddenly reach up, grab his dad around the neck, and cry. But that, of course, was what kids did. He was glad his dad hadn't seen his tears just moments afterward.

Later, when Mariam came into the house, she had walked straight for the children's bedroom. Once again, Little Jack had been forced to scramble quickly back into his bed. Mrs. Salinger only peeked into their room briefly, though, so when she turned to leave, closing the door quietly behind her, Little Jack had climbed out of bed again. He was determined to keep a watchful lookout for his mother. There, at least, would be *some* comfort. Besides, he kind of felt that he needed to protect her. From what, though? He couldn't quite understand the feeling, but it seemed important to him and wouldn't go away. He might be all she would have.

A short time later, after listening with difficulty to Alex and Mariam talking on the couch in the living room, Little Jack heard the familiar sound of the garage door opener as it vibrated against the strain of lifting the heavy garage door.

His mother was home.

Little Jack could see the kitchen door perfectly. Alex and Mariam were on their way into the kitchen. He wondered how long they would be there. He wished he could be the one to tell his mom about his dad's urgent call. But, of course, since Alex and Mariam were the grown-ups, they would have to handle it. Little Jack would just wait.

"Alex? Mariam?" Linda said, obviously startled at seeing the couple in her kitchen. "Where's Jack? The Porsche is gone!"

"Hi, Linda," Alex said, trying to sound gentle and reassuring. "Jack got a call from the base commander, or something like that. I guess there's been a crisis, and—"

"That wasn't supposed to happen for two more days!" she interrupted, while showing clear signs of creeping panic. "He told me about the deal, about the mission. In fact, we were going to go on a ski trip, and when I found out about the cancellation . . . I guess I was angry, and—" Tears welled up in Linda's eyes.

"Hey, it's okay, Linda," Mariam whispered, moving up and putting an arm around her friend for comfort. "Jack said to tell you that he'll be back in just a couple of days, or so . . . and for you not to worry. And, oh yeah, he made it real clear that we were to tell you that he loves you very much, and is sorry about tonight."

"Oh, Jack!" Linda sobbed. "I've got to go and catch him! How long ago did he leave? I'll drive—"

"Wait a minute, Linda," Alex stated. "He's definitely on the base already. It's a crisis situation! They're not going to allow you—"

"That doesn't matter, Alex! We've got friends who'll let me onto the base, for sure! I've got to see Jack before he goes." Linda started to turn toward the garage door, and it was quite clear to Alex and Mariam that with her mind made up the way it was, there was little they could do to stop her. But then, as if cued by another pressing concern altogether, Linda asked, "What about the kids? Are they all right?"

"They're fine, Linda," Mariam assured her. "They're both in their beds asleep. I just checked on them a few moments ago."

"Do they know Jack's gone?"

Alex and Mariam looked at each other questioningly. It was obvious that neither of them knew the answer. "Well . . . I'm not sure, to be honest, if Jack told them or not," Alex finally answered. "He never mentioned it to me. . . ."

"Me, neither," Mariam confirmed.

"Would you mind," Linda started to say, "staying here for just a while longer, while I go—"

The telephone rang.

"Hello, Jack?!" Linda asked hopefully.

"Mrs. Garrity?" a voice said, "This is Senior Airman Sharleen Thomas. Do you remember me?"

Linda did. Sharleen was a good friend to her husband—a very beautiful and articulate woman who was married to one of Jack's friends, a colonel who was also the best surgeon on the base. He, Sharleen, and their five daughters were making a family career of the service.

"Yes, Sharleen . . . uh . . . hi. . . . How are you?"

"I'm fine, Mrs. Garrity."

"Linda . . . please call me Linda, Sharleen."

"Thank you. Uh . . . Linda . . . but I'm calling for the major . . . uh, your husband, ma'am."

"Yes, Sharleen, what's up? I was just coming out to the base to say good-bye to him. But if you'll put him on the phone—"

"He has already left, Linda . . . flew out in a transport about ten minutes ago."

"Oh, no!"

"I'm sorry, ma'am! He was really worried about you . . . wanted me to call . . . tell you he's okay . . . and that he loves you."

"Oh, no . . . no! . . . no!" Linda sobbed again. "He can't be gone already! So fast, I mean! Is there some way I can call him aboard the transport?"

"I'm afraid that's impossible, Mrs. . . . uh . . . Linda . . . communication'll be limited."

"Well, where's he headed?" Linda asked demandingly.

"I'm sorry, ma'am. That's classified information."

"You're telling me there's *no* way at all that I can reach my husband?"

Linda was visibly angry—perhaps more frustrated than angry.

"I'm sorry, Linda. I wish there *was* something I could do. Really!"

There was a long pause on both ends. Sharleen felt a real concern for the major's wife, and she really did wish that she could help. But what could *she* do? She waited patiently for Linda to say something, and then after hearing what clearly sounded like painful, but controlled, emotional struggles coming over the line, she said, "Linda, I know it's difficult, but he's going to be okay. Really. He'll come back. Just remember what he said, ma'am, when he left. He said he loves you!"

Again there was a pause.

"Oh, Sharleen, I love him, too!" Linda said, at last, and then broke down and wept in Mariam's arms.

Down the hallway from the kitchen, the door into Trish's bedroom was slightly ajar. It closed now, and the boy walked to his temporary bed in dark silence. He reached over to a box of Kleenex on his nightstand, withdrew two tissues, then wiped his own tears away. He had to be brave. His mother would need him more than ever in his entire life—and he would be there to give her strength, that was for sure!

12

When Alex and Mariam felt relatively sure that Linda was emotionally stable enough to deal with the stress of Jack's leaving, they said their good-byes and went home. And, although she had derived a certain amount of comfort from her neighbors' presence, she was glad to see them off. She needed time alone.

Linda closed the door after them and turned the locking device to bolt the door shut from the outside world. She leaned, as if physically exhausted, against it for a moment, then took in a deep breath of warm, southern California air.

"Better peek in on the kids," she whispered to herself.

Linda found them both asleep, again in the same bedroom, and so she closed their door quietly. Once in her own bedroom—hers and Jack's room, the lack of sound was disturbingly difficult for her. She walked to her side of the bed and turned on the soft bedside lamp she had received from Jack only the week before. Then she sat down on the bed and began mentally replaying the events of the past several hours. There was a picture of her and Jack on the dresser, which she stared at just long enough to usher in another trickle of tears that seemed to come no matter how hard she tried to push them back. She then grabbed her pillow, symbolic of the shoulder she needed. And there, through a blurry film of moisture, she saw the note that Jack had left. Linda was now neck-deep in depression.

She read the note, experienced the myriad of emotions it emitted, and then curled up in a fetal position and wept.

Little Jack had finally fallen asleep. He had lain in bed for some time, listening to the faint conversation between his mother and the

Salingers. As he turned his head this way and that, trying to pass through the portal leading to a restful sleep, he fought desperately to remain brave, despite the ever-increasing pessimism welling up inside him. Finally, teetering on the edge of consciousness, the last thought to come into his mind was an image that had taken up residence somewhere in the back of his brain, an image of something dangerous, something he wished would go away and leave him alone—an image born of a nightmare . . .

It was a field of tall, green grass. The two of them, father and son, stood together, looking out at the distant horizon.

"You think the weather conditions are all right for a test flight, son?"

"I think so," Little Jack said nervously. "But . . . maybe we better wait for a while, okay, Dad?"

"Nonsense, Little Jack! I'll take her up myself, and show you how easy it really is. You just wait right here!"

"No, Dad! Don't!" But for some reason his dad couldn't hear him. The boy then looked down and saw that his feet had sunk a foot deep in mud. He struggled to pull himself free, but as he did, he seemed to sink deeper and deeper into the muddy abyss.

"Dad!" he screamed. But when he looked up, his dad was already climbing into the cockpit of the old, rusty-looking biplane. Little Jack knew that his dad would never hear his screams, because in addition to being far away—which seemed odd because only a second ago they had been standing next to each other—his dad had also put on some sort of combat helmet that cut out all outside sounds. The only sound he could possibly hear at this point, Little Jack reasoned, were commands over the radio. That was the real problem! That darn radio was set up over there on the picnic table, and if Little Jack was unable to free himself from the muddy quicksand, he'd never be able to warn his dad in time!

The storm!

"Oh . . . no!" Little Jack screamed. "I forgot to tell Dad about the storm!"

The boy then watched helplessly as his dad—never even bothering to look over at his son's hopeless predicament—revved up the engine and turned into the wind.

Didn't he see the storm? Little Jack thought, still struggling to pull himself free from the mud, which by this time had swallowed him up to just below the waist.

"Dad! Please don't fly, Dad! There's a bad thunderstorm with dangerous lightning! Come back, Dad! Come back!"

It was too late. The airplane was airborne.

"What can I do?" Little Jack said aloud.

The little radio! The one in the pocket! It's not very big, and Dad might barely be able to hear it, if at all, but it's the only chance!

Little Jack quickly reached inside his hip pocket.

"Yes!" he shouted, pulling the miniature device free—and just in time, too, because he had now sunk up past his hips in the mud, and the little transceiver would have surely been ruined from the moisture.

He flipped the switch. Plenty of power. Great!

"Dad," he said into the small mike. "Do you read me? Oh, please, Dad! If you can hear me, there's no time to explain . . . you've got to bail out! Get out, Dad! Please, Dad . . . jump! Jump out of the plane!"

Suddenly there was a massive explosion! Little Jack had been watching his dad fly perilously close to the thundering storm front, and in the blinking of an eye, the plane had been struck by lightning! . . .

"Dad!" he screamed, bolting upright in his bed, and wrenching himself free from the clutching arms of sleep. He then opened his eyes and stared out at the predawn light, barely perceptible behind the curtains. He was perspiring profusely, and shaking eerily from the nightmare's lingering images. He thought once more about the paralyzing vision of his father's exploding airplane, and although he realized it had only been a dream, he fought again to hold back the tears.

Now that he was awake, however, Little Jack remembered all of the events of the previous night. He felt a lump in his throat as he recalled his mother's dear face in tears, and he realized again how much she was going to need him.

"Be brave!" he commanded himself, and then remembered a little poem his dad used to recite when times were tough:

> If ever there's a time of need,
> With back against the wall . . .
> Just lift your eyes and ask for help
> From Him who gives to all.

Little Jack recited the poem twice, and realized that he probably needed help more now than ever before if he were going to stay brave for his mother and little sister. So, without further hesitation, he crawled out of bed and got down on his knees.

13

Thursday, 26 December 1991—
Aviano Air Force Base, Italy

Operation Screaming Ghost was now fully underway. Gathered in a small room next door to the base's Office of Special Investigations, where there was plenty of needed solitude and ample privacy from curious outsiders, a contingent of ten persons gathered around a small conference table.

It was a handpicked team of professionals that included a three-star lieutenant general named Mick Ludlow; Brigadier General Matthew (Matt) Walker; the base commander, Colonel Allen Mavers; the two pilots, Major Jack Garrity and Norman "Hawk" Barry; Colonel Steven Monson, who was the senior officer and pilot of the 141; Captain Jerry De Bourge, crew chief of the 141; and three other lesser ranking officers—First Lieutenant David Guant, and Second Lieutenants Rickie Lee Weiss and Jeanene Bergin.

Besides these individuals, only a handful of politicians and top brass officials at the Pentagon and White House knew anything at all about the operation.

The Navy, trying to keep a watchful eye, but distancing itself from the "hot spot," had two aircraft carriers, the *Nimitz* and the *Saratoga*—flanked by the muscle of the USS *Wisconsin*—floating in the Mediterranean just outside Libyan territorial waters.

Patrol units, including F-16s and F-14s, flew regular surveillance missions from west to east and back again, monitoring what they could from Tripoli and Benghazi to as far east as Tubruq—but unwilling to engage or intimidate Libyan-owned, Russian-made MiGs.

Spearheading the Mediterranean fleet was Admiral Carl Doxey, who was the only other individual with any knowledge of the F-31 and its mission. The admiral was in direct communication with the secretary of defense and the president, and had the specific directive of maintaining a "distracting" profile.

"Do not, under any circumstances, engage the enemy, Admiral," the secretary had told him. "If, in fact, your pilots are fired upon, move them out of the way!"

This directive had disturbed the admiral greatly. He couldn't understand the ideology of turning tail and running. Not with Navy "Top Gun" pilots, and certainly not from any inferior Russian aircraft or the so-called Libyan air force pilots that flew them. But, given the nature of the crisis and its disastrous potential, Doxey had stepped down from his pride and hoped for the best concerning the Screaming Ghost team.

As far as he was concerned, he would continue distracting the Libyans with aerial shows and military maneuvers that would keep them on their toes, but never give this Haman Al-Rashid any serious cause for alarm. He certainly didn't want to be responsible for the unpredictable leader's detonating any more nuclear devices.

There were other concerns.

The Russians, not easily persuaded to "let the Americans handle it," had dispatched two powerful naval vessels of their own—the *Kishnev*, a flat top, and the *Milinov*, a formidable destroyer, both of which prowled through the Mediterranean like a couple of hungry cats just barely out of sight of the American fleet.

Admiral Doxey was very much aware of the presence of these ships, and of course kept a watchful eye. His primary concern was that the Russians keep their distance. But more important, he did not want *them* to provoke the Libyans any more than he did his own men. They could not, however, discuss the objectives of Screaming Ghost, and so it was somewhat of a challenge to convince the Russians to stand patiently *behind the lines*, so to speak. Nevertheless, Doxey referred these political problems to the capable hands of those in Washington, who he hoped would keep the two vessels out of sight and out of mind.

As it was, much of the world looked to the Americans to solve the crisis. America was, after all, the peace-keeping police force of the planet, as the war with Iraq demonstrated.

"Gentlemen, and of course our distinguished colleague, Lieutenant Bergin," General Ludlow began solemnly, "I would certainly have wished for perhaps a more pleasant set of circumstances for our little gathering here this morning. But I'm afraid a very real threat has surfaced, and onto our shoulders has fallen the burden of neutralizing that threat."

The old general had a stern look on his face. His silver-white hair and dashing blue eyes gave him distinct Paul Newman features. He looked at each face around the table, as though attempting to memorize what he saw, and then proceeded. "I would expect that by now each of you has been briefed?" He took note of the heads nodding up and down and continued. "We do not have a lot of time. . . ."

"Not having a lot of time" turned into a *lot* of time! Of course Major Garrity knew that the three-star lieutenant general had not been referring to the meeting when he spoke of time. And much of what had been discussed here he had already learned in his briefings with General Walker. But Jack sat quietly, nonetheless, and followed the discussion with a determination to learn anything he could that might prove useful at some critical moment during the operation.

He learned a little about some of the F-31 team, as the general had labeled them, sitting around the table in front of him. Specifically, he learned who they were and what their specialties were.

At times when meeting people, Jack had discovered a kind of sixth sense that would tell him, in advance, if a given individual's character was of quality material—or if the person was, in fact, someone he might not care to know or associate with. And, as he looked around the table now, his first impression of the electronics specialist, Lieutenant Guant, was definitely a resounding red alert. The guy seemed okay from every outward appearance, but for whatever reason, Jack's sixth-sense warning signal was blindingly bright and ear-piercingly loud.

He wondered why.

The dark-haired lieutenant had been sitting on the other side of the table, pen in hand, and was clearly preoccupied with taking copious notes. Meanwhile, the general, using a pointer stick, directed the team's attention here and there at various places on the different maps that were pinned to the bulletin boards around the room.

There was nothing unusual about Guant, but Jack found himself questioningly curious. He seemed drawn to the man, not knowing if the attraction was positive or negative. Somehow, the alluring interest felt veiled in shadows of darkness, rather than light. He would remain cautious in the lieutenant's presence.

Contrary to what had been discussed earlier, the ultimate plan to fly the Banshee on its initial surveillance mission over Libya was postponed for forty-eight hours. Officials at the White House decided to convene a meeting in Washington with emissaries from Libya. Intelligence reports, which came directly to General Ludlow through the base headquarters, described the situation in terms of terroristic attempts to blackmail the United States and its allies into negotiating a significant and hopefully permanent arms deal. The president, however, had no intention whatsoever of giving so much as a single round of ammunition to the Libyan leader. Instead, he was only stalling for time, humoring the envoy with his supposed willingness to at least hear their proposals, however preposterous.

Meanwhile, Operation Screaming Ghost was given at least forty-eight more hours of precious planning and testing time, which the team immediately took advantage of. Important to Jack was valuable additional air time for night flights he would now be able to make over the Alps of Austria and the coastal regions of the Adriatic.

The time had come to familiarize himself with the stealthy screaming ghost!

14

1800 Hours, Italy Time

Major "Hawk" Barry stood just to the side of Major Jack Garrity and watched with playful satisfaction the expression on Jack's face as he placed his eyes on the Banshee for the first time.

"That's exactly how I felt the first time I set eyes on her," he said.

"She takes my breath away!" Jack answered.

"Wait'll you fly her! It is truly an experience like none other, Jack! Everything is completely automated. The engineers call it the 'fly-by-wire' system because everything you do, every move you make, is fed into a series of computers that correctly do your tasks for you.

"For instance, instead of mechanical links to any of the control surfaces, the stick is wired into the central computer, which consistently analyzes electronic inputs from the moves *you* make, and then instantaneously transforms those signals into commands of its own to a series of smaller computers and miniature electronic devices that, as I said, actually deploy the control surfaces in the wings and tail section.

"As far as flying goes, the system is so technologically advanced that in a way it does the flying for you! It is a digital flight control system that is so accurate, in literally milliseconds of time, laser gyros diagnose the slightest imbalance of excess thrust, leading to a probable stall of improper wing positions. It countermands with a repositioning of control surfaces, more or less thrust, or a proper positioning of pitch for the maximum performance in climbs, and so on.

"But that, Jack," Barry continued with measured enthusiasm, "is only a very small part of the Banshee's unique capabilities!"

He looked at the F-31 as if it were his child and said, "Come over here for a minute, Jack."

Jack followed his new friend and flying partner over to the undersurface of the Banshee's left wing.

"These here," Barry said, "are concrete-piercing, armor-piercing, 90mm laser-guided, tank-destroying, building-crushing, nasty bad boys we call hellcat rockets."

"All of that, huh?" Jack answered, smiling at his associate's lengthy list of adjectives. "I take it you don't want to be on the receiving end of one of these puppies?"

"You got *that* right, Major!"

"Where do you fire them from?" Jack asked.

"I'll show you in a sec. First, though, come over here and look at these."

"Yeah?"

"Okay now. I'll walk you around the Banshee and show you the works. First, here in the nose section, and also in the tail, you have your RWR."

"RWR?"

"Yeah, Radar Warning Receiver. Doesn't matter what it is, if someone's trying to get a fix on you, which they can't, this little baby tells you immediately where the signals are coming from. It then lights up a computer graphics imagery map and pinpoints the location. Of course your option is twofold. You can just ignore it and report it for later targeting, *or* you can whisper a sweet little message to Molly."

"Molly?" the major questioned.

"Yeah, Molly! That's what I named her. The central computer, I mean. You just speak to her through your computer-linked combat helmet, and she will, in turn, request—very politely, mind you—the assistance of one of your favorite pet hellcat rockets. They, upon request, will obediently blast off in about as much time as it takes to blink your eyes, and . . . well . . . need I say more? Let's just say, bye-bye, radar."

"What's the range of the hellcats?"

"Maximum effective range . . . seven miles."

"Not bad!" Jack was becoming thoroughly intrigued.

"Hang on, Major. You ain't seen nothin' yet!" Major Barry pointed to a small egg-shaped sensor just below the RWR. "This is the TADS unit . . . a telescopic extension of your eyes. TADS is short for Target Acquisition Designation Sight, and essentially magnifies targets—day or night—as far as five miles away. It's like having a sophisticated telescope directly linked to your left eye. What's more, Jack, is that its lens focuses automatically on *anything* you look at. Kind of a big-brother-is-watching device. Know what I mean?"

"That's amazing!" Jack replied, truly blown away with what he was learning.

"Oh, man!" Barry agreed. "And, like I said, there's still so much more."

Major Barry, who politely and jokingly asked Jack to call him Hawk, gave a complete and thorough hour-long tour of the Banshee's fierce firepower and electronic sophistication. He pointed out the 30mm chain gun cannon with its remarkable 2,600 rounds of ammunition storage capability, the more conventional 70mm air-to-ground or air-to-air missiles, and the two "smart-thinking" tunnel bombs that would seek a target, find it, bore into it, and then blow it to pieces from the inside out.

He took him through a mind-boggling, hands-on lecture inside the cockpit, demonstrating the infrared night vision equipment, the lethal phosphorous fragmenting mini-missile system, and the tail cannon with its missile decoy vapor bombs. In the end, he showed Jack, with pride, the intricate twin-jet turbos.

"This is really the single best part of the F-31, Jack," Barry said gleefully. "You see that turbo booster right by your thumb, there on the side of the stick? It's marked TBA, which is short for Turbo Boost Activator."

"This?"

"Yeah, that's it. Push that while you're fully under power, and Molly will make an announcement: 'Okay, everybody. Listen up. Major Jack Garrity's wanting to go real fast now . . . and I mean real fast! So let's just add about twenty parts of nitro-proprolyne to the jet fuel and speed things up . . . shall we?'

"And I'm gonna tell you, Jack, your thrust, which is already more than fifty thousand pounds, will instantly leap up to better than seventy thousand pounds—and your airspeed will climb to an impressive 3,300 miles per hour! That's better than Mach 4.4!"

"*What?*" Jack asked, clearly startled, yet not sure if he could really believe what he was hearing.

"I'm dead serious, Jack! Mach 4.4! I didn't believe it either, and was actually a bit leery about having to wear the bulky space-suit, flight-suit getup. But I'm tellin' you, man, she can do it! I took her two times up past Mach 4, kinda freaked for a minute or so, and sat back afterward with my mouth hanging wide open!"

"You suggesting that this baby can just about outrun most missiles?" Jack asked incredulously.

"Not suggesting anything, Jack. I'm *telling* you! Almost all Surface-to-Air Missiles will get left in your after-vapor, buddy! This thing's a screaming torpedo in the sky!"

"But Mach 4! Really?"

"I ain't pulling your leg, Jack. The F-31 is more like a forerunner to a runway-launched space vehicle. If it weren't for a possibility of overheating, I think you could launch this puppy into orbit!"

"What's its max altitude capability?"

"Ninety thousand feet."

"You're kidding me!"

"Not at all, Jack. Those little tiles underneath are purely for heat-resistant structural support, just like on the space shuttles."

Jack sat back for a moment at the controls. A shiver of excitement and anticipation pulsed through his body, causing gooseflesh to creep up his arms and back. The thought of flying the Banshee was now tantalizingly appealing! He looked up at his new flying partner hovering above the cockpit and said, "Hey, Hawk . . ."

"Yeah?"

"Can you imagine actually outrunning a missile?"

"Yeah . . . I thought about that, too. The way I figure it, about the only one made that could even get close to you with full turbos would be that new Lockheed unit they've been testing out at Nellis. What'd they call it?"

Jack scratched his head, remembered reading something about it, then said suddenly. "Yeah! I read about that at Edwards. It's called the Sidewinder V-2.

For obvious security reasons, flights in the F-31 were restricted to nighttime only. The aircraft, which had been securely hangared near the flight line, was curiously discussed by many. But no one, except the F-31 team—who in many ways were still restricted—had clearance to get anywhere near the hangar. Even the security police who ran a tight twenty-four-hour security watch were not allowed inside. And so the Banshee remained out of sight at all times, with the exception, of course, of the late-night test flights.

After spending most of the late afternoon reviewing operational procedures with Major Barry, Jack felt ready to try his hand at the controls. Together, the two of them left the hangar and headed for the culinary, where they ate a meal and made flight plans for that night. Each man in his own way was physically and mentally exhausted, and each had decided to catch some shut-eye for a few hours after dinner—agreeing to meet back at the hangar around 2300 hours.

Jack would fly tonight.

David Guant sat hunched over his kitchen table, peering intently through a double-lens microscope. He wore a white surgeon's cap on his head, a long cotton apron, and a pair of thin surgical gloves. In one hand he operated a micro-heating tool with which he worked steadily to place the final two chips into the homing transmitter in front of him. With the other hand, he guided a metal-based bonding solution under the heating element and fused the chip securely onto the base plate.

One more to go, he thought, then looked at his watch—1830 hours. Guant had originally planned to attach the transmitter sometime that afternoon. But after learning of the forty-eight-hour delay, the pressure on him to finish the work on the device had been lifted, thus granting him an extra day of testing time. And with everything that was at stake, the final touches needed to finish the work could now be checked and rechecked, thus ensuring success.

Guant knew, however, that contact with Al-Rashid would now be necessary. He had not wanted to make any further contacts at all, but Al-Rashid had no way of knowing that the surveillance operation had been postponed. Unfortunately, the lieutenant thought, he would have to make another trip into town to get to a public phone. Every time he used one, he ran further risk of exposure. But still, the overseas lines were less likely to be tapped—unlike the radio transmissions from the base itself. He'd have to take the risk.

If all went well, Guant would be able to finish the work by late this evening. He could use a couple hours of R and R, head into town for a late dinner, and attach the homing transmitter early tomorrow morning. Besides, he thought, it was already too late to approach the aircraft, knowing full well that Major Garrity was planning his first night flight. He'd let Garrity have his fun. *His* time . . . *his* fun . . . *his* victory . . . was coming! After the successful completion of his objectives, he'd be so amazingly wealthy, so fantastically rich! Oh yes . . . *his* time was coming!

15

Somewhere in Northern Libyan Waters

"What right do they have?" Haman Al-Rashid whispered, cursing to himself. "These puny Americans and their big Navy ships. They think they are so important to the world. They have no idea how truly vulnerable they are, Lucca. My only regret is that we have lost our first opportunity to blow their miserable secret super plane out of the sky!

"If it hadn't been for this outrageously illegal Naval blockade, the *Argos* would have made port by early this afternoon, and we, my friend, would have been waiting for her. The Americans had no right to stop us, let alone board us!"

"Do not worry, Haman," Lucca Rovigo whispered reassuringly to his esteemed commander. "We need only the one launch. Our friend, Mr. David Guant, has provided a fail-proof targeting system. It does not matter if we have only one shot at the American plane. We will have our target, and the Americans will never know what hit them! It will surely be a victory for you, Commander, and for our country."

"Victory . . . yes, Lucca, providing the Americans do not attempt to retaliate!"

"Why would they? They will be the ones who will fear retaliation. The whole world will know that the Americans attempted to provoke us, even after it was agreed that there would be no such attack! And besides, how will they explain their secret stealth fighter to the other superpowers? The Americans have arms agreements with the Russians *and* the Chinese that stealth technology will be shared. We will embarrass them in two powerful ways, Haman."

"How so?"

"Easily! First, they will have to explain and perhaps allow access to F-31 files when we report our findings to the United Nations. The Banshee, as they call it, should not even exist. And we will have sizeable pieces of wreckage to show the committee. But more important, the Americans will not believe that we, a small, relatively obscure country, would have the technology, let alone the capability, of destroying their supposedly invisible flying warplane. So . . . it will, at the very least, confuse them, and it may be a lot easier to convince them that we do, in fact, have nuclear capability, even though we are so far away from actually achieving this goal."

"Yes, Lucca, but they know about the warheads, already!"

"Of course they do. And, they are obviously afraid of them. That is why they do not cross over the territorial waters into Libya. But they do not know that we did not build them. I do not think that even their best intelligence reports are accurate. Mr. Guant informs us that they actually believe that we have three or four strategically placed nuclear devices in the eastern oil fields of Algeria and northern Chad. It is as we planned, Haman!"

Lucca stood up and looked cautiously around the cabin. There were only the two of them in the stately room. The yacht's captain and small crew were busy piloting the ship toward its destination—Benghazi, in the Gulf of Sidra. He walked over to the plush, exquisitely decorated bar and poured a couple of drinks.

Handing one of the drinks to Al-Rashid, he said, still in a barely audible whisper, "This device that Guant built . . . it was an impressive idea."

"It was, at that, Lucca."

"How can we miss?" Lucca exclaimed with an evil grin.

"I think it is as you say, Lucca. If we can get the launch site ready in time—before Guant sends us the signal, we should easily be able to shoot the F-31 out of the sky before it can release any of its weapons. And, yes . . . you are right, my friend. It *was* an impressive idea! Had we to rely solely upon the missile's heat-seeking sensors, I do not think—from what Guant has told us about this Banshee—that even with an arsenal of missiles we could shoot it down, let alone find it in the first place. *No* radar can see it!"

"Yes . . . I know."

"Still," Al-Rashid continued, "I would have enjoyed watching fireworks tonight. It would have been better to shoot it down before it can return to its base with the close-up video scans of our military installations. Do you think, Lucca, that the Americans, after looking at the photos, will be able to determine that we do not have the nuclear capabilities we would like them to believe we have?"

"How could they?" Lucca said. "They are under the impression that our facility is aboveground. Our detonation of the nuclear device in the deserts below Rabyanah on Christmas morning was an eye-opener for the whole world. It does not matter what they see in any photos taken by their spy plane tonight. They *already* believe! I do not think that they need further convincing, Haman. Certainly they do not doubt our strength, or our capability of nuclear combat. In time, with the information we have received from Mr. Guant, we *will* have a Fast Breeder Reactor. Our uranium mines are significant. Once we have actually built the reactor, the cycle will be complete. It is not a scientific mystery anymore, Haman! We *too* can split the atom, and from there, we *too* will produce the precious plutonium 239."

"And if they discover we have only one more bomb?"

"They will not discover this, Commander! We have, as I have said, fooled them already. And when we show them that they cannot send even their most sophisticated spy planes into our country without being easily shot down—then they will back off. And we will have two rewards for our efforts!"

"Two?"

"Of course! The plans for more nuclear weapons . . . and photographs, as well as working drawings to build a Banshee spy ship of our own!"

The two men sat in silence, sipping their drinks and contemplating a future Libya that for them would offer power and wealth beyond description. All of the key players from the figurehead Qaddafi on down would ultimately know the formidable omnipotence of being considered one of the world's strongest. Certainly with the strength of the bomb to assist them, the weaker, anemic, and frail countries to their east and to their south will surrender easily! In time, the puny governments of Chad, Niger, Tunisia, and Algeria will be collectively united as the Greater Libyan Territories—with Haman Al-Rashid as their recognized leader, and the wise but ruthless Territorial Governor Lucca Rovigo to govern them.

Meanwhile, on the bridge of the *Amalias*, Captain Jebel Tarsus, a nonpolitical Tunisian seaman who had come into Al-Rashid's employ by virtue of his skilled seamanship, received a priority signal over the decoder. The message was meaningless to him, but he knew it would be extremely important to the commander. The only two individuals on board who could make any sense of the garbled letters and numbers were, of course, Al-Rashid and the voiceless Lucca, who seemed more like Al-Rashid's shadow than a distinct personality all his own.

The incurious captain handed the note to one of the young shipmates and sent him on the errand. "Take this immediately to Commander Al-Rashid! Be quick about it, boy!"

"Yessir!"

Lucca met the youngster at the door, took the message without saying a word to the timid courier, and closed and locked the door behind him.

"What is it, Lucca?"

"Word from Benghazi."

"Is it coded?"

"Of course."

"Read it."

"It appears to be from Guant."

"Lieutenant Guant?"

"I believe so."

"He shouldn't contact us—"

"I know. But he has, and it is good news," Lucca said, studying the paper before him.

"Then read it!" Al-Rashid demanded impatiently.

"It says that talks with the president of the United States and our emissaries have begun in Washington, and that the F-31 will *not* make its surveillance flight through our country until the day after tomorrow."

"No?"

"That's what it says."

"That *is* good news, my friend . . . good news, indeed. Now we will have more than enough time to ready ourselves."

"There is more, Haman," Lucca breathed, still studying the little note in his hands.

"Read on, Lucca!"

"The *Argos* has docked."

"Excellent!" Al-Rashid said, clasping his hands together. "The V-2 should be on its way to Tubruq right now! More good news, Lucca! It appears that Allah is with us!"

The noose was drawing tighter.

16

2214 Hours—
Marsala's Restaurant,
Udine, Italy

Lieutenant David Guant sat alone at the small table in the corner of *Marsala's Trattoria* in Udine. He used his fork to twist little circles in the plate of spaghetti on the table in front of him. He had already eaten more than he wanted—the Italians were famous for overfeeding. Marsala, the chubby owner of the well-hidden restaurant, was no exception, as he was constantly overserving his regular American friend.

Guant liked Marsala and always left him a sizeable tip. There were no unnecessary waitresses at Marsala's. The old chubby man from southern Italy ran the place with his son, Pietro, and that was it. Papa cooked, and the boy served, cleaned tables, poured drinks, swept the floors, and washed the dishes. And, as far as Guant could tell, the boy was perfectly content.

Two other couples were in the *trattoria* who were busy eating and gabbing about seemingly meaningless things. Guant was not very interested in either of them.

It was getting late, but Guant didn't care. It really wouldn't matter if the other couples stayed or left—this was Guant's private place! As far as Marsala and his son were concerned, Guant could stay right where he was all night long. They wouldn't think of offending the American by asking him to leave, no matter how late it got. Most local Italian customers paid for their meals with the least amount of money, *lira*, possible. Rarely did Marsala find a tip for a meal well prepared, or well served. But the American often paid for the meal ten times over! For a plate costing ten or eleven American dollars, Guant often would leave a hundred-dollar bill! That alone paid a half month's rent! Oh no. Marsala would *never* ask the American to go. They would simply remain open until *he* chose to leave.

For Guant, the night had been a busy one. He had finished his work on the homing transmitter, had secured it in its mounting module, and had hidden it inside his closet. Then, after checking the green light on the intruder detector and finding it functioning perfectly, he closed the closet door and went to the telephone in the kitchen.

In the months he had worked with Al-Rashid, each time he'd had to leave the base he would call Marsala's, just to ensure—should things get unpleasant some day in the future—that he always had an alibi destination. The call also was necessary to ensure that Marsala would be "open" when he arrived, because often, if the old man was having a slow night, he'd close up shop early. But if Guant called, Marsala would be waiting—no matter how late! Better yet, Guant knew that if ever questioned, the old Italian would swear that Guant had been there *all night long*, even if Guant had only stepped in for a quick drink.

When Guant finally left the base, he noted that it was already 2030 hours, or 8:30 P.M. civilian time. Guant questioned again whether he would ever fully adapt to military time.

The sentry at the gate was a young fellow named Ken Myers, whose whole ambition in life was to enjoy a career in the security police detachment of the Air Force's Law Enforcement Division. Later on, following his twenty-year stint in the military, this handsome and soft-spoken E-6 staff sergeant hoped to move into civilian law enforcement and drive a city beat somewhere.

Ken was a friendly enough fellow. Guant liked that. And on his way out, so typical of Ken's character, instead of saluting the first lieutenant as he should have done, the blond-haired, easy-going SP simply stepped over to Guant's Alfa Romeo and said, "Howdy, Lieutenant! Night on the town, huh? Wish I could go with ya! But you know me . . . gate duty all night. Looks like I'll be finishing Victor Hugo's *Les Misérables*."

Guant thought that in addition to the kid's fascination with law enforcement, he'd probably read darn near every Tarzan book, Conan the Barbarian book, and Louis L'Amour book on base. It surprised him a little to see Myers reading one of the classics. Impressive.

As to Ken's not saluting, Guant didn't mind that at all. He was curious, however, about how other officers reacted, and so he said, "Hey, Kenny . . ."

"Yeah, Lieutenant?"

"You ever get chewed out for not saluting officers?"

"Oh, yeah . . . uh, sorry about that, Lieutenant." He snapped quickly to attention, and gave the proper salute.

"Oh, no, no, no, Ken. I wasn't . . . I mean, I really don't care if you salute *me*. I wasn't asking you that. I was just curious if the base commander, Colonel Mavers, or people like that . . . well, I was just wondering if they ever get tweeked a little, if you know what I mean."

"All the time," Ken admitted. "I just forgot, that's all."

"Hey, buddy!" Guant yelled, his car beginning to crawl away from the gate station, "don't sweat it, man! You don't have to salute me—unless, that is, I'm with a general, or someone like that."

Guant threw the Alfa Romeo into gear, stepped on the gas, and in an afterthought yelled, "Tell Jean Valjean hello for me!"

"Uh . . . I'll do that, sir!" Kenny yelled back, smiling as he waved the book.

Before he had gone to *Marsala's Trattoria*, Guant had stopped at a private phone booth, and had taken out a handful of telephone *getones*, or tokens.

He then placed two calls.

The first went across thick telephone lines that stretched along the bottom of the Mediterranean Sea, linking up somewhere on the continent of Africa. Instead of a connection with Libya, however, the voice he spoke with was somewhere in Alexandria, the large modern metropolis in northern Egypt where the Nile emptied into the Mediterranean. How Al-Rashid got the messages from there, he never knew—but get them he did!

This little arrangement had also been Guant's idea, initially. Again, looking to a future of uncertainty, Guant had not wanted calls placed to Libya for *any* reason. He wasn't really sure if it mattered, but every precaution seemed worthwhile.

Al-Rashid had set up the voice in Alexandria, and of curious personal interest to Guant was the fact that no matter when he called, night or day, the same thick-accented, monotonously lethargic voice always responded immediately following the first ring.

Did this guy *ever* leave the phone? Guant thought, questioningly.

The second call went to a small village off the Mediterranean coast of Spain called Cabo de Tortosa. Tucked away on a small lookout, seemingly hidden from the entire planet, was a beautiful estate, completely paid for, with a single occupant—Anna Trujillo, a remarkably beautiful woman with whom he planned to spend the rest of his life.

"Anna?"

"David!" the woman responded excitedly. "Where are you?"

"I'm still here in Italy, sweetheart." He felt his heart skip a beat just hearing her voice. Then he continued, reminding himself that even from a pay phone he should keep things short and to the point. "How did it go?" he asked.

"It's all there, David! Just like you said it would be. I made the other deposits *alla Banca di Barcelona*. Herr Rothenburg was very kind. He transferred the sums you requested immediately by telephone to the Barcelona branch. So . . . everything is done! Oh, David . . . when will you be coming home?"

"There are still a few more things I have to finish, love," Guant replied, thinking about the homing transmitter and the final communique he would be sending to Al-Rashid just prior to the F-31's initial flight over Libya. "But I promise you, hon, it will not be much longer! Now, tell me the figures, will you, please? I haven't much time."

"Okay," she answered, "I have the statements right here. . . . Can you hold a minute, my darling?"

"Certainly."

Anna set the phone down and went to collect the documents. Guant looked up and down the narrow cobblestone street. An occasional Fiat 127 lawnmowered its way slowly past him, its occupants oblivious to the shadowed figure standing in the small telephone booth.

Guant thought about his future with Anna. He knew he was in love. She was perfect for him, accepting him unquestioningly. She honored his every wish, running errands for him into Switzerland, where with the grace and skill of a highly confident professional, she managed their escalating accounts with the extremely polite and tight-lipped Herr Rothenburg.

The funds from Al-Rashid had always been promptly delivered. And interestingly, not by way of the usual bank-to-bank transferring system but by means of a personal courier who would just suddenly show up in a chauffeur-driven Mercedes in front of the bank. A man carrying a briefcase and a diplomatic pouch would emerge, make his way directly into Herr Rothenburg's office, leave the case and the pouch in the banker's hand, and without a single word, leave. The pouch always contained deposit instructions, and the briefcase always contained the contracted amount of money in unmarked stacks of U.S. bills.

Rothenburg never questioned anything. He simply deposited the currency and credited the account marked *Tortosa Enterprise, LTD*.

Two individuals could withdraw, transfer, or in any way, whatsoever, make use of the Tortosa accounts. The first was a man known to Herr Rothenburg as a voice on the phone and a signature on a letter by the name of Sir Douglas Aberdeen—a count with significant wealth from the highlands of Scotland. The second, a traveling accountant and vice-executive secretary named Mira Kisumu. Herr Rothenburg dealt exclusively with Ms. Kisumu. He did not know, nor would it matter if he did know, that Sir Aberdeen was actually a U.S. Air Force pilot, a first lieutenant named Guant—and that the beautiful Ms. Kisumu was, in fact, a native of Logrono, Spain, whose real name was Anna Trujillo.

"David?" Anna's voice said again on the phone, "you still there?"

"It is I, my love! Speak to me."

"I would rather hold you in my arms," she answered cheerily.

"And I, you, my darling. But that can wait a short while longer! What have you got for me?" he asked, getting back to business.

"Okay. In Zurich, the Tortosa account now reads twenty-one million, four hundred eighty thousand. That is the cash account only. There is an additional four point six million in precious metals, mostly gold, at yesterday's market price. Also a million three in gems. That is Herr Rothenburg's estimate, love," she added.

"What about Glasgow?"

"We haven't received this month's statement, but I went there three weeks ago to pay the taxes on the Highland estate, and there was better than two million, plus accrued interest, in the account. So it is probably close to two point one, maybe two point two. I can check it exactly if you would like, *signore*."

"No, that's all right, it's not necessary," he said quietly, again eyeballing both directions of the street. "How much did you transfer to the bank in Barcelona?"

"*El Banco de Barcelona*," she said, "has just a little. Two hundred thousand, just like you said."

"Good."

"I do good work, *no?*"

"You do good work, *yes!*" he corrected her.

"How much longer before you fly home, my darling?" she pleaded.

"I have leave coming in just two weeks. I'll be there then, and we can go wherever you want, although I'd prefer to relax right there on the beach at Cabo de Tortosa."

"Oh, David, why can't you just quit the Air Force?"

"You already know the answer to that, Anna. We've talked about it before. If I just leave, and it is discovered that certain powerfully important items are missing, it might draw a lot of heat our way. Let's just be patient, darling, and follow the plan. It won't be much longer, and I will leave the service with a full honorable discharge. And then . . . then we will vanish together, *no?*"

"*Yes!*" she corrected.

"Okay, Ms. Mira Kisumu, I've got to go now. I love you, ya know."

"And *yo te amour*, Sir Douglas Aberdeen."

And so now he was at *Marsala's Trattoria*, imbibing quite good, newly produced Italian wine. It wasn't the best, but that didn't seem to bother Guant, as his objective—that of drinking enough to emotionally ease out of the pressure-cooker mission he had consigned himself to—was more than adequately being met.

As Guant held the half-filled glass in his hand, he absently began to swirl the dark red contents around, mesmerized by the liquid's power. And as his hand swirled the glass of wine, his mind began to twist back through his memory bank, extracting data of his past that was sealed forever in the unsettled and embittered chambers of his mind.

His lip tightened in pain as Guant reflected how his life had begun with all of the handicaps possible. His mother was a large, stout, dominating woman who seemed to love only herself. She had been married three times, with her second husband suing for divorce because she frequently beat him up.

His mother's third husband, Guant's father, had died of a heart attack just a few months before Guant's birth. As a result, Guant never knew his father and rarely saw his mother—for she was always "gone to work," eking out a pauper's living for the two of them.

Guant's heart again stirred with anger as he thought of how his mother had given him no affection, no love—and certainly no discipline. She had always seemed embarrassed about her puny son, and forbade him from even calling her at work. It was ironic, Guant thought, how other children had rejected him as a child for no apparent reason other than his mother's fierce, domineering anger.

He remembered with self-pity the school psychologist's comment after Guant had taken a battery of tests in an attempt to discover the roots of his anti-social behavior. "David, at age thirteen, has no idea of the meaning of the word *love*." But that was before Anna—his stunningly beautiful Anna from, of all unlikely places, Logrono, Spain. Love at last was his, and all of the bitterness of his past was swallowed up in his knowledge that at last he was getting even with the society that did him dirt. And Anna—obedient, charming Anna—was completely at his beck and call, ready to do his bidding for the rest of his life!

"Will there be anything else, *Signore* Guant?" Marsala asked, interrupting Guant's sordid thoughts.

The lieutenant looked at the plate of spaghetti in front of him, then at his watch. Exactly 2214 hours. It wasn't that late after all. He'd just sit here for a while longer and enjoy another drink—only this time he would splurge and order some *vintage* wine. What a great idea—a bottle of vintage Italian grape. "Yes," he said, "*un altra bicherra di vino*. In fact, my dear friend Marsala, preparer of fine foods and deliverer of service *exceptionale*, not just a glass of *vino*, but let's make it a bottle of your finest, most expensive drink!"

"Only the best, *Signore* Guant!" the chubby old man said courteously. "I will have Pietro bring it to you immediately."

And with that, Marsala turned on his heels and moved quickly back into the kitchen, clearly delighted to see the American Air Force man in a mood for celebration. There would be a *big* tip tonight.

17

Midnight, 26 December 1991—
Aviano Air Force Base, Italy

While his wife, Linda, and his two children, Little Jack and Trish, spent an uneasy day in Palmdale, California, Major Jack Garrity began preparations for a unique government mission halfway around the world. A mission that was increasing in risk and importance with every passing hour.

Major Garrity stood uncomfortably still while his fly-buddy, Major "Hawk" Barry, made the final adjustments on his flight suit.

"Hold still!" Hawk said.

"I've got an itch, *Norman!*" Jack said, grinning through the helmet shield.

"Norman, huh? You must not want me to connect this oxygen hose, Major! You wanna breathe up there? Huh?"

"Norman is a *good* name," Jack said sarcastically. "You know how much Stormin' Norman loves *his* name! I can't imagine your not wanting a handle such as that."

"Keep it up, sir, and ol' Hawk here will hook you up to the exhaust and fire the turbos, just to check out the durability of this space suit you're wearin'."

"Okay, you win, Hawk. You about done?"

"Couple more seconds . . . and we'll snap this . . . ummph! . . . into place . . . There we go! How's that feel, Major?"

"I'm just glad I drank sparingly this morning!"

"Come on, Jack, climb up there now. Let me get these hoses hooked in."

"You sure you know what you're doing, Norman?"

"Duh . . . I think so, Major! Let's see here, X plugs into Y, and . . . oh yeah . . . Z plugs into . . . Hey! Where's the hole for Z!"

The two men toyed with each other long enough to get Jack securely harnessed into the cockpit and take away the nervous edge. That accomplished, Major Barry flipped a small switch just to the right of the flight stick and activated the unicom system. From then on they would speak through the radios.

"Jack, 2350 hours! You ready?"

"As I'll ever be."

"We're gonna pull ya out onto the flight line, and from there she's all yours."

"Roger that!" Jack breathed, his adrenalin pumping.

"Okay, now, listen up, Major! Remember, keep in constant communication with Molly, ya hear me?"

"Roger . . . talk to Molly."

"Good! Molly's smarter than you think, pardner. You get the least bit confused, just ask her. She'll tell ya darn near anything you wanna know. But don't, I repeat, *don't* break radio silence, especially over the Adriatic or up over the Alps. They can't see ya . . . but they *can* hear ya! So when you're airborne flip your transmitter off, but leave the receiver on. Molly'll keep you company. She'll really be like a passenger. You'll learn that soon enough. I know you wouldn't be here if you were the type to panic . . . so I'm trustin' in your supreme airmanship. Molly's gonna do most of the flyin' for ya, but she can't tell ya nothin' unless you're askin' her questions. So don't be shy, Major! Ask her as much as you care to."

"Do I call her Molly?"

"Yeah. She's been programmed, thanks to me, to respond whenever you use her name. I named her, ya know."

"Yeah, yeah . . . so you said. Does she respond to coded words?"

"That's a good question, Jack. I'm glad you asked me. She does, in fact, run several operations that are coded with key-word commands. I didn't know that myself until I was airborne and halfway across the Atlantic. But don't sweat it! Ask Molly and she will tell ya, herself, what those codes are, and what she does in response to them."

"Do I have to ask her in a computer kind of way?"

"No, no. You remember those *Star Trek* movies where Captain Kirk and Mr. Spock ask the computer fairly sophisticated, but straightforward, questions?"

"That easy, huh?"

"It really is, Jack! Molly's got a digitally enhanced voice box, very much like a robotic sound; but she'll talk back to you and respond just like the *Star Trek* computer. It's pretty wild sometimes cuz ya get to feeling like she's a real person. And, of course, if you'll keep in mind that it took *real* people literally four years to program her, it might make her seem more human than robot.

"Actually, I sort of played with Molly a bit during my flight. I was curious how many different ways she would process and comprehend a single question asked different ways."

"What'd you ask her?" Jack asked, curious now.

"I asked her how to turn on the map light inside the cockpit."

"What'd she say?"

"It wasn't so much *what* she said. Rather, it was that her response remained the same to as many different ways as I could think of to ask that question."

"Yeah?"

"Roger that! I said, 'Molly, how do you turn on the map light?' Her response, *'Panel sixteen, green disk, indication marks NL.'* When I asked her to define for me the NL initials, she said, *'Navigation Lamp.'* So again I asked her, 'Molly? Where's the map light?' Her response was exactly the same. Then I asked her where to find the little light so's I could read my flight charts; her response was again verbatim to what she had said before. It was truly amazing! The engineers who programmed her must have fed in endless, everyday-type questions, so that when we asked for information, no matter who was flying or how *we* talked, Molly would understand and not come back with that infamous *'it does not compute'* response!"

Jack found panel sixteen and pushed the feather-touch green button with the markings NL, and sure enough, a direct beam of light illuminated an area where something could be read. Of course the aircraft didn't really need navigational maps, because the entire surface of the planet was already programmed into the computer and was visual-at-command in graphic detail.

Too bad Molly doesn't have a detailed map of all of the strategic military installations as well, Jack thought.

Out on the tarmac, Major Barry politely asked the two military security policemen who had assisted in pulling the Banshee free from her hangar to please step back out of the way. Then, with his handheld unicom, he spoke to Jack for the last time.

"This is it, Major. You've got a full moon. Should be an amazingly beautiful flight, especially over the Alps. Stick with the flight plan, and I'll see ya back here when you return."

"Roger that, Hawk. Looking real nice out. Should be like a walk in the park!"

"Good luck, Major. . . . Hawk out!"

"You ready to fly, Molly?"

"*At your command, Major Garrity.*"

"Then let's do it!"

Jack advanced the throttles. Instantly, fifty thousand pounds of thrust accelerated the Banshee with inexorable power! The runway became a silken blur, and Jack rotated the nose a slight fifteen degrees.

He was airborne. The aircraft, at Jack's command, arched skyward and sped through the heavens like a missile. The experience of climbing on rock-steady wings through the night was exhilarating! This was a maximum performance aircraft in every sense of the words!

Jack raced northward, all the while gaining altitude at an impressive eighty-seven hundred feet a minute. He wondered how much faster he could climb if he hit the boosters.

The stick was profoundly light to the touch. It was as Major Barry had described, and much, much more! It was clear that Molly's unobtrusive intervention was the beauty of the craft, for it was in perfect balance.

Molly knew when to add thrust according to the speed and pitch determined by the major's own commands. She positioned the control surfaces on the wings for a continual steady and smooth maximum performance climb, and instantaneously modified each individual function to maintain a flawless balance of harmony.

Of course no computer could foresee a wind sheer encounter, and the Banshee did blaze a trail or two through some rough spots. But with the incredible sensors inside the flight stick, Molly could quickly countermand any disturbance, and reposition the control surfaces when needed.

The F-31 Banshee was nothing short of an aviational phenomenon!

Jack decided to do two high-altitude fly-overs of the base before he headed out over the Alps. And, since the luminous mountain range was so close to Aviano, he would use the flybys to gain altitude.

He flew speedily west across the high plains of Italy for a few moments, easing into the comfort zone he always sought at the controls of any aircraft. In a panel immediately before him, four computer screens provided various tidbits of information, including navigational charts, mountain ranges closest to his present position, ground level elevations, and specific high points and mountain peaks that he should keep an eye on.

He also had access to digital airspeed readings, fuel consumption rates, latitude and longitude readings—and curiously different—a topographical map which pinpointed his precise location and vector heading. This map moved like a video arcade game as he raced across the terrain thousands of feet above.

"Molly?" he asked, "can you show me how to activate the TADS device? I seem to have forgotten the procedure."

"*Will you be arming the weapons systems, Major Garrity?*" the computer voice inquired.

"No, I just want to use the infrared with the telescope enhancer."

"*The Night Vision Infrared System is activated by depressing the yellow disk, indicator marks I.N.V. on panel four to your immediate left, sir.*"

"I see it."

"*And the magnification system is also located on panel four, the light blue disk, indicator marks T.A.D.S. Do you see that as well, sir?*"

"Yes. Thank you, Molly."

"*You're most welcome, sir. May I assist you further?*"

"In a few minutes, probably."

"*Thank you, sir.*"

Jack activated both systems, and was equally fascinated and amused as a small, emerald-colored visor emerged from its resting place inside his helmet, and slid robotically into position about two inches in front of his left eye.

The visor was egg-shaped and appeared at first to be blankly transparent. It was like looking through the bottom of an old Coke bottle. Suddenly, like a small television set, the oval screen began to flicker with life. It was dim at first to allow the human eye to adjust gradually. But it grew progressively brighter until, with perfect clarity, a dramatically vivid image, three-dimensionally correct, appeared before him. It was a telescopic view of the earth passing some six thousand feet beneath him.

The greenish color in the system's lens gave an almost spooky tint to the hundreds of shapes below. Yet, dark as it was, notwithstanding the soft light of the moon on the earth's surface, the objects within the system's field of vision were dazzlingly clear.

Responding to his own line of sight, the electronic sight enhancer was in constant motion, moving this way and that and relentlessly focusing and re-focusing as it scanned the terrain below.

Molly handled the specific magnification operations of the Infrared TADS unit. For extreme close-ups and locks, Molly, at the major's command, would activate the zoom lens to whatever power Jack selected. This was one of the specific coded commands Molly responded to.

"What's the maximum power stop, Molly?" Jack inquired.

"*One hundred, sir.*"

"How do I activate that?"

"*Simple commands, sir.*"

"Example, please," Jack responded.

"*To magnify the passing terrain, sir, you need only verbalize what specific lens power you desire and I will accommodate. If, for example, you wish a power of ten, a simple command, ten power, will suffice.*"

"And to lock in on a specific target?"

"*Simple command, sir. Target lock, ten power, or whatever power you choose.*"

"Let's try it!" Jack said enthusiastically.

"*At your command, sir.*"

Jack was now approaching the base, having turned 180 degrees after reaching an AGL of ten thousand feet. The familiar landscape, the flight line, the bunkers, the PX, the officers' quarters, the main base headquarters—indeed the entire perimeter of Aviano lay like a map in front of him.

"Twenty power, please," he instructed Molly.

There was no verbal response, just immediate compliance.

He scanned with graphic clarity the scenes in front and below him.

Two security police officers were standing on either side of the hangar from which the Banshee had emerged only moments before. These were the same two men who had helped Major Barry pull the F-31 onto the flight line; and although Jack was better than ten thousand feet above them, and a good quarter mile west of the base, he could see their faces right down to a moustache just above the lip of the younger airman to the right.

"Amazing!" he whispered.

There was plenty of movement on the base. Three different security vehicles patrolled the perimeter and the flight line, keeping a constant watch on the vast assortment of F-16s, F-14s, tankers, transports, A-10s, and helicopters. Other sentries were posted on the flight line as well, each clearly visible to Jack's probing watch.

Another movement just to the side of the F-31 hangar turned out to be Major Barry, himself. Jack watched him for a second, then said, "Fifty power, please."

Immediate compliance.

"Thank you, Molly!" Jack said, beginning to feel, as Barry had suggested, that Molly was more human than robot.

"You're welcome, sir."

In the milliseconds of time it took for Molly to electronically focus and zoom in on the visual location desired, Jack watched his friend lift a small hand-held com unit to his lips and squeeze the transmitter button.

"You're looking good, Jack!" Hawk's voice said over the intercom. "I know you can't talk to me, ol' buddy, but I just wanted to remind you to stay loose. I'm sure you've realized by now how smooth she is! Just go with the flow, pardner . . . and enjoy yourself! And . . . oh yeah . . . say hello to Molly for me! Hawk out!"

Jack smiled.

"Hawk says to say hello to you, Molly."

"I recognized Major Barry's voice, sir. Does he also call himself Hawk, a bird of prey?"

"That's a nickname, Molly."

"A nickname, sir?"

"You don't know what a nickname is, really?"

"I'm afraid not, sir."

"I was under the impression you knew everything!"

"Hardly, sir. My central programming includes a vast network of memory data, but it is, to a large extent, limited to the individual and collective functions of the F-31."

"No big deal, Molly. A nickname is . . . well, just another name we sometimes call ourselves for fun."

"Do you have a nickname, sir?"

"As a matter of fact, I do. My father calls me Little Jack, and I have given the same nickname to my son."

"Little Jack, sir?"

"That's correct."

"Thank you, sir."

"Don't mention it, Molly."

Jack flew swiftly across the base, still gaining altitude and casually scanning the goings-on below. And as he was initiating a gradual nine-degree northeasterly bank, Jack's eye focused on the base's main gate area. A small convertible was just coming to a halt. It looked like a vintage Alfa Romeo.

"Target lock, seventy-five power, Molly."

The driver was First Lieutenant David Guant, whom he had met but hours earlier. He had come to a stop now and was gesturing to the sentry on duty. Jack watched while the two of them exchanged a few words, and then noted, with curious concern, the lieutenant reach over to the passenger's seat and retrieve what appeared to be a bottle of wine, which he attempted to hand to the sentry.

The young airman on duty shook his head politely from side to side and declined the offer. Then, motioning the inebriated officer onward, he lifted the gate and allowed him to enter the base.

"Molly?"

"*Yes, Major.*"

"What is the procedure for video scans?"

"*Simple commands, sir.*"

"Example, please."

"*At any time during TADS surveillance, whether in target lock or observation mode, a simple command, video record, will suffice, and I will accommodate.*"

"Are there any other functions that I should be aware of while operating the video scanners . . . I mean like slow or fast speeds . . . that kind of thing?"

"*Only audio records, sir.*"

"Audio records?"

"*Yes, sir.*"

"Example, please."

"*At any time during video record, should you wish to make a verbal record of what is being recorded at that moment, a simple command, audio record, will suffice, and I will accommodate.*"

"Anything else?"

"*Nothing, sir.*"

"How about the recording speeds?"

"*The video scanners are programmed to record at high speeds only, sir. No other adjustments are necessary.*"

"Thank you, Molly."

"*You're welcome, sir.*"

Through a lens mounted in the tail section of the plane, Jack watched the Air Force base fade from view. He was flying northwest again at an altitude of seventeen thousand feet and rapidly approaching the peaks and ominous valleys of the Austrian and Swiss Alps. He would race at mountaintop level along the snow-tipped giants until he reached the border of Austria and Switzerland at approximately ten degrees longitude and forty-seven degrees latitude. He would then veer south, down into the heartland of Italy.

From this point, following the shape of the great boot, Jack would missile skyward in a southeasterly arch until reaching and maintaining a ceiling altitude of eighty-five thousand feet, at which time he would begin a slow descent. His final objective, after turning one hundred eighty degrees north again, would be to fly at supersonic speeds along the Adriatic toward a homeward-bound destination point at Aviano.

High overhead, an endless ocean of stars and planets reminded the major of his infinitely small and significantly obscure self against the total big picture. He thought about Linda, Little Jack, and Trish for the first time since takeoff, and realized more than ever that they were literally on the other side of the planet below him—a long ways away by reckoning of measured distances on earth—yet, he thought, they too can see this same brilliant moon, or at least they would be able to in just a couple of hours as darkness came to their home in Palmdale.

As he considered the stars and the heavens above him, Jack reflected on the conversations he and Linda had shared so many times about the "sure feeling" inside each of them that seemed to whisper a reassuring "yes" to their inquiry about a watchful God—and the likelihood of other worlds and other intelligent beings. They *knew*, though he could not explain why, that the glory of the heavens was the work of an omnipotent Creator—and not, as so many believed, an unexplainable scientific phenomenon that granted minimal life, only to extinguish it eternally in a purposeless and costly waste of human soul and acquired matter and intelligence.

At this moment, Jack somehow felt closer to this God—*his* Creator—than perhaps ever before. With this emotion swelling within him, Jack thought of Linda, and at once he felt closer to her, as well.

Jack reached up to his chest and felt through the material of his flight suit for the gold medallion hanging around his neck. The simple gold piece, Linda's gift from just a few days earlier, depicted a small planet earth, a moon, some stars, and a miniature space shuttle. On the flip side was an inscribed message from the woman he loved more than life, itself. It read simply:

Like the heavens that have no end . . .
So is my love for thee.

Tears came to the major's eyes. He realized how immensely important his family was to him, and at the same instant he regarded his upcoming mission into Libya with great apprehension.

He knew that fear could not, and would not, accompany him into the heart of the operation, and realized that his trust in well-trained instincts, and a maturing faith in God would see him through. As these and other thoughts raced through his mind, he promised himself and the powers of heaven that if he could get out of this alive, he would devote more time—quality time—to the family he loved. He would better himself as a human being, as a father, and as a concerned and caring friend and companion to his beloved Linda.

He knew that they needed him, and he them! Then his mind spun to the present. Perhaps, like himself, Little Jack would also be flying *his* plane today. This thought entering peacefully into his mind caused a warm and tender smile to break across his face. He would make it! With all his heart, he knew that he would, and *could*, make it back to those who gave him reason for living!

For now, however, he would wing southward with Molly.

PART TWO

The Sacrifice

Like the heavens that have no end . . .
So is my love for thee.

18

Saturday, 28 December 1991— Palmdale, California

Linda Garrity stretched her arm toward the nightstand and tried unsuccessfully to flip the switch on the alarm clock.

It was out of reach.

The little buzzer was exasperatingly annoying, and although she knew that it was time to get up, Linda's body refused to cooperate. Instead she pulled the pillow over her head and squashed both sides of it against her ears to shut out the sound.

That worked for a minute, but even with the makeshift ear plugs she continued hearing, although faintly, the merciless buzzing vibrations. Finally, with no further options available, she exploded out of bed.

"All right! All right!" she shouted at the mechanical gadget. "Shut up already!"

Click. She switched it off.

"I've gotta get a different alarm clock," she said wearily. "One that plays soft, sweet music in the mornings, instead of some outrageously obnoxious imitation of a jackhammer pounding on pavement!"

Of course no one was listening to her, and as she progressively freed herself from the numbing paralysis of sleep, she looked about the room, stretched and yawned, and said, "Who you talking to, girl?"

Linda sat in silence for a minute or so and blinked her eyes at the clock. She stared at the little numbers in the right-hand corner representing the seconds of time ticking electronically by: 38 . . . 39 . . . 40 . . . tick . . . tick . . . 43 . . . That's odd, she thought. I've never heard the thing make noise before.

"Noise? It's electronic! It's not supposed to make—"

Tick . . . splash . . . splash . . . tick . . .

"Wait a minute," she said, still talking to herself. "That's not the clock!"

She stood up and walked to the bedroom window, pulled back the curtains, and cupped her hand over her mouth.

It was as dark as midnight outside. The complete west coast was thickly cloaked with a blanket of clouds that stretched down from high above the Pacific Northwest, to the farthest reaches of southern Baja, below Cabo San Lucas, and beyond. Rain had been splashing against the window, and though she didn't really mind the moisture, this particular storm seemed eerily dense and depressing.

For a moment Linda wondered if she had set the alarm a few hours too early—for surely, as dark as it was, it couldn't possibly be morning. Not yet, could it? She looked back at the clock. It read 6:38. She thought about the cloud cover causing the rain, and remembered that at this time of the year six-thirty in the morning was fairly dark, even on a clear morning.

It *was* morning!

Time to get moving.

Then again—maybe not. Did she really want to get the kids out of their beds on such a gloomy morning? Why not just let them sleep in—her, too, for that matter. What was the rush?

Despite the earlier setback of Jack's emergency crisis and ill-timed banishment to who knows where, Linda had gotten a grip on herself, and had determined that supporting her husband was certainly more important than lying around the house all day pouting about it. Jack would have wanted them—no, actually if she remembered right, he had made it clear that he *expected* them to go on up to Big Bear without him. Heck. They had already rented the cabin, a gorgeous place big enough for five families! Why waste all that money?

And so after consulting with Alex and Mariam, and failing to persuade them to come along, she had at last accepted their advice that she take the kids to the retreat so they could escape the monotony of dwelling on their father's absence.

The kids had been ecstatic, nearly forgetting altogether the gloomy atmosphere that had existed since their father's unscheduled departure. They teamed up as a family, packed their clothing, toys, and supplies, cleaned the house, and made all the necessary preparations to leave early Saturday morning.

Earlier, not wanting to make the trip in her Blazer because of problems she had been recently having with the radiator, Linda had called one of their closest couple friends at the base, Mark and Ladawn Kastleman, and had made arrangements for them to swap vehicles. She had met Ladawn at the gate, and had traded vehicles—thus acquiring an almost-new Bronco. Due to the "crisis" situation (what crisis Linda simply could *not* learn from Ladawn, who was employed as a civilian secretary for the base commander), she had not been allowed to enter the base, and so the exchange was made at the gate.

Debating now whether to awaken the kids and load them into the packed and ready-to-go Bronco, Linda took another look outside. It still didn't appear to be anywhere close to morning, at least there was no perceptible light. But since they had decided to get an early start, she thought, why not?

Still wearing her warm flannel pajamas, Linda turned toward the bedroom door. To her surprise, Little Jack was already awake, dressed, and standing there looking at her.

"Hi, Mom."

"Little Jack? How long have you been standing there?"

"What d' you mean? I just barely got here."

"Well, you frightened me, hon."

"Sorry, Mom. I was just coming in to wake you up."

"Well, you look like you're all eager and ready to go!" she said, with a seed of growing enthusiasm and an accompanying smile. "Come here . . . give me a hug."

"It's raining you know," he said, walking into her arms.

"Yeah, I saw that. I thought it was still nighttime!"

"Me, too," he said.

"Trish up?" she asked, standing him out a ways in front of her to make sure he was properly dressed.

"Yeah, she's getting dressed."

"Well, good! You two speedy gonzalas are way ahead of me! I guess I'd better get a move on."

"Yeah, slowpoke!"

"Well, listen, honey. You guys get your beds made, clean up the room if it needs it, and give me a few minutes to catch up, okay?"

"My bed's already made."

"I'm sure it is, honey. Go on and help your sister, then. Make sure she puts on the clothes we laid out for her last night, 'kay?"

"Yeah, sure."

Little Jack turned and started to leave the room. Then, as an afterthought, he turned and asked, "Want me to make some toast 'n jam?"

"Oh, no. . . . I got a special surprise for you guys. I'm sure you don't want to spoil it with a nasty ol' piece of toast 'n jelly."

Clearly excited now, Little Jack raced out of the bedroom and helped his little sister make her bed and get herself ready to leave. And just as Linda was closing the bedroom door for a bit of privacy, she overheard Little Jack say, "And she's got a surprise for us, Trish! So, let's hurry!"

By the time they got to the Avenue S McDonald's drive-in, which was two miles east of Interstate 14, the rain and winds had developed into a mild hurricane. Of course it wasn't really a hurricane. None of them had ever even seen a real hurricane or tornado, and Linda, in particular, was quite content to keep it that way. But this California downpour, having moved steadily southward from as far north as Alaska, was a humdinger! Linda was glad they had the sturdy engine and weight of Kastlemans' Bronco.

The kids chose the drive-thru window, rather than risking the hassles of wet clothes. They grabbed a hearty breakfast and headed east across the long stretch of highway known as Palmdale Road. Linda had forgotten that this particular piece of desert highway was a formidable challenge during the wet season. With its steady up and down camel-like passage, there was every reason to suspect sudden flash floods and other dangerous road conditions. But it was the most direct route to their eventual destination at Big Bear.

"What'd you think, guys?" Linda said to the two chow-hands sitting next to her in the passenger's seat, munching down Egg McMuffins and hashbrowns. "You think we're okay in this storm?"

Little Jack poked his head up like a submarine periscope to give his personal assessment. He looked out the front and side windows, and with a mouthful of McDonald's goodies, said, "Don't sweat it, Mom. We're gonna be just fine!"

She was glad for the optimistic overview, but was not quite convinced that Little Jack's forecast was all that professional. "Yeah . . . and what about you, sweet pea?" she said to Trish. "You think we're gonna be okay? Think we ought to forge ahead, or should we go back home and wait this storm out?"

"Forge ahead!" Trish said, dropping a piece of ham from the McMuffin into her lap.

"You don't even know what 'forge ahead' means, you hungry little weasel!" Linda said jokingly.

"I do, too!"

"No you don't, Trish," Little Jack interjected.

"Now, don't start, son!" Linda directed.

"Just teasin'."

"Trish, what *does* 'forge ahead' mean?"

"It means to drive to the mountains, so Dad can meet us there."

"Well, I can't argue with that! Let's hope your father gets there in time to do some serious skiing!"

Trish stuck her food-caked tongue out at her brother, as a symbolic gesture of the victory that was clearly hers.

"Yuck! Trish! Mom, make her put her yucky tongue back in her mouth!"

"All right! Now, both of you—"

Va-VOOM!

The unexpected thunder was so loud, and so intense, that it shook the Bronco and the traveling trio with what felt like a seven point five on the Richter scale, and Linda slammed her foot down on the brakes.

The Bronco's tires locked, and the heavy vehicle lurched sideways into an uncontrollable, horrifying skid. There was no place to recover, and the momentum sent the automobile rocketing into the soft shoulder alongside the nearly abandoned highway.

With no smooth surface to keep the Ford sliding on its wheels, the tires grabbed hold of and then dug into the mud and muck, spring-boarding it and its occupants into the air. It flew across the sand like a flat, polished rock skipping across a smooth pond. The vehicle did four complete rolls before slamming into a huge boulder and coming to rest on the driver's side, the wheels spinning harmlessly in the air.

After the first rollover, Linda had been thrown completely free from the carnage of twisting steel and certain death. She landed with the full weight of her body slamming down onto her left leg, instantly snapping the femur in three places. The shin bone belched through the skin with agonizing force, shooting blood and bone fragments into the air like an exploding grenade.

She passed out cold.

Little Jack and his sister had been wearing their seat belts as well as a shared shoulder harness. And although they shared a single seat, their collective weight did not break through the gripping strength of the three belts. They bounced around inside of the Bronco like a pair of lifeless dummies, slamming against each other and bearing jolt after body-wrenching jolt until, crashing with explosive force into the boulder, they came to rest, hanging limp and inanimately still.

Suspended in midair by the belts, the two children were left to the mercy of trauma-induced shock.

For a moment, except for the falling rain, all was still. Gasoline began to pour freely out onto the sand beneath the vehicle, and in the distance a huge bolt of lightning lit up the eastern sky, illuminating the scene just briefly—then all was dark again.

19

Little Jack opened his eyes.

For a moment he could not see. He felt like an actor in a dreamscape of slow-motion fantasy. Nothing was real. The images around him were cartoonish, and his subconscious tried to tease him into believing that what he perceived was only a dream and that momentarily he would awaken in a warm bed back home.

But the numbing and paralyzing images of reality began to materialize in front of him. He saw, through blurry eyes, the immediate scenes. The Bronco was resting on its side, the driver's seat was empty, and he and Trish were dangling sideways in the air, still strapped into the passenger's seat.

Trish!

The sudden thought of the tiny, lifeless body squashed and pinned beneath him against his arm, was overwhelming.

"Trish!" he tried to shout—but couldn't. A mouthful of blood came out instead.

He tasted it. It was salt.

"Trish!" he managed to whisper weakly. "Trish . . . please . . . wake up, Trish!"

Little Jack didn't care about the blood. His only thought was the little girl beside him—his sister! The one who played with him, and smiled and laughed at his silly jokes. He loved her, suddenly, more than ever before, and he knew that he couldn't let her die!

But what could he do? He felt paralyzed, and try as he might, he just couldn't move. Harder!

Still—nothing!

He was afraid. More afraid than he had ever been. The fear grew, and within seconds it evolved into sheer terror.

He had to get out! Panic welled up inside him, and his body shook convulsively.

"Mom," he tried to scream.

What came out was a faint, barely audible whisper. And more blood.

And then, a poem—

A *poem?*

This was not the time to be thinking about his dad's poem.

> If ever there's a time of need,
> With back against the wall . . .
> Just lift your eyes and ask for help
> From Him who gives to all.

That was *it!* He needed help in a desperate, critical way. God alone had the power to help in this crisis. He must—absolutely he must—call on God for help! And somewhere, buried deep within the very core of Little Jack's nearly fourteen-year-old heart and soul, he just knew that God would help. It was an absolute knowledge that suddenly lifted his spirits and gave him strength.

"Heavenly Father," he said, crying uncontrollably. "My sister and my mother . . . they need me—"

He stopped praying.

He was feeling a warmth that seemed to live and breathe with a life all its own, growing inside him.

"Please, dear God," he found himself whispering. "Please don't let her die." And tears fell from the boy's eyes as he wept with painful despair at the thought of her dying.

Strength poured into Little Jack's body, and he was suddenly very aware of all that had happened. His mind raced speedily with scenes up to, and including, the accident—but he was no longer afraid.

Somehow, he knew that his mother had fallen free of the tumbling Bronco and that she would be okay.

He focused his concerns and immediate attention on the small, lifeless form beneath him, and with the renewed stamina of muscle and nerve he gently wrapped one arm around her and held onto her with his might. With the other arm he found and unlatched the connecting buckle of the seat belts and shoulder harness, and hung tight to the side of the passenger seat to prevent the two of them from falling.

He set his sister down gently, alongside the mangled heap of crushed steering wheel and broken glass.

She did not move.

Little by little, the boy was able to work his way up out of the high side of the vehicle. And though racked with pain, and clearly suffering from shock, he was able at last to pull little Trish free from the rubble.

His senses and his perception of things around him had become amazingly sharp and well adjusted. And as he lifted Trish down out of the Bronco, holding her like a sack of potatoes over his shoulder, Little Jack's eyes caught a glimpse of two hauntingly fearful scenes that would remain etched into his memory forever. The first was a slowly growing pool of what had to be gasoline that had somehow made its way into a hollow spot at the base of the upturned Bronco. And the second, which he caught with his peripheral vision, was a blinking ballet dance of electrical sparks somewhere inside the engine.

The Bronco was going to explode!

Without hesitation, and with a clarity of direction he did not understand, Little Jack's legs sprang to life. He turned toward the highway and threw every ounce of energy into the run. But, like a scene so often played out in a Hollywood movie, the motion was piteously slow and seemingly ineffective.

Rain, lightning, and thunder whirled insultingly around him, and Little Jack was somehow reminded that every hundredth of a second was perilous.

He saw his mother—

He saw the brilliant flash of lightning—

He heard the explosion! It was simultaneous with the roaring clap of thunder, and yet was totally different.

An intense wave of pressure slapped Little Jack in the back, and something solid, but not sharp, hammered into the back of his head, sending him and his precious cargo flying ten feet forward, as though they had been shot out of a circus cannon together!

Trish landed less than two feet from her mother. She yelped an audible groan as she slammed into the mud on her side. But the force of the explosion and sudden jolt to her small frame acted like a slap in the face, startling her into an unfeeling daze of semiconsciousness.

Mud had gotten into the girl's mouth. She choked slightly, spit the foul-tasting defilement out, and dizzily called out to her mother.

But her mother did not answer.

Little Jack lay helplessly prostrate in the mud. He was little more than five feet away from his mother and sister, and was flattened like a pancake in the dark and damp desert quagmire. All that could be seen of his head was a two-and-a-half-inch gash where the metal fragment had done its damage from behind. There was a steady flow of watery blood trickling down through his scalp and onto his exposed neck.

Little Jack's face—his eyes, nose, and mouth—was buried in the mud.

20

Aviano Air Force Base, Italy

The Banshee was poised and ready. Her nose was in the wind. She was fueled, armed, and ominous in appearance. Her single passenger, Major Jack Garrity, was tense and perhaps even a bit apprehensive. It wasn't fear so much as nervous anxiety. He was well adjusted to the mission's complexity, but his sixth sense seemed to have been activated. Was its pulsating beacon warning Jack of impending danger? He wasn't sure.

Communication, even on the ground, had been suspended. He had been instructed, like before, to leave the receiving channels open—but he didn't expect to hear any further messages from base headquarters or General Ludlow. From this point forward, his only communications would be what verbal exchanges he made with Molly. And although he enjoyed communicating with the technological marvel's articulate, feminine voice, his perception of possible danger distracted him from the usual, almost euphoric anticipation that generally accompanied his flying.

Jack's last experience in the Banshee, flying unseen at unequaled speeds through the heavens over Italy, the Alps, and the waters of the Adriatic, had left him so completely intoxicated with excitement that he had not been able to think of anything else. The anticipation of a second and third flight had kept him thrillingly entranced. But now, either because of the peril associated with flying over enemy terrain or the apprehension of some other unseen hazard, Jack remained hesitantly and cautiously concerned.

Still, he was not afraid.

"Molly?" he said, "is everything completely operational?"

"A complete survey of all separate and collective aircraft functions registers positive, sir."

"Do you know our destination?"

"I do, sir. Headings and navigational readings indicate the continent of Africa, with a primary target location inside Libya."

"Well then," the major said, collecting courage, "what d' you say we get on with it?"

"At your command, sir."

Once again the Banshee F-31 raced down the runway at Aviano Air Force Base and rocketed skyward.

From a small window in a little building across from the PX, a pair of eyes peered into the darkness. Obscure and well hidden inside the bleak shadows of the kitchen area, Lieutenant David Guant blinked his eyes and squinted a little in a continued effort to follow the faint glow of Major Garrity's afterburners.

The Banshee, Guant thought, would not return. And what was equally important, neither would the nosy, high-handed major who sat at its controls. Both were on a collision course with death!

"Good riddance, *Jack!*" the Lieutenant whispered, slightly fogging the kitchen window. "Now maybe you'll learn not to go around snooping into other people's business!"

The previous evening, after Guant's second trip into the city to notify Haman of tonight's operational go-ahead, he had been furious to find the red light on the intruder detector brightly lit. Silently it announced the invasion of his privacy, and though it appeared that nothing had been disturbed, the video replay showed otherwise.

Clearly indentifiable on the television screen was Major Jack Garrity, as big as life, sifting through drawers, through materials scattered on the nightstand, and in and out of cupboards. Guant had no idea what the major had been looking for, or whether he found anything incriminating. When the major had disappeared off the screen, having passed directly in front of the hidden camera, it was certain that the two or three minutes of blank tape meant he had gone into the closet and had searched there as well.

The duration of Garrity's trespassing was ten minutes at most. And when Guant had later searched through the closet, it seemed to him that the curious major had attempted to pick the small lock clasped over the toolbox.

Neither the electronic detector nor the well-hidden video camera looked tampered with—but Guant wasn't sure. He'd never be sure. And that infuriated him.

Major Garrity looked at his watch. It was 0130. Airspeed was 1,490 knots—approximately Mach 2.6. Altitude was 2,400 ASL. He knew he was too high, according to what had been discussed in operations, and so he slowly descended.

Tonight there were no stars, no full moon to gaze upon. Instead, it was a cloudy night, dark above and below. Even with the night vision equipment fully operational, looking through the lens down at the Adriatic was like peeking into an abyss. No movement, no visible life, and no light. It was simply black.

Jack's mood was sullen. He did not converse as usual with Molly. She remained silent because he was silent.

That was an interesting thought.

Emotionless. That was the word for it. Molly was only a machine. It didn't matter how up or down his emotions ran, Molly could not respond to human emotion. If he died, she wouldn't be bothered by it. She couldn't!

"Did you see what I did this morning to your tail section, Molly?" the major asked.

"*I am not capable of sight, sir.*"

"What do you mean, Molly? You see through your camera lens, don't you?"

"*I do not see through the lens, as I interpret the definition of sight, sir. I am only capable of recording images that you see, and then comparing them against stored data in my memory banks.*"

"But, if I look through the lens and spot an ocean vessel, some kind of ship or small boat, you're telling me that you cannot immediately see that it is a boat?"

"*It requires approximately two hundred and eighty-seven hundredths of a second for images of video-gathered data to be identified positively, sir.*"

"I see," he answered, feeling a bit embarrassed. Why should he continue thinking of Molly as anything more than a masterfully crafted computer? "Well, anyway, Molly . . . "

"*Sir?*"

"I was just wondering if you had see— I mean, if you were aware of the lettering I painted onto the plane's tail section this morning."

"*No, sir.*"

"Well, remember . . . I mean, do your memory banks have a

record of our first conversation two days ago when we were flying over the Alps in Austria?"

"Yes, sir. Would you like me to play back the conversation?"

"No . . . I was thinking more along the lines of your referencing them. That's all."

"At what point would you like me to proceed, sir?"

"During our discussion of nicknames," he said.

"Yes, sir. We spoke of Major Barry's nickname. A bird of prey, sir. The name Hawk was referenced."

"Yeah, that's right . . . and then you asked me about my nickname, remember?"

"The records reference the name Little Jack, sir."

"Right again. You've got a good memory, Molly."

"It's a matter of records, sir."

"Yeah . . . I know. Well, anyway, I had this young airman, who I'd discovered was quite talented with a paintbrush, paint the words *Little Jack* onto the plane's tail section."

"Your nickname, sir?"

"Yeah . . . and that of my son. What d' you think of that?"

"What color are the letters, sir?"

"What did you say?"

"Excuse me, sir. I was referencing the letters. What color are they, sir?"

"That's the most human thing I've ever heard you say, Molly."

"Human thing, sir?"

"Yeah, human thing! I mean . . . does it matter to you what color the letters are, for real?"

"You asked me what I thought about your having put the letters there, sir. I was merely gathering more information about them to assess them."

"And color is part of that assessment?"

"Their color, their size, and their graphic type, sir, would adequately suffice."

"And if I told you all of that, what would be your assessment?"

"Simply factual representation, sir, recorded in memory."

"Only logical, factual, recorded information, Molly? Is that it? It doesn't matter to you what color they are, then?"

"No, sir."

"I didn't think so," he said dismally, and then added for the record, "Bright red!"

"Bright? Does that mean glowing red, sir?"

"Yeah," he answered, thinking to himself, assess *that one*, Molly.

"Glowing red with yellowish-orange blocking to make the letters stand out." Then, as an afterthought, he said, "I'll take a picture of it when we get back and let your video camera record it, okay?"

They flew southward for three-quarters of an hour, passing over Yugoslavia, Albania, Greece, and the Ionian Sea, maintaining an altitude of a little better than eight hundred feet. The Radar Warning Receiver flashed on and off constantly along the way, yet it was perfectly clear that not once had anyone—any country—detected his presence. No one had ever accomplished a radar lock, because the signals did not bounce off the Banshee. They were deflected away.

From time to time, Major Garrity used the TADS telescopic extension to visually mark and record the locations of the radar stations that were trying to get a fix on him, and who were lighting up on his computer-enhanced terrain maps. He would mentally run through each targeting sequence, arm the weapons through Molly, and blow the radar positions off the face of the map. It was all *too* easy!

At 0246 hours, Molly spoke.

"*Libyan territorial waters approaching in six-zero seconds at my mark, sir.*"

"Thank you, Molly."

"*You're welcome, sir.*"

Jack looked at his watch. It was 0247 hours.

Blip.

Unbeknownst to either Molly or Major Garrity, a small egg-shaped device attached to the underside of the Banshee's left wing suddenly came to life. A miniature red light blinked on and off, pulsating like a tiny heart.

However, instead of pumping life-sustaining red blood cells and plasma, this little heart was pumping out a death-dealing signal to four men crouched inside a concrete bunker not more than sixty miles away. It would only be a few more minutes before an electronic scanner with its unique frequency would respond with a signal of its own.

Once the connection was made, the small Libyan detachment would allow the Banshee to fly inland for about one hundred miles. Then, the customized Sidewinder V-2 would leap into the sky and strike—like the poisonous snake that it was—at the stealthy intruder, and blow the human infidel and all of his modern equipment into eternal oblivion!

The little bat-winged rodent, the Banshee, was flying right into the viper's nest. It was about to die.

21

Somewhere on Palmdale Road,
Southern California

Stars.

Stars?

Millions of them—moving around in some sort of gaseous sphere, or thick liquid. They seemed to be growing brighter, and encircling her head.

Linda Garrity somehow felt lighter than air.

It was as though the millions of small lights—the stars—were joining together and becoming one. One larger light. They had wrapped themselves around her body like a glowing blanket. And yes, she strangely felt lighter than air.

And something else.

She felt good. Warm. Incredibly peaceful.

She could see again.

Again?

Yes. Now she remembered. She had not been able to see. It had been dark. No. Not dark. Different than dark. It was strangely different. It wasn't just dark, it was, instead, well . . . it was a nothing, actually!

A void. That's more like it.

Like a blind person. What does the blind person see? Dark? No, not dark, because her eyes do not register light or dark. Her eyes see the void. Like trying to look out of your cheek, or the back of your head—something like that. Since that is impossible, since you don't have any eyes in your cheeks or in the back of your head, then you can't see darkness or light. It is a void. A nothingness.

But no longer!

Now there was light. And Linda *could* see.

Several feet from her was this . . . this boy, a poor young fellow sprawled out in the mud, whose face was buried in the mud . . .

Oh, no! Somebody needed to help the child before he suffocated to death!

Linda's eyes rolled in the back of her head as she tried to move her body. But it was no use. Again she fainted, only this time just seconds after she vaguely heard another noise above the sound of the enflamed Bronco.

The noise was the engine of a large tractor trailer. Unknown now to Linda, it came to rest along the highway. A man and a woman were inside. The man was talking to the woman.

"Stay on the radio, Ruthie! You know where we are?"

"Yes . . . ," she said as she watched her husband leap out of the cab.

"Good!" The man was huffing now. "Come over and help me as soon as you can! I'll take these here blankets, but I seen that young feller get blowed off his feet! I know he was a carryin' someone. I seen him!"

"You think it's gonna blow again?" the woman named Ruth asked between attempts on the radio.

"Nah! I think she done about all she's gonna do! But she'll keep on a burnin' . . . count on that!"

Lew Day and his wife, Ruth Anne, had seen the explosion, and had caught a glimpse of Little Jack dashing wildly away from the vehicle. The scene had been quicker than the blink of an eye, but the images seemed eternally engraven into the memories of both.

The two were horrified, and yet were on the scene in less than a minute. If there was a chance to save the children's lives, Lew would gladly risk his own. Whoever might have been caught inside the exploding vehicle, he thought morbidly, could not have survived! But the kids!

Lew had seen the kids—he *had* to rescue the kids! He raced across the highway and off into the desert mud, completely oblivious to the pelting winds and rain whirling angrily about.

The *kids!* He *had* to save the kids!

22

Benghazi, Libya

Haman Al-Rashid sat with his feet up on the desk. His office in Benghazi commanded a kingly view of the Gulf of Sidra. But strain as he did, there was nothing to see.

The waters in the gulf looked murky and gloomy. The overcast weather left the sea dark and lifeless. And, although there were lights at the seaport, their usual luster was nearly obscured by the shadowless black.

He held a telephone to his ear, neither listening nor speaking. Lucca Rovigo's voice on the other end of the line was also temporarily quiet. Their connection—a clear and noiseless link between the port office in Benghazi and a concrete bunker just south of Tubruq, code-named *The Lair*—had been made about three minutes earlier.

Lucca was merely waiting for the final order.

Haman broke the silence.

"What is his position, Lucca?"

"We have him at sixty miles inland."

"Is the homing device on the missile clearly operational?"

"Of course, Haman!"

"Then . . . let us not waste another moment, Lucca! Bring the American down! Fire the missile . . . *now!*

"What is that little glitch on the monitor, Molly?" the major asked, pointing to a rapidly moving dot on the ship's radar.

"*A missile, sir.*"

"Fired at . . . us?"

"*It appears so, sir.*"

"I thought they couldn't see us!"

"*There have been no radar locks on us, sir. All attempts were deflected.*"

"Then how—"

"*Sir?*"

The major paused.

A powerful, overwhelming sensation had just activated his sixth sense. But much differently than he had ever experienced before.

Deep inside him, he heard a voice.

"*Dad,*" he heard the voice whisper, "*get out of the airplane!*"

The small voice was clear and internally audible. He could not have heard it with his ears—but within, its resonance was thunderously loud.

But where—Jack glanced to his right, then to his left, fully expecting to see his son kneeling at his side. But there was nothing. And yet—

"*The missile is closing, sir,*" Molly stated, interrupting his thought.

"Range?"

"*Less than one mile, sir.*"

"Arm weapons!"

"*Weapons armed, sir.*"

"Fire aft decoys!"

"*Missile decoys away, sir.*"

Jack activated the twin boosters and was instantly pinned by the ominous power to the high-backed seat of the fuselage.

The Banshee leaped forward like a high-caliber bullet, bumping from their present speed of approximately 1,850 miles per hour to the screaming-ghost speed of more than 2,992 miles per hour. She was approaching a redline Mach 4.5!

The Sidewinder was quicker. It flew right through the vapor bombs and continued to close the gap between it and its lock on Guant's homing transmitter.

"Missile status, Molly?"

"*Missile closing rapidly, sir.*"

"What? It didn't detonate?"

"*Negative, sir.*"

"Range?"

"*Quarter of a mile, and closing, sir.*"

"Speed?"

"*Mach 5, sir.*"

"We can't outrun her, can we, Molly?"

"*Boosters are at maximum now, sir. A higher mixture of nitro-proprolyne will not burn efficiently.*"

"Can we add more, anyway, Molly?"

"*Not without significant risk, sir.*"

"Add the mixture, Molly . . . now!"

"*Yes, sir.*"

The Banshee exceeded the redline limit. There was a slight but noticeable vibration. Airspeed climbed slowly up to Mach 4.7, but would not go beyond.

"Can you add a little more, Molly?"

"*The injectors are at peak flow now, sir.*"

"Missile stat—"

Jack's internal receptors screamed to life again, and in his mind he heard his son's voice anew warning him to get out of the plane.

The sensation of the experience took Jack's breath away. Chills climbed up his back and spread like an ocean tide across his arms and legs—causing gooseflesh and immediate discomfort.

"Little Jack?"

"*You were saying, sir?*" Molly interjected.

"Silence, Molly!" he screamed at the computer.

"*Yes, sir.*"

"Little Jack . . . are you there, son?"

In a millisecond of time, Jack's mind was made aware of the crisis. He experienced first a chilling déjà vu, remembering the words his son had spoken in their living room on Christmas night just after Linda had stormed out of the house. Little Jack had tried to tell him about a frightening dream.

"It was about *you*, Dad," the boy had said. "I don't want you to go," he had pleaded, "because you won't come back!"

And now, here in the cockpit—in the heart of Libya—he saw images of espionage, pieces of a monstrous jigsaw puzzle: a schematic drawing he had found in a small drawer in Lieutenant Guant's kitchen, a drawing of an electronic device with the words *V-2 Receiver*—a homing device!

Major Jack Garrity's eyes widened in fear.

"I can't get away!" he whispered, unable to breathe.

"Molly!"

"*Sir?*"

"Missile range?"

"*Forty-one meters and closing, sir.*"

"Fire all weapons, *now!*"

"*Yes, sir.*"

Jack slammed the control stick to a full-forward position, pitching the Banshee into a high-speed, irrecoverable dive.

He hit the eject button.

"Good-bye, Molly!"

Fsssssttt!

As he was thrust free of the plane, he watched it rocket earthward out of the corner of his eye. He knew that the maneuver had bought him a little more time.

His plan would allow—should allow—two things to happen. First, instead of ejecting straight skyward, and possible coming down near to or around the wreckage where *they* would be hunting for him, his forward thrust from the rocket ejectors, coupled with momentum, would propel him a good ten miles or more from the crash site.

Second, since impact was less than a second or two away, the short delay would give the F-31's weapons adequate release and launch time. There would be massive explosions all over the place—especially from the hellcats! Anything on the ground within a five-mile range would be obliterated! For weeks they would be scratching their heads, wondering what went wrong.

Everything seemed to happen at once.

Safely beyond the danger zone, Jack caught a glimpse of missiles firing, hundreds of rounds of ammunition belching from the cannons, and powerful explosives jettisoning from the screaming ghost.

And in that same moment, the F-31 Banshee received a fatal bite from the Sidewinder V-2. The contact ignited a gigantic explosive ball of fire. The poisonous viper and the stealth fighter plane vaporized in midair.

It seemed like an eternity before Major Garrity's life-saving parachute ballistically fired, spreading out like a giant umbrella above him.

As he floated slowly to earth, he could clearly see the flames and chaos in the distance. He barely escaped with his life.

But—he *was* alive!

Jack then remembered his promise to God, and whispered a humble and reverent "thanks." Moments before finally touching down on the desert landscape, Major Jack Garrity tilted his head heavenward and whispered softly, "I *am* coming home, Little Jack! I am coming *home!*"

23

0258 Hours, Saturday, 28 December 1991
USS Nimitz, *12 Miles Due North of Libyan Coast*

"Admiral Doxey, sir?"

"Yes, Lieutenant, what is it?"

"There's been an explosion approximately 680 feet above Kufra, just south of Tubruq—inside Libya, sir."

"Oh, *no!*"

"Sir?"

The old admiral suddenly appeared faint. His face flushed, and he reached for a steady handhold. The young, extremely confident Lieutenant Besserman reached over with catlike reflex to steady the old man and prevent him from falling.

Besserman was clearly puzzled.

"Are you all right, sir?"

"I'm fine," the admiral answered, shooing the younger officer away.

"Can I get you something . . . a glass of water?"

"No, no, nothing. Really . . . I'm all right." He walked to a sofa in a corner of his cabin where he had been trying to keep tabs on Operation Screaming Ghost. This he had been doing through limited, well-coded conversation with Aviano. All links came through an orange telephone.

He sat down.

"Pour me a small glass of orange juice over there, Lieutenant, would you, please?" He pointed to the refreshment cabinet.

"Certainly, sir." The old man had changed his mind.

"What time did you say you monitored the explosion?"

"At 0257 hours, sir."

"Get a make on it?"

"Some sort of aircraft is all we know, sir. It was shot down by a surface-to-air missile of some kind. Extremely fast! But we had the missile on radar just seconds after the launch."

"Where'd she fly out of?"

"Tubruq, sir."

"No . . . not the missile . . . I mean the aircraft."

"Don't know, sir. We never saw her! All we saw was the missile fired out of Tubruq and then an explosion, sir. A small desert community called Kufra. It's about sixty-five or seventy miles south of the coast."

"Satellites pick it up?"

"Actually, sir, that's how we caught our first glimpse. *Orbiter Seven* had some pretty nifty photographs back to us in seconds. Course we had the missile tracked right from the start, though."

"Any word from our backdoor neighbors?"

"The Russians, sir?"

"Yeah."

"Not yet, sir. But I'm sure they'll wanna know what's goin' on." The lieutenant scratched his head, then continued. "You think the Russians have an advanced stealth?"

"No," the admiral whispered under his breath, "and now neither do we."

At that moment a faint buzzer sounded. Lieutenant Besserman noted that it came from the orange telephone.

24

The Desert Near Palmdale, California

"One and two and three and four and five and . . . *Breathe!*"

The man named Lew again tilted Little Jack's head back and blew another life-restoring breath into the boy's lungs.

"Again, Ruthie! Pump steady now . . . yeah . . . that's right . . . directly over the boy's heart. That's it! And four and five and . . . okay, let him go!"

"Do you feel any pulse at all, Lew?" his wife asked, breathing hard, then readying her hands to continue the CPR.

"Not yet," he whispered, breathing again for the lifeless form, and then positioning his ear just above Little Jack's mouth. "Ready?"

"Let's do it!" she urged.

"One and two and . . . "

The couple worked tirelessly with the boy for about seven or eight minutes, trading places just once to give the other a rest. Still, Little Jack lay limp and lifeless.

Ruth was crying. She had been ever since seeing this brave young lad hauling what appeared to be his sister to safety.

Lew and Ruth had seen the explosion, but the dark sky and the fierce winds had blurred the scenes of the accident. They were just glad that they had been close enough to arrive on the scene when things were most crucial.

The adult woman, lying nearby, was in a semiconscious state. They had placed a blanket over her, keeping a watch on the compound fracture. They didn't want to touch that; they would leave it for the experts. And thank heavens help was on its way. Ruth had made almost immediate contact with someone in Lancaster on Channel 9. This person, in turn, had called the police and ambulance.

As for the little girl, she seemed unscratched, though obviously was in shock. Ruth had wrapped her in a warm blanket, lifted her gently into her arms, carried her to the truck, and placed her in the cab, out of the driving, pelting storm.

But now she was back with Lew and the lifeless boy—who was likely the little girl's brother.

"The poor boy!" Ruth kept repeating. "I don't think you can revive him, Lew."

"Let's just keep the vitals goin', Ruthie! Ya never know. . . . He's young 'n healthy. Let's keep a pumpin' until someone gits here!"

Suddenly and quite unexpectedly, Little Jack let out a series of weak coughs. Lew's eyes lit up, and he leaned over to check for a pulse.

He found one!

"Ya did 'er, Ruthie!" he yelled excitedly. "Ya kicked that ol' heart back into gear!"

Ruth just sat there with tears running down her cheeks. The two of them were drenched from the downpour, yet were oblivious to the storm. They had the boy back!"

The paramedics and the police arrived almost simultaneously. Lew explained the seriousness of the explosion, and the need to use CPR on the boy.

The medics praised the middle-aged couple for their courage and their unusual competence, and then told them what Lew and Ruth already knew—that if they had not immediately administered first aid, the boy would have died for sure.

More police, another ambulance, and a fire truck arrived within minutes.

The Bronco was still in flames, though not nearly as intense as it was following the explosion. The firemen quickly started extinguishing what was left of the fire.

Both Little Jack and Trish were placed into the back of one of the units, and Linda, who had received an injection of morphine, was carefully rolled into the back of the other.

Lew and Ruth smiled as they held each other and watched the slowly disappearing emergency vehicles. They then climbed into the back of a police car and completed their telling of the accident.

Meanwhile, the storm was letting up.

Across the Pacific Ocean, a few astonishingly brilliant beams of sunlight punched through the massive cloud cover. A spectacular rainbow colored the sky. It was vivid in color, and its breathtaking beauty was so wonderfully bright that it cast its colors over the ocean water. The surface seemed to have been painted by a great artist.

Off toward the shore, where tremendous waves had pelted relentlessly against the sandy beaches, two little girls stared out from a beach home window, awestruck by the sight.

Melinda and her younger sister, Megan, had been playing together near the living room window, all the while watching the massive ocean waves and the heavy rains flood the beach far below. When the rainbow appeared, they suddenly lost interest in their dolls and in the game they were playing.

"Look, Megs!" Melinda said, "you see that?"

"Wow!" the little sister exclaimed. "A rainbow!"

"It's such a pretty one! I don't think I've ever seen one that was so pretty! Have you, Megs?"

"Not ever!" she sighed.

At that moment their lovely mother entered the room.

"Look at *that*, Mom!" Megan cried, pointing excitedly.

"Oh, how beautiful!" she replied. "You know what that means, don't you, girls?"

"What, Mom?"

"That means something wonderful has happened."

A tear welled up and fell down Megan's cheek. Something wonderful? she thought. She liked it when good things happened.

PART THREE

One Step at a Time

How can we, so weak and so frail,
Shoulder the burdens, or hope to prevail?
The Master has taught us "line upon line."
Said it was done one step at a time.

25

Somewhere in the Desert of Northern Libya

The tricky, last-minute maneuver had worked remarkably well. By the time Jack had finally floated back to earth, drifting south a bit from the winds, he had unwittingly positioned himself approximately fifteen miles southwest of the crash site. He felt strangely confident that he would now have a little time to prepare a strategy for escape.

Escape?

That was a nasty word. In all his years in the military, never once had Jack associated that particular word with anything having to do with him. He wondered if he were afraid of it.

No. Not really, he concluded, and his calmness intrigued him. Fear was the one emotion he could not afford. Fear disabled a man. It led to a weakening of will and to a confusion about objectives. In times of crisis, fear would eventually lead to panic, and to that ultimate emotional defect, surrender!

With renewed determination to get back home as he had strangely promised Little Jack, Major Garrity stuffed the nasty word *fear* into his back pocket and promised to leave it there. Well, at least he would try to anyway. If it slipped out, it would mean that things had taken a serious turn for the worse.

He prayed that would not happen.

The final resting place of the expelled rocket seat, with Jack in it, was a narrow valley, wedged in between a series of sandy hills and desert terrain. It had been an easy landing—thank heavens!

Having studied several maps over the past two days, Jack was already aware that he was somewhere on the outskirts of the formidable Sahara Desert, which stretched from east to west across the northern continent of Africa. The prevailing darkness prevented him from seeing much of anything in particular, but it also sheltered him from the probing eyes of his enemy.

Tucked away inside the ejector seat were several lifesaving implements. The foresight that had gone into the building of the Banshee, he thought, was truly amazing. The engineers had considered everything.

There was an assortment of high-protein, vitamin-rich biscuit packets, a flashlight, matches, first-aid kit, and extra clothing that included a khaki-colored Desert-Camo-Recon Vest with five large front pouch pockets, and a pair of Camo-Pants. The vest also contained a small backpack and an exceptional Gruen-made compass and watch combination of the highest quality. The compass was housed underneath the watch, and could be revealed by pivoting the watch face to one side or the other. There was also a canteen and a small assortment of weapons, including a knife, a 9mm Colt with a fifteen-round clip of ammunition, and one hundred extra rounds.

Jack spent about a half hour ridding himself of the bulky flight suit and exchanging it for the proper clothing. He then armed himself with the survival equipment and disposed of the surplus flight gear and other accessories that had floated to the desert floor with him. Burying most of the equipment in the sand was a difficult but necessary task.

Then, with a small flashlight in one hand, and some charts and maps from his survival pack in the other, he located his position and noted with relief that he was not that far from a small settlement. The map directed him in a southeasterly direction to a place called El-Kabir five or six miles away.

Jack checked his watch—0355 hours.

It had been about an hour since he had lost Molly and the Banshee. He wondered how much damage he might have done by jettisoning all of the weapons like he had done. He hoped it was severe enough to keep the enemy occupied for a while and give him a sizeable head start.

Jack's plan was to somehow slither away unseen into some populated region, mask himself in Muslim clothing—and then slowly work his way into Egypt, where he could undoubtedly find "friendlies."

Pivoting the watch face to the left for a directional fix from the hidden compass, he marked his position, then set out for El-Kabir.

The winter desert was fairly cold, but Jack was well equipped with protective clothing. He was intrigued with his unusually good spirits, considering all that had transpired.

The small rise and fall of the sandy dunes made the first leg of his journey quite tedious. But what made the going most difficult was the constant need to check and recheck his bearings. If there had been a clear sky out tonight, navigation—even on foot—would be substantially easier. But with the massive cloud cover the darkness was bleak.

This was a strange land, Jack thought, a strange terrain. One minute he would find himself slipping and stumbling through the loose sand, and the next minute he would be surefooted and more comfortably making progress over the solid and ancient African volcanic crust.

Nowhere did Jack see or sense human life, and he felt quite sure there was little, if any, life present. Whatever lived out here, he reasoned, had to be one tough beast to survive.

As Jack plodded forward, he thought about the unusual and unexpected events of the night. Had he only imagined his son's voice, or had something taken place that was completely out of his realm of comprehension? His rational mind continually sought to dismiss the impression he had felt as being some sort of a fluke—a mind game, perhaps. But Jack knew that, had it not been for this impression, he would have been killed.

It all made sense. Well, most of it, anyway. He had remembered, for instance, the anxiety and nausea that had swept through him prior to taking off at Aviano. Jack wasn't a superstitious man—God-fearing, yes, but not superstitious. And many times during his adult life, his instinct—what he had referred to as his sixth sense—had warned him of dangers. He did not understand how that quiet power inside him worked, but he did believe it had something to do with the powers of his Creator. And in this sense, since he had often experienced that still, small voice of warning, it had not been so unusual.

What was strange was hearing Little Jack's voice. Suddenly sensing his son's love and concern in the cockpit of the Banshee must have created an urgency that triggered his reactions.

That was probably what it was, Jack reasoned. Because the only other explanation would be that Little Jack was—dead!

"Dead?" Jack said suddenly, his heavy-breathing voice almost coughing into the darkness before him.

For a moment Jack's mind was fearfully consumed with this thought. Then he realized how completely irrational this line of thinking was. Little Jack was all right. He just *had* to be!

At that moment, Jack did something that he had never done

before. He stopped, dropped to his knees, and offered a silent prayer asking God for peace regarding the well-being and safety of his family.

Peace came, almost as immediate as the thought of asking had occurred. They were *all* okay! Linda, Little Jack, and his darling Trish!

Working his way back to his feet, Jack found himself weeping uncontrollably. When his emotions subsided, he wiped his tear-stained cheeks and continued walking into the darkness before him.

Jack, his mind suddenly calm, reflected upon the unusual woman he had married. Linda came from good earthy people—farmers from Ontario, Oregon. Her father, Terry Baker, had left the farm briefly for college and then a stint as a wide receiver for the Dallas Cowboys. He was beaten out by Bob Hays, the world's fastest human in his day, and so he had returned to the farm knowing that was where he wanted to be. After he passed away unexpectedly of a heart attack, Linda's mother, Patti, moved to California to be near them. She was such a queenly woman, and Jack had marveled again and again that Linda would be so much like her mother.

Jack knew Linda had gotten a grip on her emotions after his departure, and that she and the kids were probably snuggled around a warm fire in front of the big rock fireplace at their cabin in Big Bear.

How far away that seemed. But far away or not, his family was okay!

Jack determined at that moment that he would contact them via the telephone somewhere in Egypt and let them know he was alive and would be coming home shortly.

Certainly by now Generals Ludlow and Walker knew the mission had failed. In fact, they probably thought he was dead. And, since the whole thing wasn't supposed to have happened in the first place, they would be forced to say that he was missing in action somewhere over the Mediterranean while piloting an F-16 or other plane during exercise maneuvers.

The whole thing stunk! Linda would probably be getting a call from Walker. . . .

How was she going to handle that one?

Two hours of steady hiking brought Jack to the base of a fairly significant mountain. It wasn't anything like the Sierra Nevadas, or the Rocky Mountains in Colorado, but it was somewhat ominous, nonetheless. Since it was directly in line with his intended destination point, he began his ascent.

At the first discernible sign of predawn light, Jack heard a sound.

Not voices.

Not whispers.

But movement. A hushed, nearly inaudible sound, but definitely movement!

His usual internal warning system had failed him this time. Instinctively, the major pulled out his gun and crouched down behind what had to be a large boulder.

He was sure that something, or someone, had moved among the rocks above. He was equally sure that whoever it was had not seen or heard him.

Jack strained his eyes in the now greyish light. But he couldn't see anything beyond the shadowed silhouettes of the rising landscape directly before him.

He listened, breathing very slowly.

Time—even the passing of seconds—seemed eternal.

Jack kept expecting his internal sensors to activate, for surely his ears had heard something, and that was usually followed by an—

There it was again!

He strained harder to hear.

Still—nothing.

Once more he craned his neck to see around the base of the large rock formation that was his hiding place

Suddenly, the long-overdue warning signals pulsated through his entire frame. There was something behind him!

He whirled around, but it was forever too late.

"Move, American, and I kill you!" the deeply resonant voice said, followed by a lightning-swift kick from the man behind him, whose accurate targeting left a numbingly sharp pain in Jack's wrist, and sent his 9mm handgun sailing through the air.

Jack froze.

He completed little more than a half turn, grabbed his painfully throbbing wrist, and felt the nose of a gun barrel force itself against his left temple.

His peripheral vision caught sight of two fiercely angry eyes, and he knew that if he did move, he was a dead man.

26

Mid-morning—
29 December 1991

The American-made Huey UH1 hovered for a moment over the smoldering debris, while Commander Haman Al-Rashid assessed the wreckage. He was hoping to find the charred remains of the American pilot, but could not clearly see much of anything—at least not from the air.

"Set it down over there, Tajim," he ordered, pointing to a relatively level section of the terrain below.

The early-morning light painted the grim picture vividly. The American had managed to fire a tremendous arsenal of weapons that had scattered over the terrain in a hellish way, raining death and destruction over an area more than seven miles in diameter.

It was not presently known how many had died, but what infuriated Al-Rashid was the accuracy that apparently had been used. Obviously, the American knew that he was flying over a military installation and unfortunately had detected the incoming missile. He had then realized the hopelessness of any attempted evasive maneuvers and had launched everything he carried in a sort of kamikaze counterattack.

"An effective way of bidding farewell, wouldn't you agree, Tajim?"

The pilot was not sure what the commander was referring to, but agreed just the same.

"Do you see any signs of the ejector seat?"

"No, sir."

"Well . . . it is here somewhere, I am sure of it."

Al-Rashid left his pilot in the Huey and walked across the smoldering aftermath toward a group of soldiers who were sifting through a large heap of twisted dark metal and wreckage. It was the main bulk of the Banshee.

Lucca Rovigo was in charge.

"What have you found, Lucca?" Al-Rashid asked.

"Nothing yet, sir."

"Any sign of the American?"

"I do not think he is here, Haman!"

"He *has* to be here!"

"The wreckage area is large, and we have covered it completely. Still, we cannot find even the smallest piece of evidence suggesting he was destroyed during the explosion. I . . . I think he got away."

"Nonsense, Lucca! Where could he have gone? Even if he ejected safely, he could not have landed far from the area! Have your men searched the perimeter."

"Yes, sir."

"Nothing?"

"I tell you, Haman . . . he is not here! Somehow he vanished into the desert—was picked up by a rescue team, or whatever."

"Lucca, be reasonable! Our radar detected no further aircraft!"

"I do not know how he escaped, Haman, but I sense that he did . . . and though I do not have the answers just yet, I will have them soon. We will find the American! We *will* find him!"

"Use as many men as you need, Lucca. He is here somewhere. He cannot be that far away!"

The two men stood silent, their eyes continuing to scan the horizon in all directions as if hoping that through superior insight and intuition they would be able to pinpoint the location of one called Major Jack Garrity.

Lucca, unbeknownst to Al-Rashid, had a different motive for finding the American. Here, lying among the dead, charred bodies of more than three dozen Libyan soldiers, was his only brother, Gemsa Rovigo. They were not close like most brothers, but they were flesh and blood.

Immediately following the explosion, Lucca had seen something in the sky from his position in the bunker. Using a high-powered telescope to follow the trajectory of the V-2, Lucca had caught a brief glimpse of the Banshee just seconds before impact. Lucca watched, with curious fascination, as the Banshee dived suddenly earthward and simultaneously ejected an object.

The miniature object clearly had been propelled by a small rocket. Its trajectory sent it forward in a southerly arch—the same direction the Banshee had been traveling—and within seconds, it had vanished from view. Initially, Lucca supposed it was just another one of the quickly jettisoned weapons he had seen launched from the aircraft. But after thinking about it, he began to suspect that it was Major Jack Garrity, the infidel Lieutenant Guant had spoken of.

Garrity was out there—somewhere to the south—and Lucca, whose eyes were blazing with determined vengeance and rancorous hate, whispered malevolently, "You will not escape, murderer!"

El-Wahat, located approximately seventy miles inland and perhaps another sixty or so miles west of the border of Egypt, was a Libyan military storage depot. Nearly five hundred military personnel worked and were housed at the installation.

When the Banshee had deployed her weapons, missiles and firepower of unfathomable force rained down upon the base. If Garrity had tried, he could not have been more accurate with his aim.

The main installation, a sizeable bunker, had been a warehouse filled with weaponry of all kinds. At least fifty heavy armored vehicles, including tanks, deuce-and-a-half transports, jeeps, and field artillery cannons were destroyed by a single hellcat. And if that weren't enough, a second bunker, filled with more than two thousand Chinese-made AK-47s, U.S.-made Laws rockets, M-79 grenade launchers, cases full of claymore mines, and even a small collection of hand-launched Surface-to-Air (SAM) stinger missiles were blasted into oblivion when another hellcat lit into an enormous stockpile of C-4 plastics. It had been a fireworks display, the likes of which had never been seen by the surprised Libyan force caught stranded during the second barrage.

Ultimately, the casualty list grew from three dozen to more than a hundred. An additional 137 others were seriously-to-moderately wounded, and were transported directly to a hospital in Kufra.

Haman left the side of his friend Lucca and walked over to the main bulk of the Banshee's mangled fuselage. Soldiers under Lucca's command were still picking through the rubble, but quickly stepped aside and snapped to attention when they recognized the second most powerful military commander of the country.

Al-Rashid paid no attention to the men. Instead, he looked curiously about the scattered ruin and tried to visualize what the stealthy aircraft must have looked like before they so expertly shot it down.

"Come here, Lucca," he said, picking the piece out from the pile. "What do you make of this?"

He held up the charred tail section of the plane, and showed it to the pensive, but clearly curious Lucca.

"Ittle Jack?" he questioned.

"There is another piece over there, Lucca. I think the words say *Little Jack*."

"What is *Little Jack*?" Lucca asked.

"I don't know," Al-Rashid answered, turning the letters toward the sun. "Maybe some kind of a code name."

"Maybe so, Haman, maybe so."

27

Sunday Evening—
Antelope Valley Hospital, Lancaster, California

Linda wasn't asleep. She had only pretended sleep because she wanted to be alone with her thoughts. It was extremely difficult to talk with anyone without crying, and that had embarrassed her.

Was her world falling apart?

It wasn't typical of her to sit in a corner feeling sorry for herself. In fact, she understood the foolishness and wasted energy that was so easily spent on self-pity. But the continuing wave of dismal events in her life were beginning to take their toll. What she really needed right now was a psychologically therapeutic expenditure of physical energy—a good run or even a brisk walk!

"Yeah, right!" she whimpered sardonically, "with my shattered leg in traction?"

Whether she was willing to admit it or not, the culminating grief was beginning to metastasize into a bleak spell of depression.

The winds of renewed anguish began whirling around inside Linda's head, and with no one looking, she allowed herself another cry. Intense weeping spells were the most painful moments. But they were also, oddly enough, somewhat soothing. Everything was still so vivid to her. The doctors had wanted to sedate her again, but after pleading with them to allow her to keep her eyes open, they finally stopped pushing so hard. Besides, the regular injections of morphine were more than enough sedative. Valium, on top of that, would have knocked her completely out. No . . . she surely needed no further medication.

Little Jack, Linda considered, still had not regained consciousness. The doctor said that he was suffering from a concussion, and that it might be a day or two before he could shake free from the mild comatose state—and even then he might not remember a great deal.

Oh, how she prayed that he would be all right!

As far as Trish was concerned, they'd said she would be just fine—thank the Lord for that! She had suffered from a few scratches, but was mostly just bruised. Early this morning, in fact, Alex and Mariam had come by and had agreed to take her home if the doctors okayed it. After some consultation, however, they thought it best to keep her at least one more night for observation.

Linda looked over at her little girl. She was sleeping peacefully under the blanket, likely dreaming of peaceful Christmas memories.

"What on earth would I have done if I had lost you, precious?" she whispered. More tears welled up and slid effortlessly down her cheeks.

Trying again to gain her composure, Linda focused her mind on the date and time of the here and now. Let's see, she thought, looking up at a clock on the wall above the door. It's 9:30 P.M., Saturday night? No—Sunday night. The accident had occurred Saturday morning on their way up to Big Bear. They hadn't gotten far, had they? It must've happened—let's see—sometime right after they left McDonald's. That would have been sometime around 9:30 or 10:00 yesterday morning. They'd been in the hospital for about thirty-six hours.

She felt dizzy and shook her head in an effort to clear it. Instead of helping, the slight movement sent a shock wave of pain into her leg, striking her with such force that she yelped like a kicked puppy. However, the pain brought her mind back to reality. The recent injection of painkiller had apparently numbed her senses as well as the pain. What had she been thinking, that she could just get up and walk away from the hospital, fully recovered after only thirty-six hours?

It had been a serious accident! Yet for her, the event itself was dreamily unreal, as though it had never happened.

There hadn't been time to discuss the accident in detail with anyone—and thinking about it, Linda suddenly realized that she wasn't sure *what* had happened!

How odd, she thought. What *did* happen? There was the blinding flash of lightning—she remembered that. And of course the magnificent explosion of thunder . . . but then what? Had she hit somebody? No! No, no, no! She remembered the skid. Yes! There had been a lengthy skid, and in the end they had slid off onto the shoulder of the road. That much was clear.

Someone had said that she had been thrown from the car. Didn't she have her seat belt fastened? But Little Jack and Trish? What happened to them? Were they thrown from the car as well?

Everything was so blurry, so—

"Well, good evening, Mrs. Garrity," the voice whispered softly. "Are we feeling any better this evening?"

Linda cocked her head just slightly to the right and opened her eyes. It was the nurse.

"I'm . . . all right," she said, sobbing a little.

"Oh, come now, ma'am, everything's gonna be just fine. You'll see!"

"I . . . I know . . . I'm sorry . . . but I just can't seem to get a handle on my feelings." She held her hand up in front of her face and thanked the nurse for the needed tissue paper now being handed to her.

"Really, Mrs.—"

"Please call me Linda."

"Okay, Linda. You're gonna be all right, though. Sometimes heavy doses of pain medications, especially those with an opiate base, can really make a person emotional."

"It's not that," Linda answered, recovering slightly. "It's . . . well . . . the kids . . . they could have been killed!"

"Hey," the nurse countered, "now you listen to me, Linda. . . . They weren't killed, and that's what's important! There's certainly no sense in worrying yourself about what *might* have been, now is there?"

"Is . . . is Little Jack all right?"

"Yes, ma'am. He's just fine."

"The doctor said he's in some kinda coma."

"That's only temporary, ma'am. We think he'll be coming out of that anytime now. You just watch! He's gonna be fine, I'm tellin' ya."

"Why won't anyone tell me what happened?"

"It's not that no one's willing to tell you, Linda. It's just that . . . well . . . we've been waiting for you to come around, yourself—so to speak. You've drifted in and out of shock since you were brought here yesterday morning, and the doctors felt it best to wait until you were fully coherent."

"I'm perfectly coherent right now, so why don't you explain to me what happened?"

"Well . . . that's for the doctor to decide," the nurse said, shaking a thermometer in her hand.

"Decide *what?*" a voice said. It was Doctor Richard Moody, the attending physician.

"Oh, hello, Doctor," the nurse answered calmly. "Our patient here is concerned about possible amnesia. She's afraid we're all conspiring against her 'cause we won't tell her about the accident. I simply suggested that you would tell her when you felt she was ready." The nurse leaned over as she spoke, motioned for Linda to open her mouth so that she could insert the thermometer, and then concluded, "You wanna explain it to her, Doctor?"

"Well," he said, considering the request and then walking over to Linda's bedside, "I don't see any problem with that, really. But first of all, Mrs. Garrity, how are you feeling tonight?"

"Mmm . . . I'm . . . mmm . . . mfine," she mumbled, keeping the thermometer pressed between her lips.

"That's good," he smiled, looking over the recently completed work of the plaster cast. "Does that bother you in any particular place on the inside?"

"Mm . . . mmmm," she mumbled, shaking her head from side to side.

"How about right in there?" He was pointing at the shinbone area.

"Mmmno . . . "

"You want to talk for a bit, Mrs. Garrity?"

"Mmyes . . . "

"Here, let me take that silly thing out of your mouth." He reached over and retrieved the thermometer, looked at it closely, and said, "Temperature's gone down." He marked the chart, again smiling, at the same time gesturing for the nurse to close the door so the two of them could visit.

"Makes it hard to talk with those things in your mouth, doesn't it?"

"Yeah."

"How are you feeling, *really?*"

"Well, the shots you're giving me seem to be doing the trick . . . but when they wear off . . . "

"Oh, sure. You're going to experience three, maybe four days of some uncomfortable moments. But we'll do all we can to ease that for you."

The doctor paused for a brief moment, shined a tiny light into her eyes, and then continued, "I was pretty concerned when I first saw the fracture—"

"My leg?" she asked, her eyes widening a bit.

"Well, sure. . . . Compound fractures . . . you know what I'm talking about?"

"Yeah . . . you mean where the bone breaks through the skin? That kind of thing?" She looked down at her leg hanging in the mesh of suspended cables and ropes, and then continued, "Mine's a compound fracture?"

"Yes, it is, Mrs. Garrity."

"Would . . . a . . . could you please call me Linda?"

"Certainly, Linda. Yours is not a typical compound fracture. In fact, you should understand that yours was . . . well . . . *is* a far more serious break."

"Oh?"

"Now, understand," he said, gently sitting down on the side of her bed and taking one of her hands into his, "that in time you'll be walking just fine. But it *will* be a while."

The doctor paused to assess her reaction, and finding her unusually calm, continued, "It appears that your own body weight was the culprit. You must have had your leg terribly twisted upon impact, because the injury was severe in several areas."

"How severe?" she asked.

"Putting it delicately, Linda, the bones just above the ankle literally shattered. The fragments shot out of the skin like tiny missiles. They also did their share of damage on the way out. You suffered injured nerves, broken arteries, and severe lacerations. I had you on the operating table for nearly five hours."

"How . . . how much of the bone was damaged, Doctor?" Linda felt the panic creeping in.

"Are you sure you're up to hearing all of this?" He was reading her like a book.

"I'm okay, aren't I?" she asked courageously.

"Actually, considering the brain we had to use for the transplant—"

She smiled.

"Yes," he assured her, "you're doing well, and you will heal if you take things one step at a time."

"Why am I in a cast from the waist down, Doctor?"

"Okay . . . right here," he pointed to his pelvic area. "Your pelvis has been fractured in four places, and—"

"My pelvis?"

"That's right . . . and . . . ," he added, "it'll heal!"

"What else?"

"The ankle's broken."

"Like the compound fracture?"

"No, not at all. The serious breaks are in the shin area. It took some pins—"

"Pins?"

"Yeah, and they'll give you real problems every time you walk through a metal detector!"

Linda could see that the doctor was doing his best to ease the burden of understanding. But, as difficult as it was to absorb the truth—and the hard facts—she persisted, trying equally hard to remain calm.

"How many pins? Big pins? With screws in 'em?"

"Four. Not very big, and yes . . . with screws. But in time, like I said, if you'll take things easy, a step at a time, I promise you that you'll adjust just fine. You'll walk normally, and even run to your heart's content." He looked into her eyes, saw that they were justifiably anxious, and then asked, "Do you trust me, Linda?"

"Yes, Doctor, of course."

"Okay, then try not to worry."

"I'll try, but now that I know about me, I want you to tell me about my son."

"Well," he sighed, looking more concerned than he had previously seemed, "we're quite sure he has suffered a mild concussion. Something walloped him pretty good on the back of his head. It took about eight stitches . . . " He paused. "Now, Linda, I'm not one to play doctor/patient games when it comes to diagnosing symptoms and revealing facts, but I also won't promote unnecessary worry—especially in the heart of someone's mother, who is also hospitalized.

"So let me be clear on this with you right from the gate, okay? I know you have been through a very harrowing experience, and that your husband is unreachable, several thousand miles away. And I know you have the need and right to be concerned for your children's welfare. Still, I do not want you to worry unnecessarily about Jack. You are only *barely* recovering from an intense amount of shock, and excess worry is not a very good restorative liniment for an emotional wound. Do I make myself clear on that?"

"Yes," Linda answered, trying to show courage.

"All right, then, let's understand this much together. Jack, we think, is suffering from a mild coma. We're quite sure he'll snap out of it soon, but he may experience some symptoms of amnesia. And, as much as I dislike saying this to you, there is a small chance that he may not come out of the coma . . . at all. . . . "

Linda stared at the doctor with sad, pleading eyes, trying to comprehend his words. It broke his heart to look into her pain. She squeezed lightly on the hand that still held hers, and said in a quiet and emotionally moving voice, "Thank you, Doctor. I . . . I needed to know."

"Linda, there is something else you should know about your son, Jack."

"Oh?" she answered, in an almost inaudible whisper.

"Yes. The couple who were at the scene of the accident quite literally saved your son's life. If they had not happened on the scene right as the accident was occurring, the little guy would have died. They found him face down in the mud. He wasn't breathing. The man, a Mr. Day, I believe, immediately administered mouth to mouth, which kept air flowing into the boy's lungs. At the same time, his wife kept Jack's heart pumping for more than ten minutes before paramedics arrived. Just moments before the emergency teams arrived, Jack suddenly resumed breathing on his own . . . and living on his own."

"My goodness, Doctor—"

"There's more."

"Please, continue."

"The police report indicated that this couple witnessed a remarkable feat of bravery and near miraculous strength. It seems that just before the Bronco blew up—"

"It blew up?"

"Yes, I'm sorry about the vehicle."

"Do . . . do the owners, the Kastlemans, know?"

"I understand they've been notified, and that they've asked for special permission to visit you. I signed a card for them, so I'm sure they'll be visiting with you shortly.

"But to continue." The doctor cleared his throat. "You were unconscious, and in a state of extreme shock, Linda. That's what I meant earlier . . . "

Linda did not respond, but instead stared at the doctor, trying to comprehend the words he was speaking.

Resuming, he said, "But here's what's important. It seems that your little man was a noble hero! He evidently climbed into the vehicle, lifted little Trish right out of the window, and carried her over his shoulder to safety, and was actually running with her away from the Bronco when it exploded, throwing both of them to the ground."

Linda was speechless. Tears had formed in her eyes and were flowing steadily. She wasn't ashamed in the least to be crying in front of the doctor. She nodded for him to continue.

"It was, according to the observer's report, timing at its best. Had your son not rescued his sister from the Bronco, she could never have survived the explosion and fire. The vehicle was charred to a skeleton by the time the firemen arrived and extinguished the blaze. What appears to have happened, Linda, is that something from the explosion hit young Jack in the back of his head. He fell face down in the mud not more than five or six feet from where you lay.

"Thank God the couple were there to bring him back to life . . . because, clinically speaking, your son probably was already dead."

Linda said nothing more. She was suddenly very tired and asked Doctor Moody if it would be okay if she would be able to sleep for a while. It was difficult to control her emotions, but instead of the usual pain that accompanied a good cry, this one seemed sweet and strangely comforting.

Doctor Moody patted her hands gently, and did his best to reassure her that things were in the Lord's hands, and that ultimately all would be well. Although visibly concerned, he sensed Linda's need to deal with things her own way, and on her own. She was clearly a strong lady, and, yes, a good sleep was exactly what she needed.

On the way out he instructed the nurse to sedate her with a mild dose of Valium—despite Linda's earlier objections. Obediently, the woman went to Linda's side and quietly did as she had been instructed.

The Valium stung a bit as it flowed up through her arm and finally into her heart, but it had an immediate soothing effect—and Linda simply closed her eyes and waited for the moment when she would drift into a forgetful sleep. Her last thought was about her husband, and she prayed that he was, at least, okay.

"I love you, Major Garrity . . . ," she whispered drowsily, and slept.

28

Monday, 30 December 1991—
Somewhere in Northern Libya

The small room was dark, cold, and unnervingly quiet. There were no windows. The room was locked from the outside, and the single wooden door was the only exit. The concrete or plaster walls and floor were ice-cold to the touch.

Major Jack Garrity remembered a time, years ago, when his two brothers and he had discovered an abandoned mine near their home in Reno, Nevada. Their curiosity had been typical of boys their age, and so without hesitation they went inside to explore.

The network of tunnels and defiant vertical shafts was a young boy's paradise, but to Jack and his brothers, the eery, bat-ridden place became nightmarish. After a short while, with no flashlights or candles to light their way, the bleak and loathsome obscurity became *so* completely black and hauntingly thick that the boys experienced an attack of paranoid claustrophobia. They could not retreat quickly enough.

In a sense, Jack's present surroundings reminded him of the mine. He was gratefully free from the panic that had consumed him as a youngster, but was entombed, nevertheless, in a lightless, dusty murk. This time, however, he could not retreat by following some path toward the light. He was a prisoner. Whose prisoner, he did not know. But clearly the solid wooden door was tightly secured without; there was simply no escape!

Jack felt resoundingly dispirited. The whole idea of the maneuver that launched him free from the doomed Banshee had been conceived with the highest of hopes for a successful escape from his enemies. He knew that avoiding immediate capture was his only hope for a chance of freedom. But now, he had fallen right into their hands!

Jack remembered the mental wrestling match he had had with fear—how he had been able to symbolically stuff the emotion and its paralyzing grip into his back pocket. How he had prayed that it would not escape. Yet, as it was, the needle-sharp claws of fear had ripped their way free, and were now slicing away at his emotional stability.

He was truly afraid.

Subconsciously, his fears revolved around an imagined scene of horror—excruciating encounters with some barbaric beast of a man, twice his size and relentlessly sadistic, whose sole purpose in life was to extract information from infidels and spies. He shuddered to think what they could, and *would*, do to him if all he ever offered was his name, rank, serial number, and date of birth. He wondered if his captors even acknowledged the Geneva convention. Most assuredly not.

There were other reasons for fear, as well. Fear of the unknown beyond the door was nerve-wracking. Who were these people who had imprisoned him? How did they think? Why hadn't they come already with their spikes and chains, whips and hot irons? What did they want from him?

Jack fought the soul-shattering effects of fear with every weapon he possessed. He reasoned that he would somehow be able to escape. He also believed that the spiritual encounter in the plane had been given to him for a reason. Surely, a spiritual voice of warning would not save his life one moment, only to allow it to be snatched away just hours later!

There seemed to be a lot of pieces to the puzzle. For instance, why hadn't his captors simply executed him out in the desert? The gun that had been bluntly shoved against his head had been frighteningly effective. He remembered standing as immovable as stone—not even wanting to breathe. Then the man backed away, and Jack figured he might not shoot, after all.

"What are you doing here?" the voice asked in remarkably clear English, though with a thick guttural accent.

Not knowing what to say, Jack feebly responded, "Oh . . . I'm just hiking my way over to Egypt."

A moment of dreadful silence followed, and then suddenly and unexpectedly, the man shot him!

It had taken a fraction of a second to comprehend what had happened. Yet, just before falling over the edge of consciousness, Jack realized that instead of a handgun ripping a death-dealing hole into his body, the stinging point of a needle had driven its way into his neck.

The world around him became an instant blur. Solid landmarks, including the ground on which he had been standing, began to rotate and twist into a series of changing patterns and kaleidoscopic colors. His knees and other muscles used for stability weakened, and he fell into a seated position, his back against the same boulder he had been hiding behind. His arms, his fingers even—all had gone numb. His tongue felt twice its normal size. He could feel the light weight of the dart still stuck in his neck, and with considerable effort, he lifted his left hand and yanked the needle out. He was able to look at it briefly as he held it in front of his face. An orange, spongy-looking ball of cotton yarn was at one end, and a blood-stained needle was at the other. The image of the crippling device twirled around in his head like a ring of orange fire, until finally losing all strength, his arm fell, his head tilted to one side, and everything went dark.

He woke up to a living world of dark. Of course he hadn't known immediately that he was simply in a dark, stone room. He discovered that by crawling around on his hands and knees searching for a way out.

After finding the old wooden door, he felt surprised that he'd been unable to detect any light whatsoever beyond it. He had craned his neck trying to peek underneath, but to no avail. Wherever he was, it was dark in the immediate area of internment, as well as beyond.

Judging by his growing need for water and food, Jack reasoned that he had been locked up for some time. As for the effects of the tranquilizer dart, he had no idea how long he had remained unconscious. One thing was for sure—despite the warm clothing they had allowed him to keep, he was chilled to the bone—and he believed wholeheartedly that if he didn't find warmth soon, he would freeze to death.

Suddenly he heard a faint noise, the first since he regained consciousness. It sounded far away, as if originating at the far end of a long hallway outside the door.

Jack strained to see something, anything, and before long a faint but steadily growing light flickered under the door.

Soon there was a familiar sound of human footfall, and conversation, though clearly not in English.

The old, heavy-duty bolt that had held the door closed groaned in resistance. It finally slid back and the great oak door was pulled open.

Three men walked into Jack's cell. Two stood silently by the entryway, holding candles in one hand and AK-47s in the other. All three wore Muslim attire, but were uniquely armed with knives, ammunition, and grenades.

Jack looked at the three of them without flinching a muscle. They didn't seem ominously sinister, but were well armed and obviously his jailers.

Finally, after what appeared to be a visual assessment of Jack, the one in the middle began to speak.

"How are you feeling, Major Garrity?"

Jack knew that they had taken his dog tags, as well as his billfold, and so had learned his name.

"I'm all right," he answered, "but it's a bit chilly in here."

"*Chil-lee?*"

"Cold."

"Ah, yes . . . it is a bit cold, Major. We are sorry that you have been forced to remain here for so very long. We were not sure who you were. It was necessary for finding out the truth."

"Who are you?" Jack asked.

"I am Sahid Tashwan, the leader of the Libyan Resistance."

"Resistance?"

"We are a small army, Major Garrity, but we are very effective in many ways, and most pleased to have you here with us."

"Pleased? How so?" Jack was curious now.

"Before your arrival, Major, we were planning an offensive against El-Wahat. It would have been a great cost of lives for us. But then quite suddenly, there is Major Garrity in the sky, firing rockets and heavy artillery at our target. We thought that Allah had come to do our work for us! You did, by yourself, what might have taken us two weeks to do. . . . And even then, my friend, we could not have hoped to succeed without so much lost!"

"Wait . . . just a minute . . . Mr. Sa-hee?"

"Sahid," the man said.

"Okay, *Saheed.* I'm not quite sure I'm following you there, friend. Who is El . . . whatever it was you called it?"

"El-Wahat, Major. It *was* a significant military installation near Kufra where weapons of destruction against our people were stored. It is only one of many, but because of you it has become one less."

Sahid explained to Jack how he and some of his men had been secretly positioning themselves around the military encampment. Then, using his hands and surprisingly good English, the self-acknowledged rebel leader painted scenes of a fired missile, a man ejecting from the cockpit of a doomed F-31, and a jubilant chorus of cheering rebel fighters at the successive sights of mass destruction at their intended target.

A combination of nerves and the pressing cold had taken their toll on Jack. He found himself suddenly shivering uncontrollably.

Sahid saw the discomfort and responded.

"I beg your pardon, Major. How foolish of me to have neglected your needs. Come! Let us go from here." With that he gave a quick glance at the two men standing at the door, who in turn led the way out of the small room. There was, as Jack had envisioned in his mind, a long ascending hallway to the right, and curiously another descending hallway directly ahead.

Jack could only imagine what kind of place this was. The hallways, as he had called them, were not hallways at all. Rather they were tunnels that led in all directions. It was as though two independent, underground arteries met here in an L-shape, with the small room cornering the junction. What the room was originally used for, or where the tunnels led, remained a mystery for the moment. But Jack was clearly delighted with the idea of going up, rather than forward and down.

"Where are we, Sahid?" Jack whispered.

"Inside the tunnels of the dead," the man answered.

"Tunnels of the *dead?*"

"It is, Major—how do you say it?—a sacred place of resting for the souls of the ancient dead. There are many more tunnels. They lead to separate paths underneath the mosque."

"You mean this is an underground cemetery?"

"Exactly."

"Where are the bodies?"

"Much, much deeper . . . in the catacombs."

"What was that room I was in?"

"It was used, many years ago, as a—how do you say?—a temporary place where the dead were kept, before finding a more permanent location in the catacombs."

"A morgue?" Jack quizzed, suddenly a bit queasy.

"Yes, that is it . . . a morgue."

"And you say these tunnels are under some old church?"

"A Muslim mosque, Major. It is called Adi Haliab. It is old, but it is a place of beauty where the true followers of the prophet

Mohammed have for centuries gathered for prayer and fasting. It is still a home for the devout monks who continue the traditions of their predecessors. But it is also a sanctuary for the movement's strategic command post.

"Under your command?"

"Yes, most certainly."

"How many insurgents are there in your army?"

"We are spread thin, Major. It is not a big army—perhaps two thousand with weapons—but many thousands more seek independence from the tyranny of the government and the politically strong Haman Al-Rashid.

"This is the moment of our greatest struggle, and has become a holy war that will free our country from its chains! We are gathering in strength, but unless we can convince the Americans to assist us, we will fail. It is for this reason that we praise Allah for your coming. He has sent you to us so that we can show your country the great tyranny that is upon us! You see, Major, we know about your secret airplane—what do you call it, the Banshee?"

"What?" Garrity was dumfounded. "How could you—" He stopped abruptly in midsentence, catching himself just before acknowledging his participation in the Screaming Ghost operation. He wondered whether this whole scene of nice-guy attitudes was nothing more than a ploy to trick him into a confession.

Jack thought back to the tranquilizer injection and imagined having received an equal dose of sodium Pentothal. Maybe, just maybe, these guys knew something. Could he have actually told them something under the effects of the drug?

He decided to play it off. Play dumb. Assess the situation further—at least until they were free from the murky tunnels—and by then, formulate a fast-action play for escape.

"Banshee?" he asked stupidly.

Sahid looked at him with clear surprise and momentary disappointment, then turned forward once more, continuing the slow ascension. He thought about the American's sudden denial, then realized that it was perfectly normal for a military mind. There was no way for the major to know that Sahid was speaking truthfully—at least not at the moment. In a few minutes, however, he would be able to give Major Garrity a comfortable explanation and all the proof necessary. Meanwhile, not at all offended by Garrity's response, Sahid continued. "Forgive me, Major, I can see that I have . . . let's see . . . how do you Americans say it? Oh, yes . . . placed my foot in my mouth. I have expected you to trust me without showing you a reason. But no matter. Shortly we will sit in conference, share some food and wine, and I believe at that time you will be much interested in what we have to show you."

Silence followed.

The four men walked briskly upward through the last shallow arch of the underground passageway until, at last, they emerged into a small, oval-shaped room. A narrow flight of stairs ascended even further upward where there was another wooden door under which a refreshing luminescence of natural light could be seen. It was an entryway into a remote corner of the ancient desert mosque. Sahid and his men then left Jack alone, promising to return shortly with his equipment, plus food and drink.

Like a ridge-top citadel, Adi Haliab dominated the farm village of El-Kabir. The town was flanked on all sides by heavily eroded volcanic escarpments that seemed to protect the precious soils farmed by Muslim and Christian villagers.

From a large window in the front of the room, Jack could see nearby fields of wheat, lentils, peas, and beans. He thought briefly about the hardships and struggles of a people living in the heart of a vast desert. The survival of these nomads depended largely on a narrow river that flowed down through the middle of the valley, which watered the fields and provided the life-support system in the desert wasteland.

The village, which could be seen in its entirety from the mosque window, wound through the valley like a giant snake. It was not modern, but was old and colorless. The streets were dusty, hard-packed earth where people moved about on foot or with a camel in tow. There were no automobiles in view.

Also visible from the mosque's cliff-side perch was a panoramic view of the desert to the north, toward what Sahid had described was the severely damaged military base Al-Wahat, and the larger city Kufra, where civilization was a bit more modern.

Jack wondered how long he had been down in the underground room. It appeared to be mid-morning, according to what he could tell from the still-rising sun in the east. He studied his current surroundings, a very ornately decorated room, while waiting for Sahid to return.

There was a large table in the center of the room on which was spread a detailed map of Libya and its surrounding countries. Jack stared at it for several moments, determining that it was a military strategy map. All of the countries and cities were spelled out in English, but at the bottom two rows of words were written in Arabic—or at least something close to Arabic. He had no idea what the words meant.

Probing the room further, Jack was impressed with the colorful splendor of its decor. Tall marble pillars outlined the ceiling-to-floor windows, which appeared to have been hand-carved centuries ago by skilled rock masons. The ceiling and the floor, themselves, were unique and colorful works of art. Millions of translucent ceramic tiles had been fitted together to create ancient gothic scenes of civilizations long gone, but mysteriously preserved by the painstaking puzzle-piecing that had gone into the creation of these porcelain frescoes.

The furniture, besides the table, was nothing spectacular—just old, early-twentieth-century wooden chairs and other smaller tables. It seemed that this was some sort of planning room for Sahid's revolutionary forces—if, in fact, he had revolutionary forces.

The only other interesting feature about the room was the door through which they had emerged from the deep earthen chambers moments before. Looking directly at it, Jack could not tell that it was a door at all, but rather it appeared to be an extension of the faded plaster walls. There were large potted plants on both sides. It was a hidden entry.

He wondered how many other entries might be in the old mosque—and how many endless tunnels had been dug over the centuries by faceless, nameless human beings.

Sahid returned with a woman.

"Major Garrity," he said politely, "I would like you to meet my wife, Nisha."

"How do you do, ma'am?" Jack responded cordially.

"I am fine, thank you, Major. We hope you will forgive us for your short internment. But as you have been told, we had to be sure who you were before we could confide in you for help."

Nisha was a strikingly beautiful woman with pearl-black hair and dark brown eyes. Her cheekbones were a photographer's paradise. She was slender, clearly agile, and impressively strong-looking for a woman. She spoke English with the same clarity as her husband, and with the same enchanting accent. Jack suspected that at one time or another, with the impressive vocabulary they had each acquired, they must have been associated with Americans or Englishmen. He tended to link them with the former, only because he was able to detect occasional American idioms or expressions. He made a mental note to inquire later about their background.

The three of them sat at one of the smaller tables while food and drink were served. Jack made every effort to be polite, and wondered what the proper protocol was in a Libyan setting. He waited for one of them to initiate the ceremony of dining—if indeed there was such a thing. But again sensing his discomfort, Sahid spoke.

"Major Garrity, we are *not* your enemy. Please, help yourself to the food. You must be very hungry."

"Thank you," he said. "I am a bit hungry at that."

As the meal got underway, Jack felt more and more at ease with his hosts. They seemed to be very polite people, and more important, not at all evil or dangerous as he had earlier suspected.

The woman Nisha was not dressed in the traditional veiled and cumbersome attire typical of Islamic women. Instead, like her husband, she wore what appeared to be loose-fitting robes of a sort, and fitted, as was her husband, with various combat weapons. Obviously she, too, was highly active in their political reform.

No one but the three of them remained in the room. The only interruption was an occasional delivery of more food and what appeared to be a red wine—which Jack did not drink. Instead, he had politely requested water. When the woman inquired why, he simply revealed his distaste for alcohol and his life-long commitment to abstinence. Interestingly, aside from that simple verbal exchange, nothing else was said during the meal. He wondered why, but supposed that it must be the custom.

When at last it was clear that each had eaten their fill, Sahid spoke. "Can we get you anything more, Major?"

"No, thank you," he answered. "That was more than enough, and very good, I might add. You have been very generous."

"Then let us move once more, if you don't mind, over to the main table. We would like . . . oh . . . how do you Americans say the phrase? Yes, we would like to 'bend your ears' for a short while. That is, of course, if you will permit us to do so."

"Fine," he quipped, "but I have a question or two of my own, if you don't mind."

"Certainly," Sahid smiled. "Speak!"

"Well, for starters, I'd really feel a lot more comfortable if I could have my belongings back."

"Ah, yes, how foolish of me." Sahid turned his eyes toward Nisha, who immediately excused herself and left the room. Jack overheard her speaking in Arabic to a person just outside the door, and then she turned and walked back into the room. Once again he was taken by her beauty, and found it difficult to move his eyes away from the stunning features of her sculpted face. He thought that if he were a photographer of a prominent fashion magazine, he would pay dearly for an opportunity to capture her beauty on film. She was strikingly photogenic.

As she made her way toward them, two men entered the room a few feet behind. They carried with them Jack's survival pack and a small box, which apparently contained his loose items. They set the items down and left the room.

As Jack requested, Sahid returned all of his personal belongings. Jack was delighted to find his weapon, the 9mm Colt, undamaged. He took this and his knife and put them on his person. As he did, he strangely felt an increased sense of safety.

"Anything else?" Sahid asked.

"Yes," Jack said, "one more thing."

"Please . . . "

"Before you show me whatever it is you intend to display over on the table, I would like some answers about the two of you."

"Nisha and me?"

"Exactly. But additionally, I would like to hear your explanation about the Banshee project. You brought it up. You apparently know quite a bit about it."

Jack was no longer concealing his personal knowledge of the Screaming Ghost operation. Still, he was not willing to offer any more information, should his captors be only remotely informed. His curiosity was piqued. He felt it necessary to learn what he could if he was going to trust them.

"That, Major, is no problem. Come, let us take the more comfortable chairs over here around the table—then we will tell you everything you desire. Fair enough?"

"Fair enough."

Jack felt more relaxed as he approached the table. At last he would get the information he needed to plan his next move—that is, if the two spoke the truth.

A strange swelling of excitement and intrigue filled his entire being. This moment, he thought, would reveal his entire future—if, in fact, he had a future. Beads of perspiration appeared on his forehead, and Jack knew that his life weighed in the balance of what he would now learn.

29

A little more than a year or so ago, you Americans aligned yourselves with many countries of the world and gathered a great army in Saudi Arabia and the Persian Gulf. Your objectives were clear to the whole world, and with remarkable speed and irrefutable military might, your Allied contingent swept into Kuwait. There you forcibly expelled Saddam Hussein and his armies from that which you claimed was not his."

"Well, it wasn't! He was—"

"We do not dispute your motive here, Major, nor do we condemn you. Actually, we believed in your country's cause. As he showed the civilized world, Mr. Hussein is an evil, irrational man. And, from what we have learned of the coup attempts, he has been fortunate not to have been assassinated long ago. Had this happened, so many people, Christian Kurds as well as Muslims, would not have suffered and died as they have! He is much the same as our Haman Al-Rashid—a callous and compassionless dictator who thrives in luxury and wealth at the costly expense of human grief and suffering!

"What you may not know, Major, is that prior to your massive invasion of Iraq and Kuwait, Mr. Hussein and Mr. Al-Rashid were working on a secret military project code-named Holy Power. The ultimate objective of this project was to acquire, however possible, an arsenal of nuclear weapons from the West, from Russia, or from China.

"Our country, Libya, is not one of the wealthy countries rich in oil deposits, diamonds, or other commodities. But, unlike Iraq, we have deep deposits of uranium . . . plenty of uranium. Mr. Hussein signed a special pact with our president to have free access to our radioactive minerals when the time was right. This he did in exchange for financial assistance and twentieth-century military technology.

"Before and after the Gulf War, Hussein and Al-Rashid never stopped progressing with their Holy Power project. And, while world attention remained focused around the Gulf region, Hussein—how do you say?—ah, yes . . . 'bankrolled' our president, who was able to purchase two nuclear devices along with the plans and resources to build a nuclear reactor. He continued to provide this clandestine support even after the United Nations disarmament experts revealed last July that they had discovered two unfinished uranium enrichment plants north of Baghdad. And so, while the Allied countries *thought* they had disposed of the nearly completed nuclear plants in Iraq, two separate nuclear weapons were being developed here in Libya."

"*Two* nuclear weapons?" Jack questioned.

"Yes, Major, *two*."

"We were under the impression that there were maybe three or four others."

"Only two. It was cleverly arranged—how do you say?"

"Propaganda?"

"Yes, that is the word, *propaganda*. It was part of the strategy to persuade your country and others into believing that other weapons existed, and that they were strategically placed in neighboring countries where much suffering and much life would be lost if you tried to stop us from building a reactor."

"You have a reactor, then?"

"No, not yet. But it *is* under construction . . . completely underground."

"In Tripoli?"

"No."

"We have intelligence reports—"

"More propaganda . . . more part of the plan."

"Well, where then?" Jack quizzed.

"Look here on the map, Major." Sahid pulled the table map Jack had seen earlier toward them.

With explanations from Sahid the markings on the map began to make sense. "With Iraqi money, Al-Rashid has purchased huge stockpiles of military weapons. We have hundreds of jet fighters hidden around our country."

"Hold on a minute. I thought that we shot most of Hussein's air force out of the sky! Or blew them up while they were still hidden underground. In fact, if you remember correctly," Jack said, suddenly growing more emotional, "Hussein trusted the Iranians with a great number of the planes . . . remember? And . . . "

"Yes, Major . . . you tell *me*. What do you think the Iranians did with those planes?"

"They confiscated them! Don't you —"

"Yes? You were saying?"

Jack's eyes widened, then he exclaimed, "Are you telling me . . . are you suggesting that those airplanes actually made their way here, to Libya?"

"You are an intelligent man, Major Garrity! And, yes . . . to answer your question, that is exactly what happened. You see these little jet airplanes here, here, and here?" he queried, pointing to locations on the map.

"Yes, I've counted five of them," Jack said, looking at the small figures on the map.

"Five. Yes, that is correct. There *are* five of them, and each one represents one hundred and fifty fully armed and fully operational jet fighters!"

"You've got seven hundred and fifty able aircraft?" Jack asked, his eyes wide again.

"And more weapons! Much more weapons! Also, a reactor under construction right here." Sahid pointed to an obscure spot on the Libyan map just south of Gharati, where some of the uranium mines were located.

"You see, Major, Nisha and I were once part of the Libyan Elite, which, as you know, is equivalent to Hussein's highly touted, though highly suspect Republican Guard.

"As Al-Rashid's power continued to grow, there were those in this special military force who rose quickly to power. One of these individuals is a man perhaps more dangerous than even Hussein or Al-Rashid—a ruthless, power-hungry man named Lucca Rovigo. Have you heard of him?"

"Yes . . . as a matter of fact, I have. The State Department knows about him. They, too, fear that he is dangerous, as you say."

"He is that, Major . . . very dangerous, indeed! He is perhaps the most powerful man other than Al-Rashid in all of Libya! And at times I believe that even Al-Rashid could not stop him if Rovigo wished to lead an insurrection. But he does not need to. Al-Rashid has granted him full powers of state! He is General Rovigo now, and controls the Libyan Elite."

"What is the size of the Elite?" Jack pressed.

"Nearly six hundred thousand, with more than two hundred thousand active reserves. It is a formidable army, Major Garrity . . . truly a power to fear!"

"Six hundred thousand? We had no idea!"

"How could you? Your country has concerned themselves with problems in the Gulf region. The watchful eyes of the American satellites are focused more on Iraq than on Libya. This is true, yes?"

Jack didn't know what to say.

"It would—how do you say it—stand to reason, yes?"

"I think so. The Gulf has been the center of attention, that's for sure. But tell me, Sahid, you say that you and your wife were part of this Elite force?"

It was Nisha who answered Jack. She had been sitting quietly throughout the conversation.

"We were, Major," she said, folding her hands in her lap. "Our positions were respected, high-ranking positions."

"Even you? . . . I mean, a woman? I was under the impression that women in Islamic culture were not normally called on to serve in their country's armed forces."

"That is true, Major. We are *not* normally called on, as you say. But my husband and I had lived in America for several years, and we were of special value to the Libyan forces."

"That explains it," Jack stated. "Your occasional use of American slang. I noticed it earlier, but couldn't quite put a finger on it. But tell me . . . where in America did you folks live?"

"Both Sahid and I have doctoral degrees in archaeology. We taught at the prestigious Yale University in New Haven, Connecticut."

"Really?"

"Yes, Major," Sahid added, "but that is not important right now. You asked about us in particular, yes?"

"That's right, I did."

"Well, then you should understand that because of our diplomatic status with America, our command of your language, and so on, we were . . . I am not sure how you would put it . . . perhaps *forced* is the word . . . yes, forced to join the Libyan special forces, the Libyan Elite."

"You mean you were drafted?"

"Yes, that is the word. Drafted. Neither of us were politically minded. We only wanted to continue our work in America. But Al-Rashid's henchman, Rovigo, convinced Al-Rashid that we were a valuable asset to the political movement."

"You mean the Holy Power operation?"

"Exactly," Nisha confirmed.

"I'm not sure I understand—"

"The fact that we lived and worked in America," Sahid began, picking up where his wife had left off, "provided Al-Rashid with eyes and ears in your country."

"You mean you were spies?"

"No! Never spies! Commander Al-Rashid wanted us to be spies, yes, but we had friends . . . many wonderful friends in America. We did not want to be banished from your country . . . branded, as you say, as traitors and spies. But Al-Rashid tried to use us. He offered us everything—wealth and power and positions of strength in the Elite forces. But we continued to resist—politely, mind you—for we were afraid!"

"Of what?"

"Of Haman Al-Rashid!"

Sahid stood up from the table and walked to the huge gothic window. He was silent for a moment, rubbing a hand over both eyebrows as though attempting to soothe a headache. Nisha looked worried, or fearful, of something. Jack wasn't quite sure how to read emotions he was seeing.

At last the silence was broken, and Sahid continued. "They took our son, Major Garrity."

"Excuse me?" Jack countered, not really certain he heard correctly. "Your son? *Who* took your son?"

"Haman Al-Rashid!" Nisha exclaimed, taking back the burden she felt was weighing down on her husband. "The crazy man had our son—our thirteen-year-old Kashan forcibly removed from us! We were told that if we did not cooperate completely by joining up with the special Elite forces and getting involved with the movement, Kashan would be eliminated."

"What did you do?" the major asked, compassionately curious, and thinking all the while about his own son.

"We enlisted . . . but of course."

"Yes," Sahid added, joining the discussion again, "that is precisely what we did. We decided that the only way we could possibly hope to have our son back alive was to pretend loyalty and convince Haman that we had finally begun to see the significance of the project Holy Power."

"Did you get the boy back?"

"No . . . not yet. But we have at last found him."

"Found him?"

"They interned him in a boy's camp near the border of Tunisia. It is a military camp where the children are taught to hate and despise Tunisians, Algerians, Nigerians, and others who are regarded as being weak and subhuman. You see, Major, the heart of the Holy Power movement is greed and hate! Saddam Hussein and Haman Al-Rashid are determined to invade and conquer four large countries—here, here, here, and here!"

Sahid pointed to the map again, sliding a finger in a half-moon sweep, starting with the county of Chad and arching in a northwesterly direction up through Niger, Algeria, and Tunisia.

"It is the oldest reason for conflict—land, power, and the acquisition of the two atomic bombs. The governments of these countries are afraid for their lives!"

"Let me see if I understand this now, Sahid. Your government is going to invade these four countries and compel their citizens to what? Allegiance to Libya? This Al-Rashid?"

"Yes, Major," he sighed, "all of that! Hussein and Al-Rashid are determined to control most of northern Africa!"

"With just two bombs?"

"Actually . . . only one bomb. The first one was detonated, as you know, in the southeastern deserts near Rabyanah on Christmas Day. Lucca Rovigo wanted Haman Al-Rashid to *show* his strength. And now, as expected, the governments of those four countries are much worried. But the plan was also devised to fool the Americans . . . to prevent them from interfering like they did when Hussein attempted to take over the country of Kuwait."

"Who sold the nuclear weapons and technology to you—or should I say, to this Haman Al-Rashid?"

"It goes back to the Gulf War again. There was an American officer. . . . I don't know his name. But he made the deal with Hussein, initially . . . and in a sense, while Operation Desert Storm was carried out, secret movements of military hardware—including initial efforts to secure the two bombs—were set in motion. Many of Saddam's airplanes were already here in Libya before the first shots were ever fired in the Gulf. And then after the war ended, another diversion was created. Saddam put fear and terror into the Christian and Jewish Kurds living in northern Iraq. He didn't really care about them, as they were simply decoys for mass troop and military hardware movements out of Baghdad and east over the Zagros mountains in western Iran. All of these weapons, as well as thousands of troops, trickled little by little into our country. And over the past year, Saddam's soldiers have united with Libyan soldiers, creating one of the largest forces in the world."

"And the main objective is—what'd you say?—to gain control of most of the northern continent of Africa?"

"That's correct."

"But that could be a four- or five-front war! How do Al-Rashid and Hussein hope to win?"

"They have the bomb and are not afraid to use it."

"Is there access to others . . . I mean bombs?"

"I am not sure, Major. But no matter . . . we will soon be building more!"

"This American—you don't know his name?"

Sahid thought for a moment, then scratched his head in defeat. "No," he sighed, "there were only two or three highest officials who ever dealt with him directly."

The three of them continued the discussion for another half hour, speaking of what they had learned of the Banshee project through spies still connected with the higher officials inside the Libyan Elite. They spoke of their final defection from the forces, and the establishment of an underground movement bent on overthrowing Lucca Rovigo and Haman Al-Rashid.

And, with clear grief and anxiety in their eyes, Sahid and Nisha told Jack of their determination to eventually liberate Kashan from the encampment. This was their single quest, and was optimistically based upon the assumption that their son was still alive—for they understood the complete and quickly executed wrath of Al-Rashid. It was a risk of greatest proportions to them, and yet it seemed the only route they could take and still live with themselves. Their final objective, of course, was to escape the madness of Libya and flee as a family to permanent asylum in the United States.

Jack, by this time, was totally convinced of the couple's sincerity and their accurate portrayal of the condition of Libya's government and country. He knew that even though they might be able to fabricate detailed information to feed to him, they could never fabricate the emotion that swelled within each word as they spoke.

"And so, Major Garrity," Sahid concluded, "now that you understand why we must free our people from this progressive madness, our hope is that we can get you safely out of the country so that perhaps you can tell your president the truth of what is going on!"

"The problem I still see," Jack said, "is the remaining nuclear device. I'm quite certain that our president will not want to risk massive destruction of civilian lives if the bomb has been placed in some city somewhere. You don't know its whereabouts?"

"We have reason to believe that it is just inside Algeria . . . but the exact location is still unknown. There are Elite troops along every border. It has become progressively more difficult to get in or out of Libya. And it is equally difficult to acquire reliable intelligence."

"Then how do you expect to get *me* out?"

"Major . . . Libya is over a thousand miles wide from east to west. We border six countries. Even with all of his Elite forces, Al-Rashid will not be able to watch every corner—every possible road to freedom—yes?"

"You know better than I," Jack countered. And then, feeling some inner struggle over the plight of his newfound friends, and the serious threat their country's leaders were for them and for the rest of the world, Jack found his mouth suddenly open. He then heard himself say something he couldn't possibly have imagined saying.

"Sahid . . . Nisha," his mouth uttered, his hands beginning to tremble, "before we find a way out of Libya—for me, that is—there are three things we need to do first!"

The two Libyans looked at Jack, curious as to what he was about to say. Sahid spoke. "Three things?"

"Yes, my worthy friend, three things. The first, locate and destroy the hidden nuclear warhead. . . ."

Again Sahid and Nisha stared at each other.

"The second," Jack continued, "is to destroy the nuclear reactor before it can be completed, and third—at all cost—is to free your son Kashan from the cages that keep him prisoner!"

"But—"

"There are no buts, Sahid! I will not go . . . run away . . . and leave you and your gifted wife to fight against such tyranny. Besides," he added, becoming calm and almost pensive as he spoke, "I, too, have a son, a small boy the very same age as your Kashan whose name is Little Jack. He would expect me to stay and help . . . to stay and fight!"

"Major," Sahid answered at last, clearly touched by the American's nobility. "I'm afraid you do not understand. You see, our greatest help would come if you escaped from here and solicited military aid from your government. A strong assault like the invasion of Kuwait and Iraq is what we really need . . . don't you see?"

Jack walked over and placed his hand on Sahid's shoulder. He looked deep into the man's eyes, studying the courage and determination he found there. He and Sahid were about the same age, and Jack realized that he suddenly cared very much for both him and Nisha. They needed his highly trained expertise—and he would give it to them. He said finally, "I'm afraid that it is *you*, good friend, who does not understand.

"I *will* escape, and I *will* bring the matter with all its seriousness to our president's attention. But, good people, you must understand that unless we can at least locate the warhead—even if we cannot disable it—the president will not risk another detonation. It doesn't matter that we could literally blow Libya off the face of the map with all of our nuclear weapons.

"What matters is what we call the annihilation policy. We will not use the power of the bomb because we will not be responsible for such massive human annihilation. And for that reason, we will not purposely allow another country to use it either. Do you understand? As long as there is a real threat that Al-Rashid or Rovigo will actually detonate the device, our president will keep arms distance! He won't intervene until we can assure him that we know where the bomb is, or that we have disabled or destroyed it! And, my friends, if we can find it, I *can* disable it!"

Nisha approached Jack. She stepped up and kissed him on the cheek. Then she said, "You are a brave man, Major Garrity, and in my heart I know you are a good man as well. If there is a way, we will find this nuclear warhead. We will find it, and as you say, we will destroy it!

"As a mother, I am most humbled by the kind words you spoke of getting our son free from his political prison." A tear formed and fell smoothly down Nisha's cheek, but she was unashamed. "But knowing, as I do, the great walls that bind him, I am not very optimistic. Your willingness to stay and help is a noble gesture . . . but, dear Major, I do not know how we, who are so small, can accomplish so great a task without a sizeable army to fight for us and with us! It will only be by the grace of the great God of heaven that we will ever see our dear son again, for truly I cannot see any other way!"

The words were touching to Jack's ears. All three of them were standing now in a small circle, facing one another. Jack reached out and took Nisha with one hand and Sahid with the other. He looked again into their troubled faces, then spoke:

"When I was a small boy, my father used to teach me principles of honor by reciting little poems or special words that I would remember at the right moments. I have tried to do the same for my son, Little Jack, and for my young daughter, Trish.

"You said, Nisha, that you were not very optimistic . . . that you couldn't see how it could be done. Yet in the same breath you mentioned God, which leaves me to assume that you are both God-fearing and righteous followers of our Creator.

"Well, good lady, I have an answer for you. My father taught this poem to me, and I have taught it to my children. Promise me that you will teach it to your son when we get him free—for we can achieve great tasks, lift heavy burdens, and overcome obstacles if, as this poem suggests, we take things a step at a time. The poem goes like this:

> How can we, so weak and so frail,
> Shoulder the burdens, or hope to prevail?
> The Master has taught us "line upon line."
> Said it was done one step at a time.

"We *will* destroy the warhead, we *will* wreak havoc on the nuclear reactor, no matter how far along it is, and we *will* free your son from his political prison!"

30

0645 Hours, Tuesday, 31 December 1991,
New Year's Eve
Antelope Valley Hospital, Lancaster, California

The first light of day filtered down from the heavens like a slow-moving fog. At first, only the faint silhouettes of various shapes could be seen. But little seven-year-old Trish Garrity stood at the window and watched anyway, hoping.

The street lamps along the side of the hospital were still lit, but it was the predawn light that was so beautiful to her eyes.

Up the street a ways, a person wearing a full-body sweat suit jogged steadily toward the hospital. Trish watched him, for she now realized it was a man coming closer and closer. His breath made little clouds along the way. She wondered if he were a daddy, because he looked like her own daddy. The image of the man made it difficult for Trish to hold back her tears. She missed her daddy. And what was worse, she didn't even know where he was.

The lone morning jogger never saw the little girl. He appeared to be an experienced runner, for it was obvious that his concentration was runner-perfected as he almost floated along 15th West. Maybe he was training for a race. In any case, he simply ran right on by the Antelope Valley Hospital, hardly noticing it was even there. He then turned left at a small intersection and disappeared from Trish's view.

It would still be a few moments before the sun was actually shining, but from her viewpoint at the side of her sleeping mother's bed, Trish could see that the scary cloudiness of the past stormy days was finally gone—all gone. It wasn't going to rain today. No more lightning! No more monstrous thunder! The sunshine—Mr. Sunshine—was going to shine today!

Trish turned away from the window and walked to the bedside of her motionless mother. Poor Mommy, she thought, all wrapped up in big ugly Band-Aids. Except these were different. They were hard like a wall, not soft like other Band-Aids. Alex and Mariam had told her yesterday when they had come to the hospital that Mommy was going to be okay—Little Jack, too. But they both had to wear Band-Aids for a while.

Trish was glad that she had not gone home with the Salingers. She liked them. But she felt she should stay with her mommy and her big brother.

When referring to the accident, the doctors had found that Trish simply did not accept—or had blocked from her memory—anything to do with the traumatic event. She didn't refer to it or speak about it in any way.

But what the doctors did not know, and probably never would know, was that the little girl did have an associative memory of sorts. She did not understand the magnitude of the accident or realize how dreadfully close she had come to leaving this world. Instead, the event itself was associated with the storm.

Something was born inside her fragile little mind that morning that would come back to haunt her many times over the course of her life. Simply stated, they were the monsters called *thunder* and *lightning*.

And so the beautiful view outside with the clear sky and the growing light of the sun provided peace for young Trish that even she was unaware of. Before she had dared to leave the sanctuary of her room that morning, she was determined to see if the monsters were still in the sky. She had crept slowly to the window, her heart racing with fear. Oh, how she had prayed for the storm to go away! And now it had!

Hooray! she thought. It was going to be a nice day, after all.

The nurses had kept a steady diet of sedatives flowing intravenously into Trish's mother, so even as the little girl stood at the bedside inches away from her mother's face, her mother slept on.

That was okay. Somehow, Trish knew that her mother needed the sleep.

She walked in silence over to the door. Yesterday she and the Salingers had walked a few times up and down the hallway. She had seen all kinds of people. Doctors, nurses, grandmas and grandpas, moms and dads, and even a few other kids like her and her brother.

Trish had always loved her brother. Sometimes, of course, it was more fun to tease and upset him. But right now, she really loved him a lot! She didn't want to tease him at all. She didn't want to see an angry face either.

What she really wanted was for him to wake up. She knew that he was sleeping because the Salingers had said so. But what she couldn't understand was why he didn't finish his long nap and wake up! If she was going to have to go with the Salingers today, as they told her she would, she wanted Little Jack to come home with her.

With this seven-year-old reasoning, Trish poked her head out the door and looked up and down the hospital corridor.

At one end, a long ways away, was a place the nurses called their "stationary," or something like that. It was a place where all the nurses and doctors sat and talked and watched TV and drank cold soda pop from the pop machines.

Right now it didn't look like anybody was in the hallway or at the nurses' stationary, so Trish crept into the corridor, turned left, and walked two rooms down to where she had seen her big brother yesterday. If nobody was going to wake him up, then she would have to do the job by herself.

"Little Jack?" she whispered as she reached his side. "Wake up, Little Jack. Let's go home!"

Little Jack lay prostrate on his back. Two small tubes were connected to some sort of machine. It made a noise and was stuck up her brother's nose. He seemed okay to her. His face was fine, he breathed normal, and to Trish he just seemed to be peacefully sleeping.

She whispered to him again.

"Little Jack, wake up . . . please wake up so we can go home! 'Kay?"

Little Jack did not move.

He did not twitch or respond in any way to his little sister's pleas. He just lay there—trapped—unbeknownst to the little girl, in a world void of feeling. He was also void of noticeable life. Yet somewhere out of reach of modern medicine, or science, Little Jack *did* live. He could not understand the constraints that bound him physically to the bed in the hospital. Nor could he see those around him. He tried to open his eyes, but couldn't. He tried to move his hands, or turn his head to one side, but again nothing happened. He made every possible effort to form words with his mouth, as he had always done. Yet try as he might, no words came.

Curiously, however, there *was* sound.

He couldn't hear in the same physical way he had been accustomed to—it was uniquely different. It was as though he were trapped somewhere deep inside a cave or an endless tunnel, where sounds—clear and perceptible—seemed to vibrate all around and through him.

He heard his sister, Trish, and he called back to her. But his own voice sounded different. He wanted desperately to reach out and take her by the hand—but his lifeless body would not respond.

"Trish!" he silently yelled. "I'm here, Trish! I'm right here!"

She couldn't hear him. Oh, this was so frustrating! Why couldn't he see her? Why couldn't she hear him?

"Little Jack," the small feminine voice said again, "if you don't wake up, we'll never get to go home! Please wake up, I need you! *Mommy* needs you!"

"I *am* awake, Trish! Don't you hear me?"

Silence followed, and feeling bereft and alone, Trish kissed her brother on the hand, turned, and with a heavy heart walked quietly back to her own room. Little Jack's heart sunk in despair. But almost that same instant, he felt an unusual calm or peace.

He strained his eyes—his subconscious eyes—to see, and as he did so, a faint but perceptible light began to appear just above him. It was barely visible at first, but grew brighter and brighter until it surrounded him and filled his soul with a familiar warmth and internal harmony. The promise of hope flickered as before, and Little Jack was overwhelmed with the presence of a powerful and soothing love.

"It is so hard to have hope," he persisted tearfully, and paused. "My sister calls to me from a place far away. I can hear her crying. She tells me to wake up, but I can't open my eyes. And when I call back to her, she doesn't hear me. She doesn't answer me."

Little Jack remembered well the silent commitment he had made to watch over and protect his sister and mother in his father's absence. A sense of renewed determination swept through him, and with a soul brimming with hope, he knew that if he labored diligently, he would ultimately free himself from the catacombs of darkness around him.

He knew also that he was not alone.

31

Somewhere in Northern Libya

Lucca Rovigo was trained to observe. But more than that, his temperament and attentive instincts provided him the necessary patience to *think* about what he observed.

After leaving the crash site, Lucca, with a small, well-armed contingent of skilled Libyan Elite, convoyed south. Haman Al-Rashid had long since returned to Benghazi, leaving Lucca to wrap up the investigation. Lucca, of course, had already planned on tracking the American who had murdered his brother, and although Al-Rashid was clearly the supreme commander of the Libyan Elite, Lucca was very much a general, as Al-Rashid had so recently announced.

The men feared him. They were quick to obey his every command, and to do so silently.

There had been a time, seven or eight months ago, when Lucca had hand-picked two dozen prime fighters from the force to travel with him—his own small army! Each was a skilled warrior, and each respected the raspy, thin voice that made Lucca Rovigo an utterly chilling force to reckon with. They knew that any disobedience would release the ferocity of a frenzied psychopath, whose swift retribution would mean their immediate deaths. And Lucca, of course, skilled not only in the tactics of war, but extremely intelligent as well, used their own fears against them. His leadership psychology was eerily effective.

"Pull over there to the right and stop," he commanded the driver of the deuce-and-a-half.

"Yes, sir."

The convoy consisted of two jeeps, armed heavily with M-60s, a half track, and two armored transports, all of which came to rest behind Lucca's command vehicle.

Lucca alone stepped down from the vehicle and walked into the narrow valley that ran between the two larger sand dunes. Something had caught his eye. It was a small green and white cardboard box, barely poking free of the sand. He stooped to pick it up. Wiping the sand free, he read the printing on the outside.

> Gruen-Swiss Compass Watch
> Highly accurate, rugged,
> precision quartz watch
> with an oil damped, re-
> movable Swiss charting
> compass. Heavy cast
> metal exterior casing
> provides shock resistance
> and water resistance to
> three atmospheres.
> Gruen Ltd, Switzerland

Lucca crushed the small box in his right hand and discarded it. A heinous smile drew across his lips. He adjusted his sunglasses and walked back to the jeep. Then, before climbing back into the passenger's seat, he stopped and surveyed the area.

There was a long silence, not a single individual daring to break the general's concentration.

Lucca, himself, was as immovable as stone, except for a slight sweeping motion of his head moving left to right, and back again, as he scanned the terrain. Then, convinced at last of the direction he would take, he stepped into the four-by-four and said, "Southeast. Drive slowly through this narrow valley, then turn southeast when I tell you to."

"Yes, sir."

The convoy headed toward El-Kabir.

32

The communiqué was from the supreme committee occupying the presidential palace in Tripoli. The unbroken blue seal told Haman Al-Rashid that no one but himself had seen what was inside. He pressed the large, hardened, waxy piece between his thumbs and fingers and snapped the seal in half. Then he retrieved the contents of the small pouch and laid them out on the desk in front of him.

There were two brief letters. One was addressed specifically to Haman, written by the Libyan Supreme Committee. The other was a typed memo from the office of the president of the United States. He read the latter first, and noted with disgust that it was not signed by the U.S. president—rather, by the secretary of defense, a nameless nobody!

The letter was a sham! A bold-faced lie! And Haman's single wish was that he could go public and televise the *real* truth to the world! But that could wait.

The secretary of defense affirmed that the Americans had no idea, whatsoever, about a secret military spy plane, and that if one had indeed been shot down over Libya, it would had to have been something other than U.S. make. The United States had no such spy plane, and maintained that the only military activity anywhere near Libya was a Mediterranean-based Naval fleet performing practice maneuvers only.

The communiqué also stated that the aboveground "testing" of a nuclear device was in violation of the World Test-Ban Treaty, and the coalition of governments represented in the United Nations would not stand idly by while Libya continued to pollute the atmosphere with radioactive fallout. Therefore, it was the position of the government of the United States to make a formal demand that Libya cease all such activity, or face the consequence of an angered world coalition.

If indeed Libya was now a country with nuclear strength, then formal talks should begin immediately with representatives of the other superpowers, so that the government of Libya might learn responsible restraint, and utilize the power of the atom for peaceful purposes.

In conclusion, the United States and its freedom-loving people would not tolerate Libyan aggression against any other nation, and if said government were to utilize the bomb as a means to overthrow some of the weaker nations of Africa, the armed forces of a united coalition would have no choice but to use whatever means necessary—including the use of force—to liberate the Libyan people from their bondage under the dictatorship of that government.

In essence, Haman reasoned, bomb or no bomb, the world appeared to be poised and ready to invade his country the minute he and Hussein moved their operation into action.

Good! Let them invade! By the time they do, *if* they do, several more weapons with atomic strength should be ready!

Al-Rashid set the official U.S. letter down on the table and thought about picking up the telephone and dialing the coded numbers.

"The Americans," he whispered to himself, "they are always so sure of themselves. Perhaps they require a second demonstration . . . perhaps a massive graveyard filled with Algerian infidels."

He dialed the first three numbers of the code.

Six . . . four . . . nine . . .

He paused and pictured in this mind the electronic triggering device Lieutenant Guant had built and sold to him and Lucca . . . to the Libyan people! He tried to imagine himself no longer the human commander and great leader that he was, and pretended instead that he was an electronic impulse now racing at unfathomable speeds across the east-to-west telephone cables spanning the near one thousand miles of northern Libya. The numbers six, four, and nine would momentarily reach the receiver on the other end. The soccer-ball-size metal cylinder, whose network of complicated wiring linked the sophisticated trigger to the nuclear device and the phone lines, would come to life! Command one of the coded message would alert the power mechanism to stand ready and to respond to command two.

Haman dialed the second code. This time there were five numbers: four, six, four, nine, four.

He waited for the sound.

As soon as the destructive globe processed the second set of numbers, a relay switch inside the aluminum-tinted device would activate a small timer. There would be five minutes to punch in the remaining code. The final sequence was also five numbers: two, nine, two, nine, four. But before the final signal could be transmitted, Haman would have to wait for the eery, dial-tone humming that would begin immediately following the relay switch's activation of the timer.

Ommmmmmmmmmmmmmmmmmmm . . .

The timer switch clicked on.

Beads of perspiration formed on Al-Rashid's forehead. His hand began to shake slightly . . . but he held the telephone receiver to his ear and continued to listen to the electronic drone.

Ommmmmmmmmmmmmmmmmmmm . . ., it purred.

He pictured the oil field just outside El-Hadjera and Ghardaia, two heavily populated cities, in between which was secretly hidden the massively destructive warhead.

He grinned while thinking back to the ease with which his men—Lucca's men—had stealthily secured the bomb and its aluminum-encased soccer ball trigger. It had taken some doing, but repeated moonlight jaunts to the oil field had eventually paid off.

Guant's meticulously clear wiring instructions had enabled Lucca to tie the trigger to the international telephone line that spanned the oil fields of the Algerian terrain. And after the specified tests—also provided by the American Air Force lieutenant—both Lucca and Haman were nearly overwhelmed with the obvious success.

Eventually, the Libyan team had crept silently and easily back to Libya, leaving the armed and lethal weapon behind. All that remained now was a simple telephone call, a patient hand at the telephone buttons, and the cold, callous heart of a man who would not hesitate to enter the irreversible five final digits.

Haman knew that he was just the man for the job. The bomb could be detonated from any public or private telephone, and the three sets of numbers, thirteen altogether, had to be punched in sequentially correct. He, alone, knew the sequence. The supreme committee had granted him the absolute religious responsibility of detonation, and with as much hate and animosity toward the Algerians as lived in Haman's heart, he was indeed the right man for the job!

Ommmmmmmmmmmmmmmmmmmmm . . ., the chilling sound continued. Three and a half minutes had passed. If Haman did not punch in the final code, the timer would shut off by itself and stand down from its alert call. The entire sequence of coded transmission would be required again to set the timer and its nuclear trigger ready for detonation—a second time.

Haman continued the deadly game. He wondered what, if anything, the Americans would really do if he went ahead with it! A second nuclear blast would show the Westerners that Libya was a force to be reckoned with! How *dare* they tell him . . . no . . . not tell him . . . *demand* of him subservience to their police tactics!

He dialed defiantly.

Two.

Nine.

Two.

Nine.

Ommmmmmmmmmmmmmmmmmmmm. . . . The sound was cold. It penetrated his flesh and pierced like a needle into the marrow of his bones. He held a shaking finger over the final number . . . the single element of the code that would electronically relay a message of death to the trigger globe.

Just one final effortless touch on the number four button . . . and hundreds of thousands would die!

Ommmmmmmmmmmmmmmmmmmmm. . . .

Twenty-two seconds left.

If he was going to do it, it had to be now, or the trigger device would shut down.

Twelve seconds. . . .

Ten seconds. . . .

33

Northeastern Algeria

At the El-Gassi oil fields, all was quiet. Most of the workers were still enjoying the holidays. They would have three more wonderful days to vacation with their wives and children before having to return to their duties at the derricks.

Like most places of business inside the Algerian nation, the oil fields of the rich El-Gassi plateau were monitored by a small skeleton crew.

Young Kaasar Jahil and his brother, Talim, found the metropolis of giant rigs and derricks a fascinating playground, and roamed about the churning machinery unnoticed. The older boy saw a small concrete structure just to the left of one of the bigger rigs and climbed on top of it. His brother needed a boost, but eventually got there as well.

The small structure was not very high, but it did afford the two boys an overview of the mechanical city. They sat down together and watched the endless motion about them. Every kind of oil-sucking pump seemed busily concerned with the task at hand, and like a great forest of robotic monsters, each of the funny-looking machines seemed independently alive, though peculiarly harmless.

The small concrete bunker on which they sat was simple in construction. It was approximately six and a half feet long and five feet wide. It was built mostly under the ground, and housed some sort of electronic motor that worked as a pump. Heavy electrical lines fed into the small room from a network of wiring above.

Two heavily insulated wires bound together with electrical tape snaked down through a cast-iron pipe that apparently led inside, and provided the continuous currents of energy that kept the pumps active. A small metal door with a vent in its center allowed access to the small chamber. The door was open, and so, as with most boys, curiosity led the way to exploration.

Kaasar climbed down off the structure and held out his arms so that his younger brother would not hesitate to follow.

The small metal door was usually bolted and padlocked, but someone had left the lock lying on the ground. The two boys crawled inside.

It was dark at first, but as soon as their eyes adjusted to the dim lighting from the opened door, two distinct smiles drew across the faces of the innocent intruders.

This was a really neat place! There was a big motor pump to one side, with pipes attached to both ends, continuously pushing the thick oil onward toward another pumping station. And, although the pump was a fascination all by itself, it didn't compare to the big, round silver ball bolted to the metal cone-shaped object just in front of them.

The ball was beautiful! Shiny! The brothers could see their reflections in its side. But the really great part was the small red light that blinked on and off on top.

A virtual maze of different-colored wires entered the shining ball on one side, then exited the other and linked up with the cone.

That was a weird-looking thing. Bigger than they were, it looked like the nose cone of a rocket, and at the center, spelled out in English, were three unusual words: *Pluton Nuclear Warhead.*

Completely oblivious to the ominous danger surrounding them, the two Algerian children cautiously ran their dirty fingers over the exposed surface of the spherical triggering device. They both dreamed of taking the wonderful ball home, but instinctively knew not to tamper with it. After all, it was part of their father's mysteriously wonderful place of work. They both agreed to make this their secret hideout, not just for the great machines inside, but especially for the relaxing on-and-off blinking of the pretty red light and the sweet melody that came out of the shining metal globe.

Ommmmmmmmmmmmmmmmmmmmm . . .

A little more than a thousand miles away, Haman Al-Rashid vacillated back and forth, fighting every emotion of leniency he experienced. Finally, gaining control of his emotions, he determined with two seconds left to cancel the detonation command.

With perspiration pouring down his flushed and heated forehead, the almost inhuman Libyan smiled. He would wait, for perhaps the timing would be better later. He had perspective, he had power, and in the end, he would show the world that he, Haman Al-Rashid, was *the* force that would lead Libya into the future of international prominence and prestige.

He wiped his brow with his sleeve, hung up the receiver, and walked slowly to the picture window in his office.

He stared silently out at the Gulf of Sidra. His time would come.

The humming stopped.

34

It had taken some time for Jack to convince his hosts, Sahid and Nisha, that despite their honorable intentions, he was not going to leave Libya before his three major objectives had been accomplished—or at least before he had done all within his power to see them to completion.

At last, however, sensing a growing bond of purpose and power, the three new partners silently embraced.

Then with renewed focus and expediency, they began to strategize. Together they pored over the maps and offensive tactics they would use in destroying the nuclear reactor and in freeing Kashan from the military camp in the east. They learned more and more from each other and developed strategies through their collective perspectives.

But though steadily busy, the three felt an increasing air of discomfort and downheartedness. The sullen, pensive moods were the result of a single issue—fear of the one remaining nuclear bomb.

It would not be an easy task to discover its whereabouts, for it remained the single most closely guarded secret in the country. Even before the first bomb had been detonated in the southeastern deserts, only a select handful of close associates of Qaddafi and Al-Rashid knew its precise location.

The remaining officials had been so completely irresponsible with the aboveground detonation that a small desert village, alive with men, women, and children, had not only *not* been told of the horrifying event, they had been considered with malicious indifference, and had been literally vaporized in the explosion.

With such obvious lack of concern for human life, the second bomb posed a nightmare of holocaustal proportions. It would remain the most significant objective of the three strategists to find it and disarm it. But where to even begin the search was the unspoken question that so haunted them.

Major Garrity learned that Sahid's rebel forces were scattered about the country in various key locations where a watchful eye could be kept on the movements of the Libyan Elite's powerful forces.

The center of the rebel force—the command post—was the old mosque Adi Haliab. Special civilian-looking foot soldiers acted as couriers, moving stealthily from one location to the next with information pertinent to the group's overall objectives.

There were no generals or other high-ranking military officers in the rebel army, though each unit, consisting of fifty men, was led by what they called a unit commander. This commander reported via courier to Sahid and Nisha. Each of the unit commanders had a replacement in the division, should he or she (and yes, there were at least three dozen females, well armed and well trained, in the rebellion) be killed during the highly dangerous military excursions.

Every two weeks, all of the commanders—wherever they were located—made the arduous desert journey to El-Kabir where they assembled in the old mosque to report successes or failures. Here also plans were made, oaths of freedom taken, and updates of the well-known Operation Holy Power recorded in a set of military journals personally kept by Nisha.

The rebellion force's ultimate objective was to stop the psychotic leaders inside the presidential palace from actually declaring and initiating a series of suicidal wars against the four less formidable countries—Chad, Niger, Tunisia, and Algeria.

If such plans were carried out, if such terrible wars were actually to begin, Sahid, Nisha and all the loyal commanders and warriors of the rebellion knew that, despite the remaining nuclear bomb, Libya would be ultimately overthrown—and its people shunned and despised by nearly every nation in the world!

Hussein, Al-Rashid, Rovigo, and all the others in power were men who had somehow lost contact with reality—desiring and insisting on secrecy, power, and ultimate global control!

Libya had become a facsimile of sorts. It resembled, in many ways, the Nazi-infested Germany of the mid-1930s, when the SS soldiers under the direction of Heinrich Himmler terrorized their own people and turned the entire country into a demonic police state where no one was safe. Only here, in Libya, Heinrich went by the name of Haman Al-Rashid, and Adolf Hitler by the name of Hussein!

Every major and minor road through the country was patrolled and carefully watched. Similarly, one could not make a phone call, talk on a two-way radio, or send any messages through the Libyan mail service, without being subjected to sporadic censorship that could very well lead to permanent solutions.

It was, of course, for these reasons that Sahid and Nisha's armed rebellion forces were limited to such primitive means of communication.

Each bi-weekly meeting of the division commanders concluded with specific objectives. Among these were constant, small rebellion assaults that would suddenly materialize—seemingly out of nowhere—against a number of military targets. The objective, of course, was to leave vast numbers of the Libyan Elite confused and downhearted.

And as for the top military advisors working with Al-Rashid and Rovigo, these acts of insurrection and blatant rebellion were infuriating. They fostered seeds of anger that continued to grow and develop until Al-Rashid had organized a small team of military experts, whose full-time occupation was to plan a military defeat of the rebellion—at all costs! The committee had selected Lucca Rovigo as the commanding officer of the hit squads, and Rovigo, a formidable warrior in his own right, was viewed as a general, and now a commissioned general—a hunter who always succeeded!

The meeting at Adi Haliab concluded with Jack's intervention in the deployment of a military offensive operation he hoped would bring about the swift destruction of the reactor plant south of El-Kabir. Actually, the three of them, Sahid, Nisha, and himself, had drawn up a master plan. As promised, Jack had committed himself to the three operations—the locating and disarming of the warhead, the destruction of the reactor site, and the eventual freeing of Sahid and Nisha's son, Kashan.

He was now ready to carry out objective number one.

Jack lifted the small backpack onto his shoulders, then checked to see that all of his gear was stowed properly. He then slipped a loaded clip into his Colt pistol and followed Sahid outside.

It had been decided that he and Sahid would travel alone. Of course Nisha was not particularly satisfied with this plan, but agreed to remain behind for a few days so the other political matters under their mutual direction could be dealt with professionally. In any case, she would meet up with them as quickly as she could.

The winter sun was low in the western sky, and painted a beautiful desert sunset. Jack and Sahid stared at it for a moment, then set off on foot down a narrow path that wound its way into El-Kabir. Behind them, walking in strict silence, were two civilian-clad foot soldiers. The four of them moved quickly, descending gradually until, reaching the bottom of the canyon, they set out across a small field and finally entered the settlement.

Even as the day gave way to night, activity in the small village was alive and well. Several small shops still displayed their wares, and Jack found himself curiously fascinated—thinking, of all things, how nice it would be to take something home to Little Jack and Trish.

One old woman especially impressed him. She was dressed in typical layered village garb, some of it embroidered, some printed, with a black head wrap angled just slightly to cover a blind eye. She smiled a friendly greeting to the four men as they passed by her shop. No words were spoken.

Jack found it refreshing to see the simplicity of the inhabitants of El-Kabir. Many of the townspeople were farmers, but a good number were shopkeepers who constantly displayed their goods out in the open market until daylight faded. Typical of the goods in many of the other markets, the partially blind woman's small shop was filled with everything from gold, turquoise, and silver, to ragtag notions and remnants of old Bedouin clothes.

It appeared, like so many other places in the world, that everything in the shop had a price. Yet what seemed unusual was that although the few remaining shopkeepers left an impression of visible poverty, each seemed to have a certain proclivity for precious jewelry. The expensive ornaments, gold and silver chains, necklaces and bracelets, valuable gems and rings, and even gaudy-looking ear and nose rings, seemed aversive and contradictory.

Who bought that kind of stuff? Jack thought curiously. Especially way out here in the center of a vast desert of nothingness? Perhaps, Jack reasoned, the act of wearing the costly apparel was in essence protecting it? That seemed the only logical explanation.

At the far end of the dusty road leading through the village's activity center, Sahid veered left into a small tributary alley. The four walked swiftly, but maintained their silence. Finally, they arrived at an old run-down building that had what appeared to be a small garage-size door. This opened up into an alleyway. There was no visible sign of life inside or around the old edifice.

Sahid stopped and looked around the immediate area. He then glanced back toward the main road from whence they had come, and finally tapped softly on the old wooden door. He spoke something in Arabic to one of the foot soldiers, gesturing some sort of command with his hands. Immediately the young boy responded, left the group, and vanished around the far side of the colorless building.

Moments later, Jack heard a noise inside. This was followed by a groaning sound from rusty springs and pulleys as they protested their lack of needed lubricants.

As the ancient barrier slid sideways, the silhouette of an old man appeared in the darkness beyond. He stepped into the alley and was immediately greeted by Sahid, who gave him a mild embrace and kissed him slightly on both cheeks. The silver-haired old man warmly returned the gesture.

As the two spoke quietly, Jack was suddenly aware of a furtive movement just inside the small warehouse. Instinctively, the major thought of his weapon and was about to draw it free from its holster when a stout, thick-coated husky dog crept into view. The dog had sensed the tension in the stranger and raised its head, then chuffed twice. Its intuitive protective posture alerted the old man, who was obviously its master. He, in turn, looked toward Jack.

"This is my American friend, Major Garrity," Sahid said to the old fellow. "The one I spoke of earlier."

Turning then to Jack, Sahid said, "Major, may I present my father, Ibrahim Al-Sayed."

"My pleasure, sir," Jack whispered, extending his hand.

"So, you are the one who has the great honor of destroying El-Wahat! Allah has sent you, yes?"

"Well, I don't know about all of that. . . ." Jack was a little embarrassed at the continual reference to the Islamic god's having sent him to Libya like some great warrior of hope. He answered quietly, "I think, from what your son has told me, that the demolition done to El-Wahat was simply luck. I honestly didn't know that it was a military installation, really!"

"The powers of God are often mysterious. There is no simple luck, as you call it. He is with us, my young friend, and many lives have been saved because of his supreme wisdom in bringing you here to us."

The old man walked over to Jack and took him in his arms, hugging and kissing him in a welcoming gesture of friendship and gratitude. "It is . . . like you say . . . a pleasure to meet you, young American. You are welcome in our country."

"Thank you, sir," Jack replied politely. "You speak English well."

"My son, his wife, and I speak it often to each other. We have long thought that it would one day be needed. So we practice it."

"Well, you all seem to speak it well."

"We try."

Ibrahim was a wise-looking, leather-skinned old man. From first glance, one would assume that he was long past the span of years allotted to his mortal frame. Yet Jack noted that the old fellow had a keen mind and seemed alert and spry.

Shifting his attention from Jack, Ibrahim stooped down to pet his beautiful animal. The dog had emerged completely from the shadowy darkness and was now sniffing the major's lower legs and boots.

"This is my dog, Juno," the elder gentleman continued. "He is a great Samoyed purebred from the United States. He was bred as an arctic sled dog in your beautiful state of Alaska."

"You were in Alaska?" Jack asked curiously.

"Eight years ago.

"It was a matter of business with my son—more of a holiday for me. But it is where I found Juno as a young puppy, and so I was able to bring him back to Libya. It is difficult for him in the hot summer months in the Sahara, but I cut his thick coat during these months and then allow it to grow back in the winter."

"He is a beautiful animal," Jack said admiringly.

"I am old and need a good companion. Juno watches out for me."

"You are right about that, Papa," Sahid interjected. "He *does* watch out for you. Sometimes he won't even allow Nisha to get too close!"

"Ah yes . . . a good dog watches out for his master. And you, Sahid, should have one as well! You and Nisha should have a watchdog near Adi Haliab."

"Perhaps we will one day, Papa. But come, let us go inside. We must hurry."

The small group left the alleyway and walked into the small building, shutting the portal behind them. Sahid turned to the remaining foot soldier who had accompanied them and asked him to stand watch by a small, dirty window overlooking the quiet streets beyond. The man obeyed without a word. Meanwhile, Jack followed Sahid and his father into the inner sanctum of a smaller room just past the warehouse.

There was a dimly lit candle mounted on a portable sconce, flickering in a remote corner of the room. Its light projected ghostly shadows of the three onto the barren walls. For a moment, Jack wondered where the light switch was. He then realized that the village was likely void of electricity—void of anything modern.

The room itself appeared ancient. At one end a small wooden table rested against a colorless wall. Three old and rickety chairs were spread out around it. Jack was sure that if he sat down on one of them, his weight would crush the old junker and send him crashing to the rotting tile floor. However, the old man offered neither Jack nor Sahid a seat. Instead, he grabbed hold of the chairs and the table and moved them quickly aside.

This accomplished, Jack could see the faint outline of a fairly well-hidden crawl space accessible through a trapdoor on the floor. A miniature tile was easily removed, and a finger-size ringlet was flipped up to a clasping position. Sahid's father took hold of the ring and lifted the door up and outward.

"We will need the candle over there on the table, Major," he said, pointing to the opposite end of the room. "Would you be so kind as to retrieve it?"

"I have a small flashlight in my pack," Jack offered, walking over to the corner. "Would you care to use that instead?"

"We will use them both," the old fellow nodded. "I will take the candle—you, your light."

Jack handed the still flickering candle and its sconce to Ibrahim as he and his son disappeared down through the narrow passage. Jack then retrieved the small flashlight he had been carrying from his backpack.

Stepping over to the small hole in the floor, and checking the flashlight along the way, Jack was suddenly aware of the dog Juno standing patiently at the door. The dog's tongue was hanging out of its mouth and its breathing was quick and rabbit-like.

"What about the dog?" Jack asked quietly down through the hole.

"He will be fine. Come, Major, we must hurry!"

As Jack climbed down into the extremely constrictive shaft, the last sight that caught his attention was a dimly visible figure of a man just having entered the room above. It was the foot soldier who had been left to stand watch. Jack wondered why he had left his post, but he soon learned the answer when he could hear the trapdoor above his head being quietly closed and secured, and the sound of a table being pulled and dragged across the floor.

The vertical tunnel was about fifteen feet in depth and roughly three and a half feet square. All sides were supported by a rough plywood of sorts, forming a perfect shaft with a single ladder on which Jack slowly and cautiously descended. Momentarily, he reached the bottom and set foot on what felt like solid ground. It was an underground room, rectangular in appearance. The ceiling height was a little less than five feet, requiring the three men to stoop.

Jack shined his light directly into Sahid's eyes.

"Please don't do that, Major," Sahid said, waving the light away.

"Oh, pardon me, I wasn't—"

"Look over here, Major," the old man said, pointing a finger at the other end of the stuffy chamber. "We will follow that smaller tunnel to the right. It may be a bit of a squeeze, especially with your shoulder pack. Would you like me to carry it for you?"

"Oh, no, no . . . it'll be all right. I've got it, thank you." Jack thought the old man was too kind.

Ibrahim led the way, holding the candle out in front of him. He was quick and surefooted, as though he had been through these tunnels hundreds of times before. And Jack reasoned that he probably had. Sahid followed and Jack took up the rear.

"Where are we going, Sahid?" Jack inquired with a whisper.

"An hour ago, Khalda spotted a small caravan of Libyan soldiers moving toward El-Kabir."

"Who?"

"Who what?" Sahid questioned, not sure what Jack was asking.

"Who did you say spotted the convoy?"

"Khalda Jamal, one of my men who was posted just outside El-Kabir in the foothills. He was the one who came with us from Adi Haliab, but returned to his post when we arrived at my fathers' place.

"He spotted a convoy?"

"Yes."

"Why didn't you tell me, Sahid?"

"We did not wish to worry you."

"Well, what about Nisha? Shouldn't we go back and warn her?"

"Not to worry, Major. Nisha was the first to know of the soldiers.

She is well prepared. They will never know that she is even there at the mosque. But, as I was saying—in answer to your previous question—this military caravan has come in search of *you!*"

"For me?"

"It is, I believe, General Lucca Rovigo!"

"Just who is Lucca Rovigo?"

"You do not know him, Major, other than what little we discussed back at Adi Haliab. But I can assure you, he knows all about you. He will stop at nothing to find you!"

"Find me? Why does he want to find me?"

"He is Commander Al-Rashid's—how do you say?—killing man!"

"You mean hit man?"

"Yes, hit man! He is Al-Rashid's hit man, and he is after you since they could not find you—or any part of you—at the crash site. Do you understand?"

"Yes, but what's that got to do with this tunnel business?"

"You see, Major," Sahid continued, "General Rovigo will have the village surrounded in minutes. No one will be able to go out or come back in. He will search every house, every shop, everywhere! He will not stop until he is certain you are not here! Do you understand?"

Jack considered what his friend was saying, and suddenly had an eery feeling, chilling and unsettling. He wondered how they had found him, or at least how they had followed him to El-Kabir. He had done his best to cover the tracks, but apparently not good enough.

Thinking back, Jack remembered the brief discussion about Rovigo. He also remembered that the name brought with it a certain uneasy feeling, and he knew instinctively that this man was to be feared. Jack did not want to meet him . . . period. The three men made their way rapidly through the dark tunnels, moving for the most part in silence. The corridors were narrow and once again Jack was reminded of the experience in the mines long ago when, as a youthful explorer, he had learned the meaning of the word *claustrophobia*.

Many stretches of the underground passage required them to crawl uncomfortably on their hands and knees. It was during these moments that Jack finally realized why Sahid's father had offered to assist with the backpack. Having made the journey before, Ibrahim knew that at times Jack would have to push the pack along the dirt floor in front of him, while he crawled behind at a turtle's pace.

The tunnel stretched out ahead of them like a long, straight, underground tube, leaving the major to wonder who on this good earth could have tolerated such a dreary task of excavating it? It must have taken months—no, *years* of digging, shoveling, reinforcing, and probably enduring untold numbers of cave-ins along the way.

Once or twice, while on his hands and knees burrowing his way past a constricted area, Jack would find that Sahid and Ibrahim had left him behind. It was quite obvious that they were adept tunnel rats, while Jack was not. Emerging from one such narrow passage, Jack shined his small light forward into the darkness beyond. At first glance, he was not able to see anything whatsoever of his two companions—just darkness.

He panicked!

Where had they gone? he wondered, his heart racing. He lifted himself up off the dusty ground, grabbed his small pack, and shined the light forward again.

About twenty feet or so in front of him, he noticed that the tunnel was finally beginning to angle off in another direction. He bent his head slightly and moved ahead until he rounded the small curve. It was here that the flat surface of the floor angled downward like some great amusement park slide, descending deep into the earth's crust toward some mysterious destination.

He stood at the top for a moment, hesitating and wondering if he should slide down on his back, or return to his hands and knees and crawl down.

He was anxious that Sahid and his father had left him behind as they had, and he forced himself into believing that they hadn't done so on purpose. Instead, they were likely unaware that he had lagged behind. Soon, he reasoned, they would discover his absence, stop the relentless march, and wait for him to catch up.

Jack shined his light downward into the darkened depths, hoping again to catch a glimpse of either of the two men. He saw nothing.

"For cryin' out loud," he whispered. "Where'd they go?"

He flicked the switch on the flashlight and turned off the beam of light. He strained his eyes to see down through the sloping shaft hoping to spot the faint luminescence of Ibrahim's candle—but still nothing.

How odd!

How far could they have gone?

Panic welled up inside of him again, and the nightmarish visions of ghosts and underground monsters that had been a part of his childhood fears surfaced in his mind, sending a shivering spasm of fear throughout his body.

He decided that the fear was irrational, and quickly dispelled the growing phobia. After all, ghosts and underground monsters?

Flicking the small switch on the flashlight once again to light the way, Jack recommitted himself to move ahead quickly so as to catch up with Sahid and his father. In the end, he figured that the quickest way down the narrow shaft was on his backside. So, tying his pack securely to his back, he held the light before him and sat down, feet first, in a ready position.

That was when he heard a noise.

It did not come from the direction it *should* have—down the chute in front of him. Instead, it sounded far off in the distance behind!

Jack spun around and lay on his stomach, his feet angled down the chute. He switched off the flashlight again and retrieved the 9mm Colt from its holster. He jacked a shell into the chamber and waited. Whatever was coming down through the darkness was well adept at moving through the murky underground. And yet what was more confusing was that it did so without any light whatsoever.

Jack steadied his finger on the trigger and pointed the barrel directly toward the approaching intruder. The sound was eerily quiet now, but clearly audible. Jack was frozen in a paralyzing grip of terror, allowing his imagination to run wild.

As dark as it was his eyes could not adjust. The darkness was impenetrable, stealing with it any hope of a last-minute visual fix on the ghostly target. He'd have to rely on his instincts, his hearing, his smell, and his sense of distance.

The sound grew closer. The darkness deepened.

Jack strained his eyes but he couldn't even see the silhouette of the handgun stretched out in front of him.

His finger tightened slightly on the trigger.

He could hear cat-soft footsteps. The target was less than twenty feet away and steadily approaching.

Jack heard breathing.

His finger tightened a little more on the sensitive trigger. Even the slightest additional pressure and the gun would fire.

Closer! Ten feet now!

Five feet . . .

Suddenly the movement stopped! Whoever it was lay directly in front of him, crouching motionless, peering into the shadows beyond, trying to see Jack, himself.

The high anxiety of the moment was a tremendous burden to bear, but Jack held steady.

He strained his ears to listen, and suddenly he heard a familiar rabbit-quick breathing of an animal.

He switched on the flashlight and shined it into the warm and friendly eyes of Ibrahim's dog, Juno.

35

Major Garrity," the voice called, "can you hear me?"

"Yes, Sahid, I hear you."

Jack was relieved beyond words. He and the dog had made their way down the steep chute, had rounded a corner, and had plodded onward another fifty yards or so along a straight and much less constrictive part of the tunnel.

That was when Jack had finally seen the dim glow of the lighted candle.

Both Sahid and his father were making their way back through the underground corridors in search of their lost companion, and were equally relieved that he was found and with them again.

The dog was another story.

Ibrahim had reasoned that after they had vanished down through the first shaft beneath the warehouse, Juno had probably sensed the pending danger, and had started to whine. Obviously, the remaining sentry grew impatient with the animal, not wanting it to give away the escaping trio's position. He likely had carried it down into the main chamber where it had been allowed to trail after its master.

Jack could tell that Ibrahim was pleased. The dog meant everything to the man and it wasn't right to leave him behind as they had done.

"Juno likes you, Major," Ibrahim said. "He usually does not take to strangers. There must be a lot of good in you!"

"Well, I hope so . . . and frankly, I'm rather fond of Juno, myself. He is, as I mentioned earlier, a very beautiful animal."

The underground artery had taken Jack and his friends a good two and a half miles away from El-Kabir. They ended up in a well-built, very sturdy underground bunker, carved out of the side of a heavily vegetated embankment that faced the lower end of the river.

The small ingress leading into the chamber from outside was camouflaged by the overgrowth, and so was well hidden from view.

A great deal of time and effort had gone into the construction of this final room. It was extraordinarily large for an underground structure, and was filled to capacity with weapons of all kinds. Additionally, covered with what looked like an old parachute canopy, was a sturdy and well-kept four-wheel-drive land cruiser. It was filled with petrol and loaded with explosives, grenade launchers, additional weaponry, and several thousand rounds of ammunition.

The men pulled the parachute covering free and climbed inside. Then, while Sahid got the engine running, Ibrahim lifted a latch that allowed the vehicle to pass through the narrow exit. It emerged onto a dirt road that ran alongside the river.

Sahid moved slowly out into the night. In contrast to the bleak darkness inside the tunnels, the partially lit landscape from the quarter moon and distant stars seemed wonderfully bright. It was a refreshing relief to be free from the underground passageways.

Having closed the access once again, Ibrahim and his dog climbed into the back seat, and the four travelers turned southward toward Gharati.

The journey lasted about an hour. The road, what there was of it, was not really a road at all. It was a roundabout route Sahid had taken to avoid the constantly patrolling Libyan Elite forces.

During the time they were inside the land cruiser, Jack and Sahid discussed with Ibrahim the detailed plan for neutralizing the nuclear reactor. And although Ibrahim seemed anxious and willing to participate in what espionage and combat might ensue, Sahid made his father promise to assist by acting as a lookout—not a soldier.

It was just past midnight when they finally arrived at Biskra. The Superphoenix Fast Breeder Reactor was a prototype originally designed in France. It was already in operation in various countries around the world whose peaceful use of the atom had allowed them access into the French marketplace.

Biskra was situated in a rocky valley, wedged between a forsaken terrain of moonlike volcanos and complete desolation. A single unpaved road connected the mammoth construction project with the small mid-desert city, Gharati.

Five miles to the south, Sahid had detoured through an ascending mountainous area that allowed the company a far-reaching but worthy view of Biskra, as well as the immediate area surrounding it.

Very few external lights could be seen. The Libyans had intentionally built the plutonium-producing fast breeder underground for security reasons. As for the aboveground terrain, all that could be seen was a large, chain-link fence and assorted piles of construction material.

At one end of the open valley, an enormous cave-like mouth opened up into the yard. It was through this open pit that heavy equipment could be seen relentlessly moving in and out. The construction of the facility was in its final stages, and because of the intense pressures coming so often from the presidential palace in Tripoli, the work was nonstop. Twenty-four hours a day, seven days a week, the rocky valley was a virtual underground maze of human activity.

Jack pulled out his binoculars. They were a special issue that allowed him to see clearly in the dark as well as in the daylight, and were the outgrowth of the infrared lens that had been used so effectively to monitor the Vietcong and the North Vietnamese Regulars during the Vietnam War.

According to the small map provided by a loyal undercover rebel soldier who actually worked at Biskra, there would be a small natural cave at the southwest corner of the site. Jack spotted it.

The plan called for a short rendezvous with the iron-hearted Kef Nabeul. He was a young lad, barely twenty years old, whose father had been executed in 1987 for suspected treason. Kef had taken a silent oath to one day avenge his father's death. He studied hard in school, constantly nursing an exceptional mind—and the more he studied, the more he seemed to acquire a natural talent for conceptualizing the laws of physics.

Eventually Kef had been selected to work on the Biskra project, and the opportunity had been exactly what he had hoped for. Kef had joined the rebellion during the crisis in the Gulf a year earlier, and had worked discreetly with Sahid and Nisha Tashwan to develop drawings and maps of the continued progress.

With or without the help of the Americans, Kef, Sahid, and Nisha had long since planned on destroying Biskra. Since the timely destruction of El-Wahat and the sudden added assistance of the American pilot, Jack Garrity, Kef and Sahid had stepped up the schedule for the Biskra demolition.

Tonight was that night.

Leaving Ibrahim on the hilltop with Juno, Jack and Sahid loaded two five-pound blocks of C-4 plastic explosives into their backpacks. Additionally, each carried a three-and-a-half-pound spool of electrical wiring, an electronic detonation device, four grenades, and an AK-47 rifle slung over his shoulder.

Earlier, both of the men had replaced their desert fatigues with a set of well-designed, black-colored jumpsuits with large pockets up and down the legs and vest area. Inside these, they stored extra full clips for the assault rifles.

Jack holstered his 9mm Colt, as well.

Through his binoculars, Jack was aware of movement very near the rendezvous point. He suspected the person to be Kef and hoped that it was so.

Scanning the valley floor from their vantage point up on the ridge, Jack also discovered a small military installation. There were two Hueys sitting next to a concrete helipad and a couple of armored vehicles stationed by a small tin building. A single lamppost illuminated the area, and just before Jack was about to turn his attention back to the rendezvous point, he noticed two soldiers exiting the building.

One of them lit a cigarette and tossed the match off to one side. The other walked around to the back, where Jack caught his first glimpse of what had to be a .50-caliber anti-aircraft emplacement. It was mounted on a small concrete pad, surrounded by a fortress of sandbags and obscurely hidden in the shadows.

If he could, Jack thought, he'd wire this site as well, and blow the whole operation to smithereens!

Tightening and adjusting the final buckles and straps of their equipment, Jack and Sahid looked intently at each other and then silently moved out.

The climb downward was tedious. There were numerous areas where the mountain had been well worn by the ravages of time, and had become hazardous patches of loose rock. It was difficult to find a sure and solid hold, but eventually, with just a few minor slips along the way, the two men reached the valley floor.

From here, Jack was able to see the front entry into the compound. Two sentries stationed at the gate would observe any incoming vehicle or individual. Both soldiers were heavily armed and would present a problem if they weren't eliminated quickly. Jack was more than a little relieved to learn that Sahid did not delight in the shedding of blood, and that he took great pains to immobilize the enemy rather than to take his life. Hopefully, this would be the case now.

Sahid and Jack waited patiently behind a tremendous boulder, just in view of the small cave.

Keeping a sharp eye out, Kef had spotted the two men and was carefully working his way to where they were crouched.

Jack noticed the small box in the young boy's hand, and was grateful that everything was—so far—going well and according to plan.

"You make it at last!" the boy said in English, handing the box to Sahid. "I was beginning to have my doubts!"

"We ran into a few problems along the way, Kef . . . had to take a couple of detours. It seems that General Rovigo is on the move!"

"Coming here?" Kef asked with a worried look on his face.

"Maybe . . . but not for a while. We have left him to search for us back in El-Kabir. Nisha and the others will keep a close watch on him and will send a courier if he learns we have evaded him."

"He is a ruthless hunter and skilled tracker, Sahid. . . . I hope you have done the right thing! He must not show up here before we are finished with our work!"

"I think we got away all right, Kef," Jack interjected. "We left El-Kabir through the tunnels."

"Very good! No one saw you leave, then?"

"No, *no one!*" Sahid emphasized.

Kef turned to Jack and said, "It's good to see you again, Major Garrity. Our brief meeting yesterday at Adi Haliab was not adequate time for me to thank you for your assistance. It is great and wonderful that you could destroy El-Wahat! Praise Allah that he could bring you here to help us!"

"Well, thank you, Kef. You're quite a young gentleman." Jack had grown fond of the lad.

Kef kissed the major on both cheeks, hugged him in Islamic fashion, and then returned to the business at hand.

Without speaking further, Sahid opened the small box Kef had brought, extracting two handguns similar in style to a Colt .45. However, instead of firing .45-caliber bullets, these two weapons fired simple tranquilizer darts.

Jack remembered them well.

* * *

The two guards posted at the gate were bored. It was going to be another long and tedious night of doing absolutely nothing. The older of the two, Tahar Akbou, had been trying to explain the workings of a nuclear reactor to the young fellow, but could see that no matter how simple his explanation, the young man could not grasp even the most elementary concepts of basic physics. The older man was proud of his *own* working knowledge, and looked forward to the day when Biskra would go on line so that he could observe its complex workings.

Most of his personal knowledge had come from a series of lengthy discussions with his young friend, Kef Nabeul. Kef was a youthful genius, and had made understanding easy. But try as he might, Tahar could not relay the same information to his young companion here at the gate.

Kef approached the entryway and watched the verbal exchange taking place. He wondered what the two sentries were discussing, and inwardly grinned at the ease with which he could approach them without triggering any sort of alarm. But then, how could they know what his intentions were?

Looking across the compound, Tahar caught a glimpse of a man walking toward them. He strained his eyes for a moment to see if he recognized the visitor, and then realizing it was young Kef, the guard turned to his companion and said, "Here comes my physics friend, Kef Nabeul. Perhaps *he* can explain it to you in a way that you will understand.

"Greetings, young Kef," the man continued, "I'm glad you decided to stop by. I was trying to describe the process of the fast breeder . . . how it heats the core, boils the water into steam, powers the turbines, and then produces electricity. But I can't seem to make this man understand. Perhaps—"

"Well, actually, Tahar," Kef replied, pulling the two dart guns from a belt draped around his waist, and displaying them for observation, "I found these two guns in an old box sitting alongside the main steam generators, and I wondered if *you* could identify *them*."

Tahar and his companion looked at the two pistols, their eyes wide with curiosity, but completely void of fear. Kef saw that his plan was working wonderfully.

"Two guns?" the older man said, reaching out to Kef.

In a single, well-rehearsed motion, Kef raised the two pistols and simultaneously squeezed the triggers. The tranquilizer darts embedded themselves deep into the chests of the two unsuspecting soldiers, releasing their serum at once.

The paralyzing effect was quick and effective, and the two men, their eyes wide with fear, backed away frantically, lost their equilibrium, and fell harmlessly to the ground. The drug seemed to work a lot quicker on Tahar—perhaps due to his age—but the younger sentry fought its effects, trying desperately to remain conscious.

Like Major Garrity, the younger man reached up and pulled the dart free from his chest, somehow reasoning that by doing so he would be able to regain control. Nevertheless, the drug had already been injected and was busily wreaking havoc with his central nervous system.

Drifting over the edge of consciousness, the young soldier's last visual memory was that of a man stooping over him. The man's face was nearly covered with a greasy black paint of some kind, which seemed to give the appearance of a ghost.

Jack watched the young man close his eyes and give in to the drug. As he stood stooping over the lad, he had the AK-47 ready just in case. But after realizing that the young man was not going to present a problem, he handed the rifle to Kef and bent over to pick up the lifeless body.

Sahid was already dragging the other man across the yard toward an obscure scrap pile, where the body was quickly discarded. Jack did not care to be overly abusive, and instead of heaving the poor lad aside, he gently laid him alongside his companion and whispered softly, "Sorry you have to be in the middle of this, kid. Perhaps one day you'll have an opportunity to understand the forces of good and evil."

There were only two entries into the underground facility. The main entrance was high enough to allow a bus inside. It had a boat-like ramp that descended into a huge tunnel as wide as a four-lane freeway. Heavy machinery moved in and out of this causeway with relentless regularity, making it virtually impossible for a stealthy access.

At the other end of the yard near the small cave, a second entrance allowed workers direct access into the main reactor room.

The uranium-rich metal rods that would be used to heat the liquid sodium were not yet in place. If they had been, detonating and exploding the C-4 plastics might have proved far more hazardous than Jack or Sahid were willing to risk. Indeed, there would have been a massive radioactive cloud to contend with that likely would have killed or caused cancer in the thousands of residents in and around Gharati.

The men went to work.

Kef made three inconspicuous trips down into the reactor room, carrying small, unnoticeable pre-shaped blocks of the C-4—twenty pounds altogether—to various concealed locations around the room's interior.

Twice, while moving in and out of the maze of human activity, he was stopped and consulted on different matters. Both times, however, he kept his cool, and had eventually gone about his business as though what he was doing was a routine task assigned by his superiors.

Meanwhile, Jack and Sahid were busy stringing wires. Numerous concrete and metal shafts protruded out of the rocky ground into the yard. It was through these vents that Sahid and Jack fished hundreds of feet of black electrical wire. Eventually, Kef was able to intercept the wires and splice them together so that the individual lines ran to each of the hidden explosives.

In the end, a single line merged into the construction yard. They connected this to a final two hundred yards of wiring strung along the valley floor and up the hillside toward Ibrahim and Juno, and tied it into a small electronic timer. This, in turn, was connected to a small motorcycle battery, and was wedged between two outcroppings of volcanic rock.

Once again, all preparations complete, the three met at the original rendezvous point. The timer was set for thirty minutes—allowing them time to scale the hillside and drive a safe distance away in the land cruiser.

They discarded all of the extra equipment, except for their weapons, and started the climb. Suddenly, coming from the crest of the mountain, they heard the distinct sounds of a dog barking out into the night.

A burst of machine-gun fire followed.

Jack, Sahid, and Kef froze in terror!

"What was *that!*" Sahid questioned.

"It came from up on the hill!" Jack whispered, pointing in the general direction of the sound. "Wasn't that Juno?"

"I believe it was!" Sahid answered, his eyes wide in fear. Then, with a painful moan coming uncontrollably from deep within, Sahid cried, "Papa!"

Down in the construction yard they could see a flurry of activity. The small military installation was suddenly swarming with life, and up above, the sound of machine-gun fire began anew.

Sahid, concerned for his father's life, turned toward the summit and began rebounding up and over the rough terrain.

"No!" Jack cried out, but it was too late. Sahid was determined to assist Ibrahim, and rushed blindly ahead.

There was no time to think. Jack needed some kind of a diversion.

Over to his left, not far from where he and Kef were crouched behind some rocks, Jack spotted a significant pile of what appeared to be a chemical dump site. It consisted of fifty or more metal drums.

"What's in those containers, Kef?" Jack questioned, his pulse racing.

"Not much of anything . . . I don't think."

"Well, what *was* in them?"

"I believe that many of them had diesel fuel—"

"That's all I wanted to know," Jack said, cutting the young physics major off and simultaneously withdrawing a hand grenade. "Now, duck down, friend!"

Jack pulled the pin and tossed the grenade into the midst of the old barrels. Two soldiers from the distant installation were running toward the gunfire, and happened to be passing near the dump site just as the grenade exploded. The blast sent them into the air like a pair of lifeless dummies.

The blast was far more intense than Jack figured it would be. Apparently, some of the drums were still full of fuel. An enormous fireball belched skyward, sending with it a formidable concussion that rocked and toppled everything within a seventy-five-yard radius. It was, in fact, so powerful that Jack and Kef were left frantically hanging onto the rocks for their lives.

By now, hundreds of construction workers were streaming out of the two earthen orifices like scattered and confused ants in picture-perfect pandemonium.

At the top of the hill, Ibrahim had been attacked suddenly by a small squadron of Libyan Elite. General Lucca Rovigo learned from someone in El-Kabir that the American had been seen in the village just prior to the general's arrival.

Lucca did not waste any time searching from house to house, as he had intended. Instead, after a quick survey and his usual reliance on instinct, Lucca gathered his small force and had set out for Biskra.

He was certain that the American would still try and accomplish the objectives of Operation Screaming Ghost despite the setback of losing the Banshee.

With night vision equipment similar to Jack's, it had not been difficult for Lucca to spot the land cruiser at the summit of the escarpment.

A small contingent of trained fighters stealthily scaled the mountain, catching Ibrahim unaware. The old man was watching the valley below, instead of the winding road behind.

After the small strike team was in position, ready to move in on the four-wheel drive and kill or capture those near it, Juno had caught their scent, lifted his radar-like ears, and started barking.

Ibrahim dropped instinctively to the ground, just barely out of the firing line.

"Down, Juno!" he commanded the dog. "Come here, boy!"

Bullets began to fly, several slamming into and ripping through the jeep's exterior. Others ricochetted around the turf, not one of them meeting their mark. Ibrahim rolled quickly over to a sharp-edged rock formation and unslung the AK-47 draped over his shoulder. The dog, its head lowered obediently, followed his master, and sensing the danger kept low and out of the way.

Just down the hillside, Sahid was rapidly making his ascent. He was terrified for his father, but not stupid. He knew that it would be suicide to simply run right into the heat of the battle, so as he approached the crest, he kept himself low, masking himself between the shadows of the desert moonscape.

At the moment of the fiery explosion set off by Jack's grenade, the entire hillside was instantly illuminated. Sahid saw three armed members of the strike team just seconds before they spotted him. That was all of the time he needed. He let go a massive burst of rounds from his assault weapon and pelted the startled trio. They would trouble him no more.

Two others spotted Ibrahim. They had crept closer through the cover of darkness crouched by the four-wheeler, then opened fire. The old man defended himself and sprayed the area with his own volley of machine-gun fire—but to no avail. An enemy bullet caught Ibrahim in the shoulder, ripping through the old bone and flesh tissue with a searing, painful force.

The blast spun him around in the dirt like a rag doll being kicked mercilessly by a thoughtless bully. He still had his finger pressed against the trigger of the AK-47, and the rapidly firing eruption of cartridges and lead missiled through the open air in a hundred different directions—harmlessly wasted in the void.

Barely level with the crest of the mountaintop, Sahid witnessed the ensuing horror.

Helplessly wounded, and faced in the wrong direction to save himself, Ibrahim knew he was finished. For a fraction of a second his eyes met those of his son. The area was still under the gradually fading light of the explosion, and each could see the other as well as the still crouched silhouettes of the two remaining Libyan soldiers. Neither had noticed Sahid off to their right, but instead were focused on the target in front of them.

Realizing that his seconds were few, Sahid extracted the dart gun. Then, one after the other, he silently and effectively demobilized the two soldiers, keeping his position unnoticed.

Down in the valley, Jack and Kef had their hands full. Lucca Rovigo made it to the front gate and spotted the duo to the left of the yard. The powerful explosion sent debris and dust along a wave of hurricane-force wind that slammed into the small convoy and momentarily blinded the crazed hunter. But it also gave away Jack's position.

The chaos of the moment infuriated Lucca. He was a callous and malicious man, bent on one single emotional drive—to get Major Jack Garrity at all cost! He did not concern himself with the dozens of civilians running wildly about. Instead, he simply climbed up onto the back end of the armor-plated jeep in which he'd been traveling. He then pushed the young gunner out of the way and took hold of the M-60 machine gun.

Pointing the barrel toward Jack's location, the fierce-eyed Lucca squeezed the trigger.

A massive volley of bullets exploded all around Jack and his friend. They dove behind the rocks and quickly determined, as best they could, where the fire was coming from. Luckily, every fifth round from the M-60 was a tracer bullet, and in the dimming light of the explosion's aftermath, Jack was able to get a fix on the target. He peeked warily from behind the rocks, straining his eyes to see.

Jack knew instinctively that it was Lucca.

Kef, too, was anxious to see, and slowly lifted his head for a view.

"Stay down!" Jack shouted. "You'll get your head blown off!"

Kef didn't need to be told twice, especially since he didn't have a weapon of his own.

Jack positioned the AK-47 through a gap in the outcropping and steadily aimed the weapon at Lucca. He was about to fire when another barrage of lethal lead from the M-60 rained upon them.

The deadly firepower rattled everything around them. Rocks shattered like small grenades, sending dangerous fragments in all directions. There was no doubt in Jack's mind that the rocks, themselves, could kill them if they didn't keep their heads down. Several times the rounds passed directly over their heads, and Jack flinched at the ominously frightening sound. No one could ever understand the chilling experience of a gun battle until they experienced it firsthand. The sound of flying bullets was more haunting than any nightmare any human being could possibly comprehend, and Jack prayed fervently that he would never have to experience it again!

At that same instant, unbeknownst to Jack, Sahid reached their vehicle and extracted an M-79 grenade launcher. Loading it, he took aim at the huddled forms in the dimly lit yard below, and fired.

The grenade landed short, but after several seconds that seemed like an eternity, it detonated, causing Lucca and his men to vault from the vehicle and scamper for cover.

Frozen momentarily, Jack was strangely amused that he, Major Jack Garrity, pilot par excellence, would be in such a predicament. It was but twenty-four hours since he had flown the Banshee, and yet for some reason it seemed almost to have happened in a previous life.

Suddenly the area surrounding the front entrance of the yard burst into a fiery inferno. Sahid, Nisha, and a small band of revolutionaries had tossed a dozen or more grenades on the squadron.

The spirited freedom fighters had followed Lucca all the way from El-Kabir to the reactor site. Nisha, of course, was certain of Lucca's intentions, and was not about to allow the madman to overtake her husband, his father, or the American. However, despite her best efforts, she had not been able to intervene in time to prevent the utter chaos that had encompassed the yard during the previous twenty minutes.

Joining forces with her husband, Nisha and her small band of well-armed rebels moved quickly along the ridge of the volcanic escarpment, positioning themselves just above the entry gate in front of the construction yard. Collectively, they tossed the grenades at Lucca's assault team, simultaneously spraying the area below with rifle fire.

With the momentary reprieve, Jack and Kef jumped out from

behind the rocky fortress and darted into the maze of people still cowering for shelter.

At the other end of the yard, where Jack had seen the small military installation, he was amazed to find that the little camp was now barren. No soldiers were manning the outpost, and it suddenly occurred to him that the quickest, most viable plan for escape was in that direction.

He motioned to Kef and the two of them ran quickly, glancing repeatedly over their shoulders toward the gate.

The scene was chaotic.

Rapid machine-gun fire assaulted Jack's ears, and he knew that he wasn't out of this war quite yet.

Reaching the far end of the small valley, Jack entered the camp. It was, as he had figured, deserted. Apparently the small contingent of soldiers stationed here was suddenly overwhelmed with fear, believing that an all-out attack on Biskra had begun. Jack would never know where the soldiers went as they had, through some twist of fate, retreated into the darkness. Jack was relieved for himself, and for them that they would likely escape further harm.

Just up a small incline, Jack's eyes caught sight of the .50-caliber machine-gun emplacement. He knew that he could hold back the enemy for a long time if he could just get there safely. Especially with Kef's help, he could—

Suddenly another thought sprang into his mind.

Motioning for Kef to follow him, he sprinted toward the heli-pad. Jack did not particularly like choppers, but he had flown Hueys before and he could do it again.

Arriving at the first chopper, he left the door open for Kef, leaped into the pilot's seat, and started the engines. For a moment time stood still as Jack watched the large, sagging propellers make their first complete revolution. Kef eagerly joined him, sitting to his right, and the young man smiled widely as the propellers began to whip the air outside the chopper. It was Kef's first moment in a helicopter.

Within a minute or so they were airborne, rising up and over the rugged terrain of the rocky mountain where they had left Ibrahim and the land cruiser.

Keeping out of the line of fire, Jack flew the chopper just over the back side of the summit, moving slowly down the ridge to where he was able to see his friends.

Nisha spotted the helicopter out of the corner of her eye and spun around with her AK-47. She instinctively cut loose with her weapon, riddling the side of the Huey with a burst of fire. Had she known to fire into the blades, she would have immediately brought the large, cobra-like machine back to earth.

Instead, the sudden slamming of lead against the steel siding caused Jack to pitch the flight stick forward with a startled jerk. The gunship swerved drunkishly for a moment, then leveled off and continued to hover.

Instinctively, Jack flipped on the light in the cockpit.

There was only minimal light from the blazes round about, but Jack was able to identify Nisha as she fired. Because of the light in the gunship, Sahid had likewise recognized Jack and Kef at the controls. He quickly called to Nisha, putting a stop to her second attempt to bring the helicopter down.

"It's Jack!" he yelled. Then, to the others, "Quickly! Over the ridge! Let's go!"

There were four rebel fighters in all, and each immediately responded to their commander's words. Nisha followed.

Jack hovered closer and closer to a flat-surfaced area just over the crown of the hill. There he waited while the small band made their way toward him.

As the faithful soldiers boarded, Jack glanced behind him and to the right, just in time to see Sahid lifting his father into his arms, and carrying the badly wounded man to the ship. They were close now, and Jack could see a massive dark stain where Ibrahim's shoulder had taken a direct hit.

The others saw father and son at the same instant, and within a few seconds had helped the final two men into the open side door on the right.

"Fly, Major!" Sahid yelled.

"Wait!" It was the old man, raising his left arm in a motioning manner. "Juno . . . get Juno!"

Glancing around, and barely able to hear the man's words, Jack looked urgently for the dog! This is ridiculous, he thought, he had to get going!

With that thought in his mind, he remembered the timer and the explosives wired to the reactor room. He glanced down at his watch, which was in sync with the electronic detonation device—then dropped his lower jaw. The entire valley was going to blow in less than forty-five seconds!

"There's no time! The place is gonna blow!"

"Look!" Nisha shouted, pointing to the left of the land cruiser. "It's Juno!"

Thirty-eight seconds.

There was no time to think. Jack hovered two feet from the summit while Sahid leaped out.

"Here, Juno! Come here, boy!"

The dog was frightened to death, but somehow obeyed, and Sahid lifted him into the helicopter.

Eighteen seconds.

"Go!" Sahid screamed, holding onto the side panel to the right of the permanently positioned M-60.

Jack worked the controls and skillfully piloted the Huey up and away from the doomed and nearly deserted valley.

At the front gate hundreds of feet below, Lucca Rovigo lifted his head. There was a four-inch gash in his left shoulder and a fragment of steel embedded in his lower right cheek. The grenades had blown him backwards off the jeep, which he had mounted a second time, and had nearly killed him in the process.

Lucca saw the chopper, and started piecing details together. The infidels had escaped for now . . . but he would never give up! He'd find them and avenge his brother and his fallen comrades! What was important was that the American's mission to destroy Libya's first nuclear reactor had failed. . . .

Or had it?

Lucca's eyes widened. The final pieces of the puzzle slid into place.

"By the grace of Allah!" he exclaimed, at the same time instinctively tucking his head into his chest, covering it and his vitals with his bruised and bleeding arms. . . .

Four seconds . . .

Three seconds . . .

Two seconds . . .

36

Friday, 3 January 1992—
Edwards Air Force Base, California

Brigadier General Matthew Walker was in a pensive and disheartened frame of mind. He felt as if a part of him had died. The loss of Jack Garrity was more than a tragedy—it was a personal blow of monumental proportions. In a very real way, Jack's death was like losing a son.

The aging general had long since decided that tears were often an unnecessary emotional expense, and grief too costly a luxury. The fragile human heart was easily shaken during times of trial and suffering, and Matt had this philosophy—right or wrong—that anyone succumbing to such sentiment was weak-minded and fragile in character.

Matt had cried seldom since his youth, when, as a lad of sixteen, he had lost his parents in a tragic automobile accident. This had taken place in the remote area of northern Arizona known as Christopher Creek—where they had been visiting the newly constructed Zane Grey writing retreat.

The emotional struggle he had endured back then was one of the most bitter experiences of his life. At night, alone in their Santa Monica home with just his older brother Tom to turn to, Matt wept for so long and with such intensity that every part of his inner self had known torment. He had been wonderfully close to his parents, and the sudden loss was so insufferable, so agonizingly painful, that he actually teetered on the very precipice of suicide just to stop the pain.

It was then that he decided that the price for physical emotional displays was simply too much! Never! Never again would he crawl into a fetal position inside those catacombs of despair—Never!

For this reason, Matt resisted succumbing to grief now. He placed his elbows out on the desk in front of him and held his head in his hands. Then, massaging his temples as if attempting to suppress a headache, he searched through the pages of memory, still alive and fresh inside his mind.

He felt chillingly burdened with guilt. It would have been so easy to select someone else for the Libyan assignment. In fact, literally hundreds of zealous young pilots would have eagerly piloted the Banshee into the Libyan operation—pilots with hundreds, even thousands of hours of combat experience. Men who had flown complicated missions into Vietnam through the sixties and into the early seventies, as well as younger veterans who had streaked through the skies of Iraq and Kuwait during the thousands of sorties of the recent Gulf War.

But, he had chosen Jack.

Major Garrity had simply been the man for the job, with Major Barry as his backup. That was all there was to it. He was the best, and the general knew it. But how he missed his friend! Had it really been necessary to send his "son" streaking over the Libyan terrain in an untested prototype? Had the price become too high?

So many questions were still unanswered. And foremost of these was the resounding "how?" *How* had the Libyans detected Jack's fighter? How did the Libyans acquire the technology to shoot such a sophisticated aircraft out of the sky? Had the Banshee actually been the invisible stealth its engineers had claimed it to be? And if so, what had gone wrong with the cloaking characteristics?

The weight of General Walker's self-imposed guilt was overwhelming. He wasn't absolutely sure that Jack was deceased; but he knew in his heart that if his friend had survived, he had undoubtedly ended up a prisoner of the Libyan Elite! The holocaustal nightmare for Jack—if he had survived—would not have begun in that fiery ball that the satellites had photographed when the Banshee exploded. It would, instead, begin once the major had fallen into the hands of that barbarian commander, Haman Al-Rashid!

Jack would never reveal any military secrets, the general was certain of that. But that was hardly the issue. He was convinced that Jack's training would allow him to endure whatever torture was brought upon him. Indeed, no amount of physical or mental suffering could break Jack from his vow of silence!

Morbid as it might seem, the general actually hoped that Jack had died in the explosion. It was a horrible thought, to be sure, but it was far less burdensome than the thought of his friend having to endure the struggle of some barbaric method of torture-imposed interrogation.

It had been a week since the Banshee had gone down over Kufra. The aftermath of the event was—mildly stated—chaotic. The United Nations was in a general state of turmoil—a regular whirlwind of finger-pointing and name-calling. And although there was little doubt in most minds as to who had done what and where, the formal position of the Pentagon and Washington was strict denial.

As ugly as the situation had become, the general realized that it was in the best interest of the country to keep Operation Screaming Ghost a strict military secret.

That, of course, was the problem.

Matt knew that taking the ill-timed news to Linda would require a stealthy approach, cloaked in lies and secrecy—half-truths and fabrications—all in the name of national security.

Lying to Jack's widow, Linda, would be like lying to his own daughter, if he had been blessed with one. And yes, the news of Jack's death *was* ill timed. Tragically, not only ill timed but outright disastrous.

The report of Linda's accident had been the proverbial straw that broke the camel's back. Upon arriving back at Edwards and hearing of the near-fatal accident, Matt was so overwhelmed with the collective burdens of his dear friends that he had locked himself in his office and, despite his usually successful efforts to control his emotions, had wept bitterly.

The idea of Major Garrity being shot down over Libya was, by itself, profoundly painful. And as if that weren't enough, the news of the horrifying automobile accident, which had been a chilling déjà vu for the general, was simply too much for the old brigadier to emotionally handle. How could so many terrible tragedies—one right after another—happen to one small family in so short a period of time?

The general picked up the memo from his desk and read it for the third time. It had been hand-delivered by Senior Airman Sharleen Thomas, a personal friend to Jack and his family.

The memo had described in detail the series of events that had led to the accident in the Kastlemans' Bronco. There was reference made to the family having been taken to Antelope Valley Hospital in Lancaster, where Linda and their daughter, Trish, were reported as stable and recovering rapidly.

Matt was concerned, to say the least, about the multiple fractures in Linda's hip and leg. But the real stress came from his concern over the lad, Little Jack. Apparently, the boy was in a coma.

A coma!

What else could go wrong?

Weary, and inwardly loathing the task that he knew was now his, General Walker answered the painful question. What else could go wrong was for an Air Force general to have to break the tragic news of a fallen husband—a fallen friend, a fallen father—to an already distraught and emotional shaken wife. Yet, regardless of Linda's present physical and mental state, Matt knew that she had to be told the truth.

What a quandary!

How could he possibly tell her the truth? How could he do this, especially when the actual events surrounding Jack's mission were so completely shrouded in bureaucratic secrecy? All he could mention for sure was that Jack was missing in action.

Poor Linda! He knew exactly what she would say.

37

Antelope Valley Hospital—
Lancaster, California

"Missing in action? I'm sorry, General, I didn't know that we were in a state of war! Funny how nobody tells me anything!"

"Well, actually . . . uh, Linda, we're not . . . it's past that—"

"Then tell me, Matthew, since no one else seems to know anything—if we're not formally at war with some foreign country, then how is it that my husband could be missing in action?"

"There has been a crisis—"

"Doggone it, General, I've seen the reports on television! The entire world knows that this little lunatic—what's his name—exploded an atomic bomb on Christmas Day. Is that the nature of your crisis? Is that what the big military secret is, Matthew? Are we at war with Libya?"

Linda paused, collecting her strength and suppressing the desperate urge to cry. Then with a trembling voice she added, "Is . . . is Jack dead?"

"Linda, we don't know the answer to that. All we know is that Jack was flying practice maneuvers over the Mediterranean, somewhere between Italy and Libya—"

"And was shot down . . . right?" she interjected sardonically.

The kind, aging brigadier raised a hand to his brow. He massaged his temples and eyebrows again, carefully assessing the conversation. He didn't particularly care to continue this little charade with the wife of the man he cared so much for. He knew that Linda was an intelligent and gifted woman. She was endowed with an uncanny power of discernment, and would see right through his feeble attempts at covering the truth. But here again was the real dilemma—there were simply far too many aspects of the operation he couldn't tell her. And as to the haunting and bone-chilling question of whether Jack was alive or dead, he simply did not know. Sorrowfully, however, he suspected the latter.

He walked to the hospital bed and looked directly into Linda's eyes. There was pain and pent-up tenderness, a well of emotions just waiting to flow. He chose his words carefully. "Yes," he answered, never breaking eye contact, "we believe Jack's plane was hit by an enemy surface-to-air missile. . . . But we don't know yet whether or not he was able to eject safely from the aircraft."

Tears shimmered in Linda's eyes. She bit down on her lower lip and tried, in vain, to control the quivering of nerves in her chin. Matthew moved closer, then reached out to her. She hesitated only briefly, then was suddenly overwhelmed with the need for physical contact. Matthew sensed this and bent down to where she could throw her arms around his neck.

They held each other tight, as if letting go meant certain death. And for Linda, the gloom was so impenetrable and so consuming that she wondered again if life was really worth living at all. The series of tragic events was overwhelming! She had tried to be strong—to mask the truths of comfortless reality with stern willpower and a fierce resolve to fight. But her defenses were weakening, her psychological barriers were falling, and her spirits were sinking into the dismal depths of sorrow.

Little Jack was in a coma, the depths of which only heaven knew. Trish was frightened and emotionally unstable from the trauma of the accident, and Linda, herself, had a leg and hip that were twisted and mangled, bolted together with a series of metal pins and screws—and she was desperately trying to accept the possibility, despite the doctors' assurances, that she may never walk again.

And now, adding to the painful list of collective misery, the news—the wretched, soul-piercing news—of her husband's likely death! It weighed in upon her like a heavy block of cold steel.

It was all too much!

Somewhere inside, deep within the very fibers of her soul, the nerves of iron, so characteristic of Linda's indomitable strength, melted in a fiery furnace of despair and loneliness.

She lay her head onto the comforting shoulder of the general and wept bitterly. And in doing so, she never saw the tears that fell from the wise and pensive eyes of a man that may well have been—or hopefully still was—her husband's closest friend.

38

The long hours of the afternoon dragged by at a snail's pace. General Matthew Walker returned to the base, leaving Linda alone in the hospital room that to her had become a suffocating prison.

Doctor Moody was in early and wanted to sedate Linda with a numbing injection of valium to ease the stress. But Linda wouldn't have it. Instead, she sought to clear her mind and cope with the events like a responsible woman. She knew that it was silly and selfish to allow her mind to consider suicide as an option for ending the suffering, and chastised herself for such foolish reasoning. Besides, although the odds were stacked against the probability of Jack having survived the ordeal of being shot down, there was still hope! She couldn't just toss it into the wind!

The general had been square with her—she sensed it. He told her everything he was able to without jeopardizing his own strict code of secrecy. And it was clear, from what he had said, that the military truly didn't know if Jack was dead. She would have to hold onto hope. If Jack were alive and able in time to return, what measure of grief would he then suffer to find that his wife had given up when he had not?

Still, the loneliness was a heavy load to bear. Sometimes her own imagination would create a painful scenario where her only image of Jack was that of a ghostly pale face with lifeless eyes staring up at her from inside a coffin. Then in another paralyzing vision, a single granite stone with the words, *"In Beloved Memory of Jack Garrity, killed in the service of his country. Born 6 January 1953—Died 28 December 1991."*

The scenes played havoc with her emotional stability and hurled her headlong into another deep and lasting weeping session. She felt like an abused water faucet, constantly being switched on and off, and so often gushing out of control.

Like so many who wish for one last opportunity when it is too late, Linda remembered her and Jack's final words to each other. She had been angry, and had vented her frustrations on the man she loved instead of putting her arms around him in a queenly display of support. How she wished she had expressed her love to him, and had given him encouragement instead of leaving him on the coarse coals of despair—a callous and cold good-bye.

There was a song Jack used to play to her and the kids. He was a gifted singer and song writer, often using his music to teach.

Misty-eyed, and hoping for that soothing comfort that often accompanied his poetic voice, Linda began to hum softly, then quietly sing the words Jack had composed as she imagined him sitting there beside her with his guitar. It was a song he had titled, "Before the Clock Stops Ticking."

Why was I not able
before my father died
To tell him that I loved him
or let him be my guide?

Why was I not able
when he was here with me
To learn from him the wiser ways
that only he could see?

And why was I not able
before the clock ran out
To speak kind words and honor him
instead of leaving doubt?

Oh, why was I not able
to love, instead of fight
To build and strengthen others,
or provide for them a light?

I hadn't realized way back then
how painful words could be,
Especially when I never meant
to hurt those close to me.

So now before I criticize,
or let my anger flair,
I look to find the good, instead,
and tell them that I care.

For words I speak must lift the soul
and nourish special bonds
Before the clock stops ticking—
It's too late when they are gone.

"It's too late when they are gone," she repeated slowly, allowing another tear to trickle slowly down her swollen cheek. How true the words seemed to her now. When he first came to her with the lyrics and the melody, wanting to play and sing for her, it had simply been just another song. Oh sure, she had praised his efforts, and even kissed him for the special tenderness of the musical message. But then she was back to her own business, soon forgetting that he had even written the song at all. She had memorized it only because he had sung it so often to Little Jack and Trish. But it never had been a song that entered her heart—not until now.

Now the melody, the message, and the memories were priceless! If she ever did get her husband back, she would never again be able to sing along without becoming misty-eyed and ever so grateful for a second chance.

Later that afternoon, the Salingers and Trish came by to visit Linda and Little Jack. They brought with them several items Linda had requested from the house—including a pair of warm slippers, though in thinking about it, Linda considered the need for these rather ludicrous. It seemed a bit silly to sport one slipper while the other foot was heavily wrapped in a plaster cast. They also brought the bedside photo of her and Jack, which she wanted to place next to her bed, a book she had just received from some friends at Hill Air Force Base in northern Utah titled *Prayers on the Wind,* and her journal. She had also asked for a small sack of Hershey Symphony bars to satisfy an almost overwhelming craving for rich chocolate.

Trish had been with Alex and Mariam now for three days. Linda missed having her little girl constantly close by, but felt a great sense of relief in knowing that she was under her neighbors' protective and loving care. In her own cute way, Trish held her hands behind her back and approached her mother's bed.

"Hi, Mommy! I got a surprise for you!"

"You do?"

"Oh, yes . . . but you can't have it until you make three guesses what it is."

"First a kiss, darling," she smiled, kissing her daughter with a mother's tenderness. "There. Now, let's see . . . bouquet of flowers?"

"Nooo . . ."

"Let's see . . . a hot fudge sundae from Baskin Robbins?"

"Nooo . . ."

"How many guesses do I get?"

"Only three!" Trish replied gleefully.

"So, this is my last one, then?"

"Well . . . ," Trish said, thinking the matter over, "if you don't get it this time, you could have one more."

"Okay, let me try again. It's not a bouquet of flowers or a hot fudge sundae . . . right?"

"Uh-uh."

"Well then, is it a get well card?"

"You guessed it!" Trish exclaimed, swinging her hands from around her back to display her own personally made work of art. "And I made it all by myself!"

"You did?" Linda asked affectionately, reaching over to receive the gift.

"Yeah . . . and Mariam helped me!"

"I thought you said you made it all by yourself."

"I did, Mommy! Mariam just showed me how."

Linda looked over at Mariam and winked. "Well, let's see what it says. . . ." She opened the plain white envelope and withdrew a neatly folded piece of yellow construction paper. The card was fashioned like a small book, with the words, "It's not very fun to be in the hospital," on the front flap, and a follow-up thought, "except you always get TV dinners in bed," on the inside. Mariam had obviously printed the words, but the precious addition scribbled in Trish's own handwriting was just enough to turn the faucets back on.

> Dear Mommy. I love you very, very,
> very, very much and want you to come
> home so we can be a famileee again.

So get well real real fast!

I love you infinity and googalong! Trish

Linda read the simple letter, folded the piece of yellow paper closed, and set it to the side of her bed. Tears welled up unashamedly in her eyes and fell freely. She looked over at the little doll standing proudly at her bedside and reached out to her. Trish moved in instantly for her reward, a warm and lingering hug and kiss from her mother.

"That was so special, Trish," Linda whispered. "You really know how to make your mother happy. Thank you so much!"

"You're welcome, Mommy. But how come you're crying, if you're happy? Does your leg hurt?"

Linda held her daughter out in front of her to capture the angelic simplemindedness of her sincere line of questioning. She looked deep into Trish's eyes, and knew in that precious moment that life was so full of good and wonderful things—so complete and worth every effort to live on and enjoy the business that came from being a family. Jack would have it this way. How could she have possibly considered suicide when this priceless child, her only daughter, loved her so "very, very, very much," and needed her mother alive and well?

"No, pumpkin . . . my leg doesn't hurt. I was crying because I think your card is so beautiful that tears of happy came without my even asking for them! And I'm also crying because I'm happy that you love me so much!"

"I do, Mommy!" Trish exclaimed, wrapping herself back into her mother's arms.

Alex and Mariam pulled up a couple of chairs and now sat together at Linda's side. They also brought a small bag that held Trish's Baby Suzi doll along with an assortment of doll clothes that allowed Trish to keep herself busy.

Linda was grateful for the company. She had telephoned them earlier, describing the unfortunate news about Jack—and in between sobs, asked them to come over for a visit.

Alex and Mariam were also Linda's eyes and ears when it came to Little Jack. Since she was awkwardly bedridden and suspended in a spiderweb of ropes and pulleys, she could not visit her son at all. And furthermore, it had become frustrating, if not embarrassing, to have to constantly probe Doctor Moody for possible conditional improvements.

Little Jack was still in a coma, and Linda was anxious for a detailed report from Alex, who regularly went into Little Jack's room and then came back with a clear and precise description of his breathing patterns. He also shared Little Jack's heart rates, facial and body colors, and an increase or decrease in the boy's eye movements. The latter Linda saw as a sign of his trying to free himself from the dismal state of perpetual unconsciousness.

They talked for about an hour, discussing every conceivable scenario that might have happened when Jack had been shot down. Alex was especially optimistic. He was clearly convinced that Jack was not dead, but perhaps stranded somewhere—maybe even on a rubber raft, bobbing up and down with the currents of the Mediterranean—where he would eventually be found, rescued, and brought safely home.

"Look, Linda," he said, "the general didn't say Jack was dead, right?"

"He said he was missing in action," Linda replied.

"Okay, then . . . that's not the same as being dead. If he was dead, they'd know about it. I'm sure of it! Jack's a survivor, Linda! He's the kind of guy that'll work his way out of just about any situation thrown at him. He'll survive because he loves you and the kids . . . and I'm personally not going to bet on his giving up on you guys that easily!"

"Well, what about the missile? The general said that the Libyans shot him down with a missile! Wouldn't that mean that he blew up in the sky?"

"Not at all. The fighter jet, maybe . . . in fact, for sure! But Jack told me once about the super-sophisticated radar equipment in those babies. He said that if he was ever attacked, or chased through the sky, as he described it, by one of those air-to-ground rockets, his radar equipment would give him ample warning to bail out—to eject from the jet before impact. And I'm tellin' ya, Linda, I think he did just that! I think he hit the eject button and blasted outta there before he was vaporized with the rest of the plane!"

"Ooo . . . that's an ugly word, Alex."

"Oh, sorry. . . . Yeah, I suppose it is at that. How about blown up then?"

"They're *all* ugly words!" Linda said drearily. "But do you really think he made it out alive?"

"Why don't you search your own feelings, Linda?"

"What do you mean?"

"Do you remember when Mariam and I got married?"

"In Vegas?"

"Yeah . . . at that little wedding chapel—"

"The Little Chapel of the Flowers!" Linda interjected. "Oh, yes!" she exclaimed. "That was such a wonderful time."

Linda thought back to the event. It really hadn't been so long ago. It was a pleasurable experience that was cataloged into the pages of her memory. She especially remembered how wonderfully delighted and anxious the Salingers were to finally be tying the knot. She remembered the zealous need they seemed to share of getting married right away—without delay—and the ultimate decision to go to Las Vegas, Nevada.

There had been numerous wedding chapels to choose from, it seemed, but they had selected the Little Chapel of the Flowers for its unique heaven-like cleanliness. The others hadn't compared.

How wonderfully fun that trip had been. Just the four of them—she and Jack acting as chaperons, and Alex and Mariam. The owners of the chapel, Ron and Brenda—she couldn't remember their last name—had been extremely kind and hospitable. They weren't like so many others whose sole purpose for owning a wedding service was for the profit. There had been something different about them. Perhaps it was their genuine concern for Alex and Mariam's complete happiness, and their suggesting that the two newlyweds later prepare for a lasting marriage, which they called *eternal,* by marrying in a religious ceremony.

The memories were perfect. She could almost feel Jack's hand in hers when the kindly preacher announced, "You may now kiss the bride."

"Oh, yes . . . I remember, Alex!" Linda said, wiping a fresh tear from her eye. "You two were so pretty!"

"You're right," Mariam agreed. "That was a fun evening, wasn't it? It seems almost as though it were yesterday."

Linda and Mariam looked at each other and smiled. But Alex was deep in memory. "Linda, you remember dinner that night, don't you? You and Jack were so fun to be with—even if we were on our honeymoon! You shared something with us that night that has stayed with us ever since. Do you remember what that was, Linda?"

"At dinner?"

"Yes . . . that marvelous seafood buffet."

"Well . . . I'm sure we discussed a lot, but I'm not sure I know exactly what you're referring to."

"Jack said the words and you agreed. He said that as the two of you have continued to live together, to rear your family and grow together, he had noticed a unique quality surface in your marriage. Does that ring any bells?"

"It's beginning to . . . ," Linda confirmed. "But go on. . . . What'd Jack say?"

"He said that you guys had in many ways become one . . . as if your minds and your very souls were like a single, living and breathing being. He said that you were constantly in touch with each other—sensing when there was trouble in the heart of the other, or even pending danger! Do you remember that conversation?"

"I do," Mariam interjected.

"Yes . . . I *do* remember that," Linda agreed, feeling a fresh film of moisture clouding her eyes. She remembered well. And what Jack had been referring to was true! There had been many times where either one or the other could actually sense the innermost feelings—painful or joyous—in the other. They were one, husband and wife, a single team working together for the common good of their little family.

Suddenly, with reminiscent visions of Jack alive and well inside her head, Linda wept again.

"He's all right, Linda!" Alex emphasized, trying to enforce his point. "Search your feelings . . . you know what I mean . . . so search them! You guys share a common spirit, just like Mariam and I are discovering. Search, Linda! Do you feel Jack's spirit gone, or is it alive, fighting for survival? He's not dead, Linda, 'cuz if he were, I think you'd know."

Linda was reassured by Alex's complete insight and optimism. He was right, and she knew it. She was very much in tune with her husband's spirit, and realized, like Alex had said, that if Jack had died, she would have felt it—known about it!

Just before the close of visiting hours, Linda made an unusual request of Alex and his wife. Alex had gone to Little Jack's room and had returned with his usual report. Little Jack looked fine—his color normal, his breathing regular, and so forth.

"I want to *see* him," Linda stated matter-of-factly.

"I know you do, Linda," Mariam comforted, "but that's going to be a bit awkward with you all tied up like you are."

"Untie me then!" Linda directed firmly.

"You know we can't do that, Linda," Alex interjected.

"And why not?"

"Are you serious?"

"Darn right, I am! My leg doesn't even hurt, and neither does my hip. You can carry me, and . . . better yet," she enthused, "see that wheelchair over there in the corner? Could you help me into it?"

"Come on, Linda," Alex reasoned, "the doctor's got your leg elevated for a specific purpose. I'm sure you can understand that. Really . . . all those ropes and pulleys and things . . . they're here for a reason. You can't just get up and hop into a wheelchair. Not yet anyway!"

"Oh, I know that, Alex. You're strong, and I know you can sort of lift me gently into it. Then you can just wheel me quietly into Little Jack's room."

She looked at the two with a piercing expression that clearly manifested the seriousness of her will. "I mean it, Alex. I have to see my son!"

"But—"

"Tilt that leg rest into an extended position, and my leg will still be elevated . . ."

"Come on, Linda. . . ."

"I mean it, Alex. Really! I can handle it. The hospital doesn't own my body—I do."

"But Linda," Mariam added, "it seems so . . . so risky!"

"Risky? How could it be risky, Mariam? All I want to do is see my son for a moment. Then you can wheel me right back here."

Alex and Mariam looked at each other. Then, as if searching for a clue from little Trish, who was still playing with her doll, they turned in her direction. As they did, they realized at once that Trish had been listening to their conversation, and was definitely supportive of her mother's wishes. She sat in the corner nodding her head up and down, smiling with delight at the idea.

Alex walked to the door and poked his head into the hallway. Antelope Valley Hospital was quite old, and seemed to have so many corridors, including the one they were in. He saw a nurse round the corner and go out of sight, but other than that, they were quite isolated. Doctor Moody was likely home by now, and even though Alex was not happy with Linda's request, he tried to put himself in her place. Maybe it wasn't that unreasonable after all.

Just then Alex felt someone brush up against his leg, and he looked down to see little Trish standing at his side, mimicking his look-out posture.

"I know," he whispered. "Why don't you stand right here and keep a close watch while Mariam and I help your mother into the wheelchair . . . okay?"

"All right," Trish answered, clearly enthused.

"Alex?" It was Mariam. She was a little confused, and very apprehensive about her husband's willingness to go through with Linda's request. "Are you sure this is such a good idea?"

"No . . . I think it's a terrible idea, frankly, but it's what Linda wants." He saw Linda wink at him. "And I suppose she knows better than you or I."

Mariam turned to Linda in a final attempt to persuade her friend to not go through with her plans, but Linda was unwavering in her decision.

Standing guard at the door, Trish watched both the hallway and the laborious tasks undertaken by the Salingers to unstring and free her mother from the webbing of supports. Alex had developed beads of perspiration on his forehead, not from the physical exertion, but from the mounting anxiety inside him.

For some reason or another, Alex felt like he was breaking some inviolate law. He worried about getting caught by one of the nurses, or even a doctor, and having to endure the embarrassment of a demanded explanation. It was ridiculous actually, for truly, what harm could he possibly be inflicting? Linda wanted to see her kid—that was all there was to it.

"All right now, Linda," he said, as the two readied themselves to hoist her from the bed into the wheelchair. "You tell me if this hurts, even in the least. And I mean it! If you feel discomfort or pain in any way, I want you to tell us so we can put you back . . . 'kay?"

"I'm all right, Alex. Relax, will ya?" She took a deep breath and said, "I'm ready when you guys are."

"All right then . . . on three! One . . . two . . . three! Umph! Easy now, slowly . . . slowly . . . that's it . . . easy! Good! Let her down! That hurt?"

"Not at all!" Linda lied, still clinching her fists in a tight ball and gritting her teeth in pain.

"You sure?" he probed further.

"I'm fine. Really! If you could maybe slide my leg over to the right a bit . . . it needs to be centered a little more evenly on the leg rest."

"Oh, sure. . . ." Alex delicately slid the heavy cast an inch or so to the right. "That better?"

"Yes! Thank you, Alex . . . Mariam . . . you're dolls, both of you!"

"I don't know about all of that," Mariam said in a hushed whisper. "I still think this whole thing's crazy!"

Reassessing the situation, Alex turned to Trish, who still kept a vigilant watch. "Everything clear out there in the hallway, Trish?"

"Sure it is!" she said proudly.

"All right," he said quietly, turning his head toward Linda, "ready to see Little Jack, Mrs. Garrity?"

"Oh, yes!" she said, holding back another tear.

They moved without incident into the hallway and down into Little Jack's room. Alex positioned the wheelchair alongside the boy's bed where Linda could easily look into her son's face and hold gently onto one of his hands.

The sight of the unconscious child filled her with renewed despair. She looked into his face and saw a young, brave soldier; a young boy who had literally saved his sister's life—and rivers of moisture streamed down her cheeks. Somehow knowing that Linda needed to be alone with her son, Alex and Mariam tenderly took Trish by the hand and stepped back into the hallway.

"Hello, my brave little man," Linda whispered softly, not at all concerned for the tears that steadily streaked downward and dripped onto her lap. "Do you know . . . how much I love you, Little Jack?" She reached for her Kleenex, blew her nose, and continued.

"I heard all about your brave, heroic deed back there at the crash site!" She paused, as a sob broke free. "Oh yes, Little Jack, I know what you did! And I just wanted you to know that I am *so* proud of you . . . so thankful that you had the courage to go in after your sister like you did. You know, my precious son, if you hadn't, Trish would have died."

Linda sobbed openly. It took a moment to get control of the heaving of her chest, and to stabilize the flow of tears.

"Doc Moody says you actually climbed down into the wreckage after Trish, and that you pulled her free. You did all that?

"He says something hit you in the back of the head." She choked up again. "I'm *so* sorry, darling. I wish I could take away your pain, but they tell me you're going to be all right, and that you'll be back on your feet in no time at all! What do you think of that?

"Hey," she smiled, "maybe we'll go skiing again! Maybe you and me and Trish . . . and your . . . father . . . can go up into the mountains, like we planned, and catch a few days together at Snow Valley! Would you like that, son? I just know you're going to wake up and be all right . . . I just know it!"

Linda held the limp, unresponsive hand in hers, brought it to her lips and kissed it tenderly, then continued.

"Sometimes I'm not the best mom in the world, and sometimes I guess I get a little upset at silly things. But that's just me, Little Jack. It's a foolish part of me that just doesn't think before I act sometimes . . . kind of an inward flaw in my character I suppose.

"But I want you to know that I've been doing a lot of thinking, and a lot of it has been about you, your father, and your little sister. We all love you, you know. And as soon as you're well, I'm going to be there for you anytime you need me. We're going to do things together . . . all of us . . . a family! I'll never turn my back on you, dear son, never!"

Fighting desperately to remain in control, Linda bit down on her lower lip, then held Little Jack's warm hand up to her cheek. She caressed the smooth flesh with the side of her face, bathing it with her tears and praying desperately for a miracle. She wanted Little Jack to open his eyes—to respond in any way whatsoever—so she could know that he was all right and that he would eventually recover completely, just like the doctors said he would.

Linda stared longingly into the boy's face, memorizing the soft, delicate features of his eyes, small nose, blond hair, chin, and lips. She realized that her love for her son had expanded to such an extent there simply weren't any words to adequately capture the warmth and tenderness of the feeling.

Kissing the little hand again and laying it gently down onto its resting place at his side, Linda drew another Kleenex tissue from the small box, blew her nose again, and continued.

"When I was a little girl," she said softly, "my mother once punished me for something I didn't do. It was hard, Little Jack, to stand there and not be able to convince her that I wasn't the guilty one. I got a real hard spanking and spent several hours in my room where all I could do was cry my little heart out!

"I thought I'd never love my mother again after what she'd done . . . but then sometime later that evening there was a knock at my bedroom door, and a faint whisper coming from the other side.

"'Linda,' my mother's voice said, 'can I talk to you for a moment?' I wanted her to go away, Little Jack. . . . I wanted her to go away and never come back. I felt my emotions toward her totally out of control for a while, but something inside of me told me to forgive her, and to let her back into my heart.

"Well, I was pretty amazed when, after coming into my room, my mother humbly approached me. She got down on her knees so she could be face to face with me and started to cry.

"My heart melted away, Little Jack. Mother had discovered that she had accused me wrongfully and had come to ask for my forgiveness. And you know what, son? It was *so* easy to forgive! It suddenly didn't matter anymore that she had been the one who wronged *me*, and that she had spanked me for something I hadn't done. What mattered was that she was there to say she was sorry and to tell me that she loved me. Oh, how I loved her after that . . . and I'm so grateful that she is still alive! You know what I mean?"

Clearing her mind for a moment and wiping away the fresh tears, Linda looked again into Little Jack's quiet, peaceful face. At last she continued, "I suppose there have been many things that I've done to offend you, Little Jack, and I guess what I'm trying to say is . . . well . . . I'm so sorry! In my own way, I need to know that you can forgive me . . . because . . . if you'll just wake up. . . . Oh, please, my little man! Please wake up! I'll prove to you that I'm the best mother in the whole world!"

She held fast to the little hand stretched out on the bed, kneading and massaging it tenderly, and bending down repeatedly to smother it with her kisses.

"If you can hear me, Little Jack," she continued, "wherever you are . . . just know that you are so loved!"

"And son, there's one more thing. . . . Your father is very far away right now, and he needs our faith, and our prayers. . . . He is such a special man, Little Jack, and . . ." the tears were again flowing freely, "and I hope that you grow up to be exactly like him!"

Again Linda looked longingly into the boy's face, cradling the little hand as she would a small puppy's paw. She was mentally and emotionally exhausted, but she still found the strength to lower her head in a reverent and silent plea for help.

"Dear Father," she prayed, "watch over my boy . . . don't let him die. . . . Please, oh, please bring him back to me."

Suddenly for the first time in more than a week, the small muscles in Little Jack's hand responded to the touch and moved ever so slightly between his mother's cradled embrace.

"Little Jack?" she responded hopefully. "Are you there, son? Oh, dear baby . . . can you hear me?"

There was no further movement, no further sign of his having heard anything or having even acknowledged his mother's presence. But for Linda, the slight motion had been a sign that rekindled her hope. It was a powerful new reason to fight, despite the odds, for that eventual day when her little family—all of them, her husband included, would gather together again as a complete family! She would fight for that day when this nightmare would be over, and she would overcome each obstacle one step at a time . . . until in the end the Jack Garrity family was whole again.

PART FOUR

Coming Home

The wise old man was silent now,
resting there alone . . .
He closed his eyes, then smiled and said,
"At last, I'm going home."

39

Moments After the Explosion— Northern Libya

Carefully maneuvering the vibrating Huey chopper over the nearly invisible Libyan terrain, Major Jack Garrity felt the adrenalin pumping through his system. The explosion at Biskra was nothing less than spectacular, a fireworks display that rivaled anything Jack had seen back "in the world."

Now, however, his mind raced, trying to lock into the unusual complexity of flying a Huey—something he had been trained to do, and yet now seemed almost a foreign experience to him.

"Jack . . . Jack, could you please set the helicopter down?"

Turning, Jack looked into the almost panic-stricken eyes of Nisha.

"It's Ibrahim, Jack," she stammered. "Sahid is cradling him against the vibration, but I . . . I'm not sure he's going to make it."

Sensing a need to simply respond to the unexpected request rather than persuade her to continue, Jack mechanically reprogrammed his mind into compliance. As he brought the chopper out of the sky, he thought of Molly in the Banshee, and of the computer's ability to do as it was directed. In a strange way, he felt as though he were Molly.

Moments later, as the chopper's blades came to a whispering standstill, Jack crouched to the right of Nisha and Sahid as they held Ibrahim and wiped the perspiration and blood from his face.

"Major Jack . . . ," the old man breathed, a weak smile appearing on his face. "You . . . *we* did it . . . no?"

"You were marvelous, Ibrahim, as was Juno." The words came effortlessly for Jack, yet somehow he simply did not know what to say to the severely injured resistance fighter.

"You've lost a lot of blood, Father," Sahid interjected. "We'll need to get you to a hospital immediately, and then you will—"

"Sahid," the old soldier sighed, "your wishes . . . are not . . . in keeping with . . . with your training. I . . . I am ready to go, my son. The . . . feeling is there, and you . . . and Nisha . . . must accept it."

Slightly turning his head, Ibrahim looked weakly into his daughter-in-law's tearstained face. She was clasping his hand and doing all within her power to control her emotions—but the tears would not stop flowing.

"We . . . we love you, Father," she whispered, searching for the right words. "Juno also loves you," she smiled, turning to the large Alaskan dog lying at her side. "Don't you, Juno?"

Almost human-like, Juno raised his head and lapped gently at the hand of his dying master.

"You're . . . you've been the best . . . of companions, Juno," Ibrahim sighed, trying to swallow as he spoke. "As have both of *you,*" he coughed, turning his eyes back to Nisha and Sahid. "You . . . you will be successful . . . you know. . . . I . . . I will somehow be near you . . . giving you what assistance I can . . . so please . . . listen for my spirit, my beautiful children. I love you all . . . more than words can . . . reflect. And please," he continued, his body wrenching forward as he attempted to conclude his thought, "give my grandson . . . Kashan . . . my love . . . and my sacred medal."

With the mention of Kashan's name, Sahid suddenly was unable to hold back his own emotions, and he wept unashamedly as he rocked his father in his arms. "You'll make it, Father," he cried. "You must believe—"

Then, with a tear working its way along the seasoned crack in the old man's right cheek, he blinked several times, smiled, and then quietly slipped away, leaving a world of complex turmoil, and entering a sphere of peace . . . an unusual bright and tranquil sphere where his parents and his lifelong wife and companion welcomed him with open arms. For Ibrahim, the sense of joy was overwhelming, encompassing his entire person with a light that was impossible to describe. He, at last, had come home.

40

0230 Hours, Monday, 6 January 1992— Nearby, in Nalut, Libya

The pearly luminescence of the newly visible moon filtered in through the small gap in the curtains. Major Jack Garrity was too high-strung to sleep, and although this was the first decent accommodation he'd experienced since first setting foot on the Libyan desert land, sleep simply refused to come.

It had been more than a week of exceptionally rough going since the anxiety-ridden combat experience at Biskra. More than once Jack had felt a somber and wearisome sense of dread enter his heart. It was as though some crafty, shadowy presence was forever following him—never quite close enough for him to make a positive identification, but always there, just out of sight.

He knew from past experience that it was generally a wise decision to follow his instincts—to trust in them. Early that morning, while Sahid and Nisha had made the short journey to Taza, the adolescent military compound just outside Nalut, where their son, Kashan, was being brainwashed and prematurely prepared as a future soldier for the Libyan Elite, Jack sensed a peculiarly familiar shadowy shape very near to his side. Spinning around with catlike quickness, he was sure he had spotted movement.

But he hadn't.

If there were someone following him, it was an individual with cunning instincts. Someone who was, as Jack himself was, gifted with an exceptional physiological sensory capability . . . perhaps more refined and acute than even his own. In any case, Jack never did, and seemingly never would, catch a glimpse of the silent furtive stalker.

As he lay on the bed inside the small hotel room at Nalut City, looking out at the slivered moon through the two-inch gap in the curtains, a tidal wave of emotionally charged thoughts plummeted through his mind. They were of the past, the almost incomprehensible present, and the extremely tentative future that lay before him.

The Huey they had salvaged from Biskra had given them a formidable lead against any pursuers. But Jack was constantly concerned with the possibility of an air attack, and during the early hours of their escape, had maintained a vigilant watch on the chopper's on-board radar readings. Luckily, however, there wasn't a single encounter, even though every shadow through the night sky seemed eerily reminiscent of a Soviet-made MiG.

Plotting their course westward across the great desert, the weary freedom fighters said very little to one another. In fact, instead of a chorus of jubilant voices raised in victory, the mood of the small crew had been solemn and grim. The loss of Ibrahim had been a strain for Sahid and Nisha, to be sure, but they both seemed able to endure the adversity.

Sahid directed Major Garrity to the outskirts of an oasis hidden deep in the heart of the desert, similar geographically to other areas in Libya that reminded Jack of a lunar landscape.

The small patch of greenery and barely visible life became the final resting place for Sahid's father. They buried the old man in a shallow, hastily prepared grave near a small, bubbling spring where grass and wild flowers clung desperately to life.

Just above Ibrahim's grave, a small altar of foraged rocks marked the site as something mildly significant. After an informal religious incantation—the words of which were definitely foreign to Jack—Nisha produced a small piece of wood on which she had inscribed the words, which were interpreted for him to read: *Ibrahim Al-Sayed Tashwan, Fighter for Freedom. Born 10 August 1921—Died 2 January 1992.* The small wooden marker was wedged between the rocks.

Eventually, putting the ordeal behind them, they flew westward again until, running short on fuel, Jack landed the chopper a third time just south of another settlement called Al-Bayadh. It was here that the team linked up with one of the stronger rebellion commando squads.

Al-Bayadh was an oil-rich community heavily guarded by the Libyan Elite. Still, through a series of coded transmissions from the Huey's shortwave transmitter, Sahid had been able to establish contact with the rebellion.

It had been a tricky maneuver to pilot the Huey through the early-morning hours of darkness, but it was far more of a challenge to avoid detection from the radar emplacements at the Al-Bayadh military outposts. Nevertheless, with a professional combination of skill and determination, Major Garrity had carefully snaked his way across the scantily lit desert terrain and landed just two miles south of the city.

They were met by a fellow who called himself Benian. Jack noted a characteristic in Benian that seemed peculiarly similar to nearly every freedom fighter serving in the rebellion. He didn't waste a lot of time on idle chitchat as one would expect when two friends reunited—and like all the others under Sahid's and Nisha's command, Benian seemed to possess an almost reverent respect for the husband and wife duo.

Thinking back, Jack began to feel that perhaps there *was* some sort of divine intervention following his exploits amidst the people and unique situations that seemed to surface from place to place. Indeed, neither Sahid, Nisha, nor Jack had any clue whatsoever of the bizarre events that might accompany them there at Al-Bayadh.

Benian had seemed physically winded when he greeted Sahid and Nisha, as if he had run instead of driven the two miles from the city to where they had landed. He was a tall man, narrow-waisted, and powerfully built in the upper torso. He had a thick, dark beard and moustache, and a pair of sinister-looking green eyes. Of course Jack didn't notice the eyes until later when the party was assembled in a well-lit conference room.

Benian's respectful greetings to Sahid and Nisha were brief. The sense of urgency in the man's voice sent a chill through Jack, even though he was unable to learn the nature of the crisis until Nisha and Sahid later explained it to him in English.

Al-Bayadh, Jack learned, was a small, but thriving metropolis inside the northwest corner of Libya's upper desert region. It was exactly two hundred miles due south of Tripoli, on the twelve degree longitudinal line that ran straight through the capital city. As one of the newer cities, it was teeming with life and significantly more modern than any other settlement Jack had previously seen. Most of the three hundred thousand plus residents had job-related reasons for living there. The main wells of economy, of course, were the rich oil fields of Sidi.

Despite its technologically and economically advanced prosperity, a fiendishly wretched plague had swept over the city—a menace that was spreading like a cancer, and had such a profound crippling effect that entire families, men, women and children, had fallen into the darkest depth of fear and trepidation.

"What is this plague, Benian, my old friend?" Sahid had asked.

Speaking now in broken English, Benian responded. "It is an infestation of the highest form of evil, Sahid . . . a perverse wickedness brought by the soldiers of the Elite!"

Benian's green eyes were grimacingly twisted with a curious mixture of grief and anger, but held steady with Sahid's concerned gaze. He stood silent for a moment, collecting his thoughts and selecting his words carefully. "During the past two weeks, Al-Rashid's army of tyrannous butchers and oppressors have moved from house to house conscripting young thirteen-, fourteen-, and fifteen-year-old boys into active training for the Elite!

"The numbers are alarming, Sahid! They are gathering hundreds of youngsters and shipping them off to training camps along the borders."

"Who is doing this?" Sahid questioned, not having fully understood his friend.

"The military!"

"The Libyan Elite?"

"Yes, Sahid . . . under the direction of Lucca Rovigo and Haman Al-Rashid."

"Rovigo is *here?*" Sahid queried, glancing at Jack.

"No, not here . . . but it is *his* men who carry out the perverse gathering of our children . . . who search from house to house, village to village, recruiting our young sons into service against their will! It is Rovigo's orders they follow!"

Nisha, who had been quietly contemplating the seriousness of this horrific new twist, turned to Benian and said, "Tell me, Benian, how many children have they taken?"

"Two, maybe three hundred so far," he said, pausing just a moment to turn himself toward her so that he might address her more politely. "Why do you ask?"

"Where do they take them . . . the children, I mean?" she asked, continuing her line of questioning without pausing to answer his own.

"We have followed them, Nisha . . . and have learned that there are three camps west of here—two hundred, maybe three hundred miles. The closest camp is called *Akbou.* It is heavily fortified and filled to capacity with young recruits. The second is called *Timgad.* It is closer to the border of Algeria, by the city of Ghadamis. It, however, is only partially built, yet operational nonetheless. There are more than four thousand young boys in both of these camps . . . but the largest, and we believe the most cruel and ruthless of them all, is *Taza,* just outside of Nalut. It, of course, falls near the border of Tunisia."

Benian paused for a moment, suddenly remembering that Sahid and Nisha's son, Kashan, a thirteen-year-old child of innocence, was one of those unfortunate souls incarcerated at Taza. His eyes dimmed sorrowfully and he looked deep into Nisha's heart. "I fear for your son, Nisha . . . Sahid . . . for I know that Taza is a place that is said to steal the souls of the children and harden their hearts like stone. The strongest willed children go to Taza and come out broken! They are taught to hate our neighbors to the south and west, to think of the Tunisians, Algerians, and others as mere infidels!

"And now these inappropriately named soldiers are here in Al-Bayadh, stealing more children. So it is by the grace of God that you have received our urgent message and have come to assist us . . . at last."

Benian turned back to Sahid and said, "Have you made contact with other battalions inside the rebellion? Are others following you here?"

Sahid, Jack, and Nisha glanced around at each other questioningly, apparently attempting to discover if one among them was aware of this holocaust, and for some unknown reason had not shared it with the others.

Each drew a blank, and then turned their gaze back to Benian.

"What urgent message?" Sahid asked.

Benian stared at his commanding officer, then at Nisha and Jack, with a puzzled expression of disbelief on his face. He then spoke. "You did not get our message?"

"We received no messages, Benian. But we have been a few days gone from El-Kabir and the headquarters at Adi Haliab on an important mission of our own." Then, realizing that there was an extraordinary communication gap between them, Sahid described the events that had occurred since Major Garrity's arrival. He then introduced his friend Jack to the commander of the Al-Bayadh rebel battalion.

It turned out that a courier had been sent more than a week before with a message to Sahid and Nisha. They had missed him by one day. The urgency was evident now that they were, coincidentally, in Al-Bayadh, itself. The Al-Bayadh rebel force was in serious need of reinforcements to mount an attack against the military installation near the Sidi oil fields.

The Libyan Elite's central command post for the specific operation of child conscription was at the installation at Sidi. But an equally important target was the daytime operation conducted in an enormous central plaza, downtown in the heart of Al Bayadh.

Each day, soldiers from the Elite gathered truckloads of innocent youngsters and herded them through a processing operation—of sorts—right there in the city. Names, birth dates, and other records were cataloged in a large field tent. Each of the boys was then issued a pair of military fatigues, boots, and other clothing, and sent to one of the three indoctrination camps.

As Sahid and Nisha learned more and more of the terrible events transpiring at Al-Bayadh, and continued translating the conversations into English for Jack, the three were heartsick. But for Sahid and Nisha, whose son was part of the holocaust, the pain was terrifying.

During a confidential meeting later on that morning inside a well-guarded room overlooking the Al-Bayadh plaza, Benian described a detailed offensive that he hoped would send a powerful message to the high-ranking officials of the Libyan Elite.

The proposal, now set before Sahid and Nisha, was that a contingent of the highest skilled freedom fighters would encircle the plaza from strategic positions in and through many of the buildings that faced the square, and mount a predawn attack against the hundred or so soldiers who were carrying out the illegal adolescent draft. Currently, Benian had reported, the rebel force under his command consisted of about seventy-five well-trained fighters, many of whom had seen their own sons whisked away by Haman's Elite. All of them were bitterly angry at the Nazi-style policing of their country, and more important, at the appalling conscription of their young sons, so they eagerly awaited the call to battle.

The second phase of the early-hour offensive called for a simultaneous attack on the military outpost near the Sidi oil fields, but Benian had hesitated initiating either incursion due to his dreadfully inadequate strength in numbers. He estimated the Libyan army was three to four hundred strong at the installation, and he reasoned that it would be mass suicide for his men to invade.

Another problem was the short supply of heavy artillery that would inevitably be required to penetrate the well-fortified base.

It was for this reason that Benian had sent the courier to Adi Haliab at El-Kabir. He'd hoped to appeal to Sahid and Nisha for two additional battalions, as well as diversional support at other locations around the country to confuse Haman Al-Rashid and thus emerge victorious.

Little by little, Jack had come to respect the intellectually apt rebellion commander, and he found himself emotionally concerned for the trials and great struggles his friends were fighting against.

Most of those with whom Jack came in contact were curious about the American and his odd-looking dog, Juno. Since Ibrahim's death, the all-white, thickly coated Samoyed husky had adopted Jack as his new master. The two went everywhere together, and although Sahid felt a strong kinship for the animal, which in a way was an extension of his father, he never once voiced opposition to Jack's apparent attraction to the dog. In addition, he understood the dog's natural attraction to a native American, whose voice and commands were innately familiar.

"Juno has found a new master, Nisha," Sahid had whispered while they were still airborne in the Huey.

"So he has, Sahid . . . so he has," was all she had said.

In the end, it was clear that Juno was Jack's dog . . . and since huskies are rarely, if ever, found in Middle East countries, he was regarded by some as a devil animal, and by others as a great and terrible warrior beast who would protect his American master at all costs.

Temporarily detoured from their main objective, which had been to move quickly to Nalut and formulate an offensve operation to free their son from Taza, Sahid and Nisha decided to stay in Al-Bayadh and assist in any way they could with the incursion scheduled for the following morning.

Still exhausted from the battle at Biskra, Sahid, Nisha, and Jack worked nonstop throughout the day, positioning men and equipment stealthily around the open-air plaza.

Jack watched in horror from a small window in his room the endless parade of young boys being shuffled through the circus-size army tent, and herded away to whatever destination they had been assigned. The soldiers of the Libyan Elite seemed, for the most part, to be a collection of Libya's trashiest transients. Barbaric and crude, most appeared to take pleasure in abusing and intimidating the young children with swift and callous kicks, or painful slaps to the face.

The more Jack watched, the angrier he became.

"We need a diversion!" he exclaimed suddenly, spinning around from his place at the window and facing his friends. Benian asked for a translation.

"A diversion?" Sahid questioned.

"Yes, a well-timed diversion at the first sight of light. We must draw attention to the processing tent in the main square, so that the sentries manning the guard posts will turn their attention inward. That way, we can take them by surprise with a small number of our own. Besides, if we can somehow blow up the main tent, we will have successfully destroyed the combat readiness of more than half of the soldiers stationed here at the plaza."

"That is an excellent idea, Major Garrity . . . but we cannot possibly penetrate the perimeters of the plaza without alarming the rest of the forces inside the tents . . . let alone attack the middle without the support of heavy artillery. We have no way of getting in there."

"Oh, but we do, Sahid . . . we do indeed!" Jack countered, concentrating on the possible risks of the operation he was about to propose.

"How, Major?"

"Have you forgotten, my dear friends, that we have a fully armed and operational Huey UH1 sitting just outside the city?"

Sahid and Nisha looked at each other and quickly translated the suggestion to Benian, who suddenly beamed with delight.

"We have no pilot, Major," Sahid said, his brow furrowed in thought.

"Give me a break, Sahid!" Jack exclaimed. "I didn't come here for my health! I want those child abusers stopped! You just get me some aviation fuel and I'll drop in on those troops like an angry hornet. Once I fire the Huey's rockets, half of your job will be over. . . . You guys can move in and pick up the pieces, taking captives who will be more than willing to comply."

"You have risked your life already, Major. . . . You seem to forget the important role you must still play for our cause. If you are killed, there will be no one to take the message to your president. . . . Don't you see? We must not allow you to risk your own safety . . . we need you alive and free!"

"Well, then," Jack concluded, smiling with confidence, "you'll just have to cover me and Juno real well now, won't you!"

The freedom fighters worked steadily through the rest of the day and long into the night. The element of surprise was the single key for their hoped-for success.

Meanwhile, word in the underground had spread significantly so that a steady trickle of capable militiamen joined up with Benian's rebel battalion, until by three or four in the morning, the skillful commander had a fairly sizeable army—about 140 altogether, with many more on the way.

While Benian continued strategically positioning his forces around the plaza and the army outpost at Sidi, Major Garrity, Sahid, Nisha, and the four rebel fighters who had traveled with them to Al-Bayadh retired to a small, well-hidden room where they received a hastily prepared dinner. They then retired for a few hours of desperately needed sleep.

Even Juno was able to curl up close to Jack and peacefully sleep for a time.

At four o'clock Saturday morning, long before dawn, Benian came into the room to awaken the wearied traveler-comrades. Juno, however, was not eager to see his master awakened—or even approached—and as Benian stepped quietly in through the doorway, the husky chuffed and bared its fangs. But Jack was awake immediately and gave the dog a reassuring signal that all was well . . . thus pacifying the animal and divesting himself of the clinging drunkenness of sleep at the same time.

Throughout the night, Benian had somehow requisitioned a fair supply of aviation fuel and had the Huey refueled. Jack was curious as to how and where the commander had found the supply, and meant to question him on it, but decided later that it really didn't matter.

During the drive back to the chopper, while Nisha remained in the city, Benian described the night's progress to Sahid and Jack. He explained that although somewhat limited in numbers, the freedom fighters had both the plaza and the army outpost completely surrounded, and were ready for the signal to attack. And, since Jack would initiate the incursion, the entire force would hold back until the first shots were fired from the Huey.

The final plan had called for a massive surprise attack, as discussed the night before. A special unit of commandos with an assortment of 40mm grenade launchers and bazookas was positioned at the outskirts of the army base. From there, a first strike on the barracks filled with sleeping Libyan soldiers would even the odds . . . and the battle would begin.

All was ready.

The Huey lifted off at 4:40 that morning and Jack felt the sensation of breathlessness nearly overwhelm him. He had to gasp for air more than once as he struggled to cope with his fast-beating heart and apprehensive jitters. But once airborne, the highly skilled airman took over. He charted his course with expert competence and flew rapidly across the open desert toward the city at a barely maneuverable three to five feet above the sandy terrain.

On board with Jack were three non-English-speaking Libyan volunteers. Two of them, whose names Jack couldn't remember, manned the 60mm machine gun at the port side of the Huey, and the other, whose name Jack remembered as Misaan, or Mizan . . . something like that . . . sat "right-seat" in the cockpit, and assisted Jack with the visual navigation. And of course, with the new relationship developed between Jack and his proud-looking husky, Juno was not about to be left behind. He remained curled up in a corner right behind Jack, never exhibiting the least bit of fear during the entire highly turbulent flight.

The Huey approached the outskirts of the city doing a rapid eighty knots, rose effortlessly up and over the rooftops, and sped toward the open plaza about four miles inside the city limits.

The Libyan navigator was the first to spot the target site, and he mentioned to Jack in a clearly discernible sign language that it was just about time to arm the weapons. Jack turned his head toward the port side, and signaled the gunners to prepare.

The weapons were locked and loaded.

Slowing the aircraft down to a reasonable attack speed, Jack skimmed across the final outcropping of rooftops, then dove shallowly into the stadium-size public square and launched two rockets at the large green tent centered in the plaza, which was the central command post.

"Fire!" Jack screamed to his rear gunners, whose immediate compliance and skill instantly neutralized a pair of sentries. Their aim had been as he had directed—to their legs. Again, Jack's philosophy of preserving life wherever possible, even in a wartime combat situation, dominated his thinking. He knew now, though, that life *would* be taken—and even though he was compelled to help free the citizens of Libya from the oppressors Al-Rashid and Rovigo, the thought deeply concerned him.

As the Huey moved closer, Jack felt grateful to have gotten the jump on this particular band of ruthless militiamen who had no idea of the atrocities they were committing. He prayed for a speedy and successful victory.

As he swung around for a second assault on a specific row of makeshift supply tents, he caught his first clear vision of the plaza war. Men were running wildly about, some poised and defiant, firing their weapons boldly in defense. Others were dodging in and out of explosions from hand grenades tossed from high vantage points in the surrounding buildings and rooftops.

The Huey was equipped with a 30mm chain gun cannon mounted in the nose section. Jack spared no rounds as he opened up the high-speed rotary gun and joined in the battle.

But suddenly, as if shot by some mysterious phantom, a half-dozen slugs from a .50-caliber machine gun riddled the Huey's tail section and cut the stabilizing blades of the tail rotor in two. Fragments of metal debris exploded into the atmosphere, sending the Huey spinning out of control toward a far corner of the blazing, war-ravaged plaza.

Jack, the three other men, and Juno, who instinctively sensed the impending doom, braced themselves for the inevitable crash. Jack was furious at having been so quickly shot down, and he wondered where the high-caliber machine gun had been positioned. He would have liked to have destroyed that weapon.

Now, however, that idea was forever too late. For Jack and the small crew, the battle was over—and the only thing he could do now was use all of his skill to land the craft without killing himself and the others.

Around and around they went, spinning like a wobbly top, until finally Jack yelled, "We're gonna hit! Brace yourselves!" And even though the soldiers could not understand a single word their American pilot-commander uttered, they each knew exactly what the intended message contained.

Upon impact, the tail section of the chopper slammed into the corner of a building and was violently ripped off. Both of the gunners were injured seriously when huge fragments of the tail whirled around and crashed with immense force into the side of the aircraft, burying themselves into the hull. Jack later learned that both men miraculously escaped death. Juno, who was still crouched down behind the cockpit, also escaped with his life when the twisted metal shot across in front of his head in one giant sweeping arch. Jack and his co-pilot were both badly bruised and cut, but likewise survived.

Later, reminiscing about the harrowing experience, Jack recalled that something had hit him across the side of the head, and although it did not knock him out, the blow was powerful enough for the major to remember little more than pinpoint-size stars and swirling lights. He remembered the awkward struggle trying to free himself from the wreckage, and the numbing pain that ricocheted through his shoulder and arm. He felt extremely fortunate to have survived at all, and silently offered an abbreviated prayer of thanks that the chopper was on the ground and had not blown up.

As Jack crawled out of the smoldering rubble, he experienced another chilling déjà vu as he pictured the fiery ball of the Banshee plummeting earthward after being hit by the Sidewinder missile. "A second air crash!" he coughed, almost to himself, "and neither fatal!" It had been a sobering thought, for indeed, Jack did not believe that the odds were in his favor to survive a third crash—if ever there was one.

As he pulled himself to his feet, dizzy and weak-kneed, Jack's internal sensors that so often warned him of danger suddenly sprang to life. Grabbing hold of the side of the building in order to steady himself, he simultaneously reached for his 9mm Colt, and swung around to look behind him. What he saw chilled him to the bone.

Standing less than ten feet away from the crushed and mangled wreckage of the Huey was a Libyan soldier wielding an AK-47. Although the major was suffering from shock and was extremely light-headed, he knew that this angry warrior was real and was going to shoot him!

Once again, time—that fractional nanosecond of intense uncertainty and mounting fear—seemed to slow down while thoughts of Linda, Little Jack, and Trish raced through the major's mind. He didn't want to die, but knew that this soldier was going to take his life. It would all be over in the blink of an eye.

With one desperate surge of hope, Jack raised the 9mm Colt and prayed for a miracle.

Just as the soldier was tightening his squeeze on the weapon's trigger, the miracle happened. Juno leaped out from the wreckage like a screaming ghost, barking and frothing at the mouth, simultaneously bounding onto the man's weapon arm and tearing into the flesh with a frenzy.

Jack, his head swirling, responded instinctively. He stumbled to where the soldier was fighting for his life and cuffed the fallen man over the head with the butt of his Colt. The man slumped lifelessly in the sand, and Juno at once retreated to his master's side.

Jack, sensing his drained strength and weakened mental capacity, collapsed awkwardly to the ground. Juno moved in and began licking Jack's face, but he was simply too weak to thank the dog, *his* dog, for saving his life.

From that point, Jack's memory became fuzzy. He barely remembered Sahid carefully whisking him away from the battle zone, or Nisha's skillful, tender hands bandaging his head and wounded shoulder in a small room somewhere out of the immediate war zone. But what he *did* remember was the continued sound of distant gunfire and ongoing bombardment of the Al-Bayadh plaza. He hoped beyond hope for a speedy victory.

The surprise incursion was successful. The freedom fighters, having continuously multiplied in numbers, simply overwhelmed the small army inside the city square. Jack noted with curious pride and growing admiration for the freedom-loving people around him that in the end, many of the rebellion fighters were young boys and mothers standing alongside their brave fathers, wielding weapons and defending their country and beliefs without hesitation.

The entire battle had been fought and won in a little more than forty-five minutes. To Jack, it seemed more like an entire day, instead of less than an hour. And when it was over, Sahid and Benian, flanked by a small contingent of watchful guards, brought a tightly bound prisoner into the room where Jack was recovering.

The man's name was Jadid—Captain Nador Jadid, the commanding officer of the plaza outpost. He was captured almost immediately when the battle had first begun.

Sahid, Benian, and a small squad of commandos had positioned themselves at the far end of the square where they'd kept a vigilant watch on the commander's quarters. When Jack fired the first volley of missiles, four sentries posted at Jadid's tent jumped into action, retrieving their weapons and readying themselves to defend their commanding officer. But as soon as the men stood up, they were immediately immobilized by Benian's commandos, and they fell wounded to the ground. Meanwhile, Sahid and Benian, covered by their support team, rushed into the tent and took Captain Jadid prisoner, whereupon he was kept under strict watch by posted guards in another room adjacent to the one in which Jack would later recuperate.

Interestingly, the middle-aged Libyan officer was not nearly as aggressive in nature as his subordinates. In fact, the captain was very much the opposite—a friendly fellow with a cheerful rather than woeful disposition. Instead of seeming bitter and angry about his capture, he seemed almost pleased, and actually relieved.

During the ensuing interrogation, Jack felt a growing sense of concern and affection toward the man. He learned that Captain Nador Jadid, like Sahid and Nisha, had been unwillingly drafted into the Libyan Elite. He, too, had lost a son to Haman's relentless effort to build the world's strongest army, and similar to his captors, he also hoped to eventually free his own son from one of the training camps. He anticipated returning to his wife and two daughters in Tripoli and escaping from the country as a family. The plan was similar to Sahid's and Nisha's in that through serving in the Elite, he hoped to win the trust of Haman Al-Rashid and Lucca Rovigo, and ultimately learn the whereabouts of his son. He planned to then formulate his own rescue effort, and to act upon it at the most opportune moment.

Captain Jadid explained that his reasoning for taking this particular assignment of enlisting the young boys into the service was so that he could learn where his son, Kala, was—and to then make his move. Essentially, he summarized, his being captured by the rebellion was a gift from God.

Nador Jadid had become an ally. And more important, he was not just some ordinary uninformed Libyan defector—but was a stealthy, highly intelligent strategist who had been Haman Al-Rashid's and Lucca Rovigo's personal friend.

When Jadid had finished speaking, he quietly and almost casually produced a small portfolio which, when viewed by Sahid and Jack, left them with their mouths gaping wide open.

It was a series of highly classified government documents, all photocopied and reduced in size to fit neatly into a small folder that the captain kept on his person at all times.

Included in these documents were several extremely interesting and powerfully informing records—manuscripts and maps that so startled Sahid and Jack they stared at each other in complete disbelief.

The first section was a twelve-page brief, which Sahid translated into English as reading *Project Holy Power—Top Secret.* Benian, who was not quite as informed as either Sahid or Jack, said, "What is Project Holy Power?" Sahid assured him that he would be briefed later that evening.

The second section of literature was a detailed list of Libya's heavy armament and their locations around the country. It also included detailed plans of the reactor at Biskra—which was now destroyed—and underground bunkers where munitions and smaller weapons were stored.

In addition to this information, this second section contained a classified briefing of the United Nations Security Counsel's discovery of Iraq's hidden nuclear facility north of Baghdad, near Al-Sharqat. It mapped Al-Sharqat's location between Mosul and Tikrit, and confirmed the coalition's report that, like its acknowledged twin facility in Tarmia, nuclear capability at the plant was approximately eighteen months away from production. This report was dated 17 July 1991, just one day after the United Nations inspectors made their disclosure to the Western press.

Jack was totally engrossed in leafing through the documents while they were being interpreted for him.

The final section of the packet contained a rather informative document titled *The Youth of the Nation.* It described in detail the overall plan to enlist one million young boys ages thirteen to sixteen to create an underlying army of highly energetic and extremely well-trained soldiers. Their primary task ultimately would be to infiltrate Algeria and initiate a terrorist strike that would set the country into a state of confusion and overall panic. The operation was to begin with the detonation of a nuclear bomb—

"A nuclear bomb!" Jack and Sahid said in unison, looking at each other with wide, disbelieving eyes.

That was it!

They had finally located the second nuclear device!

They quickly turned the final pages of the document until they found what they were looking for.

It was a detailed drawing of an oil field in the northeast quadrant of Algeria—a place called the El-Gassi oil fields. It showed a series of numbered pump stations, oil derricks, and storage tanks, all situated inside a webbing of access roads and aboveground pipelines.

Marked in red on the map was Pump Station Number 28. And in a clearly traceable series of dotted lines, the mapmaker had detailed a telephone cable that spanned the oil field and eventually linked up with Pump Station Number 28.

Jack glanced at the silent captain, then at Sahid and Benian, who were standing at his left. He cupped a hand over his mouth, looked once more down at the map in front of him, and exclaimed, "Gentlemen, they have the device wired into the telephone system! All they have to do is dial a coded series of numbers . . . and . . . *Kaboom!* Every city or small village within twenty or thirty miles of these oil fields will be vaporized! And . . . everyone within a radius of two or three hundred miles will die from radiation exposure!" Jack stared into a void of pensive concern, then added, "And then . . . the cancer!"

No one spoke.

The room had become ghostly quiet, and Jack felt a fear he'd never before known. He wondered if he and Sahid could ever hope to get to the warhead in time. . . . How could they get across the border and warn the Algerians? The bomb could be detonated any moment!

On the next page of the document were detailed drawings of the warhead and the triggering device. Jack was fascinated by the global sphere and its complicated detonation mechanisms. The designer was extraordinarily skilled in electronics. But complicated or not, Jack was sure he could disarm it *if* he could just get to it in time. The idea of actually doing so . . . sitting close to the bomb, itself, . . . was eerily haunting.

But it was the final page of the document that pierced his soul like a needle filled with poison, causing his knees to weaken, his hands to tremble, and his heart to palpitate.

It was a letter outlining the terms for the delivery of two fully armed nuclear warheads and three custom-built triggering devices—signed by First Lieutenant David Guant!

Memories of the meeting with Captain Jadid, the startling discovery of the classified documents, the armed incursion at Al-Bayadh, and the hastened journey here to Nalut with Sahid, Nisha, Nador, and Juno, gave Jack the chills hours later.

Kef Nabeul, along with the four other freedom fighters with whom they had journeyed since leaving Biskra, remained behind to assist in the ongoing battle at the Sidi oil fields, just outside Al-Bayadh. Jack already missed his young physics friend and offered a small prayer in the lad's behalf.

He was glad to have the documents, and he longed for the opportunity of going home . . . if he could just get out of Libya alive! Jack shuddered to think what the president of the United States would do when he delivered these documents—along with his own written accounts. Somehow, he had to get home! Somehow, he had to disarm the bomb, and hopefully, if all went well, he would be able to rescue Kashan and Nador's son, Kala, from the dreadful internment camp, Taza.

Jack looked down at his watch and depressed the light button. It was nearly 0300 in the morning, but still he could not sleep. He stared out at the little sliver of moon that cast its faint glow through the gap in the curtains, then closed his eyes again in an attempt to become drowsy.

But it didn't work.

He just couldn't sleep!

Suddenly Jack noticed Juno. The dog was curled up on the floor of the small hotel room and had appeared to be sleeping. But his ears abruptly stood up. Then his head. His gaze was focused on the small doorway leading into the hallway.

Juno chuffed.

Jack rolled over quietly and grabbed the 9mm Colt laying on a small nightstand inside its holster. He checked the clip and jacked a shell into the chamber—then quietly slid off the bed and onto the floor opposite the doorway.

"Shssssss!" he whispered urgently to the dog.

Juno padded slowly over to Jack and crouched beside his master. Then the two heard a distinct sound—an ever-so-soft footfall outside in the hallway.

Someone was approaching!

Juno chuffed again and growled softly.

"Shsssss," Jack whispered again. "Easy, big fella."

Jack then lowered his gun with a steady hand, pointed to the center of the door, and waited.

The footsteps stopped. And in the faint glow from the falling moon, Jack could see the doorknob beginning to turn slowly clockwise.

41

Say it again, Lucca," Haman Al-Rashid demanded, glaring at the bruised and bandaged general sitting on the sofa in his command headquarters. "You say that Major Garrity is alive . . . and you let him get away!"

"There were others, Haman . . . Sahid and Nisha, and the accursed freedom fighters! They took us by surprise—"

"But tell me, Lucca . . . why did you withhold information from me? Why did you not tell me that the infidel American is alive? Is it possible that you knew this all along?"

"I only suspected, Haman—"

"You should have told me of your suspicions, Lucca . . . then perhaps I could have saved you from the embarrassment of defeat by sending a battalion of soldiers to assist you!"

"Haman, I *tried* to tell you! But you would not listen! It was I who believed that the American was alive . . . and not killed at the crash site over El-Wahat! *You* are the one who insisted that he was dead—"

"Silence, Lucca!" Haman screamed. "I will not have you point the finger of blame at me! If you knew that Garrity was alive . . . you should have made that clear to me! Is that not so!"

Sensing the precarious nature of his position with Haman, Lucca suddenly became quiet and appeared contrite. "It is so, Haman. I was wrong . . . forgive me, Commander."

Haman Al-Rashid paced the floor of the Benghazi office, stopping now and again to look out at the Gulf from his oversized picture window. He turned his fierce gaze from Lucca and walked to the desk where he picked up and read the latest reports from Central Intelligence.

"Our Major Garrity seems to have been a busy man, Lucca. . . . Are you sure your men are accurate on this surveillance?"

"I am sure of it, Haman. One of my best soldiers said that he personally saw the major's helicopter . . . *our* helicopter . . . shot down during the battle. At the time he did not know the American was at the controls—but he eventually got close enough to the wreckage to see the major's body being carried away by rebellion forces."

"That accursed rebellion!" Haman squawked, pounding his fist on the table. "Will we ever be rid of the infidels?"

"They captured Captain Jadid . . . ," Lucca said wearily.

"Yes, I know. . . . Yet, if your men are accurate in their report, then we know where he is being kept, correct?"

"Yes, Commander . . . that is correct. And, yes . . . the reports *are* accurate. We know that he and his captors are located in a small hotel in Nalut . . . and we will have them, Haman, I assure you. . . . They will not escape us this time!"

"For your sake, Lucca, I hope they do not!"

As his commander said the words, Lucca's blood ran cold, an icy fear creeping up his spine that strangely forced perspiration onto his forehead.

Haman, allowing his words to have impact, began flipping again through the pages of the report. His anger flared like a scorching furnace within him. He would execute justice! The nuclear reactor had been only weeks away from completion, yet now it was nothing more than a massive heap of rubble, abandoned and left to decay in the merciless desert sun.

He did not care about the lives that had been lost at Biskra, at the Al-Bayadh plaza, or at the ongoing battle at the Sidi oil fields. He felt as though the weight of the world were on his shoulders, and that this weight could be lifted and disposed of only if he could rid himself of the American! Everything, he was sure, was falling apart because of one lone crusader who had been able to somehow penetrate the increasingly complex network of the rebellion. Haman reasoned that Major Jack Garrity had been, and still was, a formidable threat, and so determined that he would be . . . he must be eliminated, no matter what the cost.

42

Jack applied a little more pressure onto the trigger of the 9mm Colt, but he did not fire the weapon. Instead, he held steady, his arms outstretched and unwavering in his determination to shoot the intruder—whoever he was—the second he set foot into the hotel room. Jack hated the thought of death now even more than at the conclusion of the Gulf War, yet he also knew that he must survive—and succeed—if the Middle East was to normalize permanently.

The silence was eery and unsettling. Jack could hear the rapid beating of his own heart as if keeping time with the quick short breaths coming from Juno at his side. He waited nervously for the door to open. But then, as if sensing the trap within, the hushed trespasser suddenly let go of the door, whirled around, and fled down the hallway, down a narrow stairwell, and out into the dark street beyond.

Hearing the commotion, and realizing what was happening, Jack sprang to his feet and ran to the door. Juno eagerly followed as he yanked the door open, waved his gun out in front of him, and then rebounded quickly out into the night—hoping to catch a glimpse of the stranger. Or better still, to overtake him.

But the street was ghostly silent and vacant. Not even Juno could decide which direction the night stalker had fled.

Jack stood there in the middle of the road, waving his gun first left, then right, then left again. . . . But search as he might, he simply had no idea which way the curious stranger had gone. The elusive character had simply vanished.

Trembling and chilled by the cold night air, Jack hesitated a moment longer, then turned and slowly made his way back into the hotel room. Inwardly, he knew that the shifty, ghost-like meddler was linked somehow with Lucca Rovigo. The thought was unnerving.

Closing and locking the door behind him, Jack wondered how it was that the stranger could be so crafty and evasive as to actually escape undetected by Juno. Surely the man—if it was a man—couldn't be more intuitive than Juno . . . could he? Was it possible for a human being's natural instincts to surpass those highly perceptive physiological sensors so common in the animal kingdom? Yet somehow this slippery, persistent shadow was not only elusive, but shrewdly psychic.

Jack knew the man was close by . . . somewhere watching . . . waiting for the right moment. But for what? Was he in danger? Did this man mean to take his life? And if so, why hadn't he done so already? Certainly there had been many opportunities . . . and undoubtedly there would be others. For Jack, the stealthy menace was a dangerous force to reckon with, and he instinctively understood the need to remain mentally and physically on guard at all times.

Checking the time again, and noting that it was just a little past 0400 hours, Jack decided to try once more to catch a little sleep. He walked cautiously to the small window and parted the curtains a little wider with his hands. The moon had vanished over the horizon, leaving the night sky bleak and dark. He strained his eyes, searching for something . . . hoping to pinpoint the hidden location of the annoying stranger. But the streets remained silent and hauntingly dark.

Jack turned to the dog.

"Is he out there, Juno?"

The animal's ears perked up and his tail flittered receptively.

"He's there, boy . . . ," Jack whispered pensively. "I can feel him."

Juno chuffed.

Across the street, and well hidden inside the shadows of a dark room on the third floor of the building, Kozani Pinios, a dark-skinned, Greek-born Libyan immigrant, peered out into the night. From his vantage point three floors up, he could see the American's window . . . and although he could not visually pierce the darkness beyond, he sensed that the U.S. pilot was there. In fact, Major Garrity was standing right by the window, peeking through the curtains . . . searching . . . scanning for mental images that would lead him to the Greek's temporary surveillance post.

This was an unusual man, Kozani thought. Not at all typical of the usual frail and powerless victims he'd so often been assigned to follow. His cousin, Lucca Rovigo, had been correct in his assessment of the American. There really was a difficult challenge in secretly approaching this man, Garrity . . . because like Kozani, himself, the Air Force pilot was very skilled with his own powers of discernment.

It troubled the brawny-faced Greek to know that there was someone else in the world as gifted as he was. He disliked the American immediately because of it, and he wished that he could have been given orders to execute the pilot instead of the trivial assignment of surveillance. Nevertheless, he was a professional. He worked for the increasingly powerful government of Libya, and although intelligence gathering was sometimes a bit boring, and keeping an eye on people rather trite for his superior talents, he always did as he was told. There was no other choice . . . especially if he wanted to keep his highly lucrative, government-paid commission.

Lucca would be arriving sometime late tomorrow, and Kozani would watch the American and the others as they were captured and executed. It would be a tremendous pleasure to witness the events, especially the American's demise. After all, Lucca had said that the Air Force major had killed Lucca's only brother—a fellow Greek—and a dear cousin.

He, the adept and very much in control Kozani, would now sleep.

43

Major Jack Garrity opened his eyes but could not see. Strange, he thought, trying to understand the pitch black. He thought that the sun would be out by now, shining brightly and filtering in through the curtains.

He looked down at his wrist searching for his watch. He'd press the little electronic button, illuminate the miniature light inside, and get a fix on the time. Perhaps he hadn't been asleep that long. . . .

The watch was gone!

What?

It was so dark. . . .

He felt up and down his arm, but nothing.

How weird.

Wait a minute . . . hold everything . . . what was this?

His skin felt very peculiar. In fact, it didn't feel like skin at all. . . . It was strangely different . . . rough, cracked . . . torn apart in many places!

"Hey," he exclaimed, "what's going on here?"

Frightened, Jack tried to sit up—but he didn't make it all the way. Instead, his head bumped into something hard and extremely rough.

"What in—" he stated, reaching up through the lightless void in search of the hard object.

His hands probed the surface. It had a texture that was strangely familiar . . . something like a rough-grade sandpaper . . . but . . . yes! Now he knew! It was wood! Rough, unfinished plywood of some kind.

Wood?

"Now wait just a second!" Jack demanded. "Wood? How could

that be? A piece of wood, resting just above me . . . some sort of . . . hold on. . . . What's this? A wall? Two walls? It can't be!" he screamed.

Jack was inside a wooden box—a coffin made from unfinished plywood! But he wasn't dead! So . . . what was he doing in the— Oh, no! he thought, suddenly remembering where he was.

They'd taken him back down into the catacombs!

Hold on.

Who had taken him?

Sahid and Nisha?

No . . . someone else . . .

A man.

A bearded man.

A very strong, bearded man with dark, thick hair, and a burly-looking moustache. The same guy who'd shot him.

He'd been shot?

How did that happen?

Then he *was* dead. . . .

And what about the bodies? The endless rows of human corpses lining the walls of the inner corridors of the ancient catacombs. Some of them, Jack remembered, were mere skeletal remains of souls long forgotten, yet others were still rotting with decay . . . shriveled, leather-like skin still clinging onto the bones. . . . Old, rotted cloth wrappings still strewn around the arms, legs, and shoulders.

They'd seen him come in.

Many of the dead had seen Jack. He was sure of it! And the man with the beard . . . he'd left Jack all alone in a single chamber, surrounded by bodies . . . skeletons . . . and they were talking . . . whispering to one another.

He had to get out of the box!

He had to get out before they came for him and made him one of them!

But his leg!

The bullet had shattered the bone in his upper thigh, and he could still feel the pain . . . not to mention the fact that he couldn't walk.

He wished he could look at it . . . if he could just see long enough to—

Wait!

What's that?

They're coming . . . he can hear them! Ten . . . maybe twenty . . . maybe even more!

They started to pound on the box . . . ugly . . . rotting, skeleton hands, banging now, calling his name, slamming their fists down onto his coffin!

"Jack?"

More pounding.

"Are you in there, Jack?"

Tap, tap, tap, tap . . .

Jack jerked himself upright, expecting to smash headlong into the wooden box . . . but there was nothing there.

He opened his eyes and let out a scream.

"Jack?" he heard the voice say. "Open the door, Jack!"

Everything finally came into focus. He wasn't inside some airless coffin, deep in some dank-smelling catacomb. . . . No . . . not at all!

It had all been a dream! He was sitting in the hotel room in a small bed, perspiring profusely.

"Are you in there, Jack?!"

Tap, tap, tap, tap . . .

Jack got up, shaking himself free from the remaining paralysis of the nightmare, and limped over to the door.

His leg was sore. Then he remembered.

He'd been so unnerved about the prowler last night that he'd gone to bed with the Colt laying at his side under the covers. Apparently, toward the final hours of the night, he'd rolled over on top of the weapon, allowing it to dig into his hip and upper thigh for who knows how long, thus leaving a tender spot to contend with this morning.

The sun was up and shining brightly. Beams of light filtered in through the curtains, and Jack felt very relieved as he unbolted the latch on the door.

It was Sahid.

"Are you all right, Jack?" Sahid questioned immediately upon seeing the weary, haggard-looking major. "I heard a scream. . . ."

"Yeah . . . I'm okay. . . . I guess you woke me up while I was having a nightmare." Jack rubbed his eyes, scratched an itch on the back of his neck, then invited his friend into the room. Immediately, Juno, who had been curled up alongside the bed, stood and padded cheerily over to Sahid.

"Ah, Juno," Sahid said, bending down to pet the animal on the head. "How are you, boy?"

Juno wagged his tail in response, seeming to link Sahid's presence with his former master, Ibrahim.

"There was someone trying to get in here last night," Jack said, dressing himself. "They came right up to the door. Juno and I both heard him—or them—or whoever it was. The guy actually started turning the doorknob!"

"Oh?"

"Yes, and he must have heard us, or something, cuz' he stopped suddenly, then turned and ran away! We followed him out into the street, but the guy just vanished."

"Vanished?"

"I'm telling you, Sahid, the guy was a pro!"

"A *pro!*"

"A professional. He was outta here faster than we could have believed possible, ran somewhere out into the street and then just vanished into thin air. It was spooky! I didn't get to sleep until about five or so this morning."

"Was this the nightmare you referred to?" Sahid questioned.

"No," Jack responded, slapping some water onto his face in preparation of shaving, "not at all. I'm serious, my friend, someone was here last night and it wasn't the first time."

"What do you mean, Major?"

"I'm saying that this guy has been following us, Sahid. I can't prove it, but I'm absolutely certain of it! I sensed his presence yesterday when you, Nisha, and that captain fellow . . . what's his name?"

"Captain Jadid."

"Yeah, that's right . . . Jadid. When you guys took off for Taza yesterday, I came back to the hotel, here, and suddenly felt a strong presence . . . like someone was watching me . . . watching all of us! But when I looked around, there wasn't anybody there!"

"Do you often feel or sense the presence of others?" Sahid inquired, with a strange look on his face, indicating that he was both curious and a little suspicious.

"Not always," Jack said. "Mostly when there is a reason for concern."

"Concern?"

"Yes, Sahid, concern! When something isn't quite right, or maybe even dangerous. And I'll tell you, my friend, I've learned to trust in that sixth sense. It never lets me down . . . which, by the way, is how I knew to eject from the Banshee before it exploded."

Sahid walked to the curtains and was about to draw them back when Jack suddenly shouted, "No! Please . . . leave them closed!"

"But it is morning, Major. There is sunlight outside. No one will be able to see us in here."

"I'm aware of that, Sahid, but I'd prefer to keep the curtains closed, if you don't mind."

"Not at all," Sahid countered respectfully.

"Did you locate your son?" Jack inquired, changing the subject.

"We know where he is, yes."

"Well, that's great! How about Jadid's kid? Were you able to locate him as well?"

"The boy is not there, Jack. At least, we don't think he is. It was a terrible blow for Captain Jadid. I fear they have taken him to another camp south of here. But we will find him, I assure you!"

"I'm sorry to hear that," Jack responded humbly. "It must be terribly difficult for Jadid."

"Truly," Sahid agreed.

"In any case, what about the radio? Were you able to locate the communications post?"

"We did. . . ."

"And . . . was there a shortwave?"

"Two of them, my friend."

"Excellent! How many operators?"

"Three."

"In a secured area?"

"It is a small building away from the rest of the encampment. We were not able to stay long . . . we did not wish to draw attention to our interest in the radio transmitter. Besides, we had not yet found Kashan. We needed to see as much as we could, without . . . how do you say it?"

"Blowing your cover?"

"That is one way, yes . . . not blowing our cover. The base commander was anxious to show Captain Jadid the central training school."

"So . . . he bought it then?"

"Bought it?"

"You know . . . believed your story?"

"Yes, Jack, he believed us. And he is expecting to give you the grand tour—as you Americans say—and invite you to dine with him in the afternoon. I am to be your official translator. You will, of course, have to speak German . . . or at least pretend to speak it. I will answer his questions for you and ask appropriate ones, as well. Are you a good German actor, Major Garrity?"

"Oh . . . I spent a few weeks of TDY in Frankfurt just a year ago . . . during the Gulf War . . . so I think I can handle myself."

"Very good, then. Shall we go? It would seem that the show is about to begin, yes?"

"Frankly, Scarlett . . . I thought you'd never ask."

44

The Juvenile Military Training Facility, Taza, Libya

The juvenile military training compound, Taza, would have looked very much like a college campus if it weren't for the tall fencing that surrounded the perimeter. In that sense it had the characteristics of a prison, a more realistic mark of its design and purpose.

Like all military camps there was a guard posted at the main gate, beyond which Jack could see a large yard area filled to capacity with marching cadets, each clad with desert fatigues and assault rifles.

The place was a boot camp. It brought back unpleasant memories for the major.

Punctuality in what they were attempting was vital, Jack was acutely aware of that. He and Sahid had met up with Nisha and Captain Jadid only five minutes before, just a couple of blocks away, and had changed automobiles. They were riding in an elegant Mercedes Benz limousine, which Jack noted to be luxurious and nearly brand new.

Jack and Captain Jadid were sitting in the back seat, while Nisha and her husband occupied the front. Sahid played the part of the chauffeur.

"Where did you get this limo?" Jack questioned, clearly impressed with Sahid's ingenuity.

"We are not without our ways, Major."

"You stole it then?" Jack teased, chuckling a little.

"Hardly, Major," Sahid said, glancing briefly over his shoulder at his American friend. "We have a full battalion of personnel posted here in Nalut, there is much undercover intelligence work that goes on here, so we must have vehicles . . . and this is one of those."

"Nice ride!"

"We are glad that you approve. But please, ready yourself, Major Garrity. We are about to enter the base."

"Ya vol, Herr Kommandant!"

Sahid and Nisha suppressed their smiles.

Without incident, the limo drove past the front gates and into the compound. It was clear that they'd been expected, and they were greeted appropriately when they arrived at the headquarters building.

The base commander was a middle-aged, dark-skinned Libyan with an unusually long nose and thick moustache. He was introduced to them as Colonel Ras Berkan. Colonel Berkan was a strict military commander, using sometimes less than human tactics to properly condition the young recruits sent to his facilities. He did not like the idea of this "meddler," although his outward mannerisms toward the German were very courteous and professionally respectful.

Berkan met the party at the steps leading into the central command post. He was flanked by two soldiers, perhaps no older than fifteen or sixteen, each armed with assault rifles and wearing battle fatigues. Jack was dismayed at the sight of so many young people wielding weapons and facing the extraordinary challenge of a military-imposed maturation.

Acting as a proper chauffeur and clever diplomat, Sahid parked the Mercedes, exited, and politely opened the door for Jack and the others.

"Ah . . . Lieutenant Hamadan!" Berkan said to Sahid, reaching out to shake his hand. "How good to see you . . . again."

"The pleasure is mine, Colonel," Sahid lied, returning the gesture.

"And of course, the general and his wife are with you this morning?"

"They are indeed, Colonel, and are looking forward to the luncheon."

"And Herr Stromberg? He has arrived safely then?"

"Just this morning, in fact. We are all here."

"Wonderful!" Berkan chimed politely, rubbing his hands together, then greeting the others as they exited the limousine one at a time.

"This must be Doctor Stromberg?"

"Yessir," Sahid said, courteously introducing Jack to the Colonel.

"How nice to meet you, Herr Doctor."

Sahid pretended to translate.

"Danke shon, Colonel Berkan. Der bericht vor Taza ist angezeichnet!"

Sahid looked at Jack with disbelief. He hadn't known that the major spoke German, and although the wording was broken and unpolished, Sahid recognized the statement and translated it for the colonel.

"The good doctor says it is nice to meet you, too, and that the reports he has read on Taza have been excellent."

"*Danke,* Herr Doctor. I'm flattered that you think so."

Again Sahid pretended to translate for Jack, and again the witty Major responded accordingly. Then, after a moment of exchanged pleasantries, the group climbed the steps and entered the building.

Jack had been introduced as a well-known, highly decorated education specialist for military schools with terminal graduate degrees in psychology and philosophy. He was noted to have taught thousands of students in the "Old" Germany principles of strict discipline through skilled techniques of mental conditioning that now promised to be extremely useful for the Libyan adolescent military camps.

Jack played the part of the doctor with such finesse and credibility that at times, Nisha, Sahid, and Jadid couldn't help but pass astonished glances back and forth.

Meanwhile, the three did their own share of playacting—Sahid as the bilingual chauffeur and obvious spokesman for the party, and Nisha and Jadid as military advisors from the presidential palace, whose primary responsibility was to ensure the success and safe passage of Doctor Stromberg. They, however, remained silent for the most part, acting rigid and unfriendly, allowing Jack and Sahid to play out the charade.

Colonel Berkan was an admirable host. He gave the emissaries a grand tour of the facilities, pointing out various programs that had been initiated to ensure the best possible outcome for each and every cadet. Along the way, he would occasionally discuss training techniques with Sahid and ask him to translate the ideas to Jack. And, of course, Jack—as the good German doctor—was only too happy to provide his own opinions, nodding his head this way and that in symbolic gestures of approval or disapproval.

At length the party arrived at the communications post. There was an impressive display of electronic gadgetry representing the highest quality and most up-to-date computer technology. Jack noted, with obvious delight, that instead of three military operators, as presupposed from the earlier discussions with Sahid, there was, in fact, only one man sitting at the station. And he was an extremely young fellow at that.

As soon as the group walked through the door, the vigilant communications officer sprang to his feet and stood at attention. He was young, to be sure, but very aware of the high-ranking officials who had entered his domain.

"As you were, Lieutenant," Colonel Berkan said, relieving the boy. He saluted, then returned to his post, replacing the headset he'd discarded while standing in respect.

Jack glanced at Nisha.

She winked briefly, American-like.

Captain Jadid saw the signal as well, and gave a slight nod of his head to Jack.

Jack returned the gesture, then in his broken German, suggested that they move on to the central command center from whence they had come, and look over the military training records of some of the boys.

"Fine!" the colonel said, "this way then."

"Excuse me, Colonel," Nisha said suddenly. "Is there a ladies' room nearby?"

"Certainly, Madam Marand. . . . Just down the hallway to your right."

"Thank you, Colonel." She turned, as if to proceed down the hallway, then spun around and added, "Why don't you all go on ahead. I will be but a moment or so, and will catch up with you then."

"Nonsense, Madam. We can wait right here! There is no hurry . . . is there, gentlemen?"

"Actually, Colonel," Captain Jadid interjected, "knowing my wife as I do, we might just as well move on ahead. Certainly she can catch up with us when she has freshened up a little . . . yes?"

"Well, that is, of course, all right with me, General Marand. But surely it is up to you."

Jadid turned to Nisha, and said, "Be quick, Kimi, and we will meet you back at the central command post."

"As you wish, Abyek," she answered respectfully. She then turned and vanished down the narrow hallway. The others exited the communications outpost and walked casually back to the main facility. Along the way, Colonel Berkan, still hoping to impress his guests, pointed to a part of the yard that was sectioned off from the rest of the outside area.

"That is the target range," he directed. "Most of the weapons we use are standard issue AK-47 assault rifles. The boys are trained in a fashion similar to the American Marines. We have acquired several training tapes, that were . . . how shall we say . . . left behind following the war in the Gulf. These tapes emphasize commando techniques proven most useful for our purposes. Most of the young recruits arrive ill prepared. Hardly a one has ever fired a weapon of any kind, let alone an assault rifle. But when they have graduated from the academy, they are skilled marksmen, and in many cases, fearless warriors for the new Libyan Elite!"

"Perhaps we might have a demonstration a bit later?" Sahid inquired, turning to Jack with another string of purposeless German gesturing and meaningless garble.

"If that is the doctor's wish, certainly! I can have some of our best squads perform a fine exhibition. . . . Doctor?"

"Heute nachmittag, vielleicht," Jack answered, responding to the question as falsely translated by Sahid.

"This afternoon, perhaps, the doctor says, if that is okay with you, Colonel."

"Certainly. This way, gentlemen."

Nisha opened the door of the bathroom slowly, just an inch or so. She peeked cautiously into the hallway, saw that everyone had left, and then walked to the Eastern-style toilet, and flushed the water through the system.

Reaching inside a small, hidden pocket sewn into a part of her upper garments, she then retrieved the coded message Jack had given to her early that morning. She then casually exited the bathroom.

Reaching the young officer, who was busy at his post, she walked up behind him and spoke. "Excuse me, Lieutenant . . ."

The boy whirled around in his chair, then started to stand.

"No, no, please. . . . Stay where you are, my friend. You do not need to get up." Nisha could see that her feminine beauty, for which she was most grateful, had not gone unnoticed by the boy. It was clear that he was greatly distracted, and uncomfortable, as he realized the two of them were alone.

"Madam?"

"I've always had an interest in radio equipment."

"You, madam?"

"Yes, Lieutenant . . . is that so unusual?"

"Most women . . . well—"

"I am not *most* women!" Nisha smiled, cutting him short. "I am the wife of a Libyan general!"

"Of course, madam," he swallowed, showing obvious signs of skittish nervousness.

"What is that unit over there, Lieutenant?" Nisha asked playfully, pointing to one of the shortwave transmitters.

The young lad turned his head respondingly. "It is a shortwave unit, madam . . ."

"Can you operate it?"

"Why, yes, madam! I am qualified on all of these systems."

"And that?" she pointed to something else. "What does that device do?"

"Oh . . . well . . . that is a decoder/scrambler." Nisha already knew what the electronic equipment was, and only pretended ignorance to bolster the boy's ego. "It is used for top priority messages from the presidential palace."

"How very interesting," Nisha again smiled. "But, are you skilled on all of these systems?"

"As I said, yes, madam. I understand them all. As a matter of fact, I enjoy this post very much!"

It was obvious to Nisha that her charms were working on the boy, as he was beginning to loosen up.

"I can see that you do, Lieutenant! May I please have a demonstration?"

"A demonstration?"

"Why not? I am bored."

"On what, madam?"

"Well," Nisha smiled, scratching her head, "how about the shortwave radio?"

"You want to listen in on some faraway conversation?"

"Sure! Why not? Can we do that?"

"Absolutely! We can listen in on any one of hundreds of channels . . . and with more than 500 watts of power in our transceivers, we can hear conversations from all over the world in many languages! I listen all the time!"

"Do you now?"

The boy put a hand over his mouth. "Perhaps I should not have told you that, madam . . . being the general's wife and all. You won't turn me in, will you?"

"Nonsense, Lieutenant. Please be at ease with me. I am, in many ways, as inquisitive as you are. I enjoy electronic equipment very much. But I do not get to play with it much, myself . . . a real pity, I assure you! Come . . . show me how the shortwave unit works!"

The young lad was beaming with excitement. He switched a couple of knobs on the panels in front of him, re-routing the audio signals from his headset to a main speaker, from which he could continue to monitor the central communications. He then moved over to the shortwave unit.

"How many channels are there?" Nisha inquired innocently.

"Nine hundred and ninety-nine, madam," he answered proudly.

"And, what if someone wanted to send Morse code over one of them?"

"Morse code?"

"Yes."

"Oh, that is easy. You see this panel over here?" The boy pointed to a small section from which protruded a single circular button.

"Yes," she answered.

"Transmissions are made by using this button . . . that is, if you know Morse code."

Pretending to be interested, Nisha reached over and depressed the button once, then a couple more times.

"Why don't we send a pretend message?" she suggested childishly.

"A pretend message?"

"Yes. Is there a channel that is not used often? One we could play with?"

"Oh, I don't think we should—"

"Lieutenant, *I* am able to do as I wish."

"But . . . ," the boy stumbled, "what if someone receives our message?"

"What of it? It wouldn't really be a message, just a pretend one!"

"Well, I suppose—"

"Good! Let's try it! What's a good, unused channel?"

"Most of them are monitored, madam, but upwards of, say, six hundred or higher are perhaps less used than most."

Nisha looked subtly down at the small piece of paper in her hand, and read the number Jack had written: *Channel seven, five, three.*

"How about . . . seven, five, three?" she queried innocently.

"Seven, five, three?" he verified, renaming the numerical figures.

"Yes . . . seven, five, three. Let's try that one, okay?"

"Fine, madam," he answered, positioning the three digital characters accordingly. "There . . . all set! Now, what did you want your message to say?"

"Please, Lieutenant," Nisha whispered, placing her hand over the hand of the boy. "Let me work the transmitter . . . may I?"

"Uh . . . sure . . . if you want to. I mean . . . do you know Morse code, madam?"

"Not really," she again lied. "I just want to try it, is all . . . see how it feels."

He got out of the seat, allowing Nisha to sit at the console.

In a mixed-up series of highly classified scrambled letters and numbers, Nisha skillfully pecked away on the little button. And although skilled himself with the international Morse code, the young lieutenant thought, with simpleminded amusement, that his beautiful, charming guest was sending out a message of complete nonsense—never suspecting that somewhere, far out in the Mediterranean Sea, activity on the USS *Nimitz* was about to change dramatically.

45

1121 Hours, 6 January 1992—
USS Nimitz, *The Mediterranean Sea*

Junior Grade Lieutenant Ritchie Robertson was about as bored as one could get. He had received a set of very peculiar orders more than a week ago that had kept him glued to a small computer console that did essentially nothing.

Its overall funtion was to scan hundreds of channels of a shortwave system and to lock onto any one of them that its operator thought prudent. But Ritchie's job had been altered. Instead of monitoring the entire shortwave band, his sole responsibility was to keep an ear tuned into one seldom-if-ever-used frequency—Channel 753.

"Seven . . . five . . . three," he mumbled to himself. "I don't want you taking your eyes or ears off of channel seven, five, three. You understand that, Lieutenant?"

That's what Besserman had told him, and in a way, he kind of resented it. Oh, sure, he knew that Lieutenant Besserman was the admiral's right-hand man. But all this "cloak and dagger" stuff was really wearing on him.

"What is it I'm supposed to hear?" he said with a disgusted inaudible voice. "Every day it's the same thing. 'Anything come through on the channel, yet, Ritchie?' 'No, Lieutenant,' I answer, 'nothing has come through! But I promise you that if there is so much as a faint buzzing sound . . . why . . . you can bet you'll be the first one to know, sir.'"

Ritchie humored himself over that particular memory. Besserman had had it coming! He drove the junior grade communications officer right to the very precipice of insanity with his constant probing. For crying out loud, didn't Besserman trust him, or what? If his only job was to monitor channel seven, five, three . . . surely the lieutenant should realize that any messages received would be promptly delivered!

There were two small lights on the panel in front of him. A red one and a green one. That was the other thing! Sometimes Ritchie wondered if Besserman thought him to be a complete moron! "Are you sure that the red light never came on today, Ritchie?"

"Lieutenant Besserman, sir? Excuse me for sounding perhaps a tad sarcastic, but your continual reference to the red light is a bit frustrating, sir. I mean, with all due respect, sir, my job is a simple one, really. It requires two things . . . and two things only—the use of my eyes, which have kept a constant watch on the red light, and my ears which are covered at all times with this uncomfortable headset, sir! I am tuned into frequency seven, five, three, sir, and have never once seen the red light illuminate! As a matter of fact, sir, if the little red light were to come on . . . it would stay on! And, as you can see, sir, it is not lit!"

Besserman, though obviously annoyed at the junior grade lieutenant's burlesque mockery, realized that he had been a bit pushy, and so he left the young officer without a word. Once again, Ritchie had wittingly made a fool out of the admiral's aide.

Looking down at his watch, Ritchie noted that it was nearly time for lunch. Momentarily, his relief would arrive and he'd be able to grab himself some chow. First, however, he'd stop at one of the machines and pick up a soft drink. He was dying of thirst.

The Communications Intelligence Center, or the C.I.C., was always teeming with life. Ritchie was fond of the electronics that gave the center its steady heartbeat. Twenty or more commissioned officers were always working at the vast array of computers, radar scanners, radios, and intelligence-gathering equipment. The dim glow from the many monitors and different colored lights scattered across the consoles gave Ritchie the feeling that he was on some sort of star cruiser, speeding through the cosmos instead of bobbing up and down—as the *Nimitz* often did—with the unsettled currents of the great oceans and seas.

He glanced across the room and noted with pride that he was an important part of the ship's overall team of professionals. And although his current assignment seemed trite, at best, its purpose was probably more important than he realized. He'd do well to bite his tongue and listen and watch for a signal, instead of bucking against the system and the tedium of his daily post.

Turning back to the shortwave console, Ritchie reached over to the volume knob for the headset and turned it up just a hair. As always he could hear the faint, steady hum of the unit's power supply—but still, no incoming message.

To his immediate right two smaller buttons activated test surges of electrical power that would illuminate the red lamp or the green one. The green, however, was always lit, indicating the active state of readiness . . . all systems go. He put his finger on the right button and pressed down. The red light lit up just as he expected, then blinked off the second he lifted his finger from the button.

"Works fine," he mumbled. "I'm sure old Besserman would—"

Suddenly the light blinked on again.

Ritchie reached over to the test button and pressed down on it a couple of times. Surely, this couldn't be a message signal—or could it?

His heart began to beat rapidly.

He released the small test button, but the red light remained lit.

Immediately above the tabletop panel, an automatic cassette recorder suddenly awoke as if from a long, deep sleep and began to turn. Another smaller light told Ritchie that the unit was recording.

Then, through the headset, Ritchie heard the Morse code. It was unusual, to be sure, but it was definitely a message of some kind—and powerfully resonant!

He pulled a pencil free from the small sleeve pocket in his jacket and began writing down the message.

D...O...(stop) Y...O...U...(stop) B...E...L...I...E...V...E...(stop) I...N...(stop) G...H...O...S...T...S...(stop) L...A...R...R...Y...(stop) I...S...(stop) 1...2...(stop) L...L...O...Y...D...(stop) I...S...(stop) 3...3...(stop) 1...7...0...1...0...0...(end)

The message repeated itself once more and Ritchie frantically copied it again to make sure he'd gotten it right.

Even after the signal ceased altogether, Ritchie quickly rewound the tape recorder, listened to the short and long blips and beeps, rewrote the message a third time, and then called Lieutenant Besserman.

Admiral Doxey was sitting at the small desk in his quarters when Besserman arrived.

There was a knock at the cabin door.

"Come in!" the admiral yelled, glancing briefly at the door. "Ah, . . . Lieutenant Besserman, what—"

"A message just came in, sir!"

"What?"

"Seven, five, three, sir . . . a message came in. . . ."

"You have it with you?"

"Yessir, right here, sir." Besserman handed the note to the admiral.

"And the tape?"

"That too, sir." He handed the recorded cassette tape to the admiral.

"Anyone know about this, Besserman?"

"No, sir. Just Lieutenant Robertson and myself, sir."

"And where's Robertson now, Lieutenant?"

"In C.I.C., sir. I left him at the shortwave console and told him to continue monitoring the frequency."

"Does he know how to keep his mouth shut?"

"Yessir."

"All right now, Besserman, you listen to me. I need you to fetch the captain on the double! Be discreet, Son, you understand me? Get him here as quick as you can—but don't make a big to-do about it! You got that?"

"Yessir—affirmative, sir!"

Admiral Doxey unfolded the coded note, read it once, then picked up the orange telephone near the bedstand. He punched in three numbers, then pressed a red button on the right side of the receiver.

In the ear piece, the admiral could hear a series of faint, but audible, clicks and tones. Then, after about ten seconds or so, he heard the on-again, off-again beeping of an electronic buzzer that sounded like a busy tone, but was—as the admiral well knew—a call signal at the other end of the satellite-linked phone system.

Second Lieutenant Jeanene Bergin heard the unfamiliar beeping noise coming from the security intelligence phone, and knew at once that an important message from the Mediterranean fleet awaited Lieutenant General Mick Ludlow.

Even as part of the Banshee team, Jeanene knew that she was *not* to pick up the orange phone. Ever! Instead, she walked to her desk just outside the general's office, opened up the bottom right-hand side drawer, and pressed firmly down onto the red button hidden under the table.

General Mick Ludlow was inside the PX. A small electronic beeper attached to his belt suddenly came to life. He instantly dropped the cereal boxes he held in his hands and asked his young aide to pay the bill and bring the groceries to his quarters.

"I'll reimburse you later," he called, rushing out of the base commissary.

He went quickly to the base headquarters and rushed into his office. Jeanene was standing in the doorway, pointing at the orange phone.

"It has been buzzing for about two minutes or so, sir."

"Stay right there, Jeanene. Grab a piece of paper and a pencil and be ready if I need you!"

"Yessir."

The general picked up the receiver.

"Carl?"

"That you, Mick?" the voice at the other end asked.

"It's me, old-timer! What d'ya got?"

Seven, five, three . . . active!"

"Oh?" The general was excited, but tried to remain as calm as possible. He shifted his eyes toward Jeanene, who was standing just inside his office, pencil and paper in hand. He covered the mouthpiece of the phone, and whispered for her to come in and sit down at his desk, motioning for her to be ready to write.

She responded quickly and professionally.

"Give it to me, Carl," the general said softly.

"All right. You ready?"

"Shoot."

"Okay . . . it's perfect! It reads exactly as it should! *Do you believe in ghosts?* You get that?"

"Uh-huh . . . got it!"

"Good. Now . . . you ready for the second part?"

"Ready." The general nodded affirmatively at Jeanene. She gestured that she had clearly written the first part of the message and was ready to continue.

"Okay, here it is. *Larry is one, two.*"

"Right . . . okay . . . Larry is one, two . . . got it!"

"Lloyd is three, three."

"All right . . . Lloyd is three, three. Okay . . . got that one, too. And the last part?"

"You ready?"

"Yeah, give it to me."

"Okay, Mick, the final sequence reads *One . . . seven . . . zero . . . one . . . zero . . . and zero.*"

"One . . . seven . . . zero . . . one . . . zero . . . zero. Got it."

The general looked at the numbers, then asked, "You guys all set?"

"That's affirmative, Mick. We're in motion as we speak!"

"Hey, Carl?"

"Yes, General?"

"He's alive!"

"He is indeed, Mick. And I think it's time we brought him home, don't you, sir?"

"Go get him, Admiral!"

"We'll do that, Mick. We'll get your boy home for ya! You just sit back and watch the magic of the U.S. of A. Navy!"

General Ludlow hung the telephone up and turned to Jeanene. She handed him the written message and made a request. "Is this the message you've hoped for, General?"

"Yes, Jeanene, as a matter of fact, it is. Jack's alive! Somehow . . . someway . . . he made it out of the Banshee, escaped capture . . . or escaped *from* capture, and made it to a radio. The *Nimitz* picked up the message just moments ago."

"What does it all mean, sir?" she questioned innocently.

"Well, it's simple, really." Picking up the paper, he read and translated it to Jeanene. "The first phrase. 'Do you believe in ghosts' is the code for Garrity having survived, is well, and is able to escape the country. The second part, 'Larry is twelve, and Lloyd is thirty-three,' means that he will rendezvous with a U.S. Naval submarine at twelve degrees longitude and thirty-three degrees latitude. And finally, the last sequence of numbers, 'one seven, oh, one hundred,' gives the date and the time for the pick up. January seventh, at one o'clock in the morning! He's coming home, Jeanene! He's coming home!"

"And what do we do now, sir?"

"What do you mean?"

"I mean, do we assist in the pick up?"

"No. Leave that up to the Navy. But we'll have him flown back here to Aviano as soon as he's picked up and safely aboard the sub."

"I hope Major Garrity's all right, sir."

"Yea . . . so do I, Jeanene . . . so do I."

46

Antelope Valley Hospital,
Lancaster, California

"Good morning, Linda."

Working to force her eyelids open, Linda Garrity found herself looking into the soft and beautiful eyes of her friend Ladawn Kastleman.

"Sorry we awakened you, Linda," her husband Mark added, "but we are on our way to Salt Lake City to visit Ladawn's folks and we just had to see how you're doing."

"Oh, thank you . . . both of you . . . for being so thoughtful. I . . . I just feel terrible about your Bronco."

"Actually, Linda," Ladawn smiled, "you did us a favor. I've been trying to get Mark to buy me a new Suburban for our growing brood of boys, and now he has done it."

"Jack has great insurance, Linda," Mark added. "We pick up our Suburban in about an hour, and then it's off to Utah."

"Oh, I'm so glad," Linda sighed. "Uh . . . have you seen Trish, or Little Jack?"

"Well," Ladawn again smiled, taking her friend's hand in her own, "we just stopped and . . . and saw Little Jack. The nurse said that he's way overdue . . . to wake up."

A tear dropped freely from Linda's left eye. She could sense the Kastlemans' discomfort in talking about Little Jack. But she also appreciated their support and their kindness.

"We'll make it somehow, Ladawn," she whispered. "Trish and I talk to him every day, and I just know that Jack is praying for us."

"Does he know about the accident?" Mark asked innocently.

"No, not really. He's on a very classified mission, and so we can't make contact with him. But he knows . . . somehow he *knows*. I just feel it."

The three friends visited for several more minutes, and then finally, without hesitating, Mark asked Linda if he could offer a special prayer for her and for her family.

Linda quickly agreed. And so before leaving, Mark and Ladawn each took one of Linda's hands and Mark offered a simple yet tear-filled prayer—pouring out their hearts to the God of Heaven for a literal miracle in their behalf. Somehow . . . someway . . . He would answer.

47

The Juvenile Military Training Facility, Taza, Libya

Major Garrity sat at the small table peering into the greenish luminescence of the computer screen in front of him. The others, Colonel Berkan, Sahid, and Jadid were there as well, each looking over the major's shoulders at the electronically recorded dossiers.

Pretending to be arbitrary in his selective search, Jack, with the help of Sahid to translate, had identified and requested to interview three young cadets. The first, an Iranian-born immigrant named Abul Tartus, was just barely fourteen years of age. He was of no interest to Jack but was simply a decoy.

The second to be interviewed was a Libyan-born youngster named Rafael Seyek, who was a bit older—nearly sixteen—and someone who showed obvious signs of military prowess. He had been a model soldier, and was the personal choice of Colonel Berkan for the interview. Jack had acquiesced respectfully.

The final lad to be interviewed, of course, was the unlikely name of Kashan Tashwan, a thirteen-year-old boy known to the colonel simply as one of the newer recruits.

The colonel dispatched one of the ever-present young sentries to locate and return with the three boys. He then turned back to the guests and discussed some of the classifying techniques used to determine whether a cadet would progress or digress in the system.

Jack pretended to be interested.

Ten minutes later, the door to the records room swung open and the three military-clad future soldiers of the Libyan Elite walked into the room.

But something wasn't right.

The young sentry who had been selected to fetch the youngsters was nowhere to be seen. In his place, standing quite literally out of place, was a full-grown man with dark black hair and a burly moustache. His left shoulder and arm were in a sling, and a large, gaping gash, sewn together with black stitching, ran along his entire left cheek. This stitching gave the man a very malicious—almost demonic—appearance.

For a moment, no one moved.

No one knew who the stranger was.

And no words were exchanged.

Then, as if signaled by some phantom mediator, two more men eased through the door. They were both dressed to the hilt in the distinct uniform of the Elite's Special Forces unit.

The two were Lucca Rovigo's men. And the man standing between them was none other than the malevolent general, himself.

It took Colonel Berkan a second or two to catch his breath. He recognized Lucca, despite the bandages and the dark sunglasses covering the general's eyes, and he greeted the man with a feeble smile and a quivering salutation.

"General Rovigo, sir . . . ah . . . what a pleasant surprise!"

Lucca said nothing. Instead, he just stood there and stared at Jack.

Jack rose slowly from the seat at the computer console, and stared unnerved back at the ghostly menace.

"So, Major Garrity . . . we meet at last," the guttural voice said, speaking in near-perfect English.

The two flanking soldiers raised their weapons.

"I am sure you realize what a great problem you have been to our country . . . yes?" He walked a few steps forward, putting his hands onto the shoulders of Kashan. "Tell me," he continued, "is this the boy you seek?"

Sahid felt his blood chill. He looked longingly into his son's eyes, and Kashan wistfully returned the gaze. But neither showed emotion, and neither showed fear.

With his free hand, Lucca withdrew an army-issue Colt .45. He raised the gun to the boy's head.

"And you, Sahid," he sneered, "did you really think that you could get away with your charade?"

"Get away . . . with what, General?"

"Oh, how charming . . . naive, are we? Innocent, are we? Surely, great Rebel Commander, you did not think that you could forever elude me . . . escape your destiny? Your pitiful freedom fighters are a laughing joke, Sahid. And the little diversion back at the Sidi oil fields . . . did you truly think you could win? We are slaughtering your pathetic band of fools! They will die for their sins! All of them! It is only a matter of days, and here you are, so pathetically predictable! The lamb in the lion's den, trapped at last!

"Oh," he continued, his voice increasing in volume, "how terribly sad you must feel, Commander Sahid. How sad, indeed! I can see that you desire to hold your son. Perhaps you have come to Taza to free young Kashan, yes? Also charming . . . and pitifully predictable.

"But I don't wish to see the great rebellion commander with sad eyes. Perhaps you are right, Sahid. Perhaps we should free your handsome young son from his miserable internment, yes?

"Perhaps a bullet to the head?"

"No!" Sahid screamed.

Lucca smiled. Then with this thumb, he released the safety switch on the Colt with an audible click.

"What is happening here?" Colonel Berkan suddenly yelped. "Who is Sahid? And this Major Garrity, who is he, General Rovigo? These are the emissaries from the presidential palace—"

"Is that what they told you, Colonel?"

"I . . . I received a coded message, General . . . a message from Haman Al-Rashid, himself!"

"Did you, now? How very interesting. You idiot! You spoke to Rashid yourself?"

"Well . . . no, sir. I . . . I received the message from the—"

"Be silent, you fool! And stand out of my way! These are not political agents from the presidential palace. Nor are they from the foreign embassy or any other governmental office inside Libya. These are spies and traitors!

"This one," he continued, pointing to Sahid, "is Sahid Tashwan, a once trusted officer of the Elite. The boy, here, is his son, Kashan. They were trying to free him, Colonel. Sahid and his wife, Nisha, lead the rebellion against the state. They are traitors, Colonel! Do you understand that?"

Colonel Berkan's eyes grew wide with anger and disgust at his own gullibility.

"Then . . . who are these two?" he asked, pointing to Captain Jadid and Jack.

"That one there," Lucca shouted, pointing to Jadid, "is also a traitor! He *was* a captain in the Elite, but he is now a dead man! He will be hanged for treason! He, too, has a son here. I am surprised that they did not trick you into bringing him here as well."

"Wha—?"

"His name is Kala, is that not correct, Captain?"

Jadid said nothing.

"Kala?" the colonel questioned. "I am not aware of any cadet by that name." He paused for a moment, then added, "What is the boy's last name, General?"

Suddenly Captain Jadid's heart began to race. Why hadn't he thought of it before? Jadid and his wife had given their son a nickname, a name by which he had grown accustomed to being called by his schoolmates and other friends. Could it possibly be that Kala had been registered into the camp by his nickname? Benji, he whispered silently, fighting back a tear. My beloved son . . . dear, dear Benji. . . .

"Jadid! You fool! This is the boy's father! Did you not listen? He is Captain Nador Jadid. His son's name is Kala Jadid. But no matter. We will deal with him later. For now, I should like to introduce you to Major Jack Garrity, the American infidel who has come to destroy our peaceful government!"

Colonel Berkan focused his eyes onto the man he'd come to know as the German doctor, Herr Stromberg, the military training specialist from the old Eastern Bloc country of Germany.

The colonel's anger grew and he suddenly wished to personally destroy the American imposter who had made such a fool out of him! But he knew that the wrath of Lucca Rovigo was far more sinister and horrific than anything he could possibly hope to inflict on the American. He would abdicate that power of life and death to his respected leader.

"Major Jack Garrity?"

"Yes, Colonel . . . an American Air Force pilot sent here to destroy our national security secrets and weapons. And I can tell you, he has been all too effective. Many of our installations are ruined or completely destroyed because of him. But what is more important, he has murdered my brother!"

Jack felt a chilling river of ice course through his veins. His brother? he thought. When had that happened?

"And now it is time for nemesis! I have waited a long time, traveled many miles, and suffered much pain, simply so that I could see this day for myself. And I assure you, Colonel, this American infidel will die for his crimes . . . and I will be his executioner!"

Lucca turned his gaze back to Sahid. It was first things first for the Libyan general. Besides, he wanted to save Jack for last.

"First, however, there is the matter of young Kashan here," Lucca smirked, still holding the loaded .45 to the boy's head. "Even if he *is* here at the academy preparing to be a soldier, it is clear to me that he will turn against the state if he has a chance. . . . For this reason, I believe it is time to eliminate them both. First the son, and then Sahid.

"Are you ready to watch your boy die, Commander?"

Sahid gritted his teeth and stood as still as stone. He was both afraid and fiercely angry—and he was equally sure that Lucca Rovigo was a complete egotistical psychopath. The sudden longing he felt for his son was so intense he thought his heart was going to melt. He wanted to rush forward and magically swoop the boy into his arms and save him from the crazed military leader. Yet there simply was no hope. He knew a single step forward would end his life with a shower of bullets from one or both of the guards posted on either side of the general.

He was helpless.

Jack, too, was breathless and immovable. He was standing less than five feet away from where Lucca was holding Kashan, but he didn't dare move any closer, for fear of being instantly shot. His mind was racing wildly. He ached for his friend Sahid and for his undaunted son. Silently he sifted through various options, searching for a solution.

Suddenly Jack remembered the *source.* The great power of celestial intervention; the one being in all the universe who could alter any earthly condition, including a single episode in a human son's or daughter's life.

His heart, teeming with the purest faith in God's ability to intervene, was suddenly overwhelmed with love.

"Beloved Father," he silently prayed, blocking out the words of the crazed man before him. "Wouldst thou this boy should die? that he and his father should be slaughtered like wild beasts? They are peacemakers, servants of their people. Love in their hearts and righteous conviction motivates them beyond simple charity. Theirs is a Samaritan kind of love . . . and I have grown close to them, as though they were my own flesh! Assist me, Father . . . show me the way . . . and I will do as thou would direct me to save their lives."

A quiet, soul-piercing response followed—similar to the impression that had guided him during the final few seconds of the Banshee flight—but peaceful and resonant, warm and embracing.

Jack's uncertainty was gone. He was suddenly spirited with strength he had never before known.

Lucca had been psychotically amused with Sahid's apparent fear, allowing valuable seconds of time to elapse while slowly tightening his squeeze on the trigger.

He was really going to do it! He was going to execute the innocent child before the horrified eyes of his own father!

Jack leaped!

A shot was fired. Then another.

Kashan felt the menacing grip of the demented captor loosen, and the boy dropped instinctively to the floor.

Jack's body hit Lucca with savage fury, knocking the leader off his feet and sending him flailing uncontrollably to the floor—landing on top of the child.

Two more shots rang out, and Jack felt an intense searing pain rip through his lower chest and left thigh. He'd been shot!

Everything around him became a whirlwind of confusion and rapidly fading sight and sound. He lost his grip on the here-and-now and saw clairvoyant images of Linda, Little Jack, and Trish reaching out to him, weeping, pleading with him to hang on.

But to what?

Life?

It was too late, forever too late. They would have to go it alone . . . find another husband and father . . . be strong without him. . . .

"Good-bye . . . ," he whispered, tumbling in slow motion toward the cold, dark floor.

His strength faded and vanished.

He came to rest on his side, staring with near-lifeless eyes across the expanse of the polished tile floor. He experienced an unusual feeling of euphoria, followed by a lengthy string of pleasant memories of people dear to him.

His mother—

His father—

His dearly beloved Linda—

His children—

His final thought was a lovely song his grandfather had taught him . . . a meaningful serenade about life's greatest treasure—the enduring, eternal relationship of families.

Jack whispered the words of the final verse, remembering the tender moment years earlier when Grandpa Garrity did the same, then passed peacefully on to that place beyond the veil.

> The wise old man was silent now,
>   resting all alone. . . .
> He closed his eyes, then smiled and said,
>   "At last, I'm going home."

Jack's eyes didn't close.

Tears welled up in them instead and flowed down across his face, falling at last to the floor.

Darkness came.

Silence complete—

And he smiled.

48

Antelope Valley Hospital,
Lancaster, California

Linda Garrity awoke with a start.

"Jack!" she cried, still living the visions of the dream. She had been so close to her husband inside the subconscious pageant that it startled her to awaken and realize it had only been a dream. And thank heavens for that, because in the twilight world of the dreamscape, her beloved husband had died.

"Oh, Jack," she cried tenderly, "please don't die on me! I need you, my love. Come home to us. . . . We all need you!"

She turned with difficulty a quarter-way around in her wheelchair and retrieved a Kleenex tissue from the bedstand next to her son. With that, she wiped away the senseless tears and resolved to stop crying so easily.

It was hard, though.

She crumpled the partially moist tissue in her left hand and reached over to stroke her son's forehead with the other.

It was dark outside. Late.

The clock above the door said two-thirty in the morning.

She had fought for the right to stay by her son, and was glad that the medical staff had finally given in. It appeared that Doctor Moody was a family man, himself, and had sensed Linda's need to be with Little Jack.

She was grateful to have a doctor like Moody. There was concern and genuine compassion in the man—a true humanitarian—the kind of individual a doctor should be.

Linda enjoyed the quiet.

At this time of the night she felt extremely close to her son, and took comfort in being able to speak to him—even if he didn't, or couldn't, respond. They had talked about everything—the hope for recovery, his courageous life-saving efforts, and the nasty accident itself. Talking into her son's ear about the accident, Linda had apologized so many times she couldn't find further words to say. They also talked about the continual uncertainty of Jack, clinging to the words *hope* and *faith* in his behalf.

Tonight, however, Linda felt a need to avoid that particular conversation. The dream she had just experienced had been bitterly realistic and painfully depressing. She had to remain positive—especially around Little Jack—if she ever hoped to keep her sanity.

Her husband was alive . . . he *had* to be!

Leaving Little Jack's side for a moment, Linda carefully placed her hands on the wheels of the wheelchair she was sitting in and pushed her way over to the window. The sky was breathtakingly beautiful—rich with a vast wilderness of stars that seemed to have a life of their own. She made out a few constellations, inwardly fascinated by the brilliant movements that seemed to give the stars their heartbeat.

"Millions of them," she whispered. "Billions!" How many alone were inside that astrological ocean called the Milky Way?

She liked to look at the stars. They seemed to provide a soothing comfort she couldn't explain. Her thoughts, however, centered on her husband. Often, while looking out into the firmament of heaven, she would pick out a constellation, a planet, or the Milky Way, itself, and make a wish. It was always a simple one—that Jack, too, could see those same stars, and that he was alive and would come back to her like he had promised in the letter.

But there was something more to the stars. It was that place, somewhere among them that was home to the God of all living things—the world some called celestial, where the Father of mankind looked longingly at his children with fervent hope that they would cease evil charades and learn to love and forgive one another.

"Father," she whispered, looking into the deep expanse of the galaxy, "I suppose it's a tad silly of me to trouble you as often as I do—and forgive me if I seem overly repetitious—but I have nowhere else to turn. I am dreadfully alone, dear Father, and I find myself doubting my own heart.

"I had a terribly sad dream tonight that has lingered inside my soul and weighs down upon me in a painful and wearisome way. It was my husband . . . Jack. I . . . I saw him die . . . and could not save him. . . . Oh, I hurt so much inside!

"I do not understand why he was taken from me, or why my only son lies beside me in a coma. . . . Father, there are many things that I do not comprehend.

"But I do know that you see all things and know all things. . . . And although it might sound selfish of me, loving my two men the way I do, my single prayer tonight—and every night—is that you will watch over them, protect them. And please . . . if it is thy will, bring them back home to me."

Linda lowered her head and wept. Then, slowly, she wheeled back to the bedside of her comatose son and took his warm hand into her own.

"Come back to me, Little Jack. . . . Come back home, please."

49

0017 Hours, 7 January 1992

Major Jack Garrity slowly opened his eyes. At first everything was blurry and rather dark.

A familiar sound was gently tickling the innermost regions of his ears. It was soothing in its own way, reminding him of days past when his world was carefree and painless—resting near the stream at his favorite spot at Big Bear.

Jack finally recognized the sound of ocean tides gently lapping at the sands. In his mind, he could see out into the sea. It was nighttime and fairly dark. But from where he was positioned, he could see the nearest three lines of the foam-crested breakers surging toward him from out of the gloom.

A sudden shiver of dreadful cold ran up through his body, causing him great discomfort.

And there was pain.

Intense pain!

"How could that be?" he whispered audibly. "No one is supposed to feel pain after they've died."

He shivered.

He wasn't just cold, he was freezing!

Was this Hades?

That was supposed to be a hot place. Besides, what was he doing in Hades anyway? Sure, there had been times in his life when he hadn't done the right thing . . . choices made that were certainly foolish at the time. But for the most part, Jack had honestly believed that his life—especially his adult life—had been honorable. It had been a military life, a bit hard on the family, and all . . . but an honest life, and basically true blue to those principles he had been taught in Reno as a child.

Then why was he so cold and feeling so much pain?

As his eyes began focusing properly, Jack noted with surprise that he was lying on his back looking up at the stars. They were beautiful—that much was certain—but not what he had expected to see when he came to.

Came to? he considered. Wait a minute. . . . I'm not supposed to come to staring at the stars, am I? I don't feel like I'm dead. I hurt too much to be dead! But if not dead, then what? Where am I?

He focused on his senses.

Sight. The view of the stars. A sliver of a moon just barely visible inside his peripheral vision. Otherwise dark. The middle of the night.

Sound. A gentle wind faintly whistling across the sky. The surf. The sea. Waves coming in one at a time and gently caressing the beach.

Smell. Definitely the smell of the sea.

Touch. A blanket covering him. A cotton blanket. Sand. He could feel it underneath his body. He toyed with it, allowing it to sift through his fingers. Cold sand. And something else . . . a wet something . . . here all of a sudden! A wet, slimy something now sliding across his cheek.

A wet something?

A slurping sound?

Rapid breathing?

A dog licking his face.

A dog?

"Juno!"

Jack opened and closed his eyes a couple of times, and finally shook free from the numbing clutches of unconsciousness—until at last he realized the reality of his situation.

He wasn't dead! He was wounded.

He wasn't in hell or heaven. Instead he was lying on his back on a sandy beach somewhere—free at last from the menacing exploits of Lucca Rovigo.

And there was Juno licking him on the face!

"Major Garrity?" the voice said just to his left. "Are you all right, Major?"

"Sa . . . Sahid?" Jack responded weakly.

"It is I, Jack! How wonderful to see you alive again! We thought you were dead!"

"You too, huh?"

"All of us! We were all so very worried for you. But Nisha found a pulse, dressed your wounds, and gave you drink."

"Gave me drink?"

"Of course, Major, so that you would get well."

Jack wondered what kind of drink Sahid was referring to, but decided he didn't have the strength or the inclination to inquire—and so he forgot about it.

Gathering more and more of his wits about him, and initiating some simple, physical movement to assure himself that he was not, in fact, dead—and that he was only dreaming this interesting scenario. Jack rolled his head to the right, then asked, "Where am I, Sahid?"

"We are at the rendezvous point. We await word from your people. That is, of course, if Nisha was successful at sending the message."

"At the beach?" Jack asked, both astonished and somewhat leery. "How did we get here? . . . And what about Lucca? And Kashan . . . is he okay?"

"One question at a time, Major. Yes, we are at the beach. We have been here for about an hour, possibly longer. It is twenty minutes past midnight, and we are—as I have said—waiting for your people to arrive, however that may be."

"They'll come by boat," Jack said softly.

"By boat, then. Good. But to answer perhaps all of your questions, I shall tell you what has happened since you fell unconscious back in the records room at Taza.

"As you may remember, Nisha did not accompany us into the records room. She was, of course, delivering your message—which, by the way, she affirms she accomplished. After she completed that task, she was about to walk out of the communications center and rejoin us when she saw General Lucca Rovigo and his men climb out of an automobile in front of the command center.

"Other guards under Lucca's command were posted immediately down at the main gates to prohibit anyone from exiting or entering the compound.

"That was when she spotted Kashan. General Rovigo had arrived at the precise moment when Colonel Berkan's errand boy was returning with our son and with the other cadets you had requested. Do you remember that much, Jack?"

"Yes," Jack answered sluggishly, "I do remember."

"Well," Sahid continued, "Lucca intercepted the children, shooed the courier on his way, and brought the young recruits to us in the records office. You, of course, know the rest of that part of the story. But what you don't know is that Nisha created a diversion just about the same time you risked your own life to save our son!

"Jack," he continued, "we are in your debt! Doubly so, as a matter of fact. For had you not thrown yourself at Lucca, he would surely have killed me as well.

"We thank you, Major."

"You are welcome, my friend. But, tell me, what happened exactly?"

"The shots that were fired came from Nisha's gun. She shot and severely wounded one of the guards who stood with the general. But she was not able to disable the second one. He turned to her and returned the fire . . . missing her . . . praise be to God!

"At the same moment Lucca fired his own weapon, wounding you. Other guards Nisha had not seen rushed into the compound, and it was then that we realized that we had to escape."

"But . . . what about Lucca? What did he do after shooting at me?"

"There was much confusion at the time, and somehow the general, himself, was shot—although I do not think he was killed—"

"You do not *think?* What do you mean by that, Sahid? He was either dead or he wasn't. You couldn't tell?"

"We did not remain in the room long enough to find out, Major. You see, it was Kashan who responded quickly and decisively. He turned on the general immediately after you were shot and took possession of Lucca's gun. It all happened so quickly! I, myself, was startled at my son's bravery, and realized right then that I had to make a move of my own.

"With Nisha outside in the hallway, and Kashan now in control of the general, who had fallen from his own wounds, I leaped onto Colonel Berkan and overpowered him. Captain Jadid and I locked the colonel, the wounded general, and the last remaining, also wounded soldier into a closet at the far end of the room. It was most fitting, Major! And I must say, very much a pleasure to have locked them up like animals, just as they have done to so many of our people!

"But that, of course, is not important! What is important is the blessed fact that we all escaped. And in answer to your question, we do not know if the general lived or died, because we did not stay to find out. We knew that you might be dead, but we were not sure. So we carried you out of a back door and eventually escaped in the confusion."

"What happened to Nisha and Kashan?"

"When we met up with some of Kashan's friends, he and his mother went for medical supplies . . . for you, Jack. Nisha had already discovered your heartbeat and we were determined to save you from dying on us!"

"Yes . . . I know . . . so that I can still fulfill my part of the mission, right?"

"Wrong, Major!" Sahid reprimanded. "We saved your life because you are like family to us! You were willing to sacrifice your own life for the life of our son!" Sahid knelt down beside Jack's prostrate body and slid an arm under the major's head, slowly and gently lifting him into a seated position. Curiously, Jack did not feel as much pain as he had expected, and so he looked calmly into his friend's eyes.

"Major Garrity," Sahid spoke softly, "we believe that your God . . . *our* God . . . sent you to us! You have learned much about our people, things that we trust you will relate to your president.

"While we were driving you here to Zuwarah—"

"Zu . . . what?"

"Zuwarah, Major. It is the name of this beach we are on. It is the longitude/latitude setting you instructed."

"Oh . . . okay."

"But as I was saying, in answer to your question, while we were driving here to Zuwarah, Nisha tended to your wounds and noted that they were not fatal. In fact, both areas where the bullets entered your body were spared the trauma of having a vital organ hit, or having a major blood vessel severed. In essence, Major, Nisha and I reasoned that your God saved your life . . . not us! He has prepared you for something. You were not meant to die on Libyan soil, my friend!"

"Well, that's wonderful, indeed, Sahid, but I am still confused—"

"About Nisha and our son?"

"Exactly."

"Do not be confused, Major. They are here with us!"

"Here?"

"Yes. They remain on the other side of that small hill of sand over there." Sahid pointed through the darkness toward a small sand dune barely visible in the dark. "They keep watch."

"Watch?"

"Yes. My son looks out into the sea with night-vision goggles, hoping to spot your people. And Nisha watches the road behind us. It is not certain that we made good our escape."

"Then," Jack said curiously, "what about Captain Jadid? What has become of him?"

"Ah . . . Jadid! Yes, but of course. He learned that his son Kala was indeed at the Taza outpost as the general mentioned. He elected to remain behind in the company of the freedom fighters in Nalut. They are guarding the temporary prison of our friend General Rovigo.

"Our son Kashan knew Kala well and gave the captain directions where he might find the boy. He shall find him, I am sure of it.

"And . . . ah, yes . . . Jadid said to tell you thank you. He would have liked to have said so himself. But under the circumstances, he wishes you well, and the best of luck for a safe, speedy return to your own family."

With those words, Jack pictured his wife and children again and ached to be with them at home in California. He felt a surge of hopeful anticipation rush through his stomach, and thought with gladness of heart that he might actually make it home, after all.

Just then, Juno, who had been sitting quietly and patiently at Jack's side, barked once, then a second time. Both men turned their heads toward the sand dune and spotted two figures approaching.

It was Nisha and Kashan.

"What is wrong?" Sahid questioned.

"There are three sets of headlights approaching, Sahid."

"How far?"

"A mile . . . perhaps a little less," Nisha said calmly, but with obvious concern as she and Kashan walked the final few steps across the sand to where Jack and Sahid were situated.

"Do I see an American major?" Nisha asked, kneeling at their side and smiling into the near-darkness.

"Yes," Jack answered, holding out his hand to the woman who had done so much for him. "It is *I*, Nisha, back from the dead!"

"Stay here with Jack, Kashan!" Sahid ordered, relieving the boy of his binoculars and assault rifle, and interrupting Jack's response.

"Of course, Father," the boy said obediently.

Jack tried to get up, but Nisha was quick to scold. "Stay down, Major! You will tear the stitches open, and begin bleeding again . . . and perhaps your wife will want you with the blood you now have."

"But—"

"No buts, Major! Please trust us. We will care for any problems that might arise. By the way, how are you feeling?" she said hurriedly, anxious to catch up with her husband who was already racing up the small hill.

"Actually, I feel pretty good—"

"Do not be fooled, Major, by the false sense of euphoria. It is morphine!"

"Morphine? So that's it!"

"You would have endured much pain otherwise. I gave you a fruit drink that is good medicine by itself, but then added a powerful dose of the painkiller. It will wear off soon."

"I'm sure it will," Jack answered.

"Meanwhile," Nisha continued, "you stay here. Take this!" She tossed him his 9mm Colt. "It is fully loaded. Use it only if you have to! But please lie still, Major! Get your rest and stay hidden! Kashan will be here if you need him."

"Thank you!" he answered, using his hands to roll the familiar gun over in his hands. It was good to have the weapon in his possession again.

Nisha turned and sprinted after Sahid.

"You saved my life, Major Garrity."

Jack was startled at the sound of Kashan's voice. He hadn't known that the boy spoke English.

"Thank you, kind American."

"Well, you're welcome, Kashan. I've been concerned about you for a long time now."

"Concern is much appreciated, Major. I would have died if you had not moved quickly. You are a brave man—much like my father, as well as my mother. They say you are sent from the great Allah to rescue our people and to save us from the great war."

"Well, I'm not sure about all of that, son, but I do know that God has played his hand in our safety and continued success. I'm just glad to see you free from that awful military camp. And I think your parents are, too. They love you very much, you know."

"Oh . . . and I love them as well, Mister Major, sir."

"Why don't you just call me, Jack, okay?"

"Okay, Jack."

Kashan walked over to the major and extended his right hand. Jack was delighted at the boy's fine manners, and extended his own hand accordingly.

"You're a fine boy, Kashan. No wonder your parents—"

His words were interrupted by the sudden clap of gunfire.

Jack tried to get up again, but Kashan wouldn't allow it.

"Stay down, Jack! Do as my mother has instructed. We must stay down inside the shadows of the sand."

Jack, Kashan, and Juno remained flat on the dark ocean front and listened intently to the exchange of gunfire.

Somehow or another, Jack reasoned, Lucca Rovigo had escaped or had been set free. He must have then received the necessary immediate medical treatment for his own wound and then continued with the chase. But what he didn't know was how. How had Rovigo been able to determine which direction he and the others had gone! It was crazy! Was this guy, Rovigo, some sort of supernatural being from another world?

The thought chilled the major, and reminded him of the pain—though numbed by the morphine—still prevalent in his leg and chest. Then Jack's mind put together the pieces of the puzzle.

Without fully understanding why, Jack knew with a calming certainty that the experience back at the hotel room in Nalut was the key. There *had been*—and continued *to be*—someone who had watched and monitored Jack's every move. A spy of sorts. A spy for Lucca Rovigo. Clearly, it was a man Lucca had chosen—because of his ghost-like qualities—to follow Jack and the others at all times, day or night, and then report the moves to Lucca, himself.

That was the reason why Lucca had come to Taza with just a couple of military soldiers to back him up! He had already known that Jack and the others were trying to free the young Libyan boys for their fathers and mothers. He had also known that it was some sort of charade they'd been playing with Colonel Berkan.

So . . . Lucca knew he could get the jump on them and take Jack and his rebel friends unguarded and unaware.

Jack thought that it was frightening how close they had all come to not only failing in their quest at Taza, but losing their lives as well. All because of some crafty snake of an individual who had been spying and then relaying information to Rovigo!

Two minutes later, while Jack was feeling a bit useless, the sound of gunfire ceased, and Juno suddenly became aware of movement over by the sand dunes.

The dog's ears stood up like a pair of radar receivers and zeroed in on the motion—but he did not growl, chuff, or even grit his teeth.

Lying on his good side, Jack steadied himself with his gun outstretched and ready for whoever was approaching. In the faint light of the starlit sky, Jack saw Nisha and Sahid. They were moving quickly down the embankment and seemed clearly concerned. Jack lowered the 9mm so that the barrel pointed at the sand instead of at his friends—then he patiently awaited their arrival.

"Dig into the sand! Quickly!" Sahid commanded as he approached Jack and Kashan. "They are coming!"

"Who? Who is coming, Sahid?" Jack responded urgently.

"It is Rovigo! He was not killed after all, and he has found us . . . with our backs against the sea!"

Jack knew now that his previous thoughts about the mysterious night stalker had been correct. It was the only logical explanation for Lucca's successful manhunt. The cloaked informer had done his job well, allowing the team to fall right into a trap!

Where could they go? The sea was to their rear, and the small army of General Rovigo's commandos was at their front door!

With a great degree of difficulty, still hurting from the gunshot wounds, Jack began the tedious task of digging into the sandy beach. If he was going to die, at least he'd go out fighting!

Seconds later, Jack was startled by two explosions just over the ridge. The fiery blasts lit up the night sky and sent a shiver of apprehension through the major's body. Quickly Sahid and Kashan helped Jack with his small trench, finished their own, and then each of them crawled in and readied themselves for the battle.

"What were those explosions?" Jack questioned.

"Grenades strung with trip wires. Hopefully, we have stopped a few more of the pursuers, perhaps evened the odds a little."

Jack was not very optimistic.

"What about ammunition, Sahid? And an extra AK-47 for myself? Do we have enough supplies to hold out for a battle?"

"It is better that you do not get into the fight, Major! Please. Keep your head down and let the three of us do the fighting!"

"You're out of your mind, Sahid! I'm not about to lie here without getting into the action! Besides, I feel fine!"

"That is the problem, Major! You are not quite your normal self. It would be foolish to see you die needlessly!"

"Nonsense, Sahid. Don't be ridiculous! Give me a weapon!"

"But Major . . . please!"

"I'm fine . . . really. Let me help you!"

Time was running out and Sahid knew it. He looked at Nisha, as if soliciting her approval, and then he grimaced as she handed a fully loaded AK-47 to her husband. She also handed over three extra clips. Sahid, in turn, gave the assault weapon to the injured American, and then whispered calmly, "May God be with us and protect us. . . ."

"Amen," Jack agreed under his breath.

Like before, Juno was the first to sense movement. A small team . . . five, maybe six men, were crawling just over the ridge. And although the sky was only minimally lit from the partial moon and stars, the figures snaking across the dark sand were visible.

From their different positions in the shallow trenches, Sahid, Nisha, Jack, and Kashan leveled their weapons and waited.

"Wait," Sahid whispered. "Wait for a clear shot before you divulge your position. There are not many of them and they do not yet know where we are. If we are patient, we may be victorious!"

"Jack?" Nisha whispered. "Are you all right?"

"Yeah, I'm okay, Nisha. I'll be all right . . . thank you."

"If I do not get the chance . . . I mean, if we do not get out of this alive . . . I just wanted to thank you, Jack. You are a brave and wonderful man. Your companion—your Linda—can be very proud of you. Thank you for saving our son's life."

"We're going to make it, Nisha! I'm sure of it! Think positively, dear lady, and you'll see. . . ."

But in the darkness, Nisha, huddled alone in her shallow sandy hole, was not optimistic—or even positive—about their chances. The odds were clearly against their hoped-for success, and although she was happy to have their small family together again, tears born of anxious fear and womanly nerves flowed unseen down her cheeks in the darkness.

"I love you, my precious family," she whispered inaudibly. "May the God of heaven and earth be our watch-guard this night. For without Him, we shall surely perish."

Perhaps sensing the tender moment, Jack, too, felt an emotional tug at his heartstrings. He wanted to reach out to the brave woman who had ventured again and again into battle with him and hold her close. He wanted to assure her that all would be okay in the end. He considered the unusual contrast of this young family of tan-skinned Libyans against his own. They were similar in so many ways, and yet so totally different.

He wondered how life would be back home in the great United

States of America if families were forced to take up arms in an effort to defend their God-given rights of freedom against unrighteous, tyrannous leaders. How depressing was the thought of Linda, Little Jack, and Trish on the run—weapons in hand—fleeing for their lives! Yet here he was, lying alongside a family of similar creatures of God! A husband and wife, whose sole activities day in and day out consisted of war games and a Russian-roulette uncertainty!

And then young . . . so very young Kashan! Was he to die tonight after all? Was this to be his last breath of freedom!

The sudden realization of the Libyan family's plight emotionally overwhelmed Jack. His eyes blurred with moisture and tears fell. He wanted to wrap each of the others inside a cozy package and mail them safely back to the states—to his house—where they could be safe and live out the rest of their lives in peaceful comfort.

"Divine Father of Heaven," Jack whispered softly, "see thou this great and awful fear in our hearts? Are we to die together in the lonely, dark sands by the sea? Or wouldst thou spare the lives of these brave and good-hearted people so that many people could be spared the agony of tyranny and death?

"It seems that our enemy is upon us . . . that they have us pinned against all hope for escape! And although I do not pretend to understand all of thy ways, I am concerned that these, my dear friends, must also die. Is there no other way?"

Jack's heart and soul had gone into his attempt to communicate with the God he had come to trust and love as his Heavenly Father. He pleaded humbly for an acceptable sacrifice—if that was what God wanted—that his life could be taken in exchange for the lives of his friends.

That willingness to die so that others might live opened the floodgates of understanding inside Jack's heart. He became filled with the truest kind of love for his fellowmen—a love called *charity.* And then he knew that all he had gone through, all that he had experienced since leaving home, was nothing more than a necessary fine-tuning of his spiritual progress.

Suddenly Jack knew that his offering was accepted in its entirety. He also knew that whether he lived from that moment on, or died, he had somehow, in some strange way, given his life to his Creator. He now belonged to the being called Christ, who had marvelously adopted him into his own family.

There *had* been a reason for his arduous journey through Libya, and it wasn't so that he could die and be forgotten. Nor was it so that he could better perfect his military skills of war, or develop a taste for human bloodshed and chaos. Instead, he had fallen into the hands of a righteous, God-fearing people who needed him. And who, like the ancient Israelites held in bondage by the pharaohs of Egypt while they looked for a deliverer, saw Jack as their chosen Moses!

He was nearly overcome by the idea and shook violently for a moment, envisioning himself before God the Father.

Peace again came into his heart.

Then a voice . . . a voice within his mind.

"Behold, my son. Look out upon the sea. . . ."

Trembling, Jack turned his head slowly, and looked longingly out into the vast expanse of the Mediterranean. It seemed empty and dark at first, but then, as if brought into focus by a power greater than he could understand, light seemed to appear out on the horizon and a great and powerful U.S. Naval submarine appeared out of the depths.

At that same instant, bright flashes of fire belched forth from the starboard side of the nuclear vessel, followed instantly by voluminous sounds of thunder.

Highly explosive shells whistled overhead and began falling on Lucca's army.

The ensuing explosions lit up the beach like a football stadium with its entire bank of lights turned on! Jack, Sahid, Nisha, and Kashan opened fire as well.

Soldiers had been crawling along the sandy dunes in greater numbers than Sahid or Nisha had previously calculated, but all for naught. Soldiers were thrown about like so many lifeless dummies in a Hollywood picture show—and fight as they might, the special commandos were simply no match for the submarine's awesome firepower.

Seconds later, to Jack's continued relief, a detachment of Navy SEALs sprang out of the water and onto the beach like phantoms, firing an assortment of M-16s and other automatic armament at the dunes.

"Major Garrity?" one of them called. "Is that you, Major?"

"Yes!" Jack screamed, tears streaming freely down the sides of his face. "Over here! Over here!"

Two of the Navy frogmen rushed over to Jack's position and jumped down alongside the little band. They were surprised to find Jack in such unusual company. A woman, a child, one man, and a large white dog! The two looked at each other with curious expressions, then turned to the group.

"Major Garrity?" one of them questioned.

"I am Major Garrity," Jack responded breathlessly. "How kind of you fellows to drop in on us like this!"

"I am Lieutenant Commander Horace Miller. My friends call me Hod. This here's Lieutenant Samson. There are six of us, Major . . . we've come to get you outta here! Ready?"

"What about my friends here?" Jack questioned, unsure of their directive.

"Sorry, Major, you know the regulations."

"We just can't leave 'em!" Jack protested. Then, without waiting for a reply, Jack grabbed Kashan by the arm for support, and motioning to Sahid and Nisha, began to work his way out into the water. The others followed, and while the two Navy soldiers held the enemy at bay, the small band was silently assisted into the waiting grey raft.

Immediately the engine was started, and Jack, holding fiercely to his aching stomach, happened to glance back into the water. There, swimming for all he was worth, was Juno!

"Hold it, boys! That dog . . . get the dog!"

The frogmen hesitated only briefly, then realizing they were taking orders from a superior officer, they quickly complied.

Four hours later, and several miles away from shore, the small band huddled around each other on the deck of the USS *Nautilus*. A helicopter was warming up nearby, having arrived from the *Nimitz*, and Jack was about to bid farewell to his friends . . . his new family.

"My friends," Jack began, his body lying on a hastily prepared cot, "your journey will be difficult and your errand treacherous. I know that you must eventually return to your people, but for now you can return to Boston, regroup, and—"

"Shsssssssh! Jack," Nisha said softly, putting a warm and tender hand over the major's mouth. "Again you prove to us your kind and charitable heart. Certainly we would like to go with you, to return to Boston to see our American friends again . . . and to meet your wonderful family. But we cannot . . . not now! We cannot abandon our duties with the rebel fighters any more so than could you. You understand that, don't you?"

"I . . . I . . . don't—"

"Of course you do!" Sahid said courageously. "We must stay now, more than ever, or all we have fought for will have been in vain. It does not matter if Rovigo, or anyone else, is still alive . . . for they fight for false power and for wealth. We, on the other hand, fight for freedom and for a life of peace with our families. And so our cause is just—and with greater urgency! Go now, Major, and tell your president the truth!"

"And go to your family, Jack," Nisha added, her eyes moist with a deep and abiding love for this man with such a strange surname. "And please," she concluded, reaching down and kissing the major on both cheeks, and then on the forehead, "tell your . . . your Linda that she is one very fortunate woman."

The two men also embraced, silently, and then Kashan knelt down and grabbed Jack around the neck.

"I love you, Major Jack," the boy said, tears forming also in his eyes. "Thank you . . . Jack . . . for saving my life! One day I would like to meet your Little Jack!"

"I love you, too, Kashan. And one day I'm sure that you will meet him. And Kashan, I can truly see why your parents feel as they do about you, as you are the perfect gentleman and the bravest young warrior I have ever known! You be sure and watch out for your mother and father for me, all right?"

Nodding, the boy suddenly burst into tears and fell unashamedly into Jack's arms.

For a full thirty seconds the boy and Jack embraced, neither wanting the moment to end.

At last, knowing that their time had come, the young warrior rose to his feet and again allowed his father to clasp arms a final time with their dear friend.

Without speaking further, and each waving with reluctant parting, the three Libyan freedom fighters backed toward the waiting chopper. Then, realizing that the moment of departure had arrived, they turned and climbed into the vibrating transporter.

Jack, meanwhile, continued to weep with full emotion, at the same time caressing the back of his dog's head.

Juno was going to make one great traveling companion.

50

7 January 1992—
The USS Nautilus

The final battle on the sands of Zuwarah had been understatedly exhausting for Jack. The lack of food, sleep, and complete medical attention had so thoroughly zapped his strength that when he was at last resting in the medical quarters of the slightly submerged USS *Nautilus,* he collapsed into a deep and lengthy sleep.

Juno, who, after a rather heated argument between Jack and Lieutenant Commander Hod had been allowed to accompany his master into the medical quarters, remained poised and stalwart at Jack's side. Nothing any of the seamen did or said could lure the husky away. Juno simply curled up alongside the Air Force major and stood a vigilant guard.

Several hours later, Jack opened his eyes and smiled. He was profoundly relieved to be free at last from the chaos in the tumultuous North African country of Libya. He struggled to hold back a fresh batch of tears. But gaining composure was paramount in importance, for he knew that his upcoming meeting with Admiral Carl Doxey was critical, and would require his utmost attention and his clear and precise thinking.

In a sealed package stuffed inside one of his pockets, Jack still carried the secret military documents Captain Nador Jadid had provided. Important among those documents was the map showing the exact location of the second nuclear device. Jack had mentioned to Lieutenant Commander Miller the extreme importance of speaking with the sub's commanding officer—and was pleased to learn that it was Admiral Doxey, himself.

Jack knew little about the Naval admiral. Nevertheless, he had remembered the name mentioned weeks ago back at Aviano Air Force

Base in Italy, and was grateful to know that the old admiral was a part of Operation Screaming Ghost since the very beginning. This knowledge would allow Jack the freedom to open up and tell all.

There was one final mission that Jack felt he and only a handful of others were qualified to do—finding and disarming the nuclear bomb hidden inside the El-Gassi oil fields in the heart of Algeria.

He was a bit dispirited by the idea of having to go back after the deadly device, but he knew in his heart that the job had to be done. And so he resolved the conflict within himself with progressive mental preparations.

Just then, two fully armed military types walked into the bay. They said nothing to Jack nor did they acknowledge him in any way. Instead, they took two positions inside the doorway and stood at full attention.

Juno chuffed his usual annoyance.

Seconds later, two more men entered the room. This time, however, Jack recognized one of them, and found his spirits suddenly lifted tremendously.

"Hawk!" he said, with obvious delight. "What . . . what are *you* doing here, ol' buddy?"

"Well, if it ain't the old screamin' ghost, himself! How the heck are ya, Jack? We thought you were a gonner!" Major Barry said affectionately, leaning over Jack's bed to give him an embrace. "Welcome home, Jack!"

"Thanks, Norman."

Major Hawk Barry only smiled at the renewed teasing, then turned to the man behind him.

"This is Admiral Doxey, Jack." The admiral extended a warm hand of greeting.

"Pleased to meet you, son. You surprised the livin' tarnation out of us, Major, with your shortwave message! We'd given you up for dead a long time ago! It's good to have you aboard, son."

"Thank you, Admiral . . . I'm—"

"Now, let's get down to business, Jack," the admiral interrupted. "Understand you got a pile of information for us." The old admiral turned to the two sentries and commanded them to leave the sick bay and close the hatch behind them. "Don't let a soul into these quarters until I tell you to."

"Aye, sir," the senior of the two replied, pulling the hatch closed from outside of the bay.

Finally, giving his full attention to Jack, the admiral sat on the bed, reached down and patted Juno on the head, then spoke. “All right, Major . . . let’s have it . . . please.”

51

Benghazi, Northern Libya

Haman Al-Rashid was seething with anger. The events at Zuwarah's beach front had been more than the Libyan commander could mentally accommodate. He was mad with vengeance, frothing at the mouth like a wild animal with rabies-induced madness.

General Lucca Rovigo was dead! "How can this be?" he reasoned angrily. Lucca was the best! He wasn't supposed to die! Yet somehow the infidel American Air Force pilot had snuffed out his comrade's life like a candle in the wind.

The sequence of events had been too much for Haman. The loss of the nuclear reactor was not only infuriating, it was outright embarrassing! One single American Air Force major had been responsible. Just one lone man! And what about the rebellion insurrection? The traitorous infidels had destroyed a small army at Al-Bayadh, taking the plaza outpost by surprise, and seriously crippling the military camp at the Sidi oil fields.

"How!" he screamed. "Are my soldiers so pathetically weak and ill trained that they are easily defeated by a band of mercenaries and freedom fighters!"

Haman thought back to the initial crash site of the Banshee and slammed his fist onto the table inside the Benghazi office. The American and his powerful weapons had destroyed the entire military compound at El-Wahat. And now . . . the beach at Zuwarah and the Youth of the Nation project at Taza!

How could it have happened? So many serious mistakes in so short a time. Hundreds of youthful soldiers from Taza had simply disappeared. Hundreds! Nothing was going as planned! Nothing.

There were dissensions within the ranks of the Elite, uncounted numbers of discontented deserters, and full military installations were being systematically destroyed! But the single event that filled Haman's heart with rage and fury beyond description was the fact that Major Jack Garrity, along with Sahid and Nisha, had escaped! "How?" he screamed again.

Haman reached for his telephone. The time had come at last to detonate the remaining warhead. His vengeance would entail the single massive slaughter of hundreds of thousands of Algerian citizens, after which press releases would blame the Americans for not having abided the terms of the treaty.

Quickly Haman dialed the coded sequence and then waited for the familiar buzzing sound inside the retriever.

But nothing happened!

It was as though the call did not go through.

He tried it again.

Still nothing.

"No!" he screamed, barely able to contain himself. "What is happening here?"

He attempted the procedure one last time, but again the results were the same—no activation buzzer, and no subsequent explosion!

It was maddening!

"And what is next?" he demanded to know.

Haman was mystified. If the bomb had been discovered, surely his field agents would have known about it. Yet if the warhead was still intact, and was still hidden inside the Alegerian oil field, then why hadn't it exploded?

Were the phone lines severed?

It was true that severe sandstorms could effectively knock out power and telephone lines; and it was also true that the lines going into the pump station had been hastily strung. But no violent storms had been in the area for some time, and certainly not since his last call to the bomb site.

His determination was resolute. The bomb had to be detonated! The world must know that Libya was now a world power and should be feared!

Haman paced the floor of his office, getting a sensible grip on himself. He understood the danger of explosive, unchecked anger, and determined to calm his spirits down.

There would be no rash decisions. No rash actions!

Slowly, the Libyan commander walked over to the door of his office and bolted the lock.

He knew what had to be done, and he could not tolerate an intrusion.

Just to the left of one of the plush sofas decorating his suite was a false panel in the wall that hid a fairly sizeable metal safe. Inside, a polished wooden box approximately eighteen inches square and twelve inches tall housed an electronic backup detonator. It was supplied by the American traitor, Lieutenant David Guant.

How typical, Haman thought, thinking back to the experience of the purchase. "Just like an American . . . everything is for sale! Buy two nuclear warheads and get a backup detonation unit free of charge!"

Haman took a moment to consider the traitor Guant. "What an honorless man," he spat in disgust. True, he *had* been useful to the cause; but in actuality, he was simply another infidel! A sand-eating grub! Guant was a man with no loyalty to others. He was a pathetic, greedy coward who would live rich, to be sure—but would also die a wretched, despised man.

Shaking free of his thoughts, Haman returned his attention to the wooden case now sitting on the desk before him. Opening the container, he carefully removed the foam packaging and retrieved the electronic gadgetry.

The device was one foot square and about ten inches high. The block was arched so that as he looked at it from the front, it reminded him of a miniature bridge. The panel covering the face plate was decorated with a single row of ten small, square buttons—each with an Arabic symbol that represented the numbers zero through nine to match those on a telephone receiver.

Setting the appliance back onto the desk, Haman removed a nine-volt battery that was wedged inside the foam. He then pulled the protective tape off its electrodes and slid it into an opening in the side of the block. It clicked into place.

With a dry smile, Haman closed the small metal door, sealing out the dust and possible moisture. He then activated the unit.

Immediately a row of miniature lights illuminated. There were ten altogether, each one a corresponding link to the ten buttons above.

The commander was satisfied.

Abdul Matulub worshipped Commander Haman Al-Rashid. He

was extremely dedicated to the great cause his leader represented, and he was likewise honored to be in the service of the Libyan Elite forces, working directly under truly the most powerful man in Libya.

He was an intelligent man, eager to serve the republic—and more important, he was the perfect man for the job.

"Ah . . . Abdul, my friend. Come in . . . please, and take a seat. Make yourself comfortable."

"Thank you, Commander. You are most kind," Abdul replied gratefully.

"You have been selected, Abdul, for a holy mission."

"A mission, Commander?"

"Yes, Abdul . . . a sacred mission. Please listen carefully while I explain."

"Yessir."

"You will pick two of your best men and will cross the borders into Algeria. You will need to pose as merchants, making sure that once inside the country, you are not followed. Do you understand?"

"Of course, Commander."

"Your primary destination will be a vast oil field just outside the city of El-Hajira. The place is called El-Gassi. It is here on this map."

Haman pointed at the destination site and handed the map to Abdul. "Should there be inquiries, your purpose is trade, and you will say that you are working for Mahdia Petroleum Company, which hopes to do business with El-Gassi."

Haman handed a small package to Abdul. "In this packet you will have your business cards, passports, and traveling visas. Do not lose them. They are vital to your success, for it is imperative that you do not fail!

"Once inside the oil fields of El-Gassi, providing you are not detained or followed along the way, you will locate and find a specific pumping station marked on the map, here."

He handed a second map to Abdul and pointed at the small drawing that depicted the pump station.

"Proceed directly to this housing station and crawl inside. There is a small door that will allow you access. Break the lock, if you must . . . although it may very well be open.

"There will be an unusual electronic device attached to a large cone-shaped cylinder. Concern yourself only with the sphere-shaped gadget. This is a photograph of the mechanism, itself." Haman showed a glossy eight-by-ten photo to his errand man. "And as you can see, it is round and shiny silver in color—about the size of a soccer ball.

"This computerized unit is the only one like it in the world."

"What does it do, Commander?" Abdul asked innocently.

"That is classified information, Abdul. Please listen, and I will explain what you are allowed to know."

"I understand, sir."

"I have here another electronic machine that will fit over the sphere."

Haman showed the backup detonator to Abdul and then continued. "On one side of the silver ball you will find a small metal strip that is sealed onto the unit with lead. You can pry this piece off with your knife. But when you do, make absolutely sure that none of the lead remains! Scrape it all away!"

"Yessir. I understand, sir."

"Now, Abdul, watch carefully. . . ."

With a quick twist of a small key on the side of the detonator, opposite the battery compartment, Haman produced ten small pins and two metal rods.

"These," he said, holding the ten pins, "will fit into corresponding holes under the lead stripping. They are electronic conductors that will allow the two units to become one in function. The other, large pieces here, are connecting rods that will work as fasteners, keeping the two computers linked electronically with the main power grid. Do you follow me so far, Abdul?"

"So far, yes, Commander."

"Good." Haman rubbed an ache in the back of his neck, looked down at the patient courier, and continued.

"Now, you need not fear that you will be joining the two devices incorrectly. They only fit together in one way. When all of the connections are made, these red lights above the program buttons will blink off, and these green ones underneath will blink on. When all of the green lights are illuminated, you will open this envelope."

Haman handed the small sealed envelope to Abdul and finished his instructions. "Punch in a series of coded numbers at that time. The numbers are inside. Is that clear, Abdul?"

"Very clear, Commander." Abdul was growing in enthusiasm and confidence. "And then?"

Suppressing a thin smile, and realizing the simple, innocent ignorance of the man's statement, Haman answered simply, "That is all, my friend. Just leave the device activated and return home."

"Nothing more?" the eager man questioned.

"No, nothing. Just come home . . . and we will celebrate your success with a special bonus."

Abdul thought about the assignment for a moment, suddenly felt very important, and then stood and faced his commander.

"I am honored that you would select me for this great assignment, Commander Al-Rashid. I will execute the operation quickly and reliably! You can count on me. And when it has been accomplished, I will return and report immediately—as you have requested."

Haman walked over to the anxious and willing comrade, and handed him the wooden box with the detonator inside. He knew that the naive soldier was completely oblivious of the suicide nature of the mission—but he could not, and would not explain the truth. His only real concern was for the success of the operation . . . the ultimate hope to wipe the El-Gassi oil fields and the surrounding communities off the face of the map!

Abdul was simply a pawn about to be sacrificed for the good of his country.

Dismissing Abdul with a blessing, Haman called his secretary, a short wiry fellow named Kalif, and said, "Abdul Matulub and his men are to be martyrs, Kalif. You will make the necessary arrangements. . . ."

"As you wish, Haman," the man replied.

"See to it that their wives and elderly parents receive a monthly endowment, and that their children are properly cared for financially so that they can attend the best universities. Do you understand?"

"Yessir."

"I, myself, will sign the official documents of Mourning and Martyrdom, and will hand carry these documents to the families."

"They will be so proud of their husbands and fathers," came Kalif's dry reply.

52

8 January 1992—
The USS Nautilus

Major Norman "Hawk" Barry stood pensively in front of the small mirror in his cabin. He looked at the reflection and stared at the deep color in his eyes. They were blue . . . and nervous. That was a good word for it—nervous. And rightfully so! The task ahead of him and his small team was perhaps the most dangerous he'd ever known. The possibilities for success before the time clock ran out seemed remote at best—and in many ways, outright suicidal!

But that wasn't the point. The operation was so important. Well, it just had to be done!

Hawk was not afraid. He and Jack were alike in many ways. Both were intelligent, both were skilled warriors in their own way, both were brave and undaunted by the many challenges the military proffered, and both were dedicated to the extent that if service of country meant laying down their lives, well . . . so be it.

In this case, however, if worse should come to worse, he might just lay down his life for the betterment of the entire planet!

Hawk thought of the four men that would accompany him on the mission. If the operation were successful, which was possible, they would be unacknowledged heroes. Yet if the venture failed, which to him seemed more likely considering the volatile, unstable mind of Libya's leader—they would simply end up as four among hundreds of thousands of anonymous casualties.

The cataclysmic implications of failure weighed on the major's mind like a giant lead weight chained around his neck. It smothered him.

What if the bomb detonated?

Would the world community act with restraint?

Hawk rather doubted it.

The recent war in the Gulf was proof to the world that this particular area of the planet was filled with angry people who still perpetuated—indeed, who amplified and exaggerated—the ancient hatreds and prejudices of their long-deceased ancestors. And, while Hawk was not extensively schooled in the history, religion, or politics of Northern Africa, he felt certain that if the Libyan leader Al-Rashid detonated the warhead in Algeria, war would be imminent. At that point, the Allied Coalition would be re-established, and in all probability a global war would transpire!

The images of a nuclear Armageddon whirled inside Hawk's head. The visions were ghostly. It didn't take a genius to see the dismal picture. Such a war could very easily transform the majestic earthen sphere into a dead globe of acrid smoke, rotted soils, and eternally contaminated waters.

Hawk shuddered at the thought.

"Dear God," he prayed silently, "I know I ain't been everything you might have counted on. But lookit here, Lord . . . this is a crisis situation, the likes of which there ain't ever been! The whole darn world's at stake here. My friend Jack's just too shot up to do the job, himself, so they chose me.

"I need ya, Lord. Man-oh-man, do I ever! I ain't gonna be able to tackle this one alone."

Lifting his head for one last look into the mirror and around the cabin, Hawk took a deep breath, flipped off the light switch, and headed through the maze of chambers and corridors inside the submarine's interior—heading toward the sick bay.

Hawk would be glad to get off the *Nautilus.* Submarines gave him occasional episodes of claustrophobia, and the little cabin he'd slept in last night was even worse.

"Good riddance!" he sighed.

Jack was also in a pensive mood when Hawk walked into the bay. He'd been concerned that the final operation of actually locating and disarming the warhead would be carried out by his friend, Major Hawk Barry, rather than himself. But then again, how much help could he proffer with one arm and shoulder inside a sling, with a chest wrap wound tightly around his upper torso, and with a set of crutches to help support his new leg cast? He was a real mess.

"You about ready, Jack?" Hawk said upon entering the room.

"As ready as I'll ever be," Jack responded, leaning on the crutches.

"What can I carry for you, partner?"

"My duffle bag, Hawk. That's about it. It's Navy issue, you know, so it should last me for some time!"

"Yea. . . . That it?"

"That's everything, Hawk. I didn't have much with me when you guys picked me up back there. Travel kinda light, you know . . . but I always carry my American Express card! You want to borrow it, Norman? You know, you're not supposed to leave home without it. . . ."

"American Express card, huh? Sure thing, Mr. Wise Guy."

"No, I'm serious, Hawk! Here, let me show you. . . ."

Jack reached over to the duffle bag, unzipped a corner of it, and withdrew his 9mm Colt in its holster. "American Express!" he said with a smile, handing the weapon to his friend. "I never leave home—especially on dangerous missions—without it!"

"You're a character, Jack!" Hawk said with a grin, "but I'm okay, really! Got my own hog's leg. I use a .45 with a special load. But hey, thanks anyway."

"Look," Jack said, "before you go making up your mind so quickly, I want you to know that this 9mm Colt went the distance with me back there in that nightmare of a place! It was like a friend to me . . . and saved my life on two different occasions!

"Now, I don't know why, exactly, but I'd sure feel a whole lot better if you'd take it with you. Even if you don't have to use it. It seems to bring good luck!"

"Well, I don't know, Jack . . . it's just a weapon."

"I know that. But that's not the point. It's silly, actually, but . . . well . . . it's like I said, the gun's been kind of a friend to me. It's part of me, if you know what I mean. And since I can't go with you guys—all bandaged up and all—well, I thought maybe you could take that part of me anyway."

Hawk hesitated for a moment, smiled lightly, and then reached out and took the weapon from Jack.

"Okay," he said graciously, "I'll take it. Maybe there's a bullet in there with that madman's name on it. You know . . . that guy you briefed us about?"

"Haman . . . Haman Al-Rashid."

"Yeah . . . that's him . . . Haman Al-Rashid."

"Well, if there is, Hawk ol' buddy, do us all a favor and put the guy out of his misery . . . will you?"

"Count on it," Hawk replied, securing the Colt, snatching up his duffle bag, and leading Jack to the main hatch.

The two Air Force majors made their way up through the different decks of the *Nautilus,* until they reached the now-surfaced bridge. There they met up with Admiral Doxey, Lieutenant Commander Miller, and Lieutenants Samson, Stoick, and Dennis. The latter four made up the special team that would go into Algeria with Hawk.

Reaching the rendezvous point just south of the island of Malta, the *Nautilus* totally surfaced and was met by a UH1 transport. The chopper pilot quickly picked up his unique passengers, hovered for a brief moment just above the monstrous nuclear submarine—and then banked slightly to the north, flying off toward the USS *Nimitz.*

Jack, who was accompanying the party to the *Nimitz,* was fascinated as he watched the open sea behind them, catching a final glimpse of the massive vessel just as it dipped and submerged itself back into the dark depths below. The sub reminded him of one of the great whales having come up briefly for air, then diving again on its never-ending hunt for food. The *Nautilus* had been an adventure by itself. Jack could finally say that he, too, had been aboard one of the Navy's formidable nuclear submarines.

During the final briefing inside the captain's quarters on board the *Nimitz,* Jack did his best to answer all of the questions posed by Hawk, the admiral, and the four Navy SEALs.

This was to be the final parting, and although Jack still regretted that he could not personally finish the job he had started, his confidence in Hawk's abilities allowed him the peaceful assurance that the job would get done, if Hawk's team could just reach the device before it was too late.

Out on the deck, Hawk and Jack said their good-byes, exchanged a hug of friendship, and promised to meet back at Edwards when the whole thing was behind them.

"I guess this is it then," Hawk said, extending his hand to Jack. "You just remember what I said about that reunion back in California. I'll get this assignment done in no time and meet you there, ol' buddy!"

"I'll be waiting!" Jack assured him. "Besides, you got my American Express card! And I fully expect you to return it!"

"Count on that, partner! But in the meantime, you get yourself well again! And more important, get on home to that family of yours! I'm sure Linda—isn't that her name?"

"Yeah . . . Linda."

"Well, Linda's probably worried sick about you, Jack. Your work's finished out here. You get back to being a husband and a father!"

"Honestly, Norman, I can't think of anything I'd like to do more than just that!"

"Norman, huh? You call me that one more time, and I'll strap you to this nuclear device we're gonna bring back with us and detonate the thing myself!"

"Okay, Norman, I won't call you that anymore . . . I promise!"

Jack grinned playfully at his friend, then extended his hand one last time.

"Adios, amigo!" he said. "Take care of yourself!"

"You too, ol' buddy! And I'll see ya when it's over!"

Major Barry and his team boarded another Huey and lifted off the flat top. Jack stood leaning on his crutches and watched the chopper as long as he could, until finally it disappeared from view. Then feeling alone, he turned and went back to his quarters. Tomorrow morning at 0700 hours he'd be on a small transport, himself, headed back to Aviano.

Tonight, if he could endure the pain, he'd finish his official report. Undoubtedly, there would be a thorough debriefing sometime tomorrow afternoon before he'd actually be relieved from duty and board the C-5 that would take him home to his family.

Jack was worn out. Yet, his mind seemed to have kicked into overdrive. His thoughts raced through him like a high-speed picture show, touching on a dozen different images of the past, present, and future.

He was grateful to be going home, and that seemed foremost on his mind. Images of Linda, Little Jack, and Trish swooping around him and welcoming him back brought tears to his eyes. He could hardly wait.

But then, thinking about the serious peril that possibly awaited his friend Hawk, Jack felt uneasy . . . even restless. How could he hope to feel peaceful until he was certain that the crisis situation was over?

And there were other thoughts as well.

Already he missed his friends in Libya. He could clearly see their faces—Sahid, Nisha, Kashan, Captain Jadid, old Benian, the rebel commander from Al-Bayadh . . . and the elderly Ibrahim. What a good man he had been. And how terribly tragic to have been forced to bury him in that grave out in the middle of the desert. All of it seemed like a dream . . . an extraordinary episode of some melodramatic Hollywood movie. But Jack knew better! It had been real, all right . . . right down to the two bullet wounds in his body.

How dreadfully close he had come to dying.

He shivered again from the memory of his struggles with Lucca Rovigo.

And those eyes!

They alone would come back to haunt Jack for years to come! He'd never seen such eery looking eyes before.

Demon eyes! That's what they were. . . .

Jack lay back on his bunk and tried to relax. He wondered if Admiral Doxey had finished briefing the president of the United States. All of the documents describing the Libyan alliance with Iraq—and that remarkable Project Holy Power—were no longer Jack's concern. From this point forward, he prayed simply that he could be left out of it.

"Let the top brass handle things," he mumbled to himself. "I just wanna go home!"

If everything was in order, the president would have contacted the Algerian government by now. He wondered what the Algerian heads of state whispered among themselves when they learned that there was an armed nuclear bomb planted in one of their oil fields? Undoubtedly, they would have dispatched a small army by now. Probably would have set up roadblocks and would have begun preparations for some sort of mass evacuation from the surrounding cities . . . all that sort of thing. In any case, he hoped that whatever preparations were made, they'd make Hawk's job a little easier.

"Good luck, Hawk!" Jack whispered softly, feeling drowsy and slowly falling over the edge of a peaceful sleep.

53

Ten minutes, Major Barry, sir," the Huey pilot called back.

"Ten minutes to Annaba?" Hawk echoed.

"Yessir."

"Good. Thank you, Lieutenant. Let me know when we start our descent."

"Roger, sir."

Annaba was a major metropolis on the northeastern coast of Algeria. It was the designated rendezvous point for phase one of Operation Hot Rock, the code name for Hawk's nuclear extraction mission. If all had gone well with the briefings and negotiations between the U.S. and Algerian governments, there would be another chopper waiting at the military airfield. Together, they would swing southward and make a quick flight toward their destination in the El-Gassi oil fields.

Hawk had never known real fear before. It simply wasn't a part of his makeup. But then again, there had never been an assignment quite like this one.

For cryin' out loud, he thought nervously, at any second that lunatic Haman Al-Rashid could pick up the telephone—providing Jack's theories about the detonation operations were correct—dial the destructive code, and blow a piece of the Algerian desert clean off the maps!

He *was* afraid.

Who wouldn't be?

Hawk looked solemnly at the faces of the men seated around him inside the Huey. He'd only recently come to know them, but he respected their Navy prowess. These were SEALs—the Navy's best! He was proud to be working with them.

Last year when he and several of his flying buddies had flown sorties over Kuwait and Iraq, he and the others had come in contact with Navy SEALs and had watched them in operation. They were great! Solid servicemen who knew their jobs and who performed them well. But that guy, Horace . . . the one everyone called Hod . . . well, he was an exception. He wasn't just great, why, he was exceptional! A natural leader. No wonder the admiral had personally picked him for this mission.

"We're on final, sir," a voice said, freeing Hawk from his thoughts. "Annaba, eight o'clock and closing. We'll touch down in about two minutes."

"Have we been cleared?" Hawk asked anxiously.

"Yessir. They're down there with a red carpet, Major!"

"Excellent. It looks like the president was successful, then. Take her in, Lieutenant."

"Roger that, sir."

Very little time was spent on the ground at the military base just outside Annaba. Hawk met briefly with an Algerian colonel named Tali Abyad. He was both intelligent and cordial, extending every courtesy to Hawk and his men.

They discussed the agreement made by the U.S. and Algerian governments, and explained that for the most part, the Algerians in power who knew of the crisis were extremely grateful for the U.S. intervention. "Algeria," the colonel said, "would gladly cooperate with the U.S. in any way possible to stop the Libyans from massing troops and weapons for an invasion." Quite frankly, they were stunned and horrified that their own security had been so lacking. It was frightening and embarrassing.

By early evening, the Operation Hot Rock team was on final approach at El-Gassi. The flight had been turbulent and physically taxing. But not so much as the mental anguish each had endured, thinking that at any moment Al-Rashid could dial the code, detonate the bomb, and vaporize their little helicopter as it grew closer and closer to ground zero. So, in a sense, the team was almost relieved to set foot on solid ground again. It was clear that none of them fancied the idea of being blown out of the sky!

The perimeter of El-Gassi was secured by some two hundred

Algerian guardsmen. The oil company, itself, had been evacuated earlier, and now appeared to be completely desolate.

Hawk wanted to move immediately. But as he was peering at the maps Jack had provided, Colonel Abyad approached him with a startling revelation.

"We have Libyan prisoners, Major Barry!"

"Prisoners?"

"That is correct, Major. It would seem that three spies were sent in with a rather unusual package to deliver. We caught them just after we arrived here in force this morning!"

"What kind of a package, Colonel?"

"It's some kind of electronic device."

"Really?"

"Yes. Would you care to speak to them? They may not answer any of your questions, but then we don't know that until we try, now do we?"

"Well . . . first let me have a look at that electronic unit you confiscated. Is it round, like a large ball?"

"Round?" the colonel questioned curiously, "Well, I don't know, Major. I have not seen it, myself."

Inside the central building overlooking the vast oil fields, Hawk studied the alternate backup detonator device. He tried to compare it with those shown in the photographs Jack supplied, but he determined that there were no similarities. Whatever it was, Hawk would learn later. Precious time was being wasted.

Hawk hopped onto a small motorized cart and drove out to the pumping station with his men. Colonel Abyad followed them in a similar vehicle with three men of his own.

There was tremendous apprehension in all of the men as they rolled up alongside the small station and pulled to a stop.

Hawk asked Miller and Stoick to assist him with the tools and with dearming the bomb. Then he slowly pulled open the small door, flipped on his flashlight, and crawled inside.

Immediately Hawk saw the warhead. Just looking at it caused his skin to crawl and his adrenalin to flow.

But something wasn't quite right.

Just above the midsection of the bomb where the words *Pluton Nuclear Warhead* were printed, a string of electronic wires and cables were hanging down like cut and useless wires inside an old radio set.

Hawk stared at them for a second, then said, "Hey, Hod . . . come here a minute!"

"Yeah . . . what's up, Major?"

"Well, look here at this photograph. . . ."

"Yeah . . . what about it?"

"You see anything different?"

"What'd ya mean?"

"Well, this is supposed to be an actual photograph of this nuclear bomb. But look here! This round ball unit has been removed!"

"Removed?"

"Yeah, Lieutenant. It's gone, man! It's the detonator! Someone's taken it!"

"Well . . . I'll be . . . ! You're right! It *is* gone! What do you suppose—"

"You see all those wires hanging out of the side of the warhead over there? And those coming in from the ceiling?"

"Yeah . . . sure do."

"Those have all been cut! They *were* connected to the sphere-shaped detonation device. But someone's come along and detached it from the bomb and has made off with it. No wonder Al-Rashid hasn't exploded the darn thing! He can't! That explains the prisoners out front. They were on their way in with another detonator of some kind."

The two men looked at each other, then at the photograph and the warhead, and suddenly burst out laughing.

54

Young Talim Jahil was playing in the small gathering room inside his family's modest Algerian home at El-Hajira. He was happy that school had been cancelled for the day because of the exciting emergency thing. Of course he didn't understand it, but he was always happy when he could be home with his family.

Papa had been sent home from work as well, and Talim felt like it was a special holiday. In fact, if what his father had said was true, then all of the families with workers at the oil fields of El-Gassi were going to have a vacation today.

How very wonderful.

Maybe he and his brother Kaasar could go to their special hideout today. Talim really liked their special place, and often looked forward to the afternoons of fun they would have playing secret agent in and around the tall oil-pumping machines.

"Hey, Talim!" his brother's voice called from somewhere back in their bedroom. "Come, Talim . . . it is working at last! Come and see!"

Kaasar was the smart one of the family. He was always making things with old radio sets and little electrical kits that looked like futuristic computers from outer space. Their room was filled with small lights of various colors, buzzers, little electronic motors, home-made fans, and other fun stuff that gave the bedroom a certain feel of its own. And for the last few days, his older brother had devoted almost all of his time to the newest and prettiest appliance of them all!

Kaasar had the thing mounted right next to their oversized tropical fish tank. The way they'd figured it, the flashing red lights and humming would give their fish something to look at and listen to while the boys were away each day at school.

Talim walked down the narrow hallway and crossed over the threshold leading into their bedroom.

"You got it fixed, Kaasar?"

"Yes, Talim! Turn off the light and close the door behind you. It is a wonderful electric ball! Watch!"

Talim sat down on his bed and watched with fascination as his big brother meticulously toyed with a set of wires coming out of the beautiful silver sphere. He thought about his brother's words, "it is a wonderful electric ball," and found himself agreeing with that assessment. It *was* a wonderful electric ball . . . and Kaasar was going to make it come alive again!

"Are you ready, Talim?"

"Yes, turn it on!"

"Okay, one . . . two . . . three!"

Click!

Suddenly, just as Kaasar had promised, the little lights on top of the silver ball blinked once, twice, and finally shined brightly. They were absolutely beautiful!

"Yeah," Talim called out, "it works!"

"Of course it works," his older brother said with uninhibited pride. "I told you it would."

He turned his attention back to a second set of makeshift switches, then looked back at his little brother once more.

"Now, Talim . . . listen to this! This is for the fishes!"

He flipped the switch.

Ommmmmmmmmmmmmmmmmmmmmmmmmmmmmmmm . . .

Talim was delighted.

55

11 January 1992—
Edwards Air Force Base, California

Major Jack Garrity could barely contain himself. He watched excitedly the familiar landscape below as the giant C-5 transport banked south for its final approach into Edwards Air Force Base in southern California.

How many times had Jack taken off and landed at this base? He didn't think he could count them all. More than a hundred? Easily! A thousand? Possibly. But in any case, this was *his* base. His home! And he was absolutely overwhelmed with the thought of being home. He hadn't been able to sleep during the entire flight over the Northern Hemisphere because the operation commander had told him of his family's accident—and had also forbade him to call ahead and let them know he was alive and coming home. Said it might traumatize them, with certain unspecified complications from the accident. And although the C-5 was a fast-flying jet transport, it was never fast enough. Jack had to get home to his family!

There was still a great deal of pain in his shoulder and leg, but both were showing signs of steady progress. Jack's mind drifted from his concern for his family as he felt grateful his body was healing so well.

The debriefing back at Aviano had been wonderfully short . . . and secret. Only two of the original members of the Screaming Ghost team had been present—General Mick Ludlow and Second Lieutenant Jeanene Bergin. Both had made Jack feel important and had commended him for a job well done.

But Jack would never forget the look on their faces when they learned about Lieutenant David Guant's treasonous exploits. Personally, Jack had hoped to catch the young lieutenant and wring his neck.

But somehow the squirrelly traitor had found out about Jack not being killed when the Banshee exploded and had conveniently vanished. That was okay, though, because sooner or later the Office of Special Investigations, the OSI, would find the little worm and put him away for life in that fun little resort hotel in Kansas known as Leavenworth.

Jack wished that he could personally bring the man to justice. But he realized again that harboring an attitude of revenge was not only wrong, but extremely unhealthy. He would let nature take its course . . . Guant would eventually be forced to pay the price.

As the C-5 touched down on the enormous runway, Jack felt at peace. A tear of mixed emotions welled up in his eyes and ran smoothly down across his cheek. He thought with gratitude in his heart of his friend Hawk. Their mission, he'd learned, had also been successful. The warhead, it turned out, had been stolen from a French foreign legion air force base inside Tunisia. Guant had been extraordinarily crafty! He'd made two phoney warheads to take the place of the stolen ones and using enormous sums of money Iraq and Libya provided, persuaded a French military officer to go along with the charade.

The idea of easy accessibility to nuclear weapons was frightening! For indeed, in the hands of terrorists like Hussein and Al-Rashid, as well as Lucca, such power was truly terrifying.

Dear Lord, Jack thought pensively, it was long past time for the world to get a tight grip on its formidable weapons of war. Put them away safely, or destroy them. For heaven only knows what can happen as the rest of the 1990s passes us by, and the modern world rolls into the twenty-first century!

Little Jack sensed the presence of his mother and his sister, Trish. They were in the hospital room with him, standing close by, and holding tenderly onto his hands. Their voices seemed rich and full, as if they were standing close behind a thin paper veil.

"Mom . . . Trish . . . ," he whispered silently inside himself, "I'm here, Mom . . . I can hear you."

Little Jack tried desperately to make his body awaken from the coma. He wanted to see his family again, to be a part of them.

"Please," he cried to the warm spirit that had accompanied him through his struggles, "Please let me wake up. I have fought for so long . . . so hard!"

There was a brief moment of silence wherein Little Jack began to feel the presence of the light that had surrounded him in the past. It grew stronger and brighter, piercing him to the very soul.

Little Trish Garrity was the first to notice her brother's movement. Tears were rolling slowly down his cheeks. Trish's little heart raced inside her chest and she grabbed with both hands onto her big brother's warm flesh.

She stood paralyzed by the sight, unable to move and unable to speak. Something was happening. And she just knew that her brother was coming home! He was finally coming home!

"Mommy!" she screamed at last, "Little Jack! He's—"

Little Jack opened his eyes.

The fluorescent lights were blinding at first, but he blinked a few times to adjust.

Slowly the images around him began to focus. His mother . . . his sister . . . the hospital room . . . the window . . . the furniture. . . . Little Jack smiled and tears fell.

"Little Jack!" his mother whimpered, falling upon him and smothering him with kisses. "Oh . . . you're back, darling!"

"Hi, Mom," he said simply.

She hugged him close and wept.

"You came home!" Trish said, her own eyes filmed over with tearful happiness. "You came home! We've been waiting a long time for you!" She too climbed on the bed and embraced her brother.

Twenty-five minutes later, after the doctors, nurses, and everyone else who had drawn close to the Garrity family had celebrated, Little Jack questioned his mother. He had become incredibly sensitive to her spirit and he felt that she was suffering a great burden.

"What's wrong, Mom?" he asked sensitively.

"Oh, nothing, my dear, dear son. I'm just so happy to have you back again."

"But there is something wrong, Mother. I can feel it! Is it your broken leg?"

"No . . . I'm all right, really."

"Then why the sad tears?"

"These aren't tears of sadness, Little Jack, my brave little man. They're—" She turned her head and wept bitterly.

Little Jack was again sensitive to the moment, and whispered in a calm, peaceful voice to his beloved mother.

"Don't cry, Mom. . . . Dad's coming home, too! He's okay . . . really!"

Linda whirled around and looked longingly into her son's eyes. How could she tell him? His father wasn't coming home . . . he'd been shot down over the Mediterranean Sea! He was *never* coming home again.

She leaned over and put her arms around the boy, holding him as close as she possibly could.

"Listen to me, Little Jack . . . your father—"

"Somebody mention my name?"

Linda and Trish spun around simultaneously and looked at the man standing in the doorway. He was tall and handsome. His eyes were blue, his hair sandy brown with streaks of grey along the sides. In one hand he held a wooden cane, which he used to support a cast similar to the one Linda was wearing. His other hand was wrapped in a sling. But what they noticed most was the bright, neatly pressed Air Force uniform—and a smile as big as all outdoors!

It was Jack!

"Daddy!" Trish screamed wildly. She ran over to Jack and threw her arms around his legs, hugging him so tightly that he nearly lost his balance and fell.

"Hello, young lady! My but it seems like you've grown two inches since I saw you last!"

Jack bent over and carefully swooped Trish up into his arms, smothering her with kisses.

Linda stood for a moment with both hands cupped over her mouth in disbelief. She could only stare.

Jack gently set Trish back down, then walked slowly over to his wife—his beloved eternal companion. She looked like an angel. Her hair was silky blonde, her eyes ocean blue. Her face seemed to shine with a radiance all its own. And as he reached down slowly to embrace her, his heart pounded like a kid experiencing his first kiss. Slowly they put their arms around one another, never once taking their eyes away from each other.

He pulled her close.

They melted together in a long and tender moment of the purest kind of love, and kissed.

"Oh, Jack, darling!" she exclaimed, "I . . . I thought you were . . . dead!"

"Nonsense, darling," he said with a smile. "I'm one of the good guys! Good guys don't die!"

Just then, Juno, who had stood patiently at the hospital room door, barked twice as if agreeing with his master. All eyes suddenly focused on the beautiful white animal.

"What's . . . who's that?" Linda asked.

"Oh, that's Juno! He hitched a ride home with me from Libya! Says he wants to meet my son."

"Libya?" she questioned, clearly curious.

"I'll tell ya later."

Together, Jack and Linda turned to Little Jack. He was propped up in his bed, waiting his turn—weeping tears of inexpressible joy.

Jack reached down and wrapped his one free arm around the boy's neck and drew him close.

"You saved my life, son!" he whispered. "And I'll always be grateful for . . . for our flying time together."

Something inside Little Jack jarred loose, and his mind reached back into the long-ago moment when he was high above the earth watching his father—and praying earnestly.

"Welcome back, Dad! I just knew you'd be coming home."

Together the family embraced, each grasping onto the others as they felt the strength and enduring quality of a family that would last. They, at last, were home.

Epilogue

29 June 1992—
Stonehaven, Scotland

The sun was out early. It was a beautiful day for a morning flight and David Guant was out of bed at the first sign of light.

In recent months, he and Anna Trujillo had moved from their winter home at Cabo de Tortosa, Spain, to their summer home at the base of the Grampian mountains in Scotland. Guant felt at home here. And with every luxury money could buy, he'd not spared a single expense on their three-acre estate.

Guant's pride and joy, however, was the highly maneuverable, highly spirited biplane—the Christian Eagle. Initially, the 340-horse-power aerobatics airplane had arrived in a series of wooden crates that had come directly from the manufacturers in Hollister, California. It was a kit. But, like everything else belonging to Guant, he'd preferred to build the aircraft himself. Once completed, the rainbow-colored bi-wing was a personal work of art—something he'd created with his own hands.

Out in the fields behind their expensive English Tudor, Guant had built a small hangar and runway. He spent numerous hours darting through the Scottish mountains and over the picture-perfect lakes and valleys. He was happy and content behind the controls of his airplane. He had everything! Truly, who could be happier?

With the money he had earned from his treasonous weapons sales, Guant had discovered that he'd achieved his fondest dreams at last.

Following the rise of the sun, Guant leaped heavenward. The biplane he named *Angie* was nearly as much fun as the high-powered F-14s and F-16s he had flown in the service. And although it wasn't nearly as responsive as the Air Force jets, it was nevertheless, a remarkably fun toy to possess.

"Toys!" he thought with a smile. "Why, with our money, there isn't anything in the world outside of our reach! Boats, cars, houses, animals, exotic vacations . . . everything! Who said money couldn't buy happiness—even for an Air Force deserter!"

David Guant grinned a fiendish grin. He had won!

Darting out across a high mountain valley, Guant thought of himself as a giant hawk in search of food. This was a favorite hideaway to fly to. It was accessible only by air, and commanded an extraordinarily beautiful view of the base of the mountains far below where he and Anna lived as Sir Douglas Aberdeen and Ms. Mira Kisumu.

Banking to his left, Guant suddenly noticed something out of place with the small stack of papers tucked into the right door packet. It was an envelope of sorts with the name *David* scripted across the top in Anna's handwriting.

Without thinking, Guant removed his seat belt and leaned over, retrieving the intriguing white packet. Then, tearing it quickly open, his heart quickened as he read the following words:

My David . . .

> My, but you have been marvelous! I shall always remember our times together, and although I have, of necessity, transferred all of our monies from the bank, I am leaving you $10,000 in the cupboard above the kitchen counter.
>
> It will be too difficult to say good-bye, and so, knowing that you will undoubtedly find someone else to share your evenings with, I must think of my future. Please do not think me mercenary for my actions. May you find happiness, my love.
>
> Anna

Stunned beyond words, David Guant ripped the letter in shreds and screamed an indescribable yell at the top of his lungs!

"Aaaarrrrrrrruuuuuuggggggghhhhhhhh!"

His fists now wrenching on the steering mechanism, Guant

turned his plane a full 180 degrees and began his descent, almost directly over his airstrip.

Suddenly something caught his eye.

Vehicles.

Military vehicles.

An entire procession of military vehicles, winding their way slowly up the small narrow road that eventually led to his Scottish domain.

"No, no!" Guant moaned audibly, his mind racing in a thousand directions at once. "It *can't* be! How could they find me?"

Shaking nervously, and almost overwhelmed with anticipatory concern and anxiety, David Guant began to panic. He wondered who they were, but knew in his heart that the charade was over. This was obviously a contingent of special investigators with the Air Force OSI. Undoubtedly, they would have a warrant for his arrest.

Guant debated briefly about attempting to land the biplane, hurry inside to get the remaining money, and seek an escape back into the skies over Scotland. But he realized there wasn't enough time for all of that. Instead, he chose the coward's way out—banking the Christian Eagle southward—escaping on his own.

"Good-bye, my villa," he said angrily, comforting himself with the twisted reasoning that there were plenty of attractive females in the world. Besides, he would find the woman who had stolen his life from him if it was the last thing he did.

His mind made up, Guant decided to fly into Europe and hide out for a while until the heat had died down.

That was when he noticed the unusually large shadow engulf his small airplane from overhead.

Colonel Jack Garrity throttled down and conversed confidently with the new computer. The voice that responded to his commands from the digitally enhanced voice box had been so similar to the earlier model, Jack had likewise named it "Molly."

"Activate radio communications, please, Molly," Jack said to the sophisticated artificial intelligence system.

"Communications activated, sir."

"Arm weapons and lock on target."

"Weapons armed and locked, sir."

"Thank you, Molly."

You're welcome, sir."

"Christian Eagle six, four, niner . . . this is Colonel Jack Garrity of the United States Air Force, special detachment OSI. Do you read me, over?"

There was a moment of silence.

David Guant's hands were shivering at the stick.

"Lieutenant Guant . . . I know you can hear me. Now, listen. I don't really want to shoot you down, despite the fact that you tried to kill me. But I have my orders, and if you don't turn around in zero three seconds and land that cute little plane back at your ranch there, well . . . I'll tell Molly here to . . . well . . . to blow you out of the sky! Fair enough?"

Guant didn't reply.

"Oh, by the way, Dave," Jack continued sarcastically, "nice place you got down there! Too bad it won't be around when you finally get out of Leavenworth." He thought for a brief moment, then said finally, "Hey, just look on the bright side, ol' buddy . . . thirty, forty years from now, who knows . . . you can always get a fresh start!"

Watching from his vantage point high overhead to ensure that the defeated ex-lieutenant would, in fact, comply with his demands, Jack slid comfortably into his usual relax-mode behind the controls of the new F-31 Banshee. This new craft was a beauty. It was even more of a delight to fly than the first prototype, and Jack couldn't remember feeling much better than this.

Far below, the Christian Eagle touched down on the grassy runway and was immediately flanked on all sides by military jeeps and OSI agents. Jack smiled comfortably, then banked southward toward the U.S. Air Force base in northern England.

"Well, Molly," he said with obvious satisfaction, "you ready to head 'em up and move 'em out?"

"Excuse me, sir?"

"Oh, yeah . . . ," Jack said, giggling like a kid, "that's right . . . I forgot . . . you don't know everything yet, do you?"

"Certainly not everything, sir. . . . However—"

"Never mind that, Molly. Why don't you just listen up for a minute and let me tell you a story. . . ."

"A story, sir?"

"Yeah . . . a story. Do you like stories, Molly?"

"I don't know, sir. I'm not sure I foll—"

"Well," Jack began, feeling a bit giddy, "this one's about a young boy . . . a young boy named Little Jack!"